IRIS HOUSE
Legacy

IRIS HOUSE
Legacy
BOOK 2

BARBARA GODFREY

Ordering Information:

For orders and inquiries, please contact:
1-888-404-1388
www.goldtouchpress.com
book.orders@goldtouchpress.com

Printed in the United States of America

Chapter 1

THE SUN WAS JUST a hazy light over the treetops, but Brenda was awake, unable to sleep, unable to shake the feeling of loss. The steam rising from her coffee cup matched the haze of fog floating across the grounds, she turned as her phone rang, switching it to mute, not answering but remembering.

It wasn't just the argument she had with Kate, or the distance that was between her and Larry, it was a culmination of events over the last twelve months, that led her to run away. Run to the place she had found as a refuge, a smile fleetingly made a move on her face as she remembered the horror of Glen and the boys when she told them she had pitched a tent in the grounds at Broadmeadows, so she could find some peace for a while. The addition, at Glen's insistence of this mobile home, he had plumbed into facilities the house would use once the council, and Heritage office decided to give the green light on the new and improved Broadmeadows Manor house, was welcome. Indeed, with the changes in her life a necessity to her sanity. Gardenia floated around her, Iris was as confused as she was, not understanding the restraints that Brenda was trying to overcome. Leaving the mobile on the table, she returned to her post in the doorway, watching the sun rise.

Reflecting on the time just passed, her mind a jumble jumping from one event to another. David moving into his finished home, the renovation of the warehouse complete. His work with Shane, now taking second place as the business venture with Peter the finding and remodelling of buildings for Iris House Retirement Homes was definitely going full steam ahead. There was a lot of laughter that night, and the party went on till the wee small hours.

Then the sadness of Hugh's wife dying too young of breast cancer, much too young, she will never get to hold the grandchild due to be born any day now. The recent unexpected joy of Linda being pregnant, trying to tell her at 38 she was not an old lady, a challenge it will be, but what a wonderful challenge.

The success of the Iris Guest House, fully booked all year and a waiting list that would see it continue to be fully booked for the next ten. Brenda was grateful that Kate had joined the group, and was taking full advantage of the new world she was living in.

She sighed as she turned back and took in the home she found herself in, Mobile Home did not do it justice, with its two small bedrooms plumbed in bathroom and kitchen. It had a generous lounge room, double glazed windows, and the best insulation found, nestled next to the ruin of the house in the shadows of the beautiful oak trees, that were giving her shelter and comfort.

Glen had realised, even if she had not, that the rebuilding of Broadmeadows was not going to be a quick fix; Iris House was not going to be duplicated. She had agreed to the arrival of this mini palace, to test if the electrical and plumbing innovations she had requested for the main house would work, in this mini manor house.

It had taken a little persuasion on Brenda's part to get Glen to bury the services, she insisted that no power poles mar the aspect of the house. They had to dig a trench to get main sewage facilities to the site, so they just made it a lot larger, a pipe big enough to stand in, and buried not only the sewage pipes, but the electrical, gas, phone lines in fact anything that would use a wire, pipe or pole utilised the buried pipe. That was in the beginning, now over twelve months later the trench had settled and you could not even see where it had been dug; only the man holes to give access if needed could be seen.

She had at first been horrified when Glen had suggested the home, but after the first autumn rainfall in that first year, realised her tent was not going to be the shelter she needed, and after using this place was grateful for her retreat, she could see how the main house, once built would weave its peaceful magic on her.

The anger that had been dissipating with her retrospection, began again as she saw the letter from the Heritage council, with still more demands for plans, more checks, more bullshit. There was nothing of the house left, apart from the beautiful sweeping front steps, all eight of them. Thinking back to her initial phone call to the Heritage Council, and being told that if it was listed, it would be the lowest level of the register. Wondering what the highest level of restrictions would be, as the ones so far were ridiculous, and why were they dithering, what political motive could they possibly have, they had been so happy when she, Glen and Dan had delivered the first set of plans drawn up by Peter, to the council chambers. The fact that Peter had drawn the exact same details from the Iris Journals, into building plans, so the main house and all others on the property, were exactly the same on the outside, as before the bombs had done all that damage was seemingly lost on both of the councils, and they had been remonstrating with them ever since.

The local council, had grudgingly given permission for the mobile home to be put on site, but were digging their heels in for everything else - it took over four months to get permission to dig the trench! She picked up the letter, reading again the part where someone had objected to the positioning of the mobile home on her grounds, her grounds. There was not a soul within half a mile of her that could actually see onto the grounds, unless they climbed to the top of Torbath's Tor, and used high powered binoculars to spy on her. If they did then they were trespassing, as Torbath's Tor the highest point around the area, boarded the lake and was on the Broadmeadows estate. Fleetingly she thought she should find out who Torbath was, he/she must have been a Lucas ancestor, and the Tor he or she built was magnificent it could be seen from the village and probably from the top floors of the Manor, proud and tall watching over the landscape. She again had the whiff of gardenia around her, a small smile tipped one side of her mouth, *"OK Iris"*, she thought, *"I know, all will be well, it is just so frustrating. I want to see all our dreams fulfilled with the restoration of the house!"*

As she watched the steam rise from her cup her thoughts roamed, *'it was going to be a long winter, it was March already and there was still snow on the ground'*, she wondered if she would be in any state of mind by the end of it. Trying to understand the restlessness that had found her, and sent her running. The silly argument with Kate, what had that been all about, and why did she feel ill-used. Kate was the real organiser of Iris Guest House, yes, she often ran things by her, but it was Kate that made all the decisions, was that what irked her? The feeling that she was no longer required in the business that she had begun.

Then Larry again putting off the weekend at Fitzgibbon Manor, she had been looking forward to her cooking classes, how many times had she put that off, at least three, and why. They had come to an agreement hadn't they, they would not live in each other's pockets, would be happy doing things separately. So why had she not gone alone, the niggling voice in her head asked her, because she could not join in the cooking classes without him, and she would miss him terribly. Yes, they had a couple of disagreements business wise, but they had really enjoyed organising Andrew and Beth's wedding, and then birth of his grandson Lucas, they had both been joyous occasions.

Then why did she feel so pent up all the time waiting for the bubble to burst, because that was the problem, she realised. Outwardly she had accepted this miracle of Lady Brenda Lucas, but in her heart of hearts she did not believe it, and was waiting for the joke at the disclosure it was!! Gardenia floated around her, the ghostly laughter she occasionally heard was there as well, it was wonderful to have that with her, but still did not allay her fears, what should she do. Who could she talk too, if anyone, she doubted that anyone could relate to what had happened to her; she realised it was nearer two years, since she arrived in the UK, and had walked through the door of Steel Street, and began this roller coaster ride that had become her life. Getting up put the cup in the sink, went to shower and dress, a walk through the grounds she could access, she decided would give perspective to her thoughts, she loved discovering more of the area, and the beauty it had once had, and would again, she vowed.

The kitchen garden, walled and with the most amazing overgrown espaliered fruit trees, that were spread against the high stone walls, was the place her feet took her. Remembering the sight of Norman doing a happy jig, as he and his team did their first walk through of the jungle just after that initial visit last year. Norman no longer in doubt that he had found the person who made him believe again in people. He was only too happy to have his name and Kew Gardens name linked to what in his wildest dreams, he could see this area becoming. He had checked in the Kew archives, and whooped for joy when he read that Capability Brown, had an input into the original design, in fact there were drawings of the terrace from the house with the markings of where the magnificent oak trees of today now lined the walk towards the lake. He was eager to see what was hidden in all the tangled undergrowth, he bounced around this walled garden area, admonishing the staff with him to equally hurry up and slow down, Tristan turning to Brenda that first day and shrugging his shoulders, but they were slowly turning this one spot, into a beautiful, restful and functional place, which Brenda enjoyed, did bring a smile. But that niggle at the back of her mind, that it should all be brought back to life, and right now, made her restless. Wondering just how she could resolve this slow pace her life was moving through and speed it up just a little.

Snow was slowly disappearing with the sun wateringly trying to dissolve it, seeing the bare ground cover, green foliage poking through the white. Then she found the daffodils in the corner, with jonquils and bluebells, coming through the ground cover, all in contrast with the slowly melting white snow, a smile formed, and tears flowed, why should the sight of some flowers make her cry, oh Brenda get a grip! She resisted the temptation to pick all of the flowers she could see, taking only the Jonquil that had a broken stem, drying her tears she walked further round the garden seeing the blossom on the fruit trees just waiting for that first burst of spring warm sunshine to help them bloom.

Knowing she could not put it off any more walked back into the home, and picked up the envelope from the Queens Council. Her investiture had been delayed, because of questions asked in regards to the legality of her title, and why she still had in her possession the orders that were given to the original Lord Lucas and not returned as they were supposed to be on the death of the last Lord. This question Hugh had taken upon himself to answer for her, as it was due to the removal of goods into the underground storage and to the various houses owned by the family, especially Iris House in London, with everything being boarded over, and the death of Iris's father. Iris had no instructions of what to do; the will her father had left gave no inkling to a problem, why should she enquire of her solicitor at that time if she had to do anything at all. In the envelope, she held was the answer to nearly a year of discussion between Hugh and the Queens Council, and she was not sure she wanted to know the outcome. This she realised was the root cause of her upset, did she really want to lose her title, even though she had never really had it.

Time had passed with no answer, was it her enemy or friend, she decided she would welcome this new life she had begun, when she could, but it was taking a long time to begin. She again put down the envelope, rose and made another cup of coffee, not willing to see if her dreams to help a world not prepared to help itself move forward, would be dashed or given the green light. Introspection seemed to be the only thing she could accomplish today, so sitting at the table, with the untouched Hugh's and the Heritage council's envelopes in front of her she decided to let her mind take her where it was wandering.

Already the Iris House Homes had welcomed their first guests and full term tenants, word of mouth was working very well indeed. Dennis had been a god send in that regard, as respite care at affordable cost, meant that the two places they had opened so far had waiting lists. Three other Iris House Homes had been stopped not due to building works, they were all nearly complete, it was the staff to run them. Not only were carers required but nurses, doctors on call, chefs, kitchen and waiting staff, cleaners – all the people you need to run a top-notch hotel really, with the added medical care, again the right fit were very hard to find. Dennis had been right, of course, they needed the right sort of help to keep the homes running smoothly, but who?

She had asked Larry for his help in finding the right fit, and that had led to an argument as he could not understand why the people he had put forward were not right, it was as if he had no idea of who she really was and what she was standing for. The four people they had interviewed, whilst having paper qualification, did not have the empathy the job required. They all came across as bottom line people, more interested in the money the homes and they could make; and not what she was looking for. Was she as Larry said being too picky, that you hired the staff that applied and then either moulded them to fit into the role you required them to fit, or you fired and hired again. Time consuming and very costly, was the argument that Brenda had shot back at him.

Again, the angry words of their argument, rang in her head, she was being too picky, and idealistic; she had to come back to the real world, the world she had inherited. She could not make him see, that she did live in the real world, he was living in the fake one.

She had for too many years struggled through hardship, it had moulded her, shaped her into the woman she was. Winning the Inheritance Lottery, she was determined would not change who she fundamentally was, at least who she hoped she was; a caring individual, who could, and would give back to the world some measure of hope, just as she had promised Iris and Grandfather Norman.

"And how do you do that Brenda? What do you do for the next trick, where do you go from here?"

David and Peter were on hold again, with her projects. Oh, they were very busy, and popular architects, especially with the way they were trying to lead builders all over the country in their energy saving techniques, getting more from what they had, and reusing where possible. They didn't want to put all the work and effort into finding suitable places, to not have either Glen and his team, or builders recommended by Glen, be able to fix them up. David had confided in her that he intended to see at least one Iris House Home, in every town and city in the UK, more if they were warranted, but of course it came back to staffing, having the right fit of people to run them. It was a worry, that she was holding them back in some way, hindering their business, with them wanting to help her.

Chapter 2

S HE GOT UP AND walked around the room, watching as rain now fell, the grey clouds had appeared out of nowhere – she was glad she had walked the gardens earlier, back to the table she went, sitting again as her mobile rang.

"Mum, I am sorry" Kate's anxious voice started before she said hello, 'I don't know what got into me, where are you, and are you ok?"

"Kate luv, no it was my fault I have no idea what got into me either. I feel lost at the moment, not able to put my mind to anything. I am so glad you are here and really getting stuck into the Guest House, I don't think it would be running as smoothly as it is without you. Or any of them, I know Linda values your work, and will be relying on you more and more in the next few months!"

"Ah well, in that matter I have to thank you for instilling in me my organisation skills, do a job right first time and you won't have problems down the track, was always your moto. Seriously mum are you ok, you left here so quickly yesterday, should I ask where you are or do I know?"

'I am at Broadmeadows, this set up is so peaceful and calming, you could join me? Sorry for running out on you yesterday, but I could not stand being in the same room as that patronising idiot one more second!'

'I know I find it difficult to keep my tongue checked as well, but Mr. Johnston really does know his stuff. I gave you a migraine, to explain your speedy exit, and he left not long after. I have no idea why Larry and Hugh think he is good for us, and yes I know we need to know what is protocol with our new standing, but does he have to be so stuffy about it?'

Brenda laughed, again in charity with her daughter, David had missed a few of the 'Protocol Lessons' that Hugh had organised, and Larry had found the tutor, Mr. John Johnston III, was as regal as his lessons were stiffly formal. The subject matter, which Brenda found absorbing, was, in his hands, as dry as the Sahara Desert, broken down into basic facts and do's and don'ts, with a lot more don'ts than do's it seemed. Brenda kept willing herself to keep going she rationalised that he would get to the good stuff soon, but after six months, he could still put her to sleep five minutes after he walked into the room!

Well that was one decision she could and would make, Mr. Johnston was a thing of the past. Lady Dorset had offered to help Brenda through the nightmare that was becoming her investiture, and she would take that kind lady up on her offer. She would learn a great deal more about the society she was (hopefully) about to enter from her.

Mr. Johnston could take his leer, and condescending attitude a long way away from them all.

'Mum, noticed you took the mail with you', Kate carried on, breaking into the thrall she had been in.

'Sorry luv, I was miles away, I think we will pay Mr. Johnston his salary, with a bonus and thank him for his efforts, but no more. We can all do without his negativity, I know I can.'

'Thanks mum, I was hoping you would see that he was not necessary. I had a phone call from Lady Dorset, she insisted I call her May which is short for Maybelle, did you know that was her first name? Anyway, she invited us both down to her place for the weekend, next weekend, and I said yes, was that ok?'

'Perfect luv, and yes I took the mail, it was all for me anyway, nothing for Iris Guest house, and yes one of the envelopes was forwarded by Hugh, he had an answer from the Investiture committee, but I have not been able to make myself open it. I thought some quiet and calm reflection would help, I am not sure it has.'

'Ha mum, the mood you were in, I doubt even Iris could have calmed you down, and I bet she is still trying! I might have added a glass or two of Champagne that could have helped, but I doubt you did, shall I bring a bottle or two up? come to think of it, how did you get there?'

'Well there is this thing called a "Train", you buy a ticket for it, and then get a taxi. Not sure the driver thought I was all there when I gave him the address, but I think he was impressed when we got here. Got a feeling the word is out, there is a new tenant for Broadmeadows, and she is an eccentric Australian!'

'I bet; we may need to get a car you know that, don't you? I am serious mum, want me to come up. We only have one guest at the moment, you know that, and he is leaving tomorrow, I love visiting the Mini Manor, as Glen calls it'

'I think that would be a wonderful idea luv, why don't you shut up the house, we don't have anyone coming in till next week right?'

'Yes, we have that family from Doha arriving, I think they are coming for a shopping trip, not sure what they are expecting, I was talking to the Secretary, trying to explain that we are not a hotel, and they have to cook for themselves no room service, not sure they got the right idea, still should be fun to see what they think, they booked the house out, I wonder if they are bringing their staff with them? Ah well we will see on Tuesday, so what time do you want me there?'

'Take your time, no rush; say goodbye to our guest first, want me to check the train times for you?'

'I think I can do that myself, but thanks for the offer. Do you need anything brought up, I can bring you some things for the weekend at May and Vincent's, it would be easier going from Broadmeadows, wouldn't it?'

'Good idea luv, let me see what I have here, I might need a few things, will send you a list. Thank you for ringing me, and I am sorry for being short, we can go over these envelopes that I am putting off together, if you don't mind giving me a bit of moral support?'

'That is what I am here for, and stop shutting us out, we can help, no matter what it is we will cope OK!'

'Ok, see you tomorrow, take care'.

Gardenia floated around, *'you approve Iris, I know Kate and her level head will be what I need, you were trying to tell me all the time I know.'*

The rain had stopped, thank goodness, but it had washed away the last of the snow, parts of the estate were very, very waterlogged, leaving Brenda wondering if there was ever a lake on the estate, and could she put one in, as the aspect of water from the front or rear of the house would be magical. Some of the plans she had found did seem to show a water feature, but on paper it was way on the opposite side of the Manor House, and an area that she had not accessed due to its unkempt state. Would that have to be put past the Heritage Council, if she wanted to reinstate what was originally there, she turned from the table, as she heard wheels on the gravel outside.

Expecting a taxi, she was a little taken back when a smiling Kate got out of a small compact SUV.

'I know, but when you sent me the list, I realised I would not be able to bring everything on the train, so I borrowed David's new car, and I am under pain of death if I get a scratch on it. It will also be helpful to get to May's on Friday and then home again!'

Brenda enveloped her daughter in a bone crushing hug, hoping to share her apology, without words, laughing at her comment.

'Actually mum, I don't think we will need a car, if we can borrow David's from time to time, and he at least has somewhere to park it.' As she talked Kate was taking the suitcases and shopping bags from the boot and back seat, handing a couple to Brenda's outstretched hands. With a nod of her head she locked the car and turned to view the home. 'Mini Manor House indeed, still looks great nestled into the trees!'

They put away the groceries Kate had brought, making Brenda laugh when she told her once she read the list, realised nothing to eat was on it, and eating was a past time Kate enjoyed. Making a coffee and tea, sat around the table, the envelopes in front of them.

'Ok, which one first, Heritage Council or Queens Council?' Kate asked.

'I have no idea, both of them could be equally bad, and I don't want bad news. Lately my life is as grey as the weather!'

'Oh mum, you really are in the doldrums. Ok I will make the choice, and I will choose the Queens Council, as I believe that is the real root of your problem, you are neither one thing or another, and can't get your head around what you should do. So, let's just see what Hugh has managed to do.'

With that Kate reached for the plain envelope with Hugh's distinctive hand writing, and with a flourish opened and tipped the contents onto the table.

"My dear Brenda,' Kate began reading the letter from Hugh, *'I know you have been anxious in regards the investiture that is your due and right. I apologise for the length of time it has taken to receive a response to our requests.*

I pointed out that correct procedures could not be followed after the demise of the correctly invested Lord of Broadmeadows death, due to both World Wars, and several fires at the estate. That Iris's father had never formally been invested again due to the fire and the war, so no information had been received by the family from the peerage council, at that time.

The house to which the family had moved once the damage had been done to the estate, was also altered in such a way that no one could know what had been moved, and what they thought was lost. Therefore, no recriminations should be given against yourself, or the family, for what were outside influences at the time.

I also pointed out that you were in fact trying to reinstate the family in the lists of peerages, to be able to rebuild and use the gift of the legacy to assist the many arms of the Lucas estate to move forward into the 20, 21 and even 22 centuries.

Finally, I believe they have realised that no fault can be levelled at anyone in the Lucas line, and especially yourself. They have advised that irregularities aside, you can be welcomed into the peerage the legacy and inheritance is giving you!

Please be assured we all feel that you will be a welcome addition to this honourable state, and my firm and I will be available to assist you in any way we can.'

Kate put the letter down, and turned to Brenda.

'Well mum, is that the answer you wanted, Lady Brenda Lucas, is yours if you want it! I take it the rest of this information is what Mr. Johnson has been trying to drum into our heads for the last six months!' She picked up a leaflet as she spoke not looking at Brenda, trying to give her mum some time to absorb the information in Hugh's letter, then picked up the very ornately waxed sealed envelope and handed it to her, with a smile. 'This, I think you should open, and I am opening a bottle of Champers, this news calls for a celebration and be damned its only three in the afternoon, it's after five somewhere in the world!'

Brenda sat as Kate bustled around the small kitchen finding glasses and opening a bottle of her favourite Andrew Garrett sparkling white, from Australia. Coming back with the two flutes automatically took the one handed to her, and after clinking glasses sipped and smiled away her fears. Gardenia floated around, 'seems like Iris approves,' Kate murmured, smiling at her mum's silence, knowing she was processing the good news, as she had been fearing it was bad.

'Ok now the Heritage Council, I just cannot imagine they could have anything else to be negative against. Although the first one you opened at home and left on your desk, I see did request more information. It is not as if we are turning the whole area into a building site and putting a new housing estate on the land, which incidentally you as in Lady Lucas and the Lucas line own, not the council. They will be able to get even more revenue in Land Tax and Rates once the house has been rebuilt!' Kate looked at her mum, who was regarding her with a surprised expression on her face, 'what, oh how do I know so much', a nod was all Brenda could muster as she took another sip of wine.

'Well I knew you were getting more frustrated every day, so I have been swatting up on the legalities involved. Hoping I could help in some way, but not much can be done until a decision has been made, both David and I have been very interested in who was on the local Council and Heritage Council making the decisions in regards the rebuilding, as far as we checked we have done everything to the letter, in regards to the paper work. So, it seemed logical to me that it is a person or persons holding us up, and not the system and definitely not the documents. I have not been able to find out much, but I asked Michael, as his law firm has been looking after the Lucas Line for centuries, so thought that a logical conclusion, as you were having such a difficult time. He hasn't contacted me yet, although I only asked for help a little over a week ago, when I came to my conclusion it was a person not the Council that was holding you up!'

'Ok luv, your logic is as ever flawless, but who? I only came to that conclusion after the last negative letter came through, and asked Glen to quietly check on who was on the council that was making what is really an easy decision very difficult!'

Kate shrugged her shoulders and using the paper knife slit the envelope open from the Heritage Council.

Dear Ms. Chalmers,

In regards to your request for planning permission to rebuild on the land known as Broadmeadows, we require the following from you to allow a decision to be made by the council!'

'Oh, my giddy aunt,' Brenda exploded getting up and pacing the small space, 'more information what in hell can they want more of now, lowest level of Heritage listing my giddy aunt!'

Kate looked at the frustration in her mum's body, oozing out of every pore, so glad that she was the one that was reading this unpalatable missive, as she could see that Brenda would have been ripping it to pieces, at this stage, but she read quickly down, 'Mum calm down hang on, they are letting you do …

'In regards to the main house we require plans submitted that show you can rebuild in the same style as was originally there. To this end, and to show good faith, we permit the plans submitted for the rebuilding of the Gate Lodge house, to allow us to see that you are intending to rebuild in the style the era of main house was originally built.'

'What, sorry luv read that again please, and I will listen this time'. After the second reading Brenda could not contain herself, paced the home going to the kitchen and back again, musing over the context of the letter.

'OK I did not realise that Glen had even submitted the plans for the gatehouse, I knew he intended to build that again, and I want it rebuilt, I am intending on putting someone in there that will be able to look after the house and lands when I am not here. This is perfect, oh they want proof do they, well we will give them proof, and this just proves to me that someone is pulling strings, giving just that much to keep me going, first the authorisation of the ground works for the electrical, sewage etc., and now this just when I was despairing of getting anything. Hmmm well we will see, I need to ring Glen and Dan, to let them know, we are rebuilding on Broadmeadows, just not what they think!'

Kate picked up her glass; another step forward, smiling as the Gardenia floated around, thinking 'they' have no idea who they were dealing with.

Chapter 3

B RENDA AND KATE WERE walking the Kitchen garden, which after the rain and the weak sunshine, was sprouting in all directions, checking on the work that Norman and the Kew team had been doing to slowly turn a jungle that was infinitely worse than the Conservatory into a thing of beauty and use, expecting more frequent visits from Norman and his team, now that Spring was just around the corner. Both of them enjoying being useful by occasionally bending and pulling some weeds so they could say they assisted in some measure.

'Hello the workers,' Glen shouted from the gate into the garden, 'nice to see that you still like getting your hands dirty Brenda, hello Kate!'

Dan grinning like a Cheshire Cat following close on his heels, gave one of his back breaking hugs to both women, laughing at Glen's comment, 'I am surprised you know what is a weed, and what is something that is supposed to be there?' nodding at the handful of weeds Brenda was going to put into the compost bin in the corner.

'I know because Norman made sure I did, and it is so good to see you both, are you here to check up on us, or is this business?' Brenda deposited her handful into the compost area, closely followed by Kate, brushing the dirt off their hands, showed the two men around the blooming and quiet space.

'We are here because of your phone call yesterday, and we wanted to make sure we could do what the Heritage Council and Local Council said', Glen could not stop the smile on his face growing broader, at last they could start to rebuild, small steps to be sure, but it was a beginning.

'We have just been to the Council Chambers and received the new authority for the building of one 'Gate Lodge', replacing the building that is there in ruins at present. Glen here got in touch with the Heritage Council, right after your call yesterday. If you had not been so secluded here in this wonderful place,' Dan spread his wide arms around, 'you would have heard the comments from the workmen at present starting to clear the site, actually it's probably better that you can't hear them!'

Brenda laughed, Kate with her hugging both of the men in front of them, immediately walked them out of the garden, back to the Mini Manor, picking up some umbrellas, and hitching a lift back down the long driveway to greet the workmen who were busy removing and carefully storing in one place the rubble that was once the Gate Lodge. Many of the dozen or so men in the group Brenda recognised from Iris House, and greeted them all warmly. She was stunned at the porta-loos and mobile offices that had already appeared behind the gate stanchion opposite the building site. Using the flat space they had originally made as a storage area for when they put in the mega-pipe, they had now cleared to make a larger space for the buildings, and a car park area. She could see workmen in them attaching all the facilities to the 'big pipe', her idea was about to be put to use in earnest; she shook her head, in wonder, but then realised whatever these two amazing men did, was definitely efficient.

'Glen,' Brenda started as they had removed themselves back to the Mobile Manor, for a cup of tea, advising the workmen that they would be welcome for a cuppa when they got a bit chilly, only to be advised that the office was fitted with running water and heat.

'Yes, what is on that mind of yours?'

'Well I just can't believe you could have organised this so quickly.'

'It has been organised for a while, when we first put that application to build the manor house, we' and he motioned to Dan as well who nodded, 'started compiling bits and pieces to make sure we could start immediately. When Peter suggested that we put in the plans to rebuild the Gate Lodge as well as the main house, seemed silly not to be ready for that as well! So, when the big pipe was put in place we also levelled the area opposite the gate lodge to eventually receive the offices and make parking spots, we realised the infrastructure would be needed, we did not think it would take this long to actually use it.'

'The upshot is Brenda,' Dan continued while Glen sipped his tea, 'that we have the majority of new pieces, steel and stone, although we can reuse most of the blocks the guys are busy digging out of the shrubbery, ready to begin once the excavation and clearing of the site has been completed, and both councils check and give us a green light. What the council doesn't know is that when we put the main pipe in, we also put a side one to the area of the Gate Lodge, so once we clear out what is there, we can extend the Utilities pipe into the site proper, and then we can start the rebuilding, neat eh!'

Brenda had wondered at the pipes that had been left in the area just behind the wall, and the dip in the road way, just inside the gates, but just put it down to erosion, never had she thought they had been so forward thinking. Gardenia floated around, and the two men smiled, knowing Iris was approving of their handiwork.

'You can then move into the Gate Lodge, yes I know you think this place is alright for you, but you don't need to be this close when we do start building, eventually.' Pulling out a set of drawings and plans proceeded to show Brenda and Kate the very modern inside but old worldly outside to the two-bedroomed revitalised Gate Lodge.

Brenda was just about to point out and ask about the second set of plans, that covered a lot larger area than one house, with what looked like a garage around a central square, when Glen's mobile rang, rolling up the plans, he motioned to them all to follow him, 'ok Jack, don't touch anything else, is everyone safe? We are on our way!'

'What's up Glen, a problem?' Dan asked as they piled into Dan's car for the trip down the driveway, Brenda again grabbing a couple of umbrellas on the way out of the home, the grey clouds had again gathered.

'No, it could have been, thank goodness Jack was looking for problems, he knows Iris, and the tricks she and her family like pulling!' was all he said, as they headed over the rise to the problems at the gates.

Approaching the site, Brenda commented on the two containers that had been set behind the office a gravelled level path giving access into what was becoming a very large and level worksite. There was space in-between the containers and space for more than the two set up at that time, she could see that the workmen were filling the spaces in between, with blocks of stone and timber from the site. Approaching as the rain started falling, all the men had retired into the office, waiting for them to arrive, Jack coming out with his own umbrella as he heard them approaching.

'Dandiest thing Glen,' he began as they moved over to the lodge, Jack making sure they stopped well short of the site. 'We had just moved all the loose stones, and taken the fallen roof timbers out so we could see what was left, Fred began pulling up the floors, with a good sanding we might be able to reuse them, good oak and wide too. He had been in what I take would have been the kitchen area, and his foot went through the floor!'

'Oh, are you thinking 'cellar', how big?'

'Well I am not sure, we need to take it all up, not sure the foundations are adequate, and we are expanding the footprint, so thought we should hold till the rain stopped and clear more of the area, we can use what Peter designated the parking spot to put the rubbish stuff we can't reuse, and we have already as you can see started the reusable area next to the workshops!'

'Workshops, oh the containers, that's what they are, what a good idea.' Brenda moved over to the edge of the clearing and realised that with all the dirt and debris of ages little could be seen, apart from the hole that Fred's foot had gone through the boards. Agreeing with Glen, that a hold for lunch would be a good idea, but she and Kate were going back to the Mini Manor, to get out of the rain. 'I can fix you lunch if you are hungry?'

'Thanks lass, but I have to get back, I just wanted to make sure this started well, and Dan has his measurements for the steel, to be able to get that delivered, once Fred and the crew have completed the clearing.'

'Ok, well you know where we are, if you need us. Kate and I will be away for the weekend, and then back at Steel Street next week, we have new guests arriving Tuesday, and need to be in the house for Stan and the crew to clean before the guests arrive. Do you have your key for the Manor, as you can use that if you need to?'

'Yes lass, we have, and I will get the lads to close the gates,' Glen smiled at her gasp, as he pointed out where Dan had rehung the refurbished original gates, Brenda had not even noticed they had been missing, handing her a couple of keys to the padlock she could see used to secure them, 'when they leave, don't need to leave an open invitation for scavengers to help themselves to the stone or timber we will be reusing!'

The walk back up the driveway, even in the rain was accomplished to big smiles and gardenia under the umbrellas.

Chapter 4

T HE WEEKEND AT MAY and Vincent's, was full of laughter, wine and May's favourite word 'Poppycock!' Especially when Kate and Brenda tried to explain Mr. Johnson's teaching, poppycock was said practically after every sentence, but they did learn a few things from May, that allayed their fears, for Kate also was a little unsure of the life that her mum had landed them all in, but did not want to say anything, realising that Brenda was having a tough enough time without having to worry about her and David.

'I enjoyed that weekend so much, hope we get asked back again?' Kate said as they drove carefully back to David's to drop off the car, and get a taxi back to Iris House.

'I know, and I feel I learned a lot from Vincent in regards to the peerage, just hope I don't forget it all. He did give me a couple of websites to look up, and I can print out what I need. Will have to get onto Hugh tomorrow, to check with him what I (we) do next? Do you think David will be home?'

'He said he would be, I think he likes his new space, invites people over rather than go out. Can you send him a text when we get closer, just to make sure?'

Brenda nodded, as her daughter carefully manoeuvred the car towards the city, at ease in this place they had all come to call home.

David was in one of his rare moods, and had made them dinner, so they stayed a lot longer than they thought, as David in one of his funny moods was not to be missed. They also had a lot to tell him about the Legacy, Hugh's letter, and May and Vincent's advice.

'You have been invited to the next weekend, at May and Vincent's, so please make sure that you are free, it will be in a month or so.'

'No problems mum, I will be happy to drive us all there, if I can get a chance to drive my own car that is?'

'No worries on that bro., it drives very well, and it is very comfortable. I like the car port out the front, give it coverage from the rain, and still lets you see into the carpark.'

'Yes, well I had always intended to have a car, and some sort of cover over it. Had to do some fancy footwork with the body corporate, in fact I had to agree to put up all the carports, so I could have my double one. I had requested garages, as they would be good for storage, but they would not go that far, so I agreed to the car ports, with clear screens you can roll up or down depending on the weather, so as not to cut up the view to the river too much. I got the firm to put mine up first, to show exactly what I was doing so the others can be built shortly. Not going to cost me that much either, contact of Dan's gave me a sweet deal on all of them!'

'David, do you mean you are paying for them all?'

Brenda was shocked, but then realised that her canny son would not have offered if he was not getting something in return. 'Ok exactly what did you get for the deal, hmmm?'

'What makes you think I got something mum? Oh, you know me too well, all right. Well the objection to the upper deck off the bedroom has mysteriously vanished, and I can finally complete the outside areas of the space. It will be nice to have both of the decks finished, I can then buy a boat!'

Both Brenda and Kate laughed along with him, saying good night shaking her head at his audacity. During the taxi ride home Brenda thinking that she will have to buy him a captain's cap for his birthday, as she was sure he was going to make his thoughts a reality.

Iris House wrapped itself around her again as she moved through to her bedroom to unpack her bag, putting the kettle on as she passed it to put the dirty washing into the hamper in the laundry, seeing Kate had already beaten her to the washing machine. Cup in hand she put music on, and wandered the conservatory, loving the peace and quiet, before the family from Doha arrived on Tuesday.

There were two children in the group, with their nanny. The Parents and two others, *'probably the cook and PA/General Dogsbody,'* Brenda thought, as they know they will have to fend for themselves, Kate had warned them. It had been simple enough to house them, the staff on the top floor, with the children and nanny in three and the parents in two. Brenda made a mental note in regards to the Iris Phones, if Kate had checked with Matt to configure them for the family, but as the waft of Gardenia floated around her, realised she would not have forgotten that important fact.

'Hey Mum, where are you?' Kates voice floated through the air, and her Iris phone warbled. Laughing Brenda moved back where she could see Kate on the steps into the conservatory, 'I am here luv, just taking a walk through the jungle, might have to get Norman over soon to check on the space, everything is growing so quickly.'

'Thought you had done a runner again,' smiling Kate hugged her mum, and led her back into the house, 'there were messages on the machine, I just checked. Hugh wants to see you at nine in the morning.' Brenda nodded, that made sense, 'Michael will also be at the meeting, hope he has news about the permits, but I won't hold my breath,' again Brenda nodded, 'and an email from Larry, that I will let you read yourself. Call him mum, he needs to speak to you and ignoring him will not make anything easier. I am going to bed will speak to you in the morning, thank you for a lovely week and weekend.'

Giving Brenda another hug, left her at the door to the study, pointing at the email on her computer screen, *clever girl, she knew I would not be able to pass it by,* Brenda thought.

'Brenda,

I am sorry, please, please call me at any time when you read this. I know things have been a bit strained on both our parts, but we can talk them through, please don't shut me out.

Call me anytime, I need to hear your voice, love always Larry.'

'Hi, sorry to call so late!'

'I am just so glad you called, how are you, where are you?'

A chuckle escaped from Brenda, as she realised that she did love this man, even though he infuriated her at times. He echoing the chuckle, realising they would get through this rough patch, as he did love her, even though she infuriated him at times.

'I am home, have been at Broadmeadows, and then had the weekend at May and Vincent's, just had dinner at David's returning his car, Kate borrowed it for the week and weekend. How are you?'

'I am better now that you have called. Can we have dinner tomorrow, we need to talk over a few things?'

'That would be lovely, do you think you can get a table at Henri's?'

'I am sure I can, ok I will pick you up at 7.30, and then we can sort everything out, are you ok with that?'

'I am fine with that, everything is ok Larry, I am just a little stressed at the moment, and you are too, so let's have dinner, and discuss. See you tomorrow at 7.30 sleep well'

'You too, don't be stressed Brenda, we can and will work things out!'

Feeling better than they both had in a while, said their goodnights and went to bed.

Chapter 5

A GREY AND GLOOMY MORNING greeted Brenda as she woke and stretched, getting showered and dressed chose a pants suit, rather than skirt, hoping as she sipped her coffee and had toast, the sun would come out some time through the day.

Kate was organising the cleaners Stan had sent over to get the three apartments ready for the new tenants, he had called and apologised for not being there himself but the people he had sent were family of course, and had been trained by Nona and Poppa as well.

Brenda walked round to Hugh's office, arriving with five minutes to spare, was ushered into his sanctum with a kiss on the cheek, and asking if she would like a coffee.

Brenda turned from saying hello to Sally sitting at her desk and ready to take notes, 'Thank you, Hugh, yes that would be welcome, still a little chilly outside'

'I hope you got my letter from earlier in the week Brenda,' he smiled at the nod of her head, 'ah good, well we can finally move forward, and I had some news on that front. The information I passed onto you from the Queens Council was mostly correct, but I have been informed as you are a nominated heir and not a familial heir we can do things a little different. In fact, the Queen herself has taken an interest in your situation, and would like to meet you privately, over tea!'

Brenda sat down with a thump, 'Meet me, privately! Hugh what does that mean?'

'Well it means we can skip, I believe, the formal investiture, which I know you were not looking forward to. As long as the Queens Council, and the Queen agree, you can be added to the Peerage Rolls, and get on with the business of being Lady Brenda Lucas. I am still confirming this part, but I believe the audience with Her Majesty is the only official requirement. The pomp and ceremony are just a secondary part to the whole thing! Great news, isn't it?'

Brenda was stunned, after all the anguish she had gone through, the lessons with that pompous Mr. Johnstone and they were not needed. A laugh escaped her, and Hugh smiled at her reaction. 'We will work something out very shortly, I am in touch with Baron Phipps he is one of the Queens trusted Equerries, and he will advise when she will be free. I will find out exactly what etiquette requires, but please be assured, it will be a very informal occasion, at least that is what I assume.'

Brenda's reply was interrupted by the intercom on Hugh's desk, 'Ok Rose please send him in.'

Michael Danish Fawkes, was a little greyer in his hair, but was still the ramrod straight ex-soldier that Brenda had met what seemed a lifetime ago. He came to her and took her hand kissing it and bowing his head in salute.

'My dear Brenda, you look wonderful, the break in the country has done you good. I hope Hugh's news has alleviated all the stress you were under?'

'Some Michael, I had a lovely time at Broadmeadows, and Hugh's letter re the investiture helped, but his news this morning is even better. Although I am not sure what her Majesty and I will be talking about at a private 'Tea', I think that is scarier than meeting her in a group, that she can just say hello and walk past me!'

Both men laughed, and Brenda remembering some of her lessons, motioned for them both to sit with her, picking up her coffee cup to help steady her nerves.

'Michael, I have been doing a lot of thinking over the last week while I was at Broadmeadows, and I have made a couple of decisions in regards to how I move forward!'

At their looks to each other, she laughed, 'Don't worry nothing changes here, but a thought I have had fermenting over that week and for a while, I believe you can help me with, or guide me in the right direction, I hope?'

Michael nodded ready for anything that this remarkable woman came up with, truly his life had been an interesting one, but the challenging one began when he met this amazing person, sitting calmly beside him.

'Well, you know we have two Iris House Homes are up and running, at least the two I have been able to find correct staff for?' he nodded again.

'One of the major decisions I made through the week was to make Dennis the CEO of Iris House Retirement Properties, IHRP Co., for short, which we,' and she motioned to Hugh, 'created to manage all the properties now and into the future. I am so glad we registered that business name Hugh, good guidance there, it is a bit of a mouthful to keep saying Iris House Retirement Properties Company. He will need the right staff not only to help him run the actual company, but also the individual homes. I have three others that are complete building wise, just need some fixing up of the grounds, but I cannot open them, as I do not have the correct empathetic staff to run them.'

Michael looked at Hugh, who nodded and smiled, wondering what was coming next.

'I would like you to check with your military acquaintances, and find me at least five or six retired/demobbed ex-army/navy/ air force I don't care which arm they come from, if they have the organisational skills I believe they needed in the forces, they will be able to organise the care homes, and have the right level of compassion. It will also give them a home to live in, as I requested in all venues at least one floor, be set up as apartments, for the use of "in house staff" depending on size of facility and staff required, to give a life to live after giving service to Queen and Country. I have seen the statistics on our armed forces once they have finished their deployments, being unable to find work, or a home, perhaps I can give them something, and if my idea works out, I will be happy to employ more of them, I need cooks, and medical staff, what better than our ex-military men and women, what do you think?'

It took a moment for Michael to digest what Brenda was asking, but he realised again she was trying to give back to the community, without it being charity. Giving opportunities to give respect to people who once they had finished their noble cause, were tossed out on the street. It was a subject dear to his heart, and immediately he thought of a dozen people who would fit Brenda's criteria, and he smiled, she had done it again.

'Well I think I can help, I still have my contacts, and I am patron of a few ex-military associations, let me see what I can find. I will let Dennis know I take it, once I have checked them out?'

'Yes please, but let me tell him first, he has been waiting patiently for me to make the CEO appointment a reality, he has been doing the work for me, from his apartment, I have no idea who else he has roped in to help, and I have to admit I had not even enquired before now, I don't know if I would have opened the other two without his help. So, Hugh, can we go ahead and get papers ready that make the job a reality for him, please?'

Hugh smiled and went across to his desk, picked up a folder and came back to the seating area, handing it to Brenda with a smile.

'I have had this ready for the last six months, Dennis has been reporting to me with details on the two homes already opened, and we have been giving assistance to him from here, but yes you do need to find the right premises for this endeavour, I thought it would be a logical extension that he was the CEO on a permanent basis. All he has to do is sign them and return to me, job done!'

Laughter and Gardenia floated on the air, as Brenda realised that the two men in front of her knew her very well indeed. Putting the folder in her brief case, she relaxed a little more, nodding when Hugh offered a top up of her coffee.

'I do have something in regards the rebuilding of Broadmeadows,' Michael said to the thinking silence, Brenda sat up straighter and looked closely at him, 'I was asked by Kate Hugh, to check into a couple of things with the rebuilding of Broadmeadows, and I agreed. Although I know the Heritage Council can be extremely slow, the time delay and the fact the whole place is a ruin, on even the acceptance of the plans was in my view, and Kate's extreme.'

Brenda nodded, 'I have news on that, not sure if you gentlemen have been advised, but we have permission to build the Gate House, and I left Glen and Dan, in the throes of beginning that endeavour. Apparently, we have to prove that the main house will be built in the style of its original, but they want more detailed plans, once that has been constructed. Oh, and while I am thinking, Michael, I will also be looking once it is completed of course so no rush, for trustworthy people, couple or single, to live in the Gate House to be my guards and help look after the place. I am excited that I will have a permanent place to live while the building of the manor happens, but still cannot understand why the delay. At this stage I envisage it will take at least another two to three years before Broadmeadows is rebuilt, once they actually start the main building, but at least the Gate House is a start.'

'That is good news indeed Brenda, and no I had not heard. They had contacted me with their concerns as well in regards to the delay.' Brenda looked at Michael, she had not known that Dan and Glen had been that frustrated, 'I am so glad they are on top of that endeavour, in their usual efficient fashion.'

Brenda laughed, and raised her cup in salute. 'Yes, they do work very well, when they are allowed to, you should see what they achieved in a week! I will be interested in seeing what they achieve by the time I go back, but with what Hugh told me this morning, may not be for a couple of weeks, or even months.'

Discussion then returned to Hugh's news from the Queen's Council, and Michael adding his information in regards to what to expect at the Tea.

Chapter 6

'WELL WHAT DID MICHAEL and Hugh say,' Kate pounced on her as she walked through the basement door, the house smelt of Nona's mixture and the ever-present Gardenia. Brenda looked around, and her daughter read the look on her face.

'Oh well as Stan's team were doing the other apartments, they volunteered to clean in here as well, I didn't like to stop them from cleaning in here as well, now could I?'

Kate could interpret her mums look and sniff easily.

Laughing, Brenda said to put the kettle on, and she would change, then they could sit and go through the very startling information she had just received.

Coming back into the kitchen, to find David and Dennis, sitting at the kitchen table a cup in one hand and looking at some plans spread out in front of them.

'Ah how did you know I was going to call you Dennis, our ESP is working well.'

'Well when Kate told me that you were around at Hugh's and Michael was there as well, I thought I should just invite myself over for lunch, and I found this reprobate on the doorstep when I arrived.'

'Hey, less of the reprobate,' David said as he moved to give his mum a hug, that she welcomed very much. 'I have been worried about you,' he said quietly in her ear, 'stop shutting us out please, I didn't get the chance to say this last night!'

Giving her tall son an extra hug she nodded not able to trust her voice which at that moment had deserted her, she doubted she could get any words past the huge lump in her throat anyway.

Quietly saying, 'Thank you luv, I know, ok, I will try, but no promises! I have to have some secrets!'

David's chuckle was as welcome as the hug, and Brenda took the cup Kate handed to her and moved round to see the plans that were on the table.

'Where are we looking at, and what are these for?'

'Oh! my newest project for the IHRP Co., this is one place that Peter and I could not pass for you. We both agreed, it was perfect in all aspects, and a great price as well.'

'Well don't keep us in suspense Dave, where is it? It looks huge, and are they individual units?' Kate asked also interested in the scale that the plans represented, this would be the biggest home so far, outstripping all of them finished or not.

'It is actually an old Holiday Camp, will need some work, and imagination, but I think this will be perfect, a village that has seen better days, right on the coast near Southend on Sea, still has a working rail line, so gives access to major rail links.' David began pulling out photos of the site, and Brenda could see it was very large, had two clubhouses, and three pools, and up to 100 cabins, and yes from the destruction she could see had seen better days.

'Haven't seen it since the deal was done, but Mum, it has such a lot of potential. Easy access to the beach which runs forever, no big cliffs just easy sand dunes. Peter and I were going to visit on Thursday, we have Dan and Glen lined up, want to come?'

'We have guests coming tomorrow luv, I can't leave Kate on her own.'

'Don't start feeling guilty now, go on mum, you will not be doing much here anyway, so go and take some before photographs, and I can see it another time.'

Brenda looked at the twinkling eyes, and straight face her daughter was giving her, and burst out laughing, 'hmm it was a bit hypocritical of me wasn't it. Ok I would love to come, and Dennis you better come as well!'

'Me, why me, you know I have been happy to help with the others, and I wanted to ask a favour if I could!' Now was the opening he had waited for, not wanting to push this friend of his, but he could not continue as he had in the past, keeping track of the paper work, or entry data in this modern time, was getting a little too much for him part time, he needed more, not only staff to help him, but to help expand on his ideas. For the first time in ages Brenda could see that Dennis was hesitant, so to give him time to compose himself she went and retrieved the folder Hugh had given her and put it in front of him.

'Why, well when you are the CEO of Iris House Retirement Properties Co., you had better start taking an interest in what and where we are building.' The startled look was replaced by an uncertain one, she had done it again, every time she deflated him by offering him exactly what he wanted.

'I am so sorry I got caught up in my own trouble it has taken me so long to get this to you. I promised you nearly two years ago that I would have a job for you in this enterprise, I am grateful for all the help you have given me in the past couple of years, but I realise now is the time to make this official, especially as we are expanding again, and I hope you will accept my job offer, effective immediately if you will take it?'

Dennis looked at this woman his sister really, who had changed his life so many years ago, and was still changing it now, then at the smiling encouraging faces of the children he thought of as his own family, and knew he had his next path to follow, and boy was it going to be a ride.

Smiling he rose and gave Brenda a hug, 'I didn't like to push, but oh you don't know how welcome this is, I quit my job yesterday could not stand it any longer. So, I was going to be homeless by the end of the week, and I was going to ask if I could bunk down here for a while?'

'You don't need to ask, of course you can'. Brenda started but stopped when David came around to them.

'Actually, Uncle Dennis, you should come over and share my place, I have the room, more than mum does. You can also keep up to date with what is going on with the buildings etc. to do with the Homes. What do you think, want to slum it in a London Warehouse for a while?'

'David, stop calling me Uncle that makes me feel older than Methuselah. I don't want to cramp your style my boy. But what you say makes sense, although I had better read my contract first, just to see exactly what I can and can't do!'

Kate came and handed a bottle of champagne to David to open and put four flutes on the table, 'this will help you read it then Uncle Dennis, I am so pleased mum finally made the decision, that was really the only logical choice. Ok Mum what else have you decided while you were rusticating?'

As she passed the glasses around Brenda told of her request to Michael, to find ex-military personnel to help run the Homes, saying that her logic was that anyone who had passed through military school or college to be in a position of organising a lot of troops, would have the brains to run her homes, also would understand what it was like to be responsible for many people not just a few, but also have the empathy that was also required of that role, and she was determined to find the best of the best.

'I have been horrified that some of our best people, who have served with distinction are thrown on a scrap heap once they demob. So, I asked Michael to look around, he will probably contact you through the week,' she looked at Dennis, he nodded and smiled, 'you can look around too Dennis; really what I am looking for are the best people we need, they don't always have to be military in background, if you have any contacts. I am not looking for people who do not know what a struggle life is; to run places that will have people living in them that have known nothing else. I don't just want Managers and Supervisors I will take cooks/chefs, medical and office staff, or even Joe Blow to be maintenance staff, but they have to be empathetic and sympathetic to help the people that have chosen to live in one of our homes, that is first and foremost. It's not about the bottom line, of course it's nice if the places can run a little profit, but it's the caring side of my Homes that I want to promote, and that does not need pencil pushing bottom line, fill my own pockets people.'

'Here, here,' David toasted and Dennis echoed.

'Sorry got on my high horse there for a second. But I get so frustrated by the resumes I have seen in regards to the Managers and Supervisors positions I have advertised. No Soul, and if I ring them, no spirit or imagination either. This has been my main worry over the last few weeks. Sorry I have been in a right mood, but I want to see more of the homes open, we have two ready to go, and that one on hold in regards to some permits, better check with Dan and Glen about that one please Dennis, but I won't open them if I haven't got the right staff to run them.'

'There is your problem Brenda, you need to leave this to me, Michael and Hugh, we will sort it out. I have an idea for how we recruit more, but wonder if I should suggest it?'

'Please don't hold back now, oh and before I get so caught up in this, please sign that document, and Kate or David will witness it, so you can go ahead with your ideas, legally, and you can take it to Hugh this afternoon to formalise, and get your salary sorted out!'

Laughing Dennis took a sip of champers, and with a flourish signed the agreement, with David happily co-signing to make everything legal.

'Ok what is your idea, come on give.'

'Well you know I have been working with the Colleges, and Education Department over the last few years. While they have been driving me absolutely bonkers, they do run some good courses,' Brenda nodded wondering where this was going, 'I think to get the people you need, you need to train them, you should run a course of your own!'

Brenda sat stunned, looking at Dennis as though she had never met him, where had this come from, and run her own course in what?

'What do you mean, Dennis run a course in what? '

'You said it yourself, you can't find people to manage your homes because they don't have the 'right' qualifications, and I know you are not worried about bits of paper that say they are qualified, although they do help. I mean run a management course, with empathise on empathy, and helping, caring for people, not just the 'academic qualification' to actually run the show. With our aging population, we are going to need more not less of people with the right stuff in years to come. So why not, I know of lesser courses for less worthy causes making it into the Education Curriculum, so why not give it a shot!'

On a roll, he took a sip of champagne, to gauge her reaction, 'You can even gear it for an older mature student, who might have a clearer idea of what they would need, and how they would like to be treated if they were living in one of the homes; then work it from there. Oh, I don't know Brenda, but it just seemed to me that to find the right people for IHRPG, you might have to train them yourself. Hey you could run a section of the course for the returned service men and women, to give them an idea of what you expect!' He shrugged his shoulders at her, and sipped his champagne, wondering if he had gone too far, but it was a logical extension of what she was trying to do, so he hoped Brenda would at least think about it.

Brenda did not dismiss the idea, she could see that Kate and David were impressed with it, so said that she would mull it over, but with the waft of Gardenia that floated around, and Dennis's nod after smelling the fragrance knew Iris approved.

'Ok I will think about it, I see where your logic is heading Dennis, so thank you for the suggestion, even with Iris's approval I will have to see who I contact to even begin something like that.

Dennis looked at her, lifting up his now signed employment letter, 'Actually no luv, you don't need to do anything, you just have to give it the green light, then it is my baby, after all I am CEO of Iris House Retirement Properties.'

She raised her glass to him, as the full impact of what he said struck, realising she had the right man for the job no doubt about it, he chuckled shaking his head, 'oh I will enjoy being on the other side of that organisation for a change.'

'Ok now, that was not all that Hugh was going to talk to you about mum, what did he say about the Investiture?' Kate came and sat beside Brenda, giving her silent support she realised.

'Well, that is very interesting; apparently, as I am a nominated heir and not a familial heir, I do not have to go through all the suffocating investiture protocol, that Mr. Johnson was trying to drum into us over the last six months!'

'What, do you mean we went through all of that for nothing!' David jumped up to object, Kate looked at him, and tapped her glass in a request for more champagne.

'Well you did manage to learn a few more manners Dave, so it was worth it for that end at least.' He chuckled as he moved around everyone filling glasses.

'But that's not all mum, surely there has to be some sort of investiture, to pass the baton so to speak?'

'Yes, David luv, there is. Apparently, I have caught the eye of one Elizabeth AM Windsor, and she would like me to have tea with her, sometime soon!'

It took a while but eventually all of them realised who Brenda was talking about. Dennis was in the process of drinking when he realised who she meant and spluttered in surprise, David and Kate followed a second later,

'Oh dear, I want to be a fly on the wall at that tea party. Afternoon Tea with the Queen, Brenda you certainly know how to deliver a line, my god. When?'

'Not sure, Hugh is making the arrangements. I expect it will be within the month, as she is keen to get everything going so I can continue with my endeavours, which she has heard about?'

'Of course, she will have heard about them Brenda. You probably now have an MI6/FBI and SAS file in the works. You will have been checked out and vetted to the Nth degree. Just be careful next time you go to an airport, and don't forget your passport.!'

Dennis sat back and chuckled to himself, imaginary scenes of tea party disasters amusing him, till Brenda tapped her glass.

'Ok what else, Michael was there wasn't he?'

Dennis sat up at Michaels name, knowing that Kate after talking to him, had asked Michael as he was the lawyer of the Lucas Estate, to check out why even the permission to lodge details for the rebuilding of Broadmeadows was taking so long.

'Well it seems, that after some digging, Michael decided to go to the top, as he was getting a run around from many of the council, and Heritage council supervisors, or Team Leaders, he had been told to contact. His talks with the top men, were very interesting, nearly all the managers in any department, had not been aware of any planning permission request, for the rebuilding of Broadmeadows!'

'What!' was the universal chorus.

Brenda let the speculation and ideas as to why fill the air for a little bit, savouring the morsel that she was about to drop, sipping her champagne watching three of the four most important people in her life putting forth ideas that became increasingly silly, looking forward to telling the fourth person the tale later that evening.

'Ok mum, what is going on, it's been nearly two years since Peter (with my help) gave you the plans and you, Glen and Dan delivered them to both the Heritage Council and the Shire Council, and you have had permission to 'improve' the land with the mega pipe, so what gives. How can most of the council not be aware of what you are trying to do?'

David sat down beside her with a thump, picking up his glass and waited for his mum to tell her tale, as he was sure it was going to be a good one.

'Well, I have to take you back a couple of years. You two' pointing to Kate and David, 'were not here right at the beginning of this mad adventure we are on. You have not met all the players in this little drama. Dennis looked at her quickly, 'No!' was all he said and chuckled sitting back sipping his wine. Kate and David looked at him and back to Brenda.

'Larry worked some of it out, he moved some of the people still checking the legacy, onto why this process, even the confirmation of the plans was being sidelined. But it was the push from Michael at your asking Kate and his subsequent contact of the top people in the head offices of both councils, that really got the detectives working on the case, especially as the Heritage listing for Broadmeadows is so low it is almost non-existent. Real detectives as well; apparently, we have uncovered a big fraud and extortion ring within the Heritage Council, and quite a few Shire councils as well.' Dennis chortled, Kate and David looked at each other 'How' was the only question all three asked.

Taking a sip of champagne, Brenda smiled and continued, 'A permission request is filed, but it never gets passed the clerk who accepts it at the counter at both the Heritage and Shire Councils. Oh, not all applications, just the ones that fitted their twisted criteria. Which is, "a very decrepit or nearly demolished building, with the owner/builder not in residence, so not checking the finer details or aware of the delay due to not being onsite," as they all drew breath. 'It is a very organised system, they sit on the request at both places, for a very long time, dodging requests, sidelining emails. Then suddenly requests for payments will come through to help 'push the process' along, need for historical digs on the property, at a cost; to check on authenticity, again at cost, all of course seemingly legal, and part of the process. People by this stage being so frustrated by the wait time, pay without even thinking.' She sipped some of the champers, enjoying retelling the tale, even though she could hardly believe it herself.

'And! Come on mum.'

'Apparently, there are a few people in the mix but the main contributors in our case are a Mr. William Gardiner and Mr. John Hemsworth.'

'Who?' came from both of them.

Dennis was chuckling as Brenda explained who the two gentlemen were.

Oh, he thought, this all fit together, he had checked as far as he could, and knew that those two fraudsters would not let Brenda off so easily, Glen and Dan had said as much to him. He had initially given all he had found out to Larry, and he must have, when Kate had asked for help given it to Michael, a gentleman with far more clout than any of them. The contacts that man had, Dennis would have loved to just glimpse his little black book.

'So, what is the outcome, come on mum spell it out, the suspense is killing me!' Kate remonstrated.

'Well the case is not closed yet, but with all the digging we have done, the men in question have flown the coup. They both left on holidays about a month ago, for a week, and have not been seen since. Not sure how I feel about that, but the minor clerks and other supervisors in on the scheme, in both Councils are being rounded up as we speak. It will take a little time before I get the final go ahead for Broadmeadows, but I am happy that Glen and Dan have the chance to build the gatehouse, it will be comfortable while we wait, I can relax a little knowing it was corrupt people not a corrupt system that was holding everything up.'

A sense of relief flooded the room, Gardenia floated around and everyone could see that Brenda was at last happy.

Dennis took his leave shortly after lunch, saying he had to get around to Hugh's, David left with him, as he wanted to check a couple of things with Hugh as well. He also invited Dennis round to the Warehouse for dinner and to pick up an Iris Phone so he could move in at his leisure.

Kate and Brenda did a last inspection of the three apartments ready for the new guests the following morning, and then Brenda went to get ready for her dinner with Larry.

Chapter 7

LARRY WAS NOT SURE what frame of mind to expect Brenda in, but was very happy to see her smiling face as he entered the kitchen to see if she was ready.

'Hi luv, ready for dinner I am starving, Henri awaits.'

'Just have to get my bag, and then we are out of here. Kate, are you going to be ok, didn't think you would want to join us?'

'No mum, I am happy here, I will heat up some noodles and add some extras, then I am curling up on my bed and watching some TV. You two go on get out of here, you need to talk!'

The taxi ride was made in companionable chatter, talking of bits and pieces, and apologies for being an idiot. Henri ushering them into the same booth they had occupied on their first visit so many months before.

A glass of champagne before them, Brenda looking into the clear blue, worried eyes of her friend and lover.

'Ok let's get the big white elephant out of the way. I am sorry I have been a worry wort for the last few weeks!' Brenda took the hand that was lying on the table between them. 'I apologise for snapping and being a shrew, but even with Iris's help I have just had a feeling of impending doom. I don't know what it is, or where it is coming from, but it is just there hanging over me, and I didn't know who to trust, talk to or yell 'help me' at, it was very silly of me.'

'Yes, it was, I am sorry to be so blunt but yes it was. I was just here and you would not let me in, would not talk to me do you know how frustrating you can be. And,' he held his hand up to stop the reprimand, 'I can be too!'

She nodded unable to speak, the grasp of the hands between them fierce to show the depth of the feelings flowing through them. Both of them relaxed, picking up the glasses clinked them gently to acknowledge the feelings of the last few minutes.

'Ok we have some catching up to do. I know Michael and Hugh were talking to you this morning, but I have a bit more. I was not there, and I know you missed me,' a tilt of his head and look, set Brenda off into a fit of the giggles, 'yes, I know you did. Well I was at the Fraud Squad section of Scotland Yard.' At this Brenda sat up and moved closer to his side, not wanting everyone to hear what he had to say, and she needed his close presence to calm her down.

'We with our initial application to rebuild Broadmeadows apparently fit the criteria of the fraudsters to a T.,' at her look, he grasped the hand again, 'rebuild on historic land and not in residence, as you were told by Michael. Also, I believe Bill Gardiner had put the word around his cronies, to delay proceeding as much as they could. We still have not worked out how he found out you were to become Lady Lucas yet, but again his contacts and I think a certain person from Sotheby's might be the leak, seem to have worked for him. Well with the lack of movement with the process, and subsequent digging by us all we have really stirred up a hornet's nest. Your application is definitely not the only one, that has been handled in such a manner, and a few greedy officials lining their own pockets have been discovered in quite a few places. Mr. John Hemsworth and Mr. Bill Gardiner were not the only offending builders and architects, they are only the tip of the iceberg so to speak and not the only ones with their fingers in the pie, you are definitely in good favour with the powers that be!'

'Me, all I did was put in an application to rebuild a house. You, Michael, and I am sure Glen and Dan have done the hard work, finding out why it took so long. If they had just given a little more rather than the silence, they might have gotten away with it!'

'You forget my love, who it was that you discredited all those months ago, Bill is a vengeful person, and probably will never forgive you for what you did.'

'That I showed him up to be a very bad builder, with suspect morals, and a greedy disposition you mean. Well I am very glad I did, he and his ilk need to be weeded out of the building industry so firms like Glen's can give the quality work people expect. Has he been found, or do they know where he is? That aspect of his disappearance I don't like.'

'Actually, the police have an idea of where he is, but they can't touch him, and they don't want to at the moment, while the investigation is going on, this is going to be big news and Michael and I have requested your name be kept out of the tabloids, you definitely don't want that kind of publicity. They are still digging and a few more rocks to be overturned, so they are biding their time. Both he and John have closed down their businesses and homes, I believe they are for sale. I hope they never set foot in this country again, jail is too good for both of them, the anguish they put you through.'

With that he picked up her hand and kissed it gently, Brenda enjoying the sensations that flooded through her at his kiss.

'So, now I hope you can relax a little and see that all will be fine, please.' He said as Henri brought the entrée to the table, and refilled the glasses.

'I will try,' Brenda commented as the hunger pangs receded, 'but I still have that prescience I just don't know how to describe it, and Iris can't either. It is just this feeling I have, that it is not all right, and there is something…oh… but I don't know what. I am sorry I am not making sense. Thank you for all you did, I am sure it was a lot. You will have to come with me next time I can get away to Broadmeadows. Did you know that Glen and Dan have made a start on the Gate House, with help from Iris of course we nearly lost Fred in the demolition!'

Brenda then told Larry about her recent sojourn and the workmen arriving to begin the first phase of the rebuilding of the dream.

'I have finally installed Dennis as the CEO of the Iris Homes, it was one of the decisions I had made through the week. I had promised him he would be working with me when all this madness began, and he has been running it for me really since we opened the first Home. Just handed him the paper work to make it legal this afternoon, and… wait for it!'

'Yes what, come on don't keep me in that much suspense,' he said laughing at her antics.

'He is moving in with David!'

'What, oh yes well that does make sense, he will be closer to the engine room of all the organisation of the new centres. He can also use the office space, staff and equipment that David has there. Although I don't think Hugh minded helping him out, it kept him busy. Did you think about staffing levels, and what are you going to do with the two that are almost ready to go?'

'Well I had another thought about that situation, and Dennis came up with a solution of sorts. I asked Michael to see if he had any contacts from the armed services, that may have been recently demobbed and looking for a job. If they have been used to organising troops, surely, they can organise a Home, and have some empathy to go with it. Also, asked him to check for nurses, doctors, chefs, even those who would just like a general handyman job, as we will need them, to look after the places. What do you think, I am looking for the right fit, and if they are there why not help those who have helped keep us safe!'

Larry leaned across and kissed her gently, conveying his pride in her, that she had come up with what was a brilliant solution, and a help to people who needed it. 'I think that is a brilliant idea, and you will have won kudos with Michael, as returned service men and the lack of assistance for them is one of his pet projects. You may get more assistance than you need. What was Dennis solution?'

'He wants me to start up my own Education courses, to train people in the right way to look after our elderly and needy people.' Brenda stopped as Larry was laughing as he tried to eat and was not doing well, she slapped him on the back and offered a glass of water. 'I know it is silly, but he was quite serious.'

'And he is right,' he said taking her hand again, shaking his head as he thought about the benefits of such a course to the community at large. 'Of course, he is, and you should take him seriously, it is a brilliant idea!'

Brenda sat back looking at Larry, wondering where his brain was taking him, and should she really be thinking seriously about this. Gardenia floated around, and she smiled, Larry looked at her and winked, 'See even Iris thinks it is a good idea, shall I look into it for you, I can chat with Dennis, as he is CEO he will be the one signing the cheques so to speak.

'Dennis also thought we should run a course for the Mature Student, and that would be helpful for the ex-armed forces we take, to show them what we are looking for. I am not sure Larry do you really think I can do this, for one thing who do we get to teach it?'

'Leave that to Dennis and me, I am sure he said as much,' she nodded, 'we will make sure the right people teach your course/courses to give you the right people to run your homes. What did Dennis do when you gave him his letter, was he surprised?'

'No as I had told him all along that he was going to be working for and with me, he was relieved I think. He had quit his job, and was going to see if he could stay with me for a while. Which he was welcome to do, but David suggested he stay with him, especially with the new place he and Peter have found.'

'New place, what new place, oh I feel as though I have been on a different planet, I have missed so much.'

'Well, why don't you come with us on Thursday I think David said they were going to inspect the new place, and we might even stay a night or two, it's just outside Southend on Sea!'

'That is a date, and I will ring David and Dennis to check on the details, and if they need another car and driver. Is Kate coming too? Oh, no you have new guests arriving tomorrow don't you'.

The main course was delivered before she could answer, and the food demolished a little before she continued.

'Kate is not looking forward to our guest's arrival, as they have been very vague with their answers to her questions, and not acknowledged the fact we are not a hotel, so no room service. Will be interesting to see what happens over the next week. I think I will send her off on holiday soon, she needs and deserves one!'

Larry could only nod with a mouth full of food, he continued a little later, after the main course empty plates had disappeared back into the kitchen.

'So, what this new place, and what is happening with the investiture, Hugh would not tell me, he said you would prefer to do that, he had a twinkle in his eye that has not been there for a while, glad he has found something to challenge him.'

'The new place is an old Holiday camp apparently, wonderful position, and space to rebuild lots of single dwelling units, with a few for staff if needed. I am eager to see the place and the plans David and Peter come up with. As to the investiture, well that is not happening, but I am apparently having Tea with the Queen!'

'What, say that again not sure I heard.?' Larry was ordering coffee for them both, and turned to give her his full attention, the mysterious devils dancing in her eyes.

'I am a hereditary heir, not a familial heir therefore the protocol is not as rigid. It seems all I have to do is have an audience with the Queen, and I can legally add my name, sorry the Lucas name back onto the Peerage rolls, job done.'

Larry looked at her, relieved that such a simple solution had been found, out of what could have been a nightmare. Raising his glass to her in salute, as the coffee arrived.

'Ok, so you just have to have an audience, but what is this about a Tea?'

'Well I have attracted her attention in such a way, that she actually wants to meet me informally, and has offered a Tea, as the meeting. Where, I am not sure, I cannot see an Afternoon Tea with the Queen at Buckingham Palace, being informal. I am waiting on Hugh to advise me, but apparently, it will be within the month!'

'I would love to be a fly on the wall at that tea!'

'You would be joining Dennis then, my love, as he also said he would love to be there!'

Laughing at the absurd thoughts they were both having, they finished the meal, thanking Henri for his, as usual, perfect attention to detail.

Outside on the pavement, Larry pulled her close, 'Your place or mine?' he asked unsure if he was stepping out of bounds, even with the wonderful sense of comradery they had had through the evening.

'Yours please, I feel like being reckless a little!'

Laughing at his immediate wild thoughts he hailed a cab.

Chapter 8

Brenda was walking up the steps the next morning just as a delivery van pulled up, she signed for the groceries, and called Kate to assist in putting them in the apartments ready for the family to arrive. Kate again saying she thought they were bringing a chef with them, judging by the groceries they took up to apartment four. Making sure on their way back to the kitchen for a morning cuppa, that each of the apartments were ready for the guests.

'Oh, I forgot to tell you, Matt came around last night, he has done some tweaking to the Iris Phones.'

Brenda looked at her daughter trying to gauge her interest in Matt, and wondering if she should push the subject. At Kate's direct stare, almost daring her mum to ask the question, she decided she would wait, at least that is what the whiff of gardenia suggested.

'Excellent, what has the magnificent Matt come up with now?'

Kate laughed, and was glad her mum did not push her relationship with Matt, she was not sure what it exactly was herself. He was funny, intelligent, and very good looking, with manners that were almost too strict at times. She only had to see the stock he came from to realise that Glen would not be happy with his sons, if they were not respectful. She would let things happen as they would, she could wait, and as they said plenty of fish in this big sea she had landed in.

'Well, he and the team realised it would be very costly to keep running the individual Iris Phones for all the apartments, so they came up with an app., that could be downloaded onto the guests own phones. Everyone has one in this day and age, and those that would like complete security not to use their home country mobile can use one of the phones we already have. The system is applicable for the period they are here, and then blocked once they leave. I have the passwords for the guests arriving, so it should be easy, but I don't think we should tell them they are the guinea pigs for this first test run.'

Laughing at the truth of her words, she hugged Kate, and went into the study to work until the family's arrival.

The family arrived without fanfare, in fact Brenda was impressed at how normal they were, arriving in two mini busses, luxury mini busses but busses they definitely were, the amount of luggage that was carried into the house for a week's stay seemed overkill to both Brenda and Kate, but the greetings they received were generous and genuine.

'Well that went better than I expected,' Kate was saying as she sat with Brenda around the kitchen table eating lunch.

'Yes, I don't think we will have to worry, Mum and Dad are extremely happy with apartment two, and once you showed the children the technical amenities of apartment three, I thought the Nanny was going to hug you on the spot, they certainly sparked up once they knew they had unlimited WIFI!'"

Kate laughed, nodding her head as she ate.

'You were right about the chef, although I was expecting a male not the very talented Doreen, her husband is a typical Major Domo, and he also was very excited about the technical aspect of the apartments, I think we should just leave a few of Matt's business cards lying around, what do you think?'

'I already have, one step ahead of you their mum. I was impressed that they are here as a break, and looking forward to doing some shopping, but also have theatre and opera tickets lined up. I did advise we were here to help if they needed it, but doubt we will as Doreen's husband is the very organised type.'

'Yes, that is my impression as well, so I think we can relax. I am just going around to Linda's to report on the new guests. Anything you want me to take round, may not be back till later.'

Kate wished her bon voyage, as she went into the study to update her files on the guests.

Linda was in the foyer, blossoming and spreading it seemed in all directions. She turned as she heard the door opening, with a smile as she realised who it was.

'Hey there stranger, how are you, haven't seen you in what seems an age!'

'Well it definitely seems a long time, when did this expansion happen? Are my calculations off, or are you nearly ready to drop this bundle of joy!'

Laughing Linda caught Brenda's arm and walked, well she waddled, her down to her office. 'I really don't know, I have an OBGYN appointment this afternoon, and Shane can't make it, so I am really worried something is wrong!'

'Would you mind my company, I would be happy to come with you love, if you would like me too!'

'You would, I didn't like to ask, but that would be the best thing. I don't want to take you away from your new guests, how are they by the way?'

'They are fine, and I don't think we have any worries, fitted in and appreciated the standard of accommodation. He was an Eton boy, and met his wife while at university here, so they are quite down to earth, arrived in jeans and jackets, five hundred pound jeans, but jeans nevertheless.'

Linda chuckled and then gasped, Brenda was a bit worried, but then saw the healthy glow, and twinkle in her eye, realised even without the Gardenia floating around all would be well. Still she was a little worried about the fact Linda was very large, so asked 'Have you packed a bag?'

'Yes, I have one packed and here, also at home I know overkill, but for us working mums to be, can't be too careful, why do you ask?'

'Where is it, as I think we might want to take it with us!' As Linda turned and pointed at the wheeled bag in the corner of the office, Brenda knew she would not be leaving the hospital, Iris agreed.

Linda looked at Brenda, this calm, serene woman who had come into her life, and now could not think of life without her. Giving her the arm she needed in a crisis, and level headedness when she found herself pregnant. It was the trip to the house in Tuscany that did it she was sure, both she and Shane relaxed and happy with life.

Brenda called Kate to let her know she would not be back till later, and why. Kate offering her words of comfort to Linda, telling her to say it would all be ok.

Brenda was right, as Linda's OBGYN took one look at her and said she was staying at least for the night, he wanted to do an ultrasound and a few tests. Linda feeling the strength and comfort in the hand securely held by Brenda's. The check in and move to a room was done quickly and efficiently, Brenda moved to the waiting room and made a couple of phone calls, while some of the tests were done.

The tests completed the ultrasound machine was wheeled into the room, Brenda again asking if she could stay, Linda asking if she would. She was a little confused, yes, she had been fine for the first six months, it was only in the last month she had been feeling a bit off colour, and very tired. This was the first ultrasound she had, as her OBYGN had not seen the need, although realising she should have not missed as many visits as she had, now she was worried at the expression on his face, she wished Shane was there.

The next minute the door opened in came Shane, with David behind him.

'Love why didn't you tell me you were coming today, I would have been here with you?'

David went over to his mum, seeing her in the corner, and knowing she would want a hug.

'You had that meeting with the new clients, and I didn't want to bother you, with just a check-up.'

'Some check-up that you land yourself in hospital. Brenda sorry thank you for ringing me, how are you?'

Brenda went and on her knees, gave Shane his usual hug, startling the nurse and doctor, David and Linda chuckling at their reaction.

Quietly Brenda said, 'she needed you, and your babies will too!'

Shocked he pulled back and looked at her, Linda was talking to the nurse, and did not hear her, but David did.

Then the OBYGN came in, as Shane was there Brenda and David moved out to the waiting room.

'Babies mum, what do you mean'.

'To fill out that fast in a month, there is more than one baby, son. In fact, I think there could be three. Judging by the movement I saw when Linda laughed before! Oh, life is going to be very hectic for that lovely couple very soon, I don't think she will be leaving hospital, and will be having those babies within the month!'

Shane wheeled into the room, and the shocked expression on his face gave the truth to Brenda's words. She knelt beside him, handed him her coffee, motioning him to drink up, after taking a gulp, he pulled her into a hug, tears of joy soaking her shoulder, but she let him cry, releasing the tension he had been under.

'You knew, how did you know, oh my god how did this happen?'

'I expect in the usual way,' Brenda said to relieve the tension, David taking the cup out of Shane's unsteady hand, then shaking the hand to congratulate the Dad on his instant family.

Shane laughed, turning around and motioning them back into Linda's room, as stunned as her husband, welcoming Brenda's hug and fighting to understand what had just happened.

'Triplets, oh my giddy aunt, what am I going to do with triplets. I had just got my head around one ankle biter, but to have three. Please do not leave me, I am going to need you and Kate, and a lot of help!'

'You have it, all the help I can give.'

'And probably some you don't,' David put in, laughing with them all.

'Now tell me, what did the Doctor say, he would not tell me anything apart from you will need a lot of rest, those little ones will be taking more and more from you so we have to make sure you rest so they can grow,' at Linda's grimace, 'just a little more. What time frame has he given you?'

'Within the next four weeks, if we can get another month along, he reckons there won't be a problem, they should all of them be ok.

Not sure what I have whether it is a mixed bag or all the same yet. I am not sure I want to know, this was a shock, I want the births to be a pleasant surprise, as much as birthing three babies will be a surprise.'

'Are you going to tell Sir James, that you are now on Maternity Leave? Or Shane do you want to tell him, I think it should come from one of you.'

'I will tell him in a little while Brenda,' Shane said still gripping Linda's hand wondering how life was going to change and not understanding any of this. They had given up on a family, decided their careers were what they would concentrate on. Shane could not of course ignore the longing and joy Linda had when helping with family and friend's children. She always shrugged it away, putting it to the back burner, not thinking about it. It was this family that had come into their lives, mother, son and daughter all with their unique talents, who let you relax and see life as something to be enjoyed. Linda had been a different person since Brenda's arrival in her life, and the joy she had brought into their humdrum world. He looked at his beloved wife, who had been beside him through every hardship this life could throw at him, and loved her even more. They would cope, she would cope and love every minute of the coming years, he just knew she would.

'I will get Kate to ring Erin in the morning to see if she needs any help, will that be ok. I am only a phone call away, so you,' she turned to Shane, 'and you' turning to smile at Linda, 'remember that, you need anything call us, ok!' David reinforcing Brenda's words, asking if there was anything he could do.

'No, thanks both of you, but I think we both just need to digest this news, sleep on it if we can. I am going to stay a while might even get Sir James to come here, then we can go back to my place together. Might call in later on if that is ok with you David?'

'Perfect and you can meet my new house mate!'.

'Housemate, what who?'

'Oh, that information can wait' David said.

'I will come back and see you tomorrow afternoon, 'Brenda leaned over and gave Linda a kiss on the cheek, 'well done my friend, very well done' she whispered. 'We are now going to get out of your hair, let me know if you need anything and I will bring it with me.

Brenda and David speculated on how the next few months would be during the ride back to Iris House. Kate when told that Linda had been admitted to hospital, was worried at first, then Brenda told her the reason, and she was overjoyed, immediately offered to go around to the office to see if she could help in any way.

'That would be better in the morning luv, we had better I think, go and do a little bit of shopping for the new mum, and her instant family. Although she would have been buying for one normal sized baby, she will not have the right sizes for three what will be premature babies, and as we don't know what mix will appear we will be very neutral. We can then take our purchases to the hospital when we visit tomorrow to show Linda that she does not need to worry, and can relax, to give those three a chance to grow and develop a little more. I am pleased the Doc., booked her in, her blood pressure would have soared, and I didn't like the tired look in her eyes even make up could not cover up her exhaustion. She would never have admitted it of course!'

'Typical of her that is for sure. But how did triplets get by the ultrasound?'

'First one she had was today, yes you may look shocked, but you know Linda, and as she said she was feeling fine, it was only when those three decided to grow big enough to realise that something was not right for one baby, she booked another appointment with her OBGYN, and we have what happened today!'

'Well as you Ladies have a shopping appointment to meet shall we go, I can drop you off on my way home. Not sure I can help in the baby shopping department, but mum can you keep me in the loop, I can ferry Shane around, that would be the least I can do.'

Assuring her son that she would keep him informed they left, with him dropping them off in Bond Street and wishing them happy shopping, headed back to the warehouse and some peace and quiet.

They arrived back at Iris House, to find Larry on the doorstep, as both her and Kate's mobiles rang, depositing the bags with Larry, motioned him into the kitchen as they answered the calls.

'Linda, what are you doing,' Kate remonstrated, 'there is no need to call me, of course I will be in the office in the morning, Erin will be fine till I get there. Will you please just relax, and look after yourself, oh and by the way Congratulations mum to be.' With a few more encouraging words, Kate put her phone on the table, nodding and accepting the glass of champagne Larry handed her.

'I take it you have heard the good news Larry, 'saluting him with the glass, 'oh my goodness there might be some changes happening at Pickworths.'

'That is an understatement Kate luv, where did Brenda go?'

The lady in question came back into the room she had changed into comfortable clothes, Kate excusing herself to do the same and change, Brenda accepted the glass with a smile and kiss on the cheek.

'Who?'

'Sir James, luv quite upset so I invited both he and Shane here for dinner and to discuss what happens now, Linda was not supposed to be on Maternity leave for another eight weeks, but that will not be happening. So, they come over and we talk about how we can help. I take it with this,' and she raised her glass to Larry, 'that you have heard the bombshell news?'

'Bombshell indeed; I had gone over to see David and Dennis to discuss the outing on Thursday. Dennis, was there David was not when I arrived, he said David had a call, and had gone with Shane for support, but didn't know what support he needed. So, as I wanted to chat with Dennis about his ideas for the Iris Homes Diploma Courses, chatted while he moved himself into his room in the warehouse. He doesn't have much to move does he, must be that wandering gene of his, never held onto too much.' A pointed eyebrow in Brenda's direction received a light slap on the arm.

'Well I am glad Norman and Iris did or I would not be here, and happy to do what I am'. Brenda was bustling around getting things out to prepare dinner for them all, making enough if David and Dennis dropped by as well. Lasagne and salad with some crusty bread would fill the hungry hordes, and easy to make up as she had the ingredients in the freezer.

'Iris Home Diploma Course?' Kate asked the question as she came back into the kitchen after changing herself, and set to help her mum making the evening meal by constructing a salad or two.

'Yes luv, something Dennis came up with; you were here yesterday when Dennis suggested it weren't you?' Kate nodded vaguely remembering something being mentioned 'You know I have been having problems finding the right people to run the homes. I told you about my solution with the ex-military staff I asked Michael and Dennis to find, well Dennis seems to think we should be running our own education courses to educate and re-educate the right people we need. Larry here seems to think it is a good idea'.

'Really, why?'

'Well,' Larry sat at the table enjoying watching as Brenda and Kate without a fuss made a meal out of containers Brenda pulled from the freezer and pantry. 'Your mum wants a certain temperament in her Office Managers, they have to be tough to deal with the day to day running of what is really a 5 Star Hotel, but; they also need the empathy to deal with the elderly and sometimes confused people living in the Homes. That combination in the commercial sector is very hard to find, but ex-military have been dealing with people in a similar circumstance; with about 30 or 40 years' age difference. Young soldiers, sailors, airmen away from home in barracks or ships, yes, they need the organisational skills, but they also need the empathy to stop the homesickness from ruining their careers. So, the analogy I am trying to badly make is that with a little bit of extra information/tuition they can transition from the military to a care home, their charges are just at the other end of the age scale!'

'Oh of course, yes I see that now, and understand where you are coming from Mum, good idea. So, when do these courses start, as I know there are two more homes just waiting for staff, with that other one nearly complete, and a waiting list of people wanting to be in them!'

'Well after my talk with a couple of people this afternoon,' came Dennis's voice from the doorway, 'we can start them at the beginning of the next semester!'

Shock ran through her, Brenda just could not believe that it could be happening that fast. Then the gardenia wafted around all of them, and they realised Iris was a very happy person. David followed Dennis into the kitchen, asking if they had heard from Shane or Sir James.

'Yes luv, and dinner is here tonight, can you and Dennis go and put an extra leaf into the dining table please for all of us. I feel like making this an occasion, to celebrate new life coming into the world. I am expecting both of the gentlemen very soon.'

With a nod, Larry, Dennis and David left the ladies in the kitchen, and with instructions soon had the dining room ready for the feast that was being prepared.

The doorbell at the cavity doors into the hall rang, as Brenda in the dining room was pulling the first dishes from the kitchen in the pantry lift.

Doreen the chef with the family was standing looking a little perplexed.

'Doreen, what a surprise is there a problem, can I help?'

'I am sorry, but I am trying to make one of the children's favourite desserts, and I foolishly did not add one of the main ingredients to the shopping list. I was wondering if you could help me?'

'I can certainly try, now what is the missing ingredient?'

'Rosewater, I understand if you don't have any, but I have no idea where to get any at this time of night!'

Brenda motioned her down to the circular stairs leading the way down and into the kitchen.

'Oh, I am sorry I didn't realise you had company,' David and Kate were finishing loading up the pantry lift with the food for dinner.

'No please its ok, this is my son David and you have met my daughter Kate!'

Doreen nodded still unsure of herself, and if she should have bothered this lady, but her husband had insisted.

Brenda could feel her unease, and taking her elbow took her into the kitchen, a gasp from Doreen as she moved into the wonderful space.

'Yes, this kitchen is the original for the house, I restored it with the help of some very talented people two years ago this week. Now, Rosewater; well I have a couple in here I was experimenting making Turkish Delight a little while ago, my friend had a craving for it. Which of these would you prefer?'

Brenda brought out four different bottles of Rosewater, with variations. Was happy to see the worried expression fade from Doreen's face. 'Oh, thank you, you are a saviour, and this is the one I need. How much can I give you for it?'

'No payment necessary, all part of the service. I am just glad I can help you out, now why don't you come this way, and use the lift up to the apartment. No need to use the stairs all the time'.

Brenda moved back into the dining room to laughter both ghostly and human.

'A problem?' Sir James said quietly to her.

'No, just a missing ingredient, and I helped with that. Now come on everyone dig in don't let this food go to waste.'

It was a wonderful evening, Shane and Sir James were congratulated on becoming fathers and grandfathers champagne flowed, and as it was a very special occasion, Brenda asked David to open a couple of Iris Vintage Red. The laughter and atmosphere in the dining room was what it was meant to be, Brenda did not need to smell the gardenia or hear the ghostly laughter to realise that this was what Iris was wanting, the house to be lived in again.

Chapter 9

THEY WERE SITTING IN the front room, soft background music playing and coffee being served, Brenda would not discuss what was on all their minds until the meal had been eaten, as she realised that both men had received quite a shock.

'Ok Sir James, how can we help you. I realise that the news you got today has shaken you very much, but what glorious happy news. Shane what are you worrying about, you have hardly said a word since you arrived. Come on gentlemen speak, we are here to help not only you but the Lady in question, who I hope is resting up. Oh, Kate can you go and bring up.' a raise of the eyebrow was all Kate needed and she went out of the room.

'Well dear lady, I really don't know where to start. I have no idea what I need at the moment, but it is nice to know we have you and Kate to lean upon. I am really happy that I am finally becoming a Great Grandfather, but three at once is a bit much. Couldn't have spread them out a bit could you my boy!'

Shane looked at Sir James, a stricken expression on his face, he still had not come to terms with his instant family. Brenda moved over to him, pulled a footstool beside his wheelchair, putting a comforting arm around his shoulders. 'I don't know where to begin,' was all he said.

Kate came back into the room the shopping bags from the afternoon in her hands, David and Dennis jumping to give her a hand.

'Perhaps these will help in the beginning then Shane, please don't worry we have it all covered. You might want to think about hiring a nurse/nanny to help in the first couple of months, but you will have willing assistants here to help you if you need them.' Kate knelt down and gave him a hug, he returning it with gratitude.

Shane looked at Brenda, and the waft of gardenia floated around them all, he realised that he had a very strong support team around him, and he was very grateful for them being there. Then he realised what Brenda and Kate had done, and were pulling out of the shopping bags. Three sets of everything, enough wraps, outfits and accoutrements that a nursery for triplets would need.

'I am not sure what Linda has at the moment, Shane, but these will probably be a good addition, so she does not have to worry, what do you think?' Brenda asked as she passed an outfit to him to check.

'How did you know, that was what Linda was worried about when I left her this afternoon. Oh, you wonderful Ladies, thank you, thank you, thank you, now I only have to worry about where the three little menaces are sleeping and what in!'

'Well now, about that,' Larry raising his coffee cup as he realised a lightening in the mood, 'you have one crib, I know you do, as I helped and urged Linda to buy the same one that Lucas is in. It is large enough, that for a while having them all in the one will be the thing to do, but as they get older, we just have to add two more!'

'Yes, but where in our warehouse are they going to be?'

'If you don't mind Shane, but I took the liberty of coming up with something, not sure you would be up for it, but!'

David moved out of the room, smiling to himself and wondering if he had overstepped himself with such a talented architect as Shane, but when he got back to the warehouse that afternoon, and walked into his space, asking what he would do in their circumstance, the plans for the conversion just flowed onto the page. As he came back with what could only be a set of plans, willing hands clearing the coffee table he spread them out in front of the startled father to be.

'This alteration just popped into my head this afternoon, I won't be offended if you throw them out, you probably have a few drafts that you have dreamed up yourself. They just felt right, you don't need much space for the first few years of their lives, and they would probably be better together. So, I thought you should follow your neighbour with a mezzanine, you have the height to make a master bedroom, with lift in the corner, across the whole back of the warehouse, under which a large bedroom with a bathroom for the triplets could fit, there is space for a third bedroom with shower room for the Nanny you will eventually hire, and even a decent sized laundry/powder room, which I assume will be needed,' everyone looking at the plans laughed at the truth of the statement, 'but it still gives a decent sized kitchen open plan living room as well!'

David was pointing out the plans to Shane wondering if he had gone too far, not sure if he was stepping on toes.

'Brilliant, just brilliant. I had always wanted to actually put in a mezzanine level, but we never got around to it, and quite honestly without the contacts we have now, didn't know how to do it! Steel right, we make the mezzanine as a free-standing internal structure, use oak for the flooring, insulated and soundproofed. Oh, David this is brilliant, thank you man!'

'Well I hope you don't mind, but I invited Glen and Dan up tomorrow to my place on Iris Home business, but I may just bring them over to your place, to see if they can help in this matter, oh and I have Brent coming around too. We will have this place of yours baby ready in eight weeks, if you agree, hell if you lot can have a house ready in four, this will be a piece of cake!'

The house rang with laughter, Iris's presence was there, her portrait hanging beside the fireplace seemed to glow, and gardenia floated around the happy people in the room.

Chapter 10

B RENDA WAS SITTING IN one of the alcoves when she heard excited young voices coming into the Conservatory. Waiting to see what they would do, realised the little scamps had escaped the clutches of the Nanny.

They stopped when they realised they were not alone.

'Hi there, are you hiding too?' Brenda asked putting down her coffee cup.

'Not exactly,' Louis the 10-year-old, and leader in mischief of sister Loren 8 years old, announced hesitantly.

'Oh, then are you trying to find the ghost of the Lady of the House?'

'A ghost, they don't exist, that is a very foolish thing to say!'

'Oh, Brenda thought *'a non-believer then, hmm what should she do, the Nanny will be frantic.'* Then Brenda noticed they were not casually dressed, in fact they were very smartly dressed as for an outing.

'Why don't I give you a tour of the gardens while we wait for your mum and dad, where are you heading out to today?' Brenda saw Kate pop her head into the conservatory, and she motioned upwards and pointed to the children. Kate understanding pulled out her Iris Phone and called the Nanny.

Loren took Brenda's hand and was very quiet as they walked around the planters, very excited when Brenda gave her one of the orchids that just matched her outfit, tucking it into a barrette in her hair. Once Louis got off his 10-year-old high horse, he also asked questions about the gardens and house, giving the information that they had more courtyards than greenhouses at home. Iris was also enjoying herself wafting around the children gardenia floated on the air.

They had just made it back to the alcove Brenda showing Louis how to make the fountains turn on and off, when his father arrived very anxious.

'My apologies Ms. Brenda, I am shocked that my children would invade your space!'

'No apologies necessary, Nasser, have you not read the information we left in your apartment. The conservatory and gardens are open to all my guests, I could not deny the joy and peace I find in here to everyone. That is why there is the access from the landing, rest assured if I don't want visitors in my home, the doors into my apartment are securely locked. But please feel free to visit the conservatory at any time, the gardens are just beginning to bloom, and we also have a gate onto the commons, securely locked I assure you, until an adult is around.'

The worried expression faded from his face as he realised what a wonderful space he was in. Wondering at the cool, and pleasant atmosphere, with a wonderful scent floating around. He must bring Adelle down to show her around, but that would be in a couple of days. He realised he was being asked a question.

'My apologies I was miles away, I will have to get Louis and Loren to show us around, once we get back.'

'Oh, you are heading out for the day?'

'Yes, I just got word, that I am required to visit an Uncle in Paris for a couple of days. Inconvenient, but only my wife, I and the children will be going. Doreen and Pierre will be remaining, we will be back on Friday, that is ok with you?'

'This is your home albeit a temporary one, you may come and go as you please. Thank you for letting me know, I have to be away on business myself Thursday and possibly Friday, but I was wondering if you would join me for lunch on Sunday about two, the whole family.'

'That sounds a wonderful idea, thank you for the invitation, now we have to go I am sure Pierre is having a fit as his timetable is being disrupted. See you on Sunday, again thank you.'

Kate came in as Nasser led his reluctant children out to the Nanny, waiting with bag in hand.

'What was that all about?'

'The children finding their feet I think. Louis is definitely the dare devil, worked out the lift actually did work, after the Nanny told him it did not. He just had to prove her wrong. Now are you off to Pickworths?'

'Yes, just going over for a while, shall I meet you at the hospital this afternoon, and I can let our Lady in waiting know that all is fine.'

Brenda laughed and walked her daughter, once she had picked up her case, out to the front door.

Chapter 11

B RENDA AFTER CHECKING WITH Shane what Linda needed, and adding a few more things she thought of, arrived to find the Lady in question having a heated debate with someone.

Surprised when she walked into the room to find Kate the object of the debate.

'I am sorry, but who in here is not adhering to the no work, no stress edict from the Doctors! Kate what is going on that you are both getting upset, come on tell please, and calm down both of you.'

Linda took the hug Brenda gave her, and the box of tissues she was handed with thanks. 'Oh, thank you, I did mention I needed some to Shane, oh you called him, of course you did. Ok well I think Kate is a little upset with me.'

Brenda turned to her daughter, who was still looking rebellious, but she sighed releasing the tension a little, and gave her mum a hug. Brenda waited for an explanation, Iris too, as Gardenia floated around the room. As she waited for a reply from either of the other women, Brenda bustled around slowly emptying the bags she had carried in.

'I have just made Kate temporary CEO of Pickworths.'

A smile spread across Brenda's face, and gardenia increased; *oh, you approve Iris, yes, I do too, but I am sure my daughter will not be happy at first.*

'I have not accepted yet,' Kate put in, still upset that it was nearly a fait accompli without any discussion at all. That was the main problem she realised she didn't mind doing the role, but it would have been nice to be asked. From what she had seen that morning when she got to Pickworths, Erin had it really under control anyway. When she handed Kate the letter from Linda and Sir James she had been shocked. The man in question was not in the office so she could not remonstrate with him, so had taken her frustration out on the one person she should be shielding.

Going over and giving Linda a hug, 'I am sorry, it was just such a shock, I thought it would be mum that you would be putting in the position, not me. Come to think of it why me, surely you have longer standing staff that will be upset that you are doing this?'

'Your mum has enough on her plate, and I know she would have refused me point blank, if I had offered her this.'

'You can bet I would!' Brenda said with a smile.

'We need what you can give, a fresh perspective, married with that good old Aussie common sense that has matured from your upbringing, and forward thinking you have inherited from your mother. You have the right qualities we need, and the longer standing staff are (and I am afraid to say) very set in their ways, I love them all dearly, as they do a great job, but only in the confines of their own areas. I, we need you and your young vitality to help move us into the next century. Even grandfather agreed that you were the one we need in the role, in a temporary capacity, to help us modernise, along with help from Matt and his team, I am planning on getting him to update all the Pickworths premises so you had better warn him!'

Laughing at the inevitable outcome, Kate nodded and hugged her again, laughing at the movement from the triplets. 'Oh, they agree, why can't I get comfortable!'

'Because they feel you getting upset, now perhaps Kate and I can take your mind off them, in a way, because we went shopping yesterday, we can take back what you don't like, so please don't worry.' With that Brenda upended the bag she was holding onto the bed, Kate following shortly with another, with a gasp from Linda and happy tears flowing down her cheeks.

'Oh, this is perfect, just perfect. I have been shopping you know, but these are what I need just to top everything off. I will need bottles though, with all the accoutrements, as even I am going to have a problem breast feeding three!'

Discussion and making of lists, about what else was required for the babies when they arrived, filled in a happy hour.

'I am worried about Shane,' Linda admitted, 'he was very quiet when he left here last night, and Grandfather well I am surprised he did not have a heart attack on the spot. I just don't know what we are going to do. He is very worried about where everything is going to fit!'

'I would not worry about that aspect Linda,' Kate put in, turning with a bag in her hand ready to put the excess away and the outfits Linda picked for the new-borns, in another bag to be taken, washed and returned for the triplets once they were delivered. A look from Linda stopped her in her tracks. 'You have your husband, my brother, Peter, Dan, Glen and whoever else they can rope in trying to come up with a solution to your housing problem. I think it is better you are in here for the next few weeks, as whatever they come up with is going to be very noisy and dusty!'

She could not help it, laughter bubbled up in all of them, as they visualised the aspect of the gentlemen in question standing in the middle of the warehouse holding forth with their ideas. It was the final release of tension that was needed in the room, Linda reaching for tissues to wipe the tears from her face.

'Oh, thank you, yes I can just see what you mean. I know they will come up with something, and I don't really want to move from the warehouse, not just yet. Perhaps in a few years, we may want to move back out to Grandfathers country house, he very rarely goes there, says it is too big and draughty for just him, he has always said it was going to be mine one day. I guess the day is getting closer!'

'It will of course need modernising before you move there, so plenty of time to come up with plans, and have them executed.' Brenda had been talking to the nurse who said the tea trolley was coming around, and she could see that Linda was relaxing so would do her checks once Brenda and Kate had left.

'Yes, there is that as well, but that move is definitely a long way off. I don't want to be that far away. You are only temporary CEO Kate, and I want to be here if you need me, really you don't need to be doing my job full time. Erin is capable of the day to day stuff, it's just when problems loom she needs help!'

'I understand Linda, and I am sorry about my reaction, but I was just so stunned. I did not expect it, as I said I thought you would ask mum!'

Chapter 12

THEY LEFT LINDA IN a better mood realising she only had to ask and it would be done, to Brenda's standards, and that was very good. Brenda remembering to tell her she would not be visiting for the next couple of days, as she was going to be away. Kate put in that she only had to call her, and she would be there quick smart. So, to relax, and enjoy the peace while she could.

When they arrived back at the house, both of them changed into relaxing clothes and found themselves around the kitchen table. Discussing the new role Kate found herself in, and looking to the future and how much time she was likely to be there.

'I was going to make the suggestion of a holiday for you luv, once our current guests are gone. We don't have anyone booked in for a couple of weeks, right?'

Kate jumped up and went into the study, coming out with her tablet to check the details. 'That's right mum, we are completely booked out from last week of March through to mid-May, and then a lull till Ascot week in June. It's quite up and down but steady, it's nice to get the break in-between. I think a holiday will be possibly a weekend away, if I have to help here and in the office as well. Thank you for the thought but let's just see how we go, I can always just bolt down to Broadmeadows for a few days, that was very peaceful!'

'That is a great idea, and you never know I might actually join you!'

'Join you where?' asked Larry as he moved into the kitchen bestowing a kiss on the top of the head to Kate, and a hug and better kiss on Brenda. David, Glen, Dan and Peter following him into the room.

'Oh, goodness I was not expecting this much company, welcome everyone!' Brenda jumped up and bestowed hugs and kisses on cheeks to everyone, quickly being followed by Kate.

'Well lass, we just had to come and see how Linda is getting on. David here said that you were visiting her today, how is she?'

'She is fine Glen, and blossoming just like Gabby did, and how are your two little rascals doing. Seems I haven't seen them in so long.' As she talked Brenda bustled around organising nibbles to go with the drinks Kate was offering.

'They have missed the visits as well, Aunty Brenda is liked not just because of the presents she brings, but the stories she tells when asked. So, when can you come down again, you always have the invitation for Sunday Dinner you know.'

'May have to be in a couple of weeks, I am busy this weekend, might be able to make it next. Depends on what arrives in my lap during that time? Now what's up with this meeting of minds. What happened at the warehouse, when are you starting work, tomorrow?'

'Ha, ha Brenda, how did you know', Dan was sitting in the strong rocking chair Brenda had bought ostensibly just for him when he visited. He liked a chair with a back, for his bad back, and could not sit at the benches. 'David's plans were a good start, and I have the steel to make the frame for the mezzanine, but we have to correlate permits, and timber, plumbing. Shane also decided that if we were going to have to alter the plumbing to get the master bathroom in, and the handicap facilities that he had always wanted they may as well do all the alterations he and Linda had been putting off for a few years. So, they are updating the kitchen with the new bathrooms to go with the redesigned downstairs bedrooms. Making the job a lot bigger!'

'Here Brenda, take a look at these.' Peter put down his beer, and pulled out the folded plan of the warehouse David had produced, with hand drawn additions in Shane, David's and Peter's distinctive styles on the plans.

'I am so glad that Linda is in the hospital, that is going to be a big alteration gentlemen, you really only have four to five weeks possibly six not the eight David said last night. Brenda looked at her son, who nodded at her remarks, 'If need be we could put the family up here for a little while, but hopefully we can work some magic and get it done. David luv you might have another temporary guest, good job both of your downstairs bedrooms have a shower room as bathrooms, Shane will be able to use.'

At the blank looks she was getting from the men around the table, Brenda looked at Kate. She understood what her mum meant, shaking her head, 'if you have to move furniture and switch off the utilities, as I can see that you are just removing everything that is in there at the moment, how will Shane survive, he will have to move out. Might be neighbourly for you to offer him a room, from now David, better that he not be on his own. With Dennis to help, he won't have time to brood on the what if's.'

'Good idea sis., he went to visit Linda after we left. So, will go over and help him pack some stuff when I see him return. Must remember to get Dennis to call Stan, if they can get some boxes they can pack up the rooms and make sure all is neat and cared for, before we start the demolition.'

He looked around at the chuckles from Glen, Dan, Peter, Larry and Brenda as they remembered Stan coming and packing up all the treasures they found in the house. Chuckling along when they told him the story, and that Stan was sure to have boxes.

'Well If you happen to be back here on Sunday, I am hosting a lunch time BBQ, yes I know, but I also know you lot. The days of the week don't matter just your time frame, so do you think you will have it all finished in four weeks. You are of course going to get Rebecca up here to check on the details?' At again the blank looks, 'she will have to purchase the new kitchen appliances and bathroom fittings. Don't forget to put a bathtub in that downstairs bathroom in the baby's bedroom, you will need it to bath three babies when they get a little older!'

'Of course, we have, she is coming up tomorrow, to see Shane, and then going to check with Linda in hospital. Are you coming with us to see the new place David and Peter have found for Iris Homes Brenda? On paper, it looks too good to be true, but we will wait and see. Ok we are out of here,' Glen drained his cup and moved over to put it in the sink. 'Have to go and do some ordering and see if I can't hustle the delivery from a month to a week.'

Everyone laughed as they realised that it would happen, getting up and moving with them all out to the door.

'We will see you at the site tomorrow around ten thirtyish,' Larry was saying to Glen and Dan, as they shook hands. Both gentlemen nodding and waving goodbye, Peter giving Brenda a hug and kiss on the cheek in farewell, hurrying off after them.

'I get to drive my new car tomorrow, and will bring Dennis with me, so see you in the morning, looking forward to seeing this place.' With that David was hailing a cab and disappeared as well.

Moving back into the house, and discussions of this new phase just beginning.

Chapter 13

I T WAS AN EASY start to the Thursday morning, with breakfast eaten and coffee in hand, overnight bags in the Range Rover, just in case. Larry and Brenda eased their way through the London traffic and enjoyed the drive to the seaside.

'Has Kate got over the shock, do you think?' Larry asked as they moved into easier traffic. 'It was Sir James idea, but not supposed to happen until Linda went on maternity leave, and she was going to bring up the subject of temporary CEO closer to the time. Guess that didn't happen!'

Brenda laughed, 'no mother nature got in the way, still I think she will be all right. She was discussing time tables for some updates to the other properties, and ways to improve the communication system for all of them with me before we left this morning, I think she had been up before dawn. I believe she will be getting Matt to call in to discuss, she was also going to check if he could update the system at David's.' A questioning look was all she got as he negotiated a bit of traffic, 'be better if they had the same system as our updated one, oh sorry you have not been told about that!' The explanation and discussion about Matt and his brilliant technological ideas took them to an area on the coast on the out skirts of Southend on Sea.

Driving down towards the sea front, through a gap in the hills the road running beside the train line, split after the station, to follow the coast, the headlands and green space giving a backdrop to what was a stunning vista as they moved down to what had once been a very busy area with shops and homes mixed together. Brenda smiled as they drove into what was once viewed as a quaint seaside village nestled in those hills, but now was a dismal sight. More boarded up homes and shops than open ones, the pub/hotel on the corner as the road curved round to the seafront, opposite the boarded over site, had seen better days, but at least it was open. A general handyman store that seemed to have come right out of the 50's and sold just about everything, was looking a little forlorn, but had a couple of people checking in the boxes at the front of the shop. The elephant in the room was the dilapidated area opposite these premises, that looked when seen through the gaps in the high intimidating fence, as though not one but several bombs had gone off, demolishing buildings and generally making the area a mess.

Seeing they were early, Larry suggested they have a coffee at the pub, a sign outside stating coffee and cake were being served. Just one more way to get business, in an area where it would be scarce to run just an alcohol only venue.

The inside was cosy and clean, could do with an update as the carpet was worn and needed to be replaced in areas. The bright shiny coffee machine standing out on the original bar, that needed a sanding and refinishing looked a little incongruous. Moving to a corner seat that gave a view out the window, so they could see when everyone arrived, ordered the coffee and cake from the very attentive man behind the bar.

'Thank you, have you been in the area a long time?' Brenda asked as the coffee was placed in front of her, the carrot cake she had chosen looked delicious, and freshly baked.

'Not really, I took over the pub when I married, my wife's father was the previous owner, and he wanted to retire. We both have a background in hospitality, my wife is the baker/chef she makes all the cakes we sell. I was the manager of one of the leading cocktail bars in London. I have plans for this place, just need to build up the business, hopefully with that eyesore being sold I might have a chance!'

'Oh, do you know who too?' Brenda innocently asked.

One of the two patrons that had been sitting in the corner by the fire, chipped in. 'We hope it's not a food store, don't need that. We don't need a multistorey car park either or high rise apartments.

I remember when the Holiday park was in its heyday, this area was a prime spot, lots of shops and people, happy holiday makers. Still people go overseas for their holidays now, cheaper too!'

The door opened, the Landlord looking up and smiling as this was the best morning he had seen in a long time, new faces and there was something about them. David and Dennis walked in and seeing Larry and Brenda, walked over, ordering a coffee each but declining the cake.

'Well what do you think?' David asked as they pulled up chairs to sit at the table.

'I think I love the spot, it has a lovely feel, Iris agrees. I also think I need to get Larry to check on the houses and shops in the area. Might be a good investment to purchase a couple, then we have places to stay while the work is going on. From what I can see from my walk up the street, this is not going to be a quick fix!'

'You are not visiting are you', the landlord brought the coffee over, leaning down as he spoke to not alert the patrons in the rest of the room.

'No,' at the look Larry gave him.

'Gus, I am Gus Lambert my wife is Janet, as I said we took over the pub Seashore Retreat, from my father in law six months ago. We have been trying to build it up, but it is a struggle.'

He shook hands all around, hope blossoming in his heart, wondering at the wonderful fragrance surrounding this group.

'Well Gus,' David continued, 'this might just be the break you have been waiting for. Don't please bandy this around, yes, we know who has bought the old Holiday Village. You can rest assured, it is not going to be turned into a high-rise apartment block, so the sea shore will still be seen, or a car park or a shopping centre. Hopefully it will bring people and business back into the neighbourhood, and we will see if we can't help you and the business's that are already here grow a little.'

'Thank you, we have all been worried, since the sold sticker went across the board a month ago. Wild theories have been abounding since then, my regulars on an evening love to speculate as to what is happening. I know you can't say, just that you have assured me that a huge shopping complex or high rise is not going to spoil what was once a pristine coast line, is enough. I will pass the word tonight, we have an open mike night and my wife does a limited food service, best we can do with the equipment we have. Still it does bring in a good crowd. Thank you again for the information.'

Gus bustled off to fill the request for a refill. David spotted Glen, Dan and Peter who had parked beside the sold sign in the high and intimidating fence that blocked most of the view. Moving out of the pub, after saying goodbye, joined them as they tried to see the scope of land, Peter opened the padlock on the gates and they all moved through, Brenda gasped.

In front of her was a vista of the sea, sparkling and bright in the sunshine. From the high advantage point on the promenade walk way which was a few steps down from the road level, she could just see to either end of the wide deep block, which reminded Brenda of an old Roman amphitheatre facing a marvellous expanse of sand and sea. By mutual silent consent, they all moved down some very rickety steps down the cliff face and towards the beach, Dan and Glen going first, to test them, as she heard their comments, realised these would be the first things to be replaced.

Walking through the site, Brenda was disgusted at the vandalism and graffiti there was everywhere, all of the buildings were going to go, she thought, they would start again so it could be rebuilt correctly. They turned at the sea wall, and looked back at the property that Brenda had purchased.

The two large buildings at either end of the space, must once have been the hotel and restaurants with other facilities of the site, along with matching pools in front. In between were lots of cabins, some still standing but badly vandalised, reminding Brenda of the bathing boxes she remembered from the Mornington Peninsula in Melbourne. Her thought that the site had to be cleared reinforced as they moved through them, and saw how badly damaged they were, in fact they were a major health hazard.

She could see the area reborn, a vision of the two main buildings rebuilt for the retirement village use, a road way from the main road down the right- hand side as she looked from the sea wall, she vaguely remembered there was a narrow road, a track really which could be updated, opposite the pub, which she could see was the better access point, to allow for both general public access to the beach, also delivery vans, once the site was being rebuilt and then used after it was completed. There had to be easy access for all the equipment she knew would be required to demolish and rebuild, also ambulances when required, that sad thought came into her mind. A low wall with seating included, would be needed on the roadside to allow a view across to the sea again, from the houses and shops that were looking so neglected.

She shrugged turned again to calm her thoughts and looked out over the sea, and the view up and down the headland, it was spectacular. In a calmer frame of mind, she turned again seeing the area with the existing cabins replaced with one and two bedroomed units with landscaping in between. Brenda began making mental notes, vowing she would replace the remnants of the boardwalks they could see coming through the buildings towards the beach edge, as they flowed towards what was left of the sea wall they were standing on it, the entire space to be demolished and rebuilt, it had crumbled to nothing in places, she could see it renewed. Then the path through the dunes to the beach, widened and made manageable by foot or wheelchair. Again, Brenda had the urge to fix this nightmare, Iris was incensed that something that had so much beauty, had been vandalised and left to ruin.

'This is just a beautiful place!' Brenda turned to the startled looks the men were giving her. 'Can't you see it, oh there is a lot of work here, cleaning up the site properly before you can even start is going to take months. But can't you see what this will be, I can and Iris can, so well done the two of you.' She gave a hug and kiss on the cheek to David and Peter, laughing at the relieved expressions on their faces.

As they started to move back towards the stairs, Brenda made another decision, it seemed Iris agreed with her thoughts, judging by the gardenia floating around, 'Larry, I want to purchase if possible at least three of the homes that I can see on the front, that are for sale and boarded up. The one in the middle I want for me, as that will give a complete view of what is going on over here while we are building and a wonderful seaside retreat. The one next to it as a place for you to call home Dennis? I want to buy the café that is boarded up, I might see if Mama wants to expand to the seaside as the workers will need their lunches delivered!'

They all looked at her, realising that the magic was happening again, and it would be as she could see it. They moved down to the base of the site, wandering over to the main buildings, inspecting the vandalised and ruined properties not daring to inspect the upper floors, Dan saying they were not safe. The smiles would not go as they could all see what Brenda was explaining. Peter and David jotting down notes so not to miss any of her ideas.

'I don't think we will need the two pools, if we make a brand new single pool move it to the middle of the site, and modernise it, that should be sufficient. With new walkways through the buildings, not the rickety boardwalks that are here, and then build a new wide boardwalk across the sand to the sea, what do you think?'

Glen moved over and gave her a hug, 'I think you are remarkable, for you to see what you do, when you have just seen the space five minutes ago, I am looking forward to bringing your visions to life!'

Dan followed Glen, 'I think we build the frames in steel,' at Brenda's look, 'we can coat them against the salt air, using posts to lift off the sandy soil a little, and allow air flow underneath, with the insulation and double glazing you always insist on, they can last a hundred years, and be a valuable addition to the area. Yes, it will work, but I had better get my lads working on the basics, once you two give me the plans of course!'

Laughing they moved out of the gates securely locking them behind them. Glen, Dan and Peter left, Peter fending off requests for designs as soon as possible, Brenda hearing him say, that she had to finalise them first, after he and David had come up with designs.

Larry suggested a walk along the street, so he could write down the real estate information on the houses Brenda wanted to buy. Dennis was in shock wondering if he had heard Brenda correctly, he was to have one of the houses as his own. Understanding she was offering him a place to work from, but something he had never thought possible, his own home. Looking around again, this time with a view of rebuilding the area, giving it back a life and purpose. Ending up back in the pub, this time with counter lunches all around, Gus and Dennis having a hard time keeping the smile off their faces.

Getting back into the car after waving Dennis and David off, Brenda asked Larry to drive around the area for a while, so she could judge what the place could become. There were quite a few 'for sale' signs in the streets on and behind the shorefront. Showing just how unpopular and on hard times the area had become. The thought also came to her they would be handy for workers to rent rather than using some of the units to be built, at her prices, to be close to the centre, once open. Her brain working overtime, Larry happy to drive and let her ponder, knowing that whatever was brewing in the complex brain would be worth waiting for.

'Larry, do you mind if we don't overnight, I think I need to go back home! I need to do some research and speak to Hugh, this is not going to be a cheap fix up, I may need more funds than I have to do what I want. You also have to find out about the houses, I noticed most of them are with the one agent. See what you can do for me, I would like to buy as many as I can, so please negotiate good prices. Especially the middle one on the front, and the one next to it that will be Dennis's. He is going to need somewhere to live and work from, and I can see the basement of his house with access to the street, being turned into the main offices of the whole shebang, what we are about to launch into is going to be the biggest Iris Home of the lot, with the problems that will come with the rebuilding, he is going to have to be here on site.'

Larry laughed, and turned the car back to London, knowing in his heart that Brenda was right. She was on the brink of building something that was going to make all the other so called Care Homes, sit up and take notice. He found he was looking forward to the challenge.

Hugh was not surprised when Brenda walked into his office at eleven the following morning, he found he was looking forward to seeing her, and the challenge that she was sure to give him. The phone call Brenda had made on arrival back into London, to see if he was free, and the warning from Larry when he had returned to the office, that she was working on something for the Iris Homes that would need quite a bit of funding, put him on his mettle. So, Hugh had turned the visit to his and Brenda's advantage by asking her to lunch.

'Hugh, sorry to bother you. But I have to check some details with you, and wanted to see you, thank you for inviting me to lunch. I was not sure how to dress, so hope this is passible.'

Hugh could not help but smile, Brenda was dressed in a lovely muted burgundy silk shirt dress, that was stylish and neat, a matching jacket in reversed colours to the dress, draped over one arm, the Iris Pearls a lovely off set to the severe outfit. 'That is just perfect Brenda, we are not going far, but I am lunching with some colleagues and don't want to go alone. Phyllis usually accompanied me, so I hope you don't mind?'

Moved that he would ask her to accompany him, she went over and hugged this gentleman 'Of course I don't, thank you for asking me.'

'Now what is it that you are wanting to do. I had Dennis and David in the office yesterday, this Southend on Sea endeavour is going ahead I take it?'

'Oh yes, but I don't think Dennis, David, Peter, Glen or Dan realise exactly what I have in mind for this area. The existing Holiday Village not only needs to be demolished and the land cleared before it can be reused, the whole Seahaven area around it needs rescuing. I am going to do something a bit different. I want to build, 'The Iris Village' for the over 55 market, the youngish retirees, who want independence in a secure place, but not the large house to have to run. I still have to talk to David and Peter but I want the care homes to be primarily centred in the refurbished hotel, restaurant /amenity blocks that are already there, when I was reading the zoning rules found that I can go up another storey from the original buildings. As I want to lodge the area, lower in the ground, to give better access to the beach, and for wheelchairs, it will not make them too high that they block the views of the water from the houses already there.

My idea is that the retirees purchase the lease of the units while they live their lifestyle, the ones that will make up the Village area. They will be a mix of one and two bedroomed homes built in the space between the actual Care Homes; they then just pay utilities etc. direct. The price they pay we invest for them, with a modest cut to help maintain the property, and then when it is time for them to move into the main care home because they are unable to maintain the villa units, they have a guaranteed space, the money invested is used for their extended care, and once the inevitable occurs, the left-over funds are given back to their families. Not sure how many units we can get in there but I don't want them to feel crowded, so hopefully fifty to sixty may be possible. What do you think Hugh, is my idea mad or what?'

Hugh sat back and looked at this remarkable woman, where had this idea come from he wondered. Then realised the time, Rose opened the door to his office, 'The car is here Mr. Pemberton.'

Brenda looked at him, 'I don't drive to these functions Brenda, I like the wines they serve!'

Laughing they both moved out to the car waiting for them in the street. Once settled, Hugh turned to Brenda, 'Go on, what else do you intend to do, surely you don't need vast amounts of funds for just the village, seems as though any cost will eventually be covered?'

'Well I want to buy a few of the houses in the area that are up for sale. Then I can guarantee the workers I am hiring for the Village a home to live in, at reasonable rents, I don't have to use any of the units then for staff. I have selected one of the houses for myself, and earmarked one for Dennis, as he is going to need a place to base himself from, and this area will be perfect for him.'

'Ok, so how many is a few?

'Well, at the moment twelve, but maybe more. I was astounded at the number of houses and business that were just boarded up, and neglected. You know I hate to see wonderful buildings neglected!'

Hugh had to laugh, he looked at Brenda sitting calmly beside him, calmly stating she wanted to buy twelve or more houses. Two years ago, that would have put her in a panic, and been the furthest from her mind. He only hoped what happened next, she would want to sit next to him on the way home.

Brenda was enjoying the drive, but realised that they were going a little further than she thought they were going for a lunch. 'Hugh exactly how much further to this lunch of yours'

It was then that Brenda saw the building up ahead, and the car slowed down and stopped. A distinguished gentleman in a pale grey suit, got in next to the driver, and Brenda realised she had been hijacked. Knowing exactly what was going to happen, when they drove through the gates at Windsor Castle.

Brenda was sitting at the kitchen table, remembering the events of the last few hours, and having a very hard time believing that it actually happened.

Baron Phipps was graciousness itself, and guided her and Hugh through to the Royal Apartments, explaining that he thought after talking to Hugh, if she was aware of time and place, panic might have set in, so wanted to avoid it, as her Majesty wanted to meet her, without any pomp and ceremony.

Brenda just nodded, unable to speak, trying to take in the grandeur of the halls they were walking through, places the general public were never allowed to be in, gave them a special feel. He was explaining a little of what to do in the beginning, echoes of Mr Johnston's lessons reverberating in her brain, a small smile formed and gardenia floated, she relaxed a little as they moved into a wonderful room, it had a view out to the inner courtyard, sunlight streamed in through the stained-glass windows. Baron Phipps requested Hugh to make himself comfortable, he would be right back. Motioning Brenda towards the door in the corner, ushering her into the room with 'Your Majesty, may I introduce the right honourable Lady Brenda Lucas!'

Her curtsy she hoped was precise as she had been taught, and she caught the smile on the face of a Lady who had witnessed a lot of life. A simple one shake of the hand that was proffered, and Elizabeth Windsor, asked her first question 'Do you take milk or lemon in your tea?'

After that it was a task to piece together what had been an enjoyable afternoon. The two corgis after the initial sniff and scratch, Brenda asked if she was ok to offer, and the Queen nodded again with that smile, sent the dogs into ecstasies. Which, led to the question did she have any pets, and discussions of whether Corgi's were working dogs. Questions then followed in regards to the Care Homes that she had been told about, and how that was being managed, to the problems with getting staff with the right qualities. Brenda's solution (she hoped) with the ex-military personnel being offered the roles, and possibly her Diploma courses. To her surprise the Queen then mentioned William and Harry and the causes they championed, and of her own contributions. It was a very easy afternoon, and both ladies were a little disappointed when the knock on the door heralded Baron Phipps to advise time was up. Brenda was offered the hand again, this time the hand shake was a firm thank you, and her curtsey a little lower than needed was accepted in the manner it was given, with respect.

Back in the car, Hugh unsure of how Brenda was taking this new step in her social standing.

'Thank you, Hugh,' Brenda startled him by saying.

'Thank me, but why do you want to do that, I hijacked you, and we didn't get lunch!'

'Thank you for giving me one of the best afternoons I have had in a very long time. What a remarkable woman, what stories she could tell, but never would. She has seen this world, good, bad and very ugly at times, but still has time to take tea with me. I feel blessed!'

It was Kate coming into the kitchen that broke her mood, and the hug she got put the world in perspective again. Asking what was for dinner as she was starving, motivated Brenda to check what was in the fridge she could make up, then making Kate laugh by saying takeaway.

Her dreams that night were a mix, but predominately positive, visions of Iris, and her father were prominent, smiling and clapping. There were more figures in the background, also clapping, as if at a garden party, everyone dressed in their finest, the sun shining, and life was very good.

Chapter 14

I T WAS AN EARLY start to the morning, Brenda having looked into the fridge and freezer realised that shopping had to be done, if she was to host the BBQ on Sunday. Glad, she had invited Hugh around, and sending messages to Larry, Shane, Dennis and David with an invite too.

Leaving a note for Kate, took herself off to the markets, and supermarket to replenish lost stock, and enjoyed the morning wandering around; catching a taxi back to the house, laden with bags. Kate running up the basement stairs to help her mum in with what she thought a very large amount of groceries.

'I am doing a BBQ tomorrow luv, invited our resident guests, and Hugh. I sent a message to David and all, want to see if Matt can come. He can then meet Nasser, and do some networking?'

'Oh, I forgot that you had done that, ok will send him a message, he did say he was coming up to see David, might put him off till tomorrow and he can stay the night!'

Realising she had gone bright red, she started stammering. Brenda just went over and hugged her. 'What you do is your business, and you could not have picked a more loving and attentive suitor. But I am not prying, and I am not pushing; this is your business, but I am here if you need to talk Ok?'

Relaxing Kate nodded, her mum's hugs were to be savoured, and her words were welcome. Putting action to words went off to ring Matt and invite him up for lunch, and the afternoon. 'Good job you have the mountain of food mum, Glen and Ben are coming up with Matt, they want to speak to Shane, about the remodel, and when they can start. Hey what happened to your sleep out, weren't you planning on staying over at Southend?'

Realising that Kate had not been brought up to speed, did so while they set about preparing meat and delectable nibbles for the hoards now arriving the following day.

A phone call from Larry as she washed her hands and picked up her tea, was welcome. 'Hey thanks for the luncheon invite, I offered to ferry Hugh over to the house, who else is coming?'

'I invited our guests, I hope they realise it is for everyone, Doreen and Pierre included. Also, David and the gang from the Warehouse, I believe from Kate that Glen, Matt and Ben possibly Rebecca are coming up too, they need to talk to Shane and finalise some details with the architects, wonder if I should invite Peter as well?'

Larry was laughing, a small intimate luncheon which he was expecting was not going to happen, he realised this when he talked to Hugh that morning. 'The more the merrier, can I do anything to assist, I have a couple of folding tables and extra chairs, would that help?'

Saying that would not be necessary, just his company was required, he rang off saying he would be round fairly early, after picking up Hugh.

Brenda spent some time with Kate in the office, making sure the reminder for the BBQ was posted on each units T. V's. Spending some time sweeping and tidying the patio, not to Nona's standards of course, but neat and ready to meet all the visitors the following day. Once she was happy with the area, Brenda did a last-minute check of the BBQ. She was very happy that her request to build it into the end of the terrace next to the lift enclosure, Glen had endorsed as a good idea. That she had also requested Ben to attach it to the main gas line, reminiscing about the times when she had forgotten to check the gas bottle was full. Remembering those times with fondness, and smiling at the happy outcomes that the race to replace the gas bottles before the handyman store closed, gave her, as well as the times they had missed that deadline, and ended up with cooking sausages in the kitchen. Knowing that Larry and David would be vying for cook's duties to make sure the 'Barbie' went well.

It was just that hush before the day began, and Brenda woke going over the things to do before people arrived. The house guests had arrived back early on the previous afternoon, and Brenda had seen them walking through the conservatory, the children's voices light and happy as they ran around showing their parents, what Brenda had shown them.

Stretching, showering and getting dressed, she set about the chores she had to do. Not that they were chores, she always enjoyed cooking, and the preparation in the quiet before guests arrived was the best. When Kate walked into the kitchen quite a while later, it was to see her mum in the midst of making magic, she was transported back to the times of her birthdays, and the parties her mum would throw for both she and David.

The wonderful smell of baking bread, and other delicacies set the world to rights again, and she gave her mum a hug of thanks, 'You have been up for a while, good morning.'

'Good Morning luv, where did you get too last night, or should I not ask.' This was muttered under her breath as Matt, a rather sheepish Matt, walked into the kitchen not sure of his welcome, as it was clear he had spent the night.

A laugh from Kate, and another hug, was the only answer she was to get she realised, going around the table and giving Matt a hug, 'You are welcome any time my friend, be kind to my daughter and we will be fine!'

Hugging her back 'I intend to if she will let me in, but I will be patient!' he whispered to her. The timer went so checking that Kate was getting coffee and breakfast for them, went to pull the first loaves of bread and buns out of the oven. Turning when more footsteps heralded Ben coming into the Kitchen.

'Oh! I met them both last night, Becca had other plans, but will be round later, I invited them both here as Glen was coming up to see Shane, they could hitch a ride back with him after lunch.'

'Morning Brenda, oh what a wonderful smell, reminds me of Mum's kitchen on a Sunday morning, you two are so alike.' He picked up one of the bread buns juggling it across to the table to put butter and jam on to have for breakfast.

It was a lively, laughter filled morning, Brenda asked Kate to organise the boys to make sure all was set up in the patio, filling the drinks fridge that was also part of the BBQ set up. Bringing out of the Workshop the trestle tables that had been found, a couple of which fit in the curve of the terrace, the other four they set out with the wooden folding chairs that had also been found. Many of which were still good, but some even with the careful preservation Iris's ancestor had done, were not safe to sit on, so Brenda had organised for Nigel Hawthorn, Glen's Master Carpenter, to make replacements, he had also made the replacement dining chairs, that even the experts could barely tell apart from the originals.

She was busy in the kitchen, when Larry walked in appreciating the wonderful smells of food being prepared, going and putting his arms carefully, as she was in the midst of chopping nuts with a rather large knife, around her enjoying the warmth and beautiful smell of warm bread and spices.

'How long have you been up, it looks as though you are opening a restaurant, what are you doing here!'

'Morning luv,' Brenda turned in his arms and gave him a welcome kiss, quickly turning back to the desert she was preparing. 'Well I am expecting a hoard there will be the house Guests that's seven, Kate, Matt, Ben, Rebecca, Glen, Hugh, David, Dennis I also expect Shane, as I doubt David will let him be alone at the Warehouse, yourself and me, by my reckoning that is sixteen, so I have catered for twenty, never know who will show up on my doorstep!'

Larry laughed, and nodded in agreement to her assessment, as Hugh came into the kitchen, with a huge bunch of flowers for her, with Iris's being prominent.

'Thought these might be a thank you for the invite to lunch Brenda, as I knew I could not bake or bring food, bit like bringing coals to Newcastle that would be. Now how can I help?'

Laughing and giving him a hug taking the flowers, kissed him on the cheek and told him to go out to the noise in the Patio and keep the "young un's" under control they were supposed to be getting plates, cutlery etc. set out on the tables, and open the French doors please. Handing both him and Larry a coffee shooed them out, both of them chuckling at her comment, moved out through the butler's pantry, and requested help to fold back the doors, allowing cool fresh air to flow through the kitchen. Before she could do anything, footsteps heralded more arrivals. David and Dennis with Rebecca guiding them, walked through the kitchen door, a rather heavy looking Esky between them. 'What?' Brenda asked, after the hugs had been given.

'Well mum, I knew you would have the wine and cold drinks for the BBQ, but it really isn't a BBQ until you have the beer to go with it. So, I had John at the pub, put together some Aussie boutique beers to go with the food. Before you ask, I know what you have prepared, it's the same as you always do and I love – sausages chicken, pork and beef, marinated steak, chicken in some form or other, your delectable vegetable skewers, and knowing where your guests are from a fish possibly your yummy salmon parcels am I right?'

Laughing with him, and advising he was right, was she so predictable, enjoying the laughter that was flowing through the house, sent them out to help Larry and the gang finish the setting up, while she finished off the preparations.

The patio could not look any different from the neglected mess it was two years ago. The kitchen garden in the terraces were in full growth, set out by Norman as it would have been when in use, the herbs were spicy and aromatic, growing in abundance with the little bit of care Brenda gave them. The tiles shone and glistened, the colours on the walls and floor as though they had just been laid. Brenda had put Hugh's flowers in a large antique vase, and brought them out, nestling them into a spot in the bottom of the terrace that just cried out for the vase to be in. Wondering again if she was reliving someone else's life, how many people had used this vase and put it into this spot in the terrace. A slight shiver ran through her, and gardenia floated in the air, a caress of breeze on her cheek, and she knew she was right, tears started in her eyes, but there was joy in the air, as she turned with the lift doors opening.

Doreen and Pierre were the first of the house guests, again wondering at their inclusion into the lunch. Brenda allaying their fears with a sweeping arm around the mainly male gathering, quietly saying her invites were for all guests of Iris House, and they were her guests, no matter what role they played with their employee. Doreen smiled and thanked her again for the invite, holding out a large plate, that had a delicious nut and pastry slice, 'for dessert, I hope you don't mind, but I could not come empty handed.'

Thanking her taking her hand and pulling both of them into the midst of the gathering, looking to Kate and Rebecca to take Doreen under her wing, took the plate into the kitchen, checking preparations were all ok. Coming back to find a lively debate on how the Australians were going to go in the test match coming up through the summer months. Pierre and Matt were in a corner in a very deep discussion, Kate gave her mum a wink, and cheeky smile. As David donned his apron to start the BBQ, Larry wearing a matching apron coming out of the Kitchen BBQ tools in hand. The lift doors opened Sir James and Shane coming out in the midst of a mock BBQ tool sword fight to see who would be the chef of the day. Laughter rang out, sunshine and rainbows sparkled the air, Gardenia floated and Brenda wondered if her heart could take any more, this was what Iris had wanted, the laughter, the bonhomie. Going and saying hello and welcome to both of the gentlemen pulling them away from the antagonists, turning to both saying, there was enough for both of them to look after, just make sure the BBQ was on!

Nasser, Adelle and the children were next, Adelle advising that the Nanny had taken the day to visit family, and she sent her apologies. They were a little shocked at arriving in the midst of such a large gathering, but the children once their shyness was overcome were delighting the adults with their conversations. Glen, with Peter in tow were the last to arrive, Peter with a roll of plans under his arm, apologised for crashing the luncheon.

'Family can't crash anything, Peter love, surely you know that, you Beverley and those two hellions of yours are welcome at any time. Now what have you here?'

Peter enjoyed the hug he was given, as he always did, Brenda was the mum he had never known. Dan and Helen were kind and he loved them dearly, being the parents of his beloved wife, but in

Brenda he had found that something, a peace, a knowledge that whatever you did would be met with pride, assurance and love, this woman's capacity for love amazed him, and he just wanted it to continue.

'Well when Dan told me that Glen was coming to lunch and Shane would be here, I hitched a ride, as I have the final plans for the alteration to the warehouse. The permits have come through, so once everything is packed up we can make a start, but I wanted to get Shane's ok on what David and I have come up with.'

David came up with a beer for him, 'here try this, John said it was a tasty light beer, but I want your opinion. Oh, you got the plans finished, hey Shane want to check these out?'

Peter took the beer automatically, wondering at the gathering in the patio. Happy laughter was in the air, and he moved over to Shane and Sir James, who were talking to a rather handsome couple, that he tagged as the Iris House guests, the two children running around must belong to them.

The plans were unrolled on the table next to Shane, and the whole company gathered around to view them. It was a neat alteration, the existing interior of the warehouse was just removed, giving a clean slate. The plumbing for Kitchen, the two downstairs bathrooms, laundry and cloak room, and the upstairs bathroom added, which according to Ben, would be easy. While this was going on, Matt and his team were going to be prepping the electrics, the updated security system, the separate line for the lift, the mechanics for that being given by Brent. Then once the preparation was complete in came the new frames and panels for the mezzanine with its internal soundproof walls. To the Kitchen – open plan to the living room of course, and the two bedrooms' downstairs, the big one with its own children friendly bathroom, with room enough for three cots that could turn into small beds. The slightly smaller bedroom with shower room for a nanny, and the space for a powder/laundry room. Then the lift in the corner of the living room, that the spiral stairs wound around, up to the mezzanine with its own wheelchair friendly bathroom.

'This is a very neat alteration,' Nasser said taking in the plans with an expert eye, 'I understand your firm has done this?' He turned to Peter, as he had brought the plans.

'Yes,' Peter nodded, looking and nodding at David, 'my partner and I have been the architects of a few remodels recently. This is just the latest, also the team that actually build the structures are here with the exception of my father in law, who runs the steel works!'

'But why the alteration, the warehouse itself looks fine?'

Shane looked up from the plans, he had toyed with the idea of altering the warehouse for years, but had never got the right feel from any of his designs. Putting his ideas on the back burner. This felt right, and would give him and his new family a place to live, until the children needed more space to run around in.

'Well the space would not work in a couple of months, you see my wife Linda is in hospital at the moment, we have just found out she is having triplets, not the one child we thought it was!'

Adelle had wandered over, realising that the adults in the group, would not let the children out of their sight, and it was safe to relax. It was a strange mix of people in the gathering that she found intriguing. She realised before her husband, that the mix of people in this group were the builders of the structures Peter had the plans for. Congratulating Shane on his instant family, and looking at the plans with renewed wonder.

'My husband, is also an architect, although he builds rather large complexes. I studied the basics, it was how we met. I can see that the way you have used the space will fit you and your family for years to come.'

Nasser, smiled at his wife, but noted she was correct. The group then discussed what was next to happen, when lunch was called. Brenda explaining what had been cooked on the BBQ to allay any dietary requirements, setting out the food on the trestles along the wall, urging people to fill plates and go for seconds.

Chapter 15

THE SECOND ROLL OF plans Peter left with David, as he wanted him to go over the Village details with his mum. Sure, he had not got them right, as there was something going on in Brenda's head that she had not voiced, and he did not think the BBQ was the place to ask the question.

Shane advised that he had Stan and some of the family with boxes arriving early the following morning, and would have the house packed up and moved to the storage place he had rented, so work could begin in earnest on Tuesday morning. Glen adding that he and at least three of his men would be there, with a skip being delivered Monday afternoon, easier if the stuff they pulled out was put in the skip straight away less mess. Then possibly by Wednesday or Thursday morning he could leave the place to Ben and Matt to put in all the pipes and plumbing, to then wait for Dan to deliver and fit the steel mezzanine, with the circular stairs, and Brent the lift.

'Baring any accidents or delays with deliveries I think we may actually have your place put back to rights within three weeks. At least that is what I am planning, as I am sure Ms. Brenda here will have more work for me to do, and will want that happening yesterday!'

Brenda was a little stunned as she had just heard the last part of the speech, being busy in the kitchen with teas and coffees, bringing out Doreen's delicious slice, and the two types of Turkish delight she had made for dessert.

'I am sure this will not be in the same class as the Turkish delight you make, but you reminded me that I had the bottles of Rosewater, so made some with pistachio nuts and some plain. The leftovers I will box up and take into Linda in the hospital when I visit her tomorrow. Now what was Glen going on about?'

Discussion over building time frames and merits of different building techniques went on for a long while, with Nasser and Adelle adding in their information from a different country, and how long it took to organise building material and builders.

The children had been very good, and now were sated but very tired, so started picking at each other, even David who with Ben had been the favourite people in the group were not able to stop the bickering. Deciding that the last few days were really taking their toll, Nasser and Adelle reluctantly left, rightly deciding, that giving the children an early night with a bath and story in bed would be the best for both of them. Doreen and Pierre leaving not long after, thanking Brenda for an enjoyable afternoon.

'Another successful afternoon at Iris House,' Sir James came up and gave Brenda a hug, everyone could smell the Gardenia floating on the air. Filling his coffee cup from the pot on the burner, and taking another piece of Turkish delight, 'I like the pistachio one, and will accept a box anytime you feel like making it for me!'

'Next time I remember I have the Rosewater in the pantry I will make a box just for you. Now how is Linda, I take it you both went to see her this morning?' They left not long after, going to see Linda that evening, to report on everyone they had met that afternoon.

It was not long before everyone else was saying their goodbyes, realising it was closer to 6pm than the 4pm she thought it was, Brenda was shocked that they had stayed.

Brenda caught Glen as he delivered more used coffee cups to her in the kitchen.

'Glen, have you some workmen that won't mind being away from home for a while?'

'Why luv, we are not ready to start on the Village, you haven't even got planning permission!'

'No, I know that, and I must have a look at the plans Peter said he had drawn up for me, I need to alter them slightly, actually we might have to scrap them and start again, but' and she ignored his chortle at her comment, 'I will need your building assistance if you can fit me in, or a reliable replacement if you know of any builders that have your sense of integrity, that are in the area, as I am going to modernise and refurbish the houses I am buying in the street, I would like them up to Iris House standard if I can. One will be for me, and one for Dennis. He will need a base to work from, and he deserves a proper home to live in, so we will need to check out what we have, once Larry and Hugh have bought them; hence my request!'

'No worries lass, I do actually have contacts over that way, good men, good reliable men, who would welcome the work. So, when you are ready, you let me know, and I will make sure they come up to town for our planning meeting, you can check them out, ok?'

'Check who out, who is Mum checking out now,' David with Dennis, were bringing in the leftovers from the BBQ and salads. Brenda could hear Kate, Ben, Rebecca and Matt folding up the furniture and putting it away in the Workshop. She put fresh coffee on, and the kettle to boil, while leaving the food on the big kitchen table to be picked at before putting in containers in the fridge.

'The builders I will be in contact with over at Southend, your mum seems to want someone to check the houses in the street with a view to updating them a la Iris House, so will get Len and his foreman Wayne, to come up to town next week, and see your mum.'

Larry walking into the kitchen, with the BBQ tools and paper towels after making sure the BBQ was clean and switched off, heard Glen say about the Southend builders.

'Well we won't need them for a week or two Glen. I still have to buy the houses, have put in a call to the estate agents, and will follow up tomorrow, but by all means line them up, and give them a boost that there is work aplenty coming up for them!'

Glen nodded and hugging Brenda, took Ben, Peter, Rebecca and Matt home, saying Julie would be furious Sunday dinner was not going to be enjoyed as it should, he was stuffed from the excellent lunch. Laughing Larry and Brenda waved them goodbye and moved back into the kitchen. Kate, David and Dennis had put most of the food away, David snagging a large container of leftovers for his place. She put an arm around him, asking him to bring out the plans for the Village.

Not even wondering how she knew he had them, brought them in from the patio, spreading them out so they could all see them.

'Ok mum, what do you think?'

'I think they are wonderful, and all wrong. No wait a second, you don't know what I am thinking, so let me explain.' Taking a pencil to alter the plans, as she had done when she wanted changes to happen continued, 'I want to demolish everything, make a clean sweep of the area, the main buildings are rubbish anyway, the foundations were not put in correctly you can see that by the cracks that are everywhere. So; I want to clean the site, settle it lower into the area, we will have to excavate to put in new footings, and I want to use the same system for the sewerage and connections as at Broadmeadows, no power poles please. Those rickety stairs we walked down, please replace with spiral staircase.'

'Made in steel', was the chorus from everyone with laughter.

Brenda nodded, 'I would like to rebuild the two main buildings, basically as they were originally intended as hotel, with restaurant, kitchens, library etc. in one, but then go two or more floors up to road level which will give the reception area and offices of the new site. I would like the top floor to be at road level, with the access from there via a walkway, and also a door from the promenade. We also need to check the existing steps from the road to the promenade, better get Brian Goddard, Glen's stonemason, or his compatriot in the area to check them and refurbish please. The land already slopes from the road to the beach at the Retreat end of the sea front, I just want to make the path that is there a lot wider and user friendly with a paved road, which will be needed to move machinery in and out of the site, so you may have to dig it out a bit further.'

They all nodded as they could see what Brenda meant.

'These two main buildings become the Iris Care Homes, oh and in one I want to add a Doctors suite, we may be able to get a live-in doctor for the homes and possibly the area, as I noticed there were no doctors in the vicinity, and my research didn't show any. The rest of the area is really going to be the "Iris Village for over 55's".' She then explained to them what she discussed with Hugh, who was sitting in Dan's chair enjoying the feel of the afternoon and the enthusiasm of the people listening to what Brenda proposed. 'Well what do you think?'

Larry looked at her, then at Hugh, who raised his cup in salute, giving his approval to what to everyone outside this room would think it to be a madcap venture. He looked at David, who was looking at the plans, that Brenda had attacked to try and get her idea over to them all. Dennis was chuckling, realising when Brenda had offered him the house, she was already twenty steps ahead of them all, and had all this planned out in her head.

'Well what do you think?' Brenda asked again, Kate had been quiet in the back of the kitchen, slowly tidying away the things from the luncheon, filling both the dishwashers, and generally making the place tidy. She moved over to Brenda, standing next to David and Larry, Dennis sitting on the bench, 'I think we had better buy a car, we are going to need one!' Laughter rang out from everyone.

Chapter 16

MONDAY MORNING, SHE MOVED out of the bed loath to disturb Larry, who was sound asleep, it had been a late night, after finishing off some leftovers, at least what David had left them, and polishing off a bottle of Iris red, Hugh had left in a cab. Larry staying as he David and Dennis were discussing how to achieve the plans Brenda was hatching.

She moved into the study after putting the kettle on and coffee to brew, her brain not able to shut down with all the details she wanted to find out. She wanted to give hope to the people living in the area she was about to transform, first of all she had to organise her brief to the council, to see if they were willing to allow the Care Home and Village to go ahead. Larry and Hugh had worked out a plan of attack for the purchase of the houses, assuring her that she would be able to afford all she had asked for, they would be careful on her part, and would start the implementation of that today. She was still restless, and wondering which way to go with the Southend Council, she had various drafts of her submission in the computer when Larry poked his head around the doorway into the study.

'There you are, thought you had done a runner again!' chuckling when she turned and swatted him on the arm.

'I have been here trying to work, your snoring woke me up!'

'I don't snore my dear Lady, and I know your brain has not switched off from Thursday. I also know what happened on Friday,' at her startled look, 'don't get anxious Hugh told me, he is a little worried you won't like him anymore because of what he did!'

'Oh, how can that wonderful man think that, hopefully the luncheon yesterday will have dissuaded him of that. It was one of the most surreal afternoons I have ever had, and I still can't believe it actually happened. One of these days I might tell you about it, but one thing she was really interested in was the Care Homes, she was really impressed by my idea for the staff to run them.'

She heard movement coming from Kate's room, 'please don't say anything to Kate, I just want to savour the moment myself for a while, before it all comes out.'

Nodding in acceptance, Larry motioned to the coffee cup and Brenda accepted the top up. Moving into the kitchen to give her daughter a very big hug, and welcome to the morning. They were all sitting down dissecting the previous day's events, all three of them with different perspectives of what worked and what did not, when Brenda's phone rang.

'Glen, good morning, didn't think I would hear from you for a few days. How was Julie when you got home, was she mad that I filled you up at Lunch?'

'No lass,' Glen's hearty chuckle came down the phone, 'she was fine, besides her Sunday dinners, become Monday lunch and Tuesday's Scampi. No, I wondered if you were free, Jack has uncovered something at Broadmeadows, and I think I have to show you what and where. You also did not get a good look at those plans, there is a little more to what we found out than just the Gate Lodge. Do you think you can get down there today, I am just about to leave?'

'Hold on Glen, Larry is still here I can ask if he can be my chauffeur?'

Brenda explained that Glen needed her at Broadmeadows, asking her to hold on till he checked what was on his diary that day, after a check on his phone, sent a text message to his secretary, said he would be happy to drive her, he hadn't seen the place in a long time. Besides the overnight bags were still in his car!'

Laughing, Brenda turned to Kate.

'It's ok mum, you need to go, looks like Iris or Grandfather Norman still have some surprises up their sleeves. I need to be around for our guests, they leave tomorrow, and we don't have anyone coming in till Wednesday next week, so go ahead, I can go over and visit Linda, fill her in with all the details'

'OK Glen, all arranged, Larry and I will be down shortly see you at Broadmeadows!'

They got on the road a little while later, Brenda packing some food to take, and a few other bits and pieces. Larry rang Hugh and told him where they were going, hoping he didn't mind and he knew he was just itching to get involved in the house purchases, if he hadn't started already.

Arriving at Broadmeadows, Larry pulling through the gates parking on a spot outside the offices; Brenda was stunned at what she saw. First, she saw the very large pile of timber rescued from the ruins of the Gate Lodge, with the equally large pile of tree trunks carefully stacked against the side and behind the wood workshop container. The rescued timber she had expected but the tree trunks left her wondering where they had come from. Getting out of the car when Glen came out of the office, looking at him, the grin on his face made him look twenty years younger, she could see echoes of both Ben and Matt in that grin.

She turned then and realised that the oak trees that had been behind the ruins of the building were gone and knew where the stack had come from. Glen motioned them to move further up the driveway, the trees had been so dense, they had hidden from view the two very substantial but damaged, stone pillars that were miniature versions of the main gates. In between the pillars was now an opening that led into a very large open space, that was completely hidden in overgrown brambles, ivy, and various types of foliage that she had no idea what it was.

'Ok I see but I don't believe, just what have you done to the Gate Lodge?' Brenda was turning on the spot trying to comprehend the changes that had occurred.

Larry walked over to the edge of the clearing, and looked at Glen, 'Iris or Grandfather Norman?'

'I think more likely Great Grandfather Norman, did this.' And he spread his arm over the partly cleared site. Fully cleared it was not, the foundations of the Gate Lodge were covered in a tarpaulin, so could not really be seen, but the area beyond could be seen to a certain extent although a lot of greenery was still obscuring their view. 'When I did my initial walk around the Lodge, I realised this area', and he pointed to the area beyond the newly found pillars, 'was too level, and had no trees at all, just shrubs and brambles. When I scraped down a bit, I could clearly see a cobbled yard, very old cobbled yard, and I got to wondering. Now I know there was a stable block up by the main house, that was demolished for the Greenhouse/Warehouse, so where do you put the stables? Here, was the answer?'

They had walked quite a way past the Gate Lodge, up the driveway and were standing in front of the newly found pillars, Brenda realised she was walking on a partly cleared wide cobbled roadway that gave a level entrance from the driveway to the area beyond. The stumps of the trees showed you where they had been taken from, and they were very big indeed, giving a brilliant camouflage to the area behind them, so dense you could not see when the trees were there, also now seen were the remnants of stone walls either side of the stone pillars and tantalising bits and pieces, it was a huge space.

'There are at least two possibly more cottages here Brenda luv, along with stables to house at least a dozen horses. What you don't know is that Peter knew about this area, he had found detailed descriptions of the buildings and out buildings in one of the really old journals. So, when he put the plans into council for the upgrading of the Gate Lodge, he actually asked for the "upgrading of the Gate Lodge and surrounding grounds and buildings", so guess what?'

Brenda just nodded at him, still trying to take in what the trees along the back of the Gate Lodge and up the driveway had been hiding for a very long time.

'What?' was the best she could muster, wondering at the length of time it was going to take to get all this planning through both of the councils.

'You, already have the planning permission for this, it was given when they gave the ok for the Gate Lodge!'

Stunned was what Brenda was, and in total awe of the commitment these people were continuing to give her. As a light drizzle began to fall, Glen motioned them back into the office, to show them the second set of plans that Brenda had seen, but not had the chance to ask about.

'You are going to rebuild the lot then Glen?' Larry asked as they poured over the plans set on the draft board in front of them.

'You bet I am, with Brenda's permission of course, I want to see this estate as it was, and not just in my dreams, or nightmares. There will be discoveries to make to be sure, and another one was when we excavated down into the Gate Lodge, realised the cellar is a lot larger than the actual house above it!'

Brenda just looked at him, blowing to cool her coffee at a loss for the words to describe her feelings.

'And!' Larry prompted, 'there was more wasn't there, I am always amazed at what Iris's ancestors managed to do.'

Glen laughed, this whole mad adventure that started over two years ago was just continuing, and he loved it, you never knew what was going to come next.

'You are right Larry, when we pulled up the floor, realised that there was a substantial cellar, haven't checked it out properly yet, hence the tarpaulin to keep the weather out, but Jack found a door in the cellar wall, once they got it open, it is a good oak door, they realised there was a tunnel going out into the darkness. Dan is going to love this, the length they walked, oh its ok Brenda they could not get too far, as there is debris in there, and I was not going to let them go digging it out just yet,' as Brenda gasped, worrying about their safety. 'Jack is no fool, but when he realised the place is made out of steel, curved steel and brick lined, realised the grandson had built it around the time when the greenhouse was done, again probably to prove to his father and grandfather it could be done. I am now wondering when we get through all the debris if the ground works for the stable would still be there, as I think they were made in steel?'

The revelations were stunning, and Brenda just could not believe the scope of what she had inherited. Looking from Glen to Larry, tried to find words, but non-came, a waft of Gardenia floated around the group, and she smiled. 'Iris is happy at least, so when do we see what is there Glen?'

Chuckling as he had also smelt the fragrance, along with Larry, he pointed out the path they had just used. 'That was what we thought a flowerbed going through the trees. It is cobbled the same as the stables, and we think the area over the cellar is like that as well. There was once a substantial road through to the main cobbled area in front of the stables, from this main road, judging by the stone pillars we discovered, it must be reinforced somehow. The cobble driveway perhaps was damaged in the bombing when the main house burnt down, which allowed the oak trees to grow. I thought the damage to the Gate Lodge was just old age, perhaps the bombs hit here as well as the main house, and mother nature took over to cover the scars. Well we will find out when we get the archaeologist down here again. They will have to see the site and do their bit and pieces. Dan is coming down tomorrow, with a few of his workers, so we will see what he thinks.

The drizzle had turned into a very steady rain, nothing much could be done for the rest of the day, so Glen, called an early finish, to start again bright and early next day. He was sure Dan would be there at first light, Brenda and Larry both agreeing with him.

Bright and early was an understatement, the knocking on the Mini Manor door was before the sun had risen. Thank goodness, Brenda thought, she was awake early too, and had coffee brewing and kettle boiling, Dan apologising as he sat down at the table accepting his cup of tea with a chuckle.

'I just knew you would be awake Brenda, eager to see what there is,' nodding at the camera on the table, 'and to note what we remove. It is a very big area, and I am sure it is bomb damage, so we will have to go very carefully, as I bet they didn't do a sweep after they hit. Ah good morning Larry, good of you to join us!'

Larry just looked at the bright and cheerful face and growled, he was never the best in the morning, and as the sun had yet to show was even more surly. Brenda gave him a cup of coffee and urged him to sit next to Dan. She was about to follow, when another knock on the door heralded Glen, with Peter following.

The hug she bestowed on the young man, was welcome 'Thank you for thinking five steps ahead, you are brilliant,' she whispered in his ear. Turning him into the room and asking if he would like tea or coffee. General chatter flowed, with all the men itching to see what was there, but Dan again put a cautious note into the dialogue.

'We can't just go charging in we have to be able to see what we are stepping on, I have an army buddy of mine coming down with a few of his cadets from the college that is just up the road, they are bringing metal detectors with them. I am sure the archaeological people will be here shortly as well, I made sure they realised what we might find, and they were very excited.'

Peter pulled out a set of plans with the new area now clearly outlined, Brenda turned to him, 'How do you know that is what is there?'

Sheepishly, he turned to them all, 'Well I got excited when Brenda said we were rebuilding, all those months ago, I sort of trespassed a little.' Brenda smiled, he knew he was ok, 'I wanted to get a feel of the place before I put drawings on paper, so for a couple of weekends, I brought Beverley with the boys to ramble over the area, it let them blow off steam a little, we sort of walked a little bit of the perimeter, just to be able to put it down correctly. I was very excited when the boys disappeared between the oaks and found the space covered in the brambles and greenery, realised it had been originally an area with farm buildings. What we saw and found in the scope of the land, I could not believe. The damage I saw here and up at the main house I realised that it had to be due to many bombs, got out of there very quickly, as I did not know if there were any unexploded shells in that debris, there would have been an awful lot falling on the area to do the damage, and demolish the main house.'

The sun was just a hazy glow on the horizon, but Brenda could not contain herself or restrain the men in the group. They piled into the cars, and drove down to the Gate Lodge, to find a crowd of people, milling around. Stunned by the numbers, Brenda was introduced to the Archaeological team, then the friend of Dan's from the military college, with his eager cadets behind him, then Dan's workers she acknowledged, with Greg coming over and giving her a hug to say hello. She turned to Glen, wondering where Jack and Fred were from his workers, only to nod as he reminded her they were starting the demolition of the warehouse, that day, so had sent the two of them off to begin, he had wanted to be here with her.

Standing at the gates, with all the people around her and the light steadily growing with the rising sun, Brenda could view the area as she had never done before. Yes, she had visited but had immediately gone straight to the mini manor, not even thinking about the area she was now viewing. It took her breath away, as the morning sun rose and gave a golden highlight to the day, opening up the vista in-front of them all. Showing her the ruins that was her gate lodge that Glen had been right, the area beyond could only be the stables.

It was agreed that the cadets with their metal detectors should cautiously go first around the outer edge to work inwards, to check what was hidden (if anything) under the ground cover. Splitting into teams, it was agreed, once the metal detectors had cleared an area, the workmen armed with spades and secateurs, would clear away the foliage. Slowly moving over towards the shells of the buildings they could now see were covered in brambles and ivy hiding them from view.

These were on the left-hand side of the square, as Brenda looked cautiously through into the space from the driveway. Following the first group, could see the outline of a cottage as the ivy and brambles were cut down, to a lot of muttered curses from Dan, who would not let her out of his sight, was helping his men with a rather large machete in hand. She could also see looking through the building, a garden space and after this a substantial ivy covered stone wall before the road which ran parallel to the estate. It was a slow process, to check if anything unexploded was lurking in the buildings themselves, but apart from finding the shell cases of quite a few bombs, found nothing else, thank goodness. It took most of the day to get half way around the perimeter to the cottages alone, and although still light, Dan after consulting with Glen called a halt. They had to remove the debris from what they had started to clear or they would make more work for themselves. After the archaeological teams and the cadets had departed shortly followed by Dan and Glens workmen, only Brenda, Larry, Peter, Greg, Dan and Glen remained. It was quiet and peaceful without all the people around.

'Well lass, I think this will work out, once we can see what is there! Now, I can see but will have to check, that there will be space to extend and bury the utilities pipe for the cottages have to check how many buildings are actually buried in that rubble, but I will extend it as far as I can. May have to make courtyards rather than gardens, but there is the room to do that, once the all clear has been given.' Glen was commenting on the area they had just cleared, standing beside one of the gate pillars, no one wanted to walk further in, caution of the unknown keeping them on the edge.

The cobblestones in the small space they could see before them, looked as good as the day they were laid, Glen and Dan had advised the workers to clear with shovels, until they had gone over the whole area, neither of them wanted heavy machinery possibly setting anything off. The outlines of two of the houses opposite the stables had been rescued from the brambles and undergrowth, Brenda hoped that the height of the foliage past them hid another one or two buildings, clearly now with the greenery taken away you could see that they had been hit by an explosion. They could see sandstone blocks and roofing tiles in amongst the undergrowth, across the space in front of them.

At the far side, opposite to where she stood, there were the remnants of an immense gatehouse which had given the fourth wall enclosing the space for the stables, she was shaking her head at the damage that had been done to a wonderfully proportioned building. She could see the side beams that had made the gate uprights, all that was left of some magnificent gates leading out into the estate, attached to the side walls of the building remnants, imagining the building that had two towers and rooms running across it, opening onto a path of some sort out into the grounds of Broadmeadows. She could see both Dan and Glen were itching to go inside the cottages, but Brenda would not permit it.

'Guys please be cautious. We have no idea how these places were demolished whether there are pot holes or worse hiding under the foliage, and we don't know if they have cellars linked to the main gate lodge, that might be hiding a more explosive welcome. Let's please just take our time shall we, and yes Glen I said let's just take our time!'

He looked at her, and chuckled putting a friendly arm across her shoulder, to say ok. Moving back to lock up the office, Larry and Brenda closing the gates after their cars had gone. Strolling back up to the Mini Manor for the evening, it was a beautiful evening, the promise of summer on a whisper of wind, rattling the leaves just beginning to appear on the trees. Loathe to be inside she took Larry on a tour of the gardens, explaining that Norman was planning great things for this kitchen garden, and the house once it was built, but was laying the ground works now.

Chapter 17

T HE MORNING START WAS not quite so early the following day, but still the sun had just appeared above the roof tops. No Archaeological team today, they had decided they were not required, so it was just the cadets, with Dan and Glens smaller teams. They worked steadily through the morning, clearing more of the debris in front of the two cottages, and cautiously making their way across the yard as craters had been found.

Brenda was on the phone to Kate, in the office explaining what was happening, when a shout went up, and everyone came hurrying out of the yard. 'What's up mum, problem?' Telling her she was not sure, and would call her later, went out of the office to meet up with Larry, standing listening to what Colonel Johnstone was saying.

'I think I had better call in the bomb squad, not sure what it is but Leon here said it looks intact, and if intact might be dangerous, also if we have found one, there might be more. So, if you don't mind I will just call up a colleague of mine, who just loves poking his nose into these types of scenarios. Me, I would be running very fast the other way!'

'Ah, well that was good timing on yours and Leon's part then Colonel Johnstone, as I had arranged for lunch to be delivered today, and here it comes by the look of it. So please get the cadets to relax, and lunch will be ready for everyone very shortly, if you ring your Bomb Disposal buddy it will give him time to get here while we eat lunch, does that sound fair?'

Dan and Glen pulled their men and machines out of the area, all of them happy when they saw the little van with catering logo written over the side setting up outside the office; realising that Brenda had again thought of offering them lunch. The cadets too, were happy to stand down, and all gave the caterer's a headache until everyone had what they needed.

They were finishing off lunch and waving the caterer away, Brenda had checked with Sam Sargent who owned and ran the catering company 'Broadmeadows Catering' that she and her team would be required whenever there were workmen on the site, and to please come back again tomorrow, they would be welcomed.

They had just disappeared from view when four large Army trucks pulled into the drive way, filling the parking area beside the office. A small jeep followed them and stopped outside of the office, Colonel Johnstone saluting as the passenger got out of the car, his driver moving off to park in front of the trucks.

'Jim, thanks for coming, let me introduce you to everyone, and tell you what we are doing, and have found.'

The man reminded Brenda of someone, it was the bearing the ramrod straight stance and the demeanour, as he turned to come over to the group, she realised he was a younger version of Michael Dranish Fawkes, she smiled as gardenia floated around everyone.

'May I introduce General James Richardson commanding officer of the Bomb Squad that trains at the campus, we are based at.'

He shook hands with the gentlemen, and took Brenda's hand and briefly kissed the back. Stunned for a second, she took in the twinkle in the eye, and small smile, even more so when a wonderful Welsh lilted voice said, 'Charmed I am sure, now Dick here was very cryptic in what you were doing, but I take it you are building and found something that should not be there?'

Larry did not miss the twinkle or the fact he still held Brenda's hand, and laughed at himself, as the Gardenia floated around. He knew that the secret was out, how, he was not sure, he was also not sure how Brenda was going to take this, the look on her face he could see she was a little confused, then it cleared he nodded his head, yes, she knew.

Leaving the main body of men beside the office, Dick and James took their lieutenants and a couple of the bomb squad with them for a reconnoitre. Dan, Glen had a discussion, decided most of the workmen could have an early day, they took John, Fred and Greg off to the storage area, to work on the stone or timber that needed sorting, cleaning and getting ready to be used again.

It was not long before the military contingent came back, a little quicker than they went.

'Yes, well I am glad that Dick here did send for us, and I could see that the unexploded device was not alone. So, I need for everyone to clear the site completely, and we will take over the clearing of the area. Can I please speak to the owner, I need to inform him of what we are doing, I also have to advise the Police that we will be detonating a few bombs, once I have found a place that will be safe to do so, as I don't think after all this time, they will travel well!'

Brenda was a little bemused, how was she going to deal with this, head on she realised was the only way, but Larry got in first.

'Excuse me General, may I have a word?' He pulled the General aside away from his men and Dick, 'I am sure you have done a little bit of research before you headed out General? You know exactly who is in charge here, I know you do. The way you greeted her makes me even more sure you know who Lady Brenda Lucas is? So, was the Freudian slip meant or do you not recognise her standing?

General James looked at Larry, realising that he could not avoid telling that he did indeed know who Brenda was, with the college in close proximity to Broadmeadows, they had wondered when improvements had begun, and had done some research, on the new owner. They had many times in the past, tried to purchase some or all of the land, now to find that the new owner was actually going to restore the area, he was not sure he was happy, they would not be able to expand the college as they wanted. He had also, called Baron Phipps to check details, he had been a past chairman, who had asked they look after the new Lady Lucas, whenever they met her. Expecting a wizened old hag, he had had quite a shock when Brenda had been in the group of workmen.

Glen and Dan, with Greg following behind, came to stand next to Brenda, realising something was afoot when Larry was having a quiet word with the General. The Colonel was quite bemused wondering what was going on, you never crossed General James, never, and here were civilians doing just that, he was intrigued, especially as it seemed to centre around the woman, who was nice but he had dismissed her as a worker like the others, possibly the PA of the owner. He had sent the cadets back to the college, no need for them now, the bomb squad would carry on, he was just waiting for final instructions, moved over to the group when Brenda smiled at him.

'Thank you, and the Cadets for all your hard work over the last couple of days Colonel. Hopefully they enjoyed the outdoor experience?'

'Yes, I believe they all enjoyed the fact they were out of the classroom, and actually using the equipment they study practically. Oh, and thank you for the lunch, it was not necessary, but welcome.'

'My pleasure, I don't like to see any workman go hungry, not when they are expending energy at my request.'

Dan, Glen and Greg all chuckled at the last remark, the Colonel giving them a querying look, just as Larry and the General came over to them, he was not ready for the shock that the General was about to give.

Stopping just short of the group, being covered from the rest of the men by the three very large bodies that were flanking Brenda, General James made a decision, and hoped it was the right one. He stopped and took her hand again, bobbing his head to her, as Mr. Johnstone in all his lessons had told her eventually men would, 'Lady Lucas, I apologise for my crassness before, I did not know if it was general knowledge that you were here? I also have to advise you that Baron Phipps sends his regards.' Immediately Colonel Johnstone realised who Brenda was, and it was not a PA, he quickly bowed his head in acknowledgement, but she seemed so normal!

Brenda sighed, realising that here was where her life as Lady Brenda Lucas began, it was fitting it should be here, with the rebuilding of Broadmeadows. Gardenia floated on the air, all the men stiffened at the smell, the old guard knew it was Iris and the men of the Lucas line giving Brenda a benediction. The two new gentlemen just liked the fragrance Brenda wore, taking it as her perfume.

'Thank you for that General, now as you have requested my help in finding an area that would be remote enough but not too far for transport, to detonate.' Brenda turned as Peter tapped her arm, 'Can I have a word with you for a moment Lady Lucas?'

Surprised by his use of Lady Lucas, she automatically nodded and followed him back into the office also surprised by the hug he gave her as they were out of sight.

'Oh, I am so pleased that the title is now confirmed, been waiting to congratulate you for so long. I overheard the General thought I should use the title, it being one of the times it should be used,' he said at her startled look. 'Now as to the disposal of whatever they have found. You said to Glen a while back you wondered if a lake or water view can be added to the site, well if you look here at the far side of the house out in the grounds, on my rambles in the past Beverly and I found a depression, I think that was a water course or lake once, it was very boggy in places, in fact one of the boys had a very good mud bath Beverly was not happy. The spot is far enough away from the house and buildings, but would be in the right place if you wanted to excavate, why not let the Germans a few years late do it for you?'

Giving him a hug back, went to the door to call the men in. Showing both the General and the Colonel the site Peter had seen, getting the approval on paper, from both of them. With the proviso that Glen and Dan could actually clear a path for them to take the ordinance safely to the site. When pointed out to them by Peter, both men looked at each other, realising it would let them clear a road, if one was not already there, around to the other side of the main house out into the grounds to where the depression was, but had not thought of exploring that far ahead, because of the lack of council permission, they put on suitable faces to check on the details, all the while trying to keep from jumping for joy.

Suddenly the quiet site was a busy place with machinery being started; the bomb squad donning gear and getting trollies and machinery out of the trucks. Larry came back into the office where Brenda had remained with Peter, while the men played with their big toys.

'Just what did you let them do?' Larry asked, 'I have not seen Glen or Dan so happy in such a long time, especially on this site. Where are they going?'

Out of the office windows, you could clearly see Dan and Glen leading the General and Colonel, with their lieutenants, to the jeeps setting off up the driveway towards the ruins of the main house, and disappearing over the first ridge. The rest of the men went back into the stable yard, with more equipment to see what else they could find. Peter showed Larry what he thought would be the best place for the bombs to be exploded, and the reason why. Saying both Glen and Dan had wanted to clear the area for a long time as they wanted to view the ruins of the main house from the other side, so it was a very valid reason to ignore the Council restrictions as they were being safety conscious. Not taking what could be very dangerous ordinance off the estate, and endangering the community.

Brenda could not help it, she went and hugged him, tears of laughter rolling down her cheeks, oh it was a joy to laugh, after all the concerns, she just knew they would get through and have everything as it should be.

When the troops returned, they said the area was indeed suitable, but it was going to take a bit of time, to get the roads that could clearly be seen, sufficiently unblocked to safely move the bombs to detonate. Once the explanations and details of what was required had been shared with Dan and Glen, the General and Colonel took their men back to the college.

Glen had been told it was safe to take his machinery across the yard to clear the fallen stones from the gateway, which he realised led to a wide bridle path completely overgrown with bushes and plants. The very wide and substantial Bridle Path, went through the gateway, out of the stable yard onto the estate, running up towards and beyond the main house, years of neglect he was happy to rip out and then repair. He had a twinge about the removal of the foliage, wondering if he should have asked Brenda to contact Norman, but realised, Norman would have been alongside him pulling the weeds out, he had bemoaned the fact they could not explore the area fully, due to the restrictions imposed. Glen warned Brenda that he needed a few more of his crew to make the job right. However, with Dan, Greg John and Fred made a start to the clearing, but it was only to see what awaited them on the other side of the broken arch.

All in all, it was a fairly busy day at the once sleepy and ignored estate, they even had a camera crew, and a journalist from the local newspaper arrive at the gates. Thank goodness, the story of the Cadets doing some field work, had covered the finding of the bombs, but she did find out later Broadmeadows featured for about 30 seconds on the news.

The following morning, the Bomb crew returned, no Colonel today just General James and his team, with a much smaller team from Glen working on the clearing and rebuilding of the path they had found going out towards the depression. Dan and Greg arriving to assist, with their machetes to help clear the rest of the buildings. Brenda was very thankful for the caution that was being taken, when another unexploded bomb was found near the ruins of the stable. The area was then deemed secure, as they had removed most of the shrubbery from the cobblestone yard and explored the shells of the buildings as much as they could with the building debris in the way.

The General and his team left after lunch, as they could do nothing, but keep the ordinance they had found secure, advising that until all the paths/roadways were finished there was little they could do.

Glen, Dan and Greg, were very happy with what they achieved in a day, as they watched the college people leave, told Larry and Brenda, they had used the excuse of clearing the area a little to find out if any more buildings or walls could be found, they smiled asking them both to follow them, laughing they said they had been doing their own archaeological dig so to speak. With Peter tagging along followed them, as they crossed the cobble yard, for Brenda to view the other side for the first time.

The bridle path at least a narrow corridor, they could see now cleared of the brambles and self-seeded foliage, was easy to walk on, Brenda enjoyed seeing her inheritance before her, it was not fully cleared, there was still a little work to do, but they could walk quite a distance to the split of the road way which in one direction, they all realised would lead them back to the front of the main house, then split again a decent way past the ruins, one road clearly could be seen heading off around the back of the house and probably towards the Greenhouse, Brenda said out loud, to nods from the men around her. The other road went further into the grounds, this was where Glen and Dan were clearing out the ground cover to allow the trolley with the bombs access to the depression. Glen turned to Brenda and explained that depression was taking more time to clear as it was quite boggy and there were more fallen trees, probably from the bombs Glen thought. The fallen trees were being removed with a lot of care, as they could be reused as beams and joists for the rebuilding of the cottages. Good matured oak with spans as long as the ones found were not to be wasted, Brenda could only smile and hug him, enjoying the very large smile that was spreading across his and Dan's face, Peter and Larry not far behind.

Friday morning dawned with the return of the Bomb Squad, and a police car, with a couple of constables to check on everything. General James, took his time at the Stables further securing both the bombs to move them for exploding. It was later in the afternoon before they were in place, the explosion not as big as Brenda thought, they had covered the ordinance with a special foam, that stopped the large spread of any scrap material, and made it easier to clean the site up, was a little anticlimactic.

It was a very happy, but exhausted crew that departed out of the gates that evening, after the clean-up had occurred. General James expressed his desire to be of assistance in any way once she had rebuilt, or even during the rebuilding of the Manor house. Dan, Glen and Peter were happy that they could safely clear the site, and rebuild it to its former glory, Peter adding that the rebuilding of the stable gates out to the bridal path and beyond would not be a problem smiling as he showed her his updated plans.

Brenda had been keeping Kate up to date with all the developments, she was keen to see what had been happening, so it was no surprise to Larry or Brenda when David's SUV pulled up just as they were closing the gates with David and Kate smiling at them offering them a lift up the driveway. Handing them some takeaway as they drove back up to the mini manor house to celebrate another step in the rebuilding of the main house.

Chapter 18

IT WAS A HAPPY group that wandered the grounds the following morning. Larry wanted David's opinion of something he found as they reconnoitred the site for the bombs to be exploded. Brenda and Kate just wanting a look at the other side of the grounds now accessible because of the newly cut roadway, it was still a cross country hike through the vegetation, but they were not disappointed. The vista that was blocked by the rubble that had been the house and still obscured in areas by rampant overgrown foliage, was stunning. The line of oaks that the tops could be seen from the first rise in the main driveway, were quite a way behind the actual house, were huge and ancient, must have been there even before the original manor house was built, yes you could see where limbs had been blasted off from the bombs, and Brenda was sure it was multiple not singular, but they still stood in all their glory.

She realised that what they were standing on was a very flat and large terrace, which would have had access from the manor house, she scraped aside some of the detritus under her feet, it was indeed a very large paved area. She tried to look further past a mountain of brambles and weeds that just had to be covering a balustrade with either a large pot or column to be able to get that high, she could just see that there was another flat area after the terrace, that went seemingly for miles in between an aisle of trees not all of them the majestic oaks. As far as the eye could see it was all overgrown with weeds and shrubs gone wild. Kate yelled at her to come over to the right side of the house, one of the oak trees had not survived and had fallen, right across what Brenda saw had been once a magnificent rose garden, squashing a few, but being resilient as roses are, they had engulfed the tree, spreading along its trunk, and surviving. This garden room would have been a wonderful fragrant access towards the greenhouse. The scope of the land, was beginning to overwhelm her, wondering if they could ever bring it back to a semblance of order.

'Oh, my Lord, but Norman and the Kew Gang are going to be ecstatic over this,' Kate muttered reading Brenda's mind. 'I think you should fortify him with a couple of bottles of Chateau Iris mum before you let him see this. I remember what he was like when he saw the kitchen and the walled garden. This will floor him!' she spread her arms to encompass what was the original terrace and lawn up to the oaks, as well as the rose garden, 'and I am sure will put him into apoplexy!'

Laughing with her daughter, heard their names being called, went back out onto the terrace, and found David jumping up and down shouting their names. Running to catch up to him, wondering what could have gotten him so excited, as that was the feeling he was conveying.

'Mum, you have got to see this,' he dragged them off to the area where the bombs had been exploded, with Larry standing looking out across the area, a very bemused expression on his face. 'Well luv, you wanted a water feature, just didn't think it would happen this quickly.' He turned as he said this pointing out a very substantial body of water filling the depression, submersing the foliage that was there.

Shocked Brenda did not know what to say, David moved them all along what would clearly be a raised walkway to the furthest point they could get, again more fallen trees blocked their path. He pointed down, and they could clearly see even further along, a bricked culvert, that a free-flowing stream was now pouring clear fresh water into the bowl.

'The explosion must have opened up the stream, it was a bit boggy the General did say, so must have been trickling for years. I dare say it got blocked with debris from the explosions, there must be an exit that the stream runs into, further down the area.' Larry offered as an explanation.

'Shall I go and see where it goes.?'

'David no, not yet, please. Let's just keep an eye on the water level, if it gets too large, we might have to get some of Glen's men to have a look at it, or better still, call Norman and the Kew team. But I think it will pool to a certain height, and then naturally drain away. As this was always here, just as you said, it got blocked when the bombs hit, and the area just filled in over time, we will have to dredge it out properly, but at the moment, we have a few more problems to deal with. Let's go and see the Gate Lodge so you can realise what all the fuss was about.!'

They walked down the newly discovered bridle path to the stables, speculating on the scope of what they would find. Brenda voicing her opinion that the newly discovered stream, would probably have been tapped for fresh water for the manor house, Larry speculating they may yet be able to use it for the new Manor House once built. Arrived at the stable yard, ogling the size of what would have been a massive archway out of the stable and onto the bridle path. Brenda finally being able to touch the massive oak beam that would have been an upright of one of the gates, still in place on the only wall that was still standing, moved into the space of the stable yard.

'Well mum, I think once rebuilt this will be fantastic, so are you going to learn how to ride a horse, as you are now a Lady perhaps you should learn how to ride side-saddle?'

'What do you mean, as mum is a Lady, she has always been a 'Lady', and of course she will be learning to ride. What's the point of rebuilding a stable block if you are not going to buy some horses to put in them. May I also point out brother dear, neither you nor I know how to ride a horse either!'

Accepting this was the time to tell her children, Brenda turned to Kate, 'What David means is that as I have had my meeting with the Queen, and how he knew I would like to know, my Lady Brenda Lucas status is a done thing. So, we had all better get used to the change of status, as it is now real. Larry and I had a taste of it with the General from the military college he knew who I was. I still have not worked out if he liked me or not, think I will have to see, exactly what the problem was with him, as there was one, he was not happy.'

Kate could not believe what her mum was saying, 'What do you mean mum, when did you have your 'Tea with the Queen', and why did you not tell us. Oh, my giddy aunt, is that why Michael and Hugh have been so formal?'

'Probably luv, but we can dissuade them from being to pompous, I am sure. Now what do you think, do you like the area? Glen is intending to rebuild as it was, the Gate Lodge, the cottages and the gate house, with the stables. Perhaps I could get Her Majesty to recommend a good place to get some horses from, in a couple of years of course, as that is how long probably it is going to be before we can live here to use them!'

Larry put his arm over Brenda's shoulder and moved them over to where the Gate Lodge was still covered in the tarpaulin, out onto the drive way, Brenda telling the three of them of her 'Tea with the Queen", on the walk back up to the mini manor house.

'At least we know everything will be built, and built to last for a very long time, world wars notwithstanding.' Larry said as they sat with drinks in hand, 'I had a very interesting email from Hugh and you have some work to do,' turning to David, 'and we need to leave your very competent builder to complete the job he is as passionate as the owner about, but, I am loathe to leave this beautiful place. How about another evening in the Mini manor, and return to reality tomorrow?'

A very firm agreement was made by all four people who had been touched by the magic of the place. Everyone could see what it could become, and the afternoon and evening was spent making plans for the future.

After lunch on the Sunday, the two cars turned onto the road way, after carefully closing the gates behind them. Peace flowed over the area, the only new sound was of water flowing again reclaiming its original place in the scheme of things.

Chapter 19

IT WAS ANOTHER GLORIOUS Monday, and Brenda welcomed the new week, with its challenges ahead. Peter had emailed her that the submissions she had sent him were good but he had tweaked them into one, and submitted her proposal and basic information in regards to the Care Homes to Southend Council. They were due to meet on the following Thursday if she wanted to accompany David and himself to the meeting she was most welcome. He was going to be at David's place the following day to check on the alterations she had made to his plans. Chuckling at herself that he knew she had changed what he had originally set down on paper.

Following a phone call from Hugh, requesting her presence in the afternoon, she left the house and went around to see Linda. She was looking a lot better after the enforced rest, and judging by the movement the babies were getting very restless, and growing. Trying very hard not to make her laugh, but not really succeeding, she retold the story of finding the Stables, and meeting both the Colonel and General, the discovery of the stream, and the rebuilding of Broadmeadows finally getting on track. Having achieved her goal of giving her something to think about, took a list of things, Linda needed, promised to be around the following day. Linda shaking her head and wondering just what she was up to, as Brenda had not told her about Southend keeping it a secret at the moment, until she could show her good friend some progress was happening.

Walking into Hugh's office, found Baron Phipps sitting at the coffee table, along with Larry. Immediately the three men rose, and nodded, Baron Phipps coming and taking her hand giving it a brief salutation.

'Sir, what a pleasant surprise. I hope all is well,' motioning the men to resume their seats, took the coffee cup that Larry handed her, and sat beside him.

'Yes ma'am, all is well in those circles, her majesty really enjoyed your meeting, and she would like to meet again in a few months, perhaps in summer when she moves to Balmoral. I will liaise with Hugh here with the details.'

Brenda was a trifle stunned, but nodded and sipped her coffee not really sure how to reply. Hugh came to her rescue, 'I was advising Baron Phipps about your recent purchases Brenda, and the hope that one of your Care Homes can be built on the new site you had bought, he was advising me about the trouble at Broadmeadows!'

'Ah, General Richardson reporting in I presume?' he raised his coffee cup in acknowledgment of the fact. 'Yes, quite a week it was, I actually have to give a big thank you to the General and his men, with the detonation of the bombs, the shock wave released a stream that ran into the depression, they used to safely dispose of them. I am sure once we can clear it out we will find it was once a fine lake on the property, at the moment landscaping is the last thing on my mind. But I was hoping Baron Phipps, that you might be able to help me.' Wondering at what was coming, he nodded.

'I have been checking the boarders of the Broadmeadows Estate, and something struck me as decidedly odd, especially with the assistance I have received from the college. Michael confirmed that my thoughts were correct, there is a parcel of land, on the edge of Broadmeadows, that runs along the border of the college,' she noted that he was very interested and sat up straighter, 'would they be interested in acquiring it do you think? Hugh, do you have the map of the estate here, can I point out the section to the Baron, perhaps I can ask you to check with the college?' Brenda knew straight away he was very aware of which parcel of land she was talking about.

Both Larry and Hugh were a bit shocked at her suggestion, Hugh going and bringing over the map of the Broadmeadows estate.

When seen the land suggested really did stick out, and seemed to flow more naturally with the college than Broadmeadows.

'If the college does still require the land, I shall be happy to donate it to them. I have been reading the really old journals and came across a passage that said one of the Grandfather Normans, had won that parcel of land off the owner in a card game, many decades ago, before the college was even thought of, I have also been made aware of the numerous attempts to purchase the land from the Lucas Estate. I am not going to need the extra land, I am going to have a problem maintaining the estate as it is, so with a couple of conditions I will donate that parcel of land back to the college.'

Baron Phipps was stunned, trying to keep a calm face, but this woman, as Hugh had told him, was something else. 'I can safely say that the purchasing of that parcel of land has been one of the main goals for all of the Commandants of the College from its inception Lady Lucas. I think I can agree to any conditions you may levy to make this a done deal!'

'Raymond, please call me Brenda while I am with friends, my title is still giving me a little trouble.' He nodded in acknowledgement and also the fact she had called him friend, which he realised he truly was. This stranger had over the last few months demonstrated she was trustworthy and loyal not only to the Queen, but to him also, and therefore one to each other had earned the status of 'Friend'.

'I need to have neighbours that will look after the Broadmeadows estate when I am not there. I do not mean patrolling the grounds or anything like that, but just keeping a watchful eye on the place, especially while I am rebuilding. We are finding a lot of useful material that we will be reusing, especially some really good oak trees, so I do not want any of it to disappear while there is no one there. I also would like to find out more about the Colleges curriculum, as I believe a course I am trying to start may be a useful addition to your teaching programme. For that I need you to contact the CEO of my Care Homes Mr. Dennis Brookes, who with Hugh here and Larry are trying to work out a programme to find staff for the homes.'

Raymond looked at Brenda, and knew he would not have any trouble in regards to the watchful eye she had requested. In fact, he knew it was already in place, with a police patrol that had started when the first digger had appeared on the property, clearly, she had no idea this was happening, Larry looked at him and raised an eyebrow, he knew the men in the room were aware of this, but were not worrying Brenda with the details. As to the curriculum, that might be a bit more challenging, and discussions would have to be had, as he had an idea it may have to do with the staffing of the Care Homes, by the returned military that Michael had talked to him about, he was all for it happening, it would give hope to the young cadets they were training, that there was something of value to come home to at the end of their military service.

'I will most certainly relay your information to the Commandant, I am actually going to have dinner with him this evening. Can I advise him that he may go down in College history as the man to restore the grounds to its rightful size?'

Laughing Brenda shook his hand, 'That is my promise Raymond, and as soon as I get a few things off my plate this week will make sure Michael who is really the legal man in charge of the Lucas estate, sets in motion the return of the 'Card Game Land', to its rightful owner! Can I ask what the land is going to be used for?'

'A new Teaching Block, and at least one if not two live-in accommodation blocks, I believe. The college is bursting at the seams, and turning away students who could not attend unless they were living off campus. These were the main items on the list!'

'If they need competent builders, I have a couple of firms I can recommend, in between working for me of course.'

Everyone laughed, Baron Phipps leaving shortly after, assuring them he would be in touch.

'Brenda, that is very generous of you. Are you sure you just want to give it away, that is a very valuable parcel of land?' Hugh had to ask the question, although he knew what the answer would be.

'I think I can afford it Hugh, and besides, I meant what I said to Raymond, I have no idea how I am going to maintain the land I have. The college really is in desperate need of more space, Michael has already approached me about it. I think I am getting the better part of this deal, really.'

Hugh nodded, and Larry took her hand, 'Well we had better warn Dennis that he is going to be contacted about the Iris Homes Diploma Courses, very soon.'

Brenda relaxed, gardenia floated around she realised she was doing the right thing. Smiling at the two gentlemen in front of her, 'Now, what were you wanting to see me about Hugh, I hope it was more than the meeting with Baron Phipps?'

Legal documents were then produced for Brenda to sign, stating she had purchased five of the homes on the shore front and a couple in the street behind in Seahaven Village, there were at least four more waiting for confirmation, and she had also bought the buildings that housed the boarded-up restaurant, and the shops either side of it.

'This is great,' she said, once the documents were signed, 'I am going to go with Peter and David to the Council meeting on Thursday, this will show that I mean to revamp the area, and help the people living there. Anything else gentlemen, I hope that I still have some money left, as there is an awful lot to do, at Broadmeadows also the Council at Southend is sure to want its large chunk of Rates.'

Hugh laughed thinking, *She really has no idea the extent of the inheritance, and I mean to keep it that way, then she will never be stifled with her ideas, however far-fetched they are!*

Assuring her that she was fine, there was plenty of money in the kitty for whatever she wanted to do at Broadmeadows. Also, that all dues had been paid, all fines covered that had been left by previous owners, the rates paid for a couple of years, Southend Council had just had a windfall, in the shape of Lady Brenda Lucas, and she of course would eventually receive money from renting out those properties. Brenda and Larry left Hughes office, taking a taxi to David's warehouse, to check on the progress of the plans for the Seahaven Care Homes.

Shane was just leaving, his taxi waiting for him, Brenda gave him a quick hug and told him to give the same to Linda, and she would see her tomorrow.

David and Dennis, were seated with a beer watching the workmen fixing up the decking over the water. Brenda did not recognise them, wondering who the efficient crew were as they tidied up preparing to leave for the day.

David jumped up and gave her a hug 'I was not expecting you today! Hi Larry, isn't this great, Dan put me onto these guys, they also built the carport. I think they are almost as efficient as Glen, but don't tell him that.'

The leader moved over to them, while his two workmates put down a folded tarpaulin just inside the sliding doors, to put the workboxes on top, protecting the flooring. Brenda was impressed.

'Thank you, Mr. Chalmers, for letting us leave the gear inside, saves us lugging it to and from the vans. We have a little more preparation to make, and pick up the railings and glass from the workshops, but once we have replaced the two missing upstairs beams we can be finished quite quickly.'

'It's quite ok, I understand what it means to have equipment safely housed. May I introduce you to my mother Brenda Chalmers, I think Dan has told you about her; Mum, Mr. John James.'

'Ah Lady Lucas, yes Dan did say for me to make your acquaintance if I could. I believe you are restoring a country house, and at some stage will need assistance with railings and decks inside and out I believe?'

'I think that is entirely possible Mr. James, and from what I have seen in the few minutes we have been acquainted you are exactly the type of craftsman I need. Have your services been requested on the warehouse remodel for my good friends Mr. and Mrs McGill, by any chance.'

'The warehouse across the way, yes indeed they have, and we are busy getting all those details ready once the reconstruction has finished.'

'Can I ask that you add a couple of child proof gates to the list, as the three babies that are going to occupy the space will grow into toddlers very quickly. You are a married man Mr. James do you have children?' At his nod of realisation, she continued, 'please just think what you did to baby/toddler/child proof your home. The same will be required in this one.'

'I can certainly do that, and I know that Dan is fabricating the staircase so will just ask him to make some adjustments so the gates will be unobtrusive till needed. Good suggestion ma'am.'

He left shortly afterward, taking his workmen with him, promising to be back in the morning with the timber required to fix the upper balcony.

David, Dennis and Larry had all watched this exchange and wondered how Brenda's brain worked. They had not even thought about child gates, Larry realising he would need to do some work at his place once Lucas found his feet, which would not be far off. 'Ok to what do I owe the pleasure of your company today,' David said handing his mum and Larry a glass of wine, and Dennis moving papers off the sofa to make room for her to sit.

'Thought I should let you know Dennis, that you will be getting either an email or phone call from a Baron Raymond Phipps,' at the quizzical look she received, from both Dennis and David, looked at Larry and smiled, oh how life was going to be so busy, and she loved it.

'Baron Phipps is one of the Queens equerries, but he is also a past Commandant of the Military College that is adjacent to Broadmeadows. We had a lot of help from the college last week with the finding of the unexploded bombs, so I have offered them something that the college has been trying to acquire for a very long time. David, do you have that map of the Broadmeadows Estate handy by chance?'

They moved to the dining table, as it was clear of clutter, and spread the map out. 'Here this bit of land that looks really oddly shaped, well I found out, that it was won by one of the Grandfather Norman's in a card game a very long time ago.' Dennis chuckled, David just looked at his mum, wondering what was coming next.

'I have offered the land back to the College, in return, I get a presence to watch over Broadmeadows, especially as we are rebuilding, I don't want any of the felled oak trees or sandstone blocks to disappear, they are to be used for the rebuilding of

Broadmeadows, not some council house remodel. I also get to run my Iris House Home Diploma course, I hope at the college?' Dennis nodded knowing that his idea had been the right one, and he wondered who they could contact who was at the college already to check details, he smiled as gardenia floated around.

Brenda and Larry left shortly after, Brenda happy with the new plans that David had come up with, and he had a proposal ready with pro's and cons' in regards to what she wanted to do with the area. David agreeing to pick her up early on the Thursday so they could review the area again, and speak to Gus and Janet Lambert about what was, hopefully about to happen.

Chapter 20

Tuesday disappeared in a flurry of forms and emails. Going back and forth between Peter, David and Brenda. A short text from Dennis, with a cryptic 'Contact Made', had Brenda chuckling, reading it as she greeted Stan and his gang to clean the apartments, before the new guest arrived for apartment two the following day.

Wednesday a visit to Linda with the lady in question asking what was going on, as she knew there was something they were keeping from her. Brenda realised that Shane had not said anything about the revamp of the warehouse, although Rebecca had been to see her, she still had no idea. Judging this to be a very bad idea for the uptight mum to be, advised her that at the moment her warehouse did not resemble a home, but a very frenetic building site, with burly workmen, in heavy hobnail boots everywhere. Laughing, and the babies agreeing Linda relaxed.

'Oh, that is what this is all about, why would Shane not tell me?'

'I think luv, he wants to keep it his surprise, so please don't ask, believe me when I say, he is not doing this alone. Rebecca, Kate and myself are working to make sure everything is finished to a high standard, so please relax.' Putting a hand on the babies, as she could see they were playing ball, 'and keep those little ones happy ok?'

'Ok I promise, oh is that why Rebecca was talking kitchens and bathroom details with me. I must be getting old, what a dummy not to realise, I thought it was a new client of hers, that she needed help with; oops it was, it is me!'

'Yes, silly goose, so if you want to rethink what you said, better contact Rebecca now, as she might have to repurchase the items, as the way they are working, they will be installed very soon! Ok I am out of here have a few things to do, and I won't be in tomorrow. No I am not telling you why, so if you need anything, Kate is around,' bending down and addressing the belly, 'and you three stop playing soccer in there, give your mum a break!'

Thursday and Brenda felt as though she was ready, the trip to Southend with David, Dennis and Peter was a strategy briefing on the go. Arriving at the Council offices with thirty minutes to spare, registered with the official, and were ushered into the Council Chamber, patiently waiting for their case number to be called.

The mood Brenda could not read, David had given the new set of plans for the area to the steward, and seen them disappear into the offices to be discussed, she realised that they would be added to the initial submission Peter had given.

Finally, case 442/b/Sea Haven Village/Redevelopment was announced. Moving down into the main body of the chamber from their seats, faced the members of the council, again Brenda could not read the mood, only one council member, a woman smiled.

Their names were given, as the supplicants on the case, the Mayor in his splendid chain of office, nodded 'Please state your case!'

David and then Peter addressed the meeting, putting forward the plans, and giving a factual account of the rebuilding of the areas. Brenda, with gardenia floating around her stood, to speak for the Iris House side of the build, Dennis smiling and squeezing her hand.

'Your Honour, Ladies and Gentlemen of the Council, may I speak?' at a nod from him, 'I have seen the area called Sea Haven Village, and I wonder if any of you have actually visited there?' stunned looks returned her gaze, 'I am prepared to, re-alight the area, giving hope to the people who still call the Village a home. Putting back business, and turning an eyesore, into a thriving community for our elderly, and those whose working life is over, but not their thirst for life itself. I intend to turn this derelict area into a place where our elderly and not so elderly relatives, can be housed safely with respect, where they can enjoy those last few years of life with dignity, but I need your help. I need you to see with my eyes, what I can achieve, with the Iris Care Homes. I will need workers, people who want to assist, want to look after our residents. To this end, I have purchased property in the area, to give housing to the workers; the care givers, the medical staff that will be needed, the chefs, and waiters, waitresses, the gardeners, and even the cleaners so they will have places to live. This in turn will boost the economy of the businesses already in the area, the pubs, the shops, the restaurants. I also intend to add a fully equipped medical centre, something the area sadly needs, as I checked and the last doctors' office closed two years ago! So please I ask you, if you have not seen the area, go and visit, then think of what we can achieve together to see life and hope return.'

Brenda sat, shaking not sure how that blunt speech had gone down, Dennis wanted to cheer, David took her hand, Peter offered her some water, smiling, his pride in her showing through. The Mayor called a short recess to discuss the proposal, still not giving anything away. The usher hurried after the council members, after asking Brenda to stay seated.

Thirty of the longest minutes she had ever had to sit through went by, before the Council reconvened.

'Ms. Chalmers,' the Mayor began, 'when the purchase of the site went through, we in the council were very interested in exactly what was going to be built. We have had various options put forward over the years the land has been vacant, before any purchase was made, which we dismissed, but you purchased the land before finding out what you could build. Please tell me what will you do with the land if we do not agree to your proposition?'

'I would bulldoze the area, clean it up, make it safe, then landscape it and turn it into a Park, giving people free access to the shore again!' was Brenda's immediate response, shocking the council as a whole.

'No building at all?' a question from the woman who had smiled.

'None, if I cannot redevelop the site, for the use of our elderly and aged population, then I shall restore it as a park for everyone to use. Of course, I am intending for the shore to be available to everyone even if I can develop the site, and will have access from the roadway to the beach made around the Care Home site, as you can see on the plans, but if I cannot build, then I will demolish and make the area free for everyone.'

The Mayor put up a hand, as the general discussion ensued. Looking down at the computer screen in front of him, stiffened noticeably. Brenda wondered just what he had read, as he looked up at her, gardenia floated around; David, Dennis and Peter smiled, looking at Brenda, who had a serene expression on her face.

In the silence that followed, which seemed to be an eternity but was really only a couple of minutes Brenda knew there had been an intervention. Looking at the Mayor she thought *'oh so you have just been informed that I am not just Brenda Chalmers would be entrepreneur/business woman, but one Lady Brenda Lucas, and my influence goes very high indeed. You are now thinking just how much can you gain by saying yes to my request, and would it be worth it. If you get to know me, let us just see!'* Brenda nodded at him, acknowledging what she knew had just happened, he quirked an eyebrow, and smiled.

It was a jubilant group that headed to the Seashore Retreat, to pass on the good news to Gus and Janet, and have lunch. The drive back was done in high spirits, just as they arrived back into London, Brenda received a text from Kate, *'wherever you are go to the hospital, there have been developments.'*

Brenda turned to Dennis and Peter telling them what the message said, they immediately asked to be dropped at the nearest underground station, as they would not be needed, sending them off with good thoughts. Brenda directed David to the hospital to find Kate pacing the corridor.

'What?'

'Linda went into labour, and they are delivering the babies now!'

'Guess they didn't have enough room to play soccer, and wanted more!' At the strange looks she was getting from both of them, she explained her last comment to the babies the day before. It was not long before Sir James with Larry arrived 'I called Larry when I found out' Kate said, 'I thought Sir James should be here, and knew Shane would not have had time, he was on the phone to me, when the waters broke, so said I would pass on the message!'

'Thank you, my dear girl, yes I would not have missed this, so glad Larry here could come with me. Do we know what is going on?'

'Last time I saw one of the nurses she said everything was going ok, but that was a while ago?'

Sir James was just going to see if he could find anything out, when the Nurse came into the waiting room.

'Oh, you are Mrs. McGill's family, good, all went well, the babies are doing fine, just have to be in the premature ward for a little while, but they are all well developed. Shane will be out shortly, he is just seeing Linda back in her room. If you don't mind just waiting here a little longer?'

She left, Brenda going and giving Sir James a hug, and moving him to a chair, as she could see he had gone a little pale. Larry made a tea for him from the supplies in the corner of the room, and they waited.

Shane coming in a little later, surprised at the number of people in the room.

'We,' David said pointing to Brenda, were just on our way back from Southend, when Kate sent us word.'

'I brought Sir James,' piped up Larry. 'Ok man, just don't sit there tell us, how is your instant family and when can we see Linda and the triplets.'

He was in shock Brenda realised, motioned for David and Kate to make coffee and teas all around, while Shane got his breath back.

'I have no idea what has just happened, one minute I was sitting there, finally telling Linda about the remodelling, which is going very well indeed. When she gasped, and asked me to buzz for the nurse, of course things happened quickly from then, the doc came in took one look, and wacked on a monitor, tut tutting under his breath. He then looked at me, and said 'Well Shane looks like your family does not want to wait!'

'Next thing I knew we were in the delivery room, and Linda was pushing out the babies, naturally! That I think was the strangest thing, as we had been dreading a caesarean.'

'Ohhhh for goodness sake please tell me what do you have, three boys, three girls or a mix, please!'. Brenda was kneeling giving him a hug, as she asked.

Shane chuckled, 'Norman Lucas, David James and Louise Brenda McGill are doing very well indeed!'

Cheers rang out, the nurse came in on the heels of his announcement, and shushed the group congratulating the father and great grandfather. Brenda asking if she could visit the new mum, Shane saying he would take Sir James to see his great grandchildren. Larry and David opted to stay in the waiting room, while Brenda and Kate went to say congratulation to Linda.

She was a little dazed, but happy to see their smiling faces, 'Guess they took your advice literally,' was what she said as Brenda gave her a hug. 'Oh, don't make me laugh, I ache in all the wrong places. But no caesarean, I am so pleased I did not have to have that!'

'The Doc., reckons he got his timing all mixed up, because you kept cancelling the appointments,' Kate said and at Linda's quizzical expression, 'the babies are all very well developed very close to full term, so well done you. He was saying they would not be in the premature ward for very long!'

'I had better tell Glen, he will need more men on the remodel, as his time frame has just changed!'

All three ladies laughed at the comment, one grimacing as it tightened strained muscles. Brenda and Kate left as Shane and Sir James came into the room, inviting the two men around for dinner that evening gathered the gentlemen in the waiting room, and went back to Iris House.

Chapter 21

B RENDA SOON FOUND SHE did not have enough hours in the day over the next few of weeks. Between visiting Linda and the babies, helping Shane with the alterations to the warehouse, looking after the guests, getting updates from Glen on Broadmeadows, answering questions about Seahaven, it was with a chuckle she walked up the steps to see Michael Dranish Fawkes. Realising her life was wonderful, and she would not change a thing.

Michael took her back to his office, almost a replica to Sir James' in the Pickworth offices. Brenda vowing that she would have to try and make her office in Broadmeadows a copy and amalgamation of the two, as she did feel safe and secure in both places.

'Now my dear,' Michael began as they sat around the coffee table, he pointed to a folder in front of her. 'I have drawn up the papers for the return of what did you call it the 'Card Game Land' to the college, but I needed to ask did you really want to give that and the other portion back as well?'

'Yes Michael, I know that you, Larry and Hugh think I am mad to give it away, but what use will it be to me. You have told me how desperate the college is, and the extra section running along behind the college is really no good to me, I would have to cross the college grounds to access it, it is really not a viable part of Broadmeadows. It was also the other part of the bet that the Ancient Lord Lucas was gambling with. It would have been lost ages back if he had not won the card game. I am just redressing a wrong, and giving the College some breathing space.'

Michael nodded, realising it was not worth it to remonstrate with Brenda, she had made up her mind, and he agreed with her. She had more than enough to deal with in the scope of land that was the main area of Broadmeadows. He was amazed at what Glen, Dan and the team had achieved, even with the planning debacle, and was looking forward to their next update on progress. Wondering what Norman and the Kew team had achieved as he knew Glen had called them in after the lake had been discovered and what to do with the water that was rapidly filling the space on the estate.

'Baron Phipps will be most pleased, I am sure' he said, 'I also think the Commandant of the College will be lauding your presence next time you visit Broadmeadows, please be polite, he is quite a boar, but a brilliant strategist, and efficient in what he does, keeping the college going!'

Brenda laughed and assured him she would be appropriate, and set him off as well.

'Now that you have been generosity itself, I have some people I would like you to meet. You asked me to find managers and supervisors for the Care Homes, well I have asked a few I think would fit in with what you are wanting, here is some basic information on them, what do you think?' Brenda was a little stunned but should have realised that Michael would have worked quickly on her idea for Care Home help. She went through the information, looking at the photos attached to each sheet, reading a little of the basic information included. 'They should be all here now, shall we?'

With that he ushered Brenda into a big meeting room at the back of the building quite light and airy, with large picture windows out to the courtyard beyond. There were a mixed group totalling a dozen men and women in the room, chatting and making general conversation, wondering themselves at the mix of people. Two were in wheelchairs and bore scars inside and out, but were making a good job of covering their confusion of being included in the group.

'Good morning, Ladies and Gentlemen, thank you for coming to this meeting,' Michael began bringing the group to order, asking them to take a seat. A chuckle escaped the woman wheeling her way towards the seating area, followed by the gentleman.

'You are all here today, because of your talents. You all have exceptional leadership skills, as well as organisational skills to match. I am the trustee of a legacy that goes back generations, was lost for a while and is now being revived. I have a role for each and every one of you, if you would like a challenge for the next part of your lives, and an ongoing career.'

Interest sparked on all but a couple of the faces, Brenda noted both of the men at the back of the group, who did not seem that interested, but the rest sat up straighter and began to look eager to hear more.

Michael motioned to Brenda to speak, standing unsure of what to say, gardenia floated around, she smiled.

'Ladies and gentlemen, my name is Brenda Chalmers, I need people to assist in a business venture I have begun, but do not have the right staff to run it. I need men and women who have not just exceptional organisational skills, but also a lot of empathy.'

The two men she had noted before looked at her, Brenda realised instinctively that they would not work. The others, especially the lady and gentleman in the wheelchairs looked eager.

'I have recently started the Iris House Retirement Properties Group. These facilities are basically Care Homes, places for our elderly who need a little more assistance, to be able to live out their lives in comfort and care, and not be what they think of themselves, as a burden on their families, or if no families around to help them, think themselves a burden on society. You are all here because Michael believes you have the right mix of organisational skills and empathy to help me run these facilities, if you think you would be able to help please I ask you to submit your full resumes and I, we will be in touch.' Nodding to Michael, she left and went back to his office waiting for his return.

'That went well, I think?' he said as he walked back in with an armful of papers.

'Hmm, yes but I don't think two of them will fit, the rest yes eager and willing.'

At his quizzical glance, she handed him the two resumes she had been checking, of the two who had stood out for all the wrong reasons.

'Ah yes, well I had added these to the mix, for a different reason,' he leaned down and kissed her cheek, 'I am so glad you picked them out. Both Roger and Max, are former special forces, and I thought of them for your security at Broadmeadows really, not for the Care Homes. I wanted to see if you picked them out of the pack, and you did. I will keep them in the background, as they both will be brilliant at keeping your estate safe *and you as well*, he thought. 'Also, Roger has another talent that would be brilliant for you, he was brought up on a big estate in Scotland, his father was the Estate Steward. He is well aware of how a big estate is supposed to be run, and by whom and how many, so will probably become your right-hand man, and keep you on the straight and narrow, with do's and don'ts as Lady of the Manor.' He smiled as Brenda chuckled and sat back in her seat.

'Max is also a very keen horticulturist, and odd job man, he likes to keep his hands busy, is what he said to me, also has green thumbs up to his elbows, loves to grow things, when he was not doing undercover operations.'

Brenda realised that he was right, and although the fit for the Care Homes was not there, the fit for herself was. She did not need the gardenia that floated around to tell her that these two would fit in very well at Broadmeadows. 'As long as they don't mind waiting Michael,' he looked at her a question in his eyes, 'it will be at least a year or two before Broadmeadows is up and running, even with Glen and Dan pushing through the lessened red tape.'

'I know that they would, but I don't believe they will have to wait that long. I have been in contact with Glen and Dan, they have advised now the site has been cleared, the building of the cottages and gate lodge will not take long, with their prefab methods. Once they are built you will need the security on site, not just the overseeing by the college. Oh and by the way, both of the lads are ex College graduates, so they will be really going home. I don't think they will have to wait that, long do you?'

Brenda was stunned at the realisation he was right, and smiled at him, 'of course you are, I just can't get my head around the fact that I will be living in the Gate Lodge within the next six months, or sooner, and the rest of the area will be completed as well. It has been such a long time since I drove up that dilapidated driveway and saw my future in ruins, that I can't believe one of these days I will drive up that beautiful driveway to live in the house in my dreams!'

Michael nodded, understanding that although accepting the good fortune that had come her way, she still had difficulty in believing it was real. Turned her attention to the resumes in front of him, going through them all, putting them in order of interest.

'Yes, now I will organise interviews with the ten candidates, so we can really check on their ideas and you can see the calibre of people they are. As I said Max and Roger are here for a different reason and I asked them to stay behind, can I bring them in to see you?'

At Brenda's nod, he left returning quickly with the men smiling and chatting behind him. Immediately Brenda was struck by the security she felt as they walked in the room, the steadfastness and solid presence was there, these two were attuned and she could see best mates. Seeing them in the different role she had expected, reinforcing that Michael was right, these were the men she needed to keep Broadmeadows safe.

'Thank you for waiting, sorry our discussion took so long.' She began, as she motioned them to the seating area, 'I can see that Michael has been very cryptic in the job offer he has proposed.' They smiled at the comment looking at Michael, and then back at her. 'Let me be to the point. I need your skills, and I don't just mean those ones that I can never read about, and yes, I know how specialised they are, but you are adaptable, and Roger you especially have an upbringing, Michael has pointed out that might be beneficial for me to tap into. I also would like your help in a security matter as I rebuild my house!'

Wondering what exactly was going on, both men again looked at Michael.

'In a security matter, Ms. Chalmers, exactly what do you mean?' Roger asked, a lovely Scottish brogue lilted his voice.

'I am sorry gentlemen, I should have introduced Brenda correctly. She recently became Lady Brenda Lucas, owner of the estate of Broadmeadows. You will both be aware of what and where that is?'

Brenda smiled, seeing the understanding cross both of their faces, immediately they both jumped up and nodded, laughing she motioned them back down into their seats.

'Our apologies ma'am, we did not realise. Michael never let on, just offered us a job, he would not tell us what it was about.' Max motioned to both himself and Roger, he was a little taken aback, but smiled at her, taking stock. Roger just smiled understanding and hoping.

'No please, gentlemen, it is not common knowledge that the Lucas Line has been revived, or that I am Lady Brenda Lucas. In fact, it was only recently approved by her majesty, and the Lucas line put back on the peerage roles. You two, are among the first outsiders, to be advised of this, and I need your help.'

Immediately they were listening, taking in the details of what Brenda required as she described the low and high points of rebuilding the manor.

'Now, the recent discovery of the Stable yard and buildings is the latest in a succession of out of the blue discoveries I keep making with this new life I have found. There was a complication with planning permission that I will let Michael fill you in on. Recently rebuilding of the Gate Lodge, which I will use for myself while the main manor house is rebuilt and the cottages began, and I wondered if you and your families would like to join me when they are built to become the newest members of the Lucas Family!'

Stunned they were, not at first understanding what this friendly Australian was asking them. Looking at each other, and the realisation that after all the struggles they had since being demobbed, could this be the offer to-good to be true, and make those struggles be a thing of the past.

'Lucas Family?' was the question Roger asked, looking at Brenda and then Michael.

'Ah that I will also leave for Michael to explain.'

Standing, and the men following suit, she went over and took their hands, shaking them in agreement, 'welcome aboard I hope you both say yes, I would like to get to know you both better.' Nodding to Michael, left the room letting Michael explain and sign up two very welcome additions to the clan.

Over the next week interviews for the Care Homes were conducted, with Dennis, Hugh and Michael sitting in on the first round. Brenda was invited to the final interview and to offer the successful candidates their positions. She was very happy with the choices, and happy to confer all of the ten with a job offer.

Mary-Beth Williams, was the wheelchair bound candidate that had chuckled at Michael in that very first meeting. Confined to a wheelchair after an altercation while on Patrol, she had not lost her spirit, and sense of fun. At her interview, Brenda confided to her that the job of Care Home manager was hers, with a twist, that the actual job site was only a distant glimmer on the horizon.

'You mean I have a job, but nowhere to actually do it?'

'Exactly,' Dennis said, laughing along with her. 'We are in the process of getting the plans for the site through council, and as we are offering you the job of Manager, would like to have your input in how the site is built, and then managed.

'What I was hoping,' Brenda continued, 'is that you and John Bennett, would be able to run this place in tandem. You cannot be there full time and I would not ask it of you, it is going to be stressful on you as it is, so as this is the best site to employ both of you with your special skills,' Mary Beth laughed and nodded, 'hoped that you would be able to work together, as joint Managers?'

'Joint Managers, I like the idea. Don't know John that well, but I do like the fact I don't have to do this alone. What do you mean by the site being the best for us?'

Dennis then pulled out the final plans that David and Peter had submitted that morning to council. Showing Mary-Beth the managers units in the grounds, the only ones Brenda was allocating to staff, and the updated and modern facilities in the Care Homes themselves.

'Of course, you have a unit each, built for wheelchair accessibility, for your homes, and I insist if you accept the role, you are put on the payroll as consultants, until the whole set up is complete. What do you say?'

'Yes, yes please, oh what a challenge you have given me, and a very generous offer. How can I help, I am willing to help in any way I can? I have been doing some research since my first interview, and love the homes that are open. My mother was one of those that thought she was a drain on me and society, so I know the struggle people have to find the right kind of care and understanding. Give me a task, ask me and I will try and help in any way I can.'

Brenda left the meeting with Mary-Beth feeling she was at last moving forward. She had Managers and Supervisors for the three homes now ready to open, also knowing that she had the right mix for the Seahaven project once they could start it. Mary-Beth's empathy mixed with John Bennet's practicality, along with the two supervisors they would employ once the site was complete, would make a brilliant team. All they had to do was wait for the council to give them the go ahead.

She had Master Builder Leonard Masters signed up within an hour of him walking in the room, introduced by Glen, they could have been twins, and with the same commitment to doing a good job and doing it right the first time. He had been the one liaising with Southend Council, going back and forward with details and resubmitting time scales etc. with David and Peter's plans. Hopefully very soon they would be able to begin the clearing of the site.

Leonard, with Dennis overseeing, was at that time refurbishing the properties Brenda had purchased making sure his and Brenda's new home was up to the high standards set by Glen's refurbishment of Iris House. Dennis had also pointed out that if they fitted out the house at the opposite end of the block to the pub, split into two units, both of which could be updated with a lift for wheelchair access, it would then give Mary-Beth and John a home not only while the

Village was being built, but after as well. Mary-Beth also pointed out that they would then only need one unit when the site opened, to be on hand. A two bedroomed one so they could each have their own bedroom when on duty, with the house being their major home when work finished. Brenda had made sure that Leonard was aware that the house refurbishment was the main priority, asking if it could be finished quickly.

Chapter 22

A FEW DAYS LATER BRENDA stopped the cab by a florist to pick up some flowers, as she was heading over to meet some new arrivals. Wanting to check all the details of a massive refurbishment were completed to her standards. Shane had updated his security with Matt's new system, he had given her the code to access the warehouse, as today was the day the triplets were finally coming home.

Brenda walked into Shane and Linda's warehouse, happy with the transformation that had occurred. True to his word, Glen had completed everything a shade under his four-week deadline, a couple of suppliers had let him down. What Brenda saw when she walked through the front door was just breathtaking, the area had been completely transformed. From the open echoing space, it had been, there was now purpose and design to accommodate the instant family. Brenda smiled, sniffing the familiar odour of Nona's mixture and realised that Stan and his team had been in for a final clean, everything was spotless. She found the vases she needed in the new kitchen space, that was very similar to the old space, open to the room, except she could see that John James had come through, and slide out child gates attached to the centre island could cut the open plan kitchen off from the rest of the room once crawling or toddling babies were around, otherwise they looked like decorative panels on the island. Into the lounge room with its new addition of the lift and its wrap around staircase in the corner, with the baby gate she could see folded back into the curve of the staircase itself. She also realised that the top part of the mezzanine was enclosed in glass, and not open as she thought it was supposed to be, then realised that it was right, it was a master bedroom, it should be closed off from the rest of the house to give the parents some privacy.

The children's bedroom with the three cots, that could be transformed to a toddler's bed, fitted well into the room, along with a couple of rocking chairs, and change tables. Everything was ready when Brenda heard the commotion outside and went to welcome the family home.

Linda looked radiant, and very pleased to be out of the hospital, welcomed Brenda with a hug, introducing the Nanny/Nurse hired the week before, Susan Swift was a tall beanpole, but had the most amazing green eyes, and red hair.

Smiling and accepting the welcome from Brenda turned to help take the baby capsules out of the taxi that had brought the family home.

'Hi mum, Linda can we help?' David and Kate appeared and eagerly grabbed babies, bags and baby gear to get the family in the house. Shane had Louise Brenda on his lap, David took hold of Norman, and Kate grabbed David James, once they had everything out of the taxi, they moved the family into their new home.

Linda gasped as she walked through the door, seeing it for the first time. Hugging Brenda, explaining to a bemused Susan that all the work to transform the place had happened while she was in hospital. Susan nodded understanding, she had moved in herself only two days before, and could understand what Linda meant, there was a warmth to the place, she enjoyed the sensation. In her lovely Irish accent, she asked David, Kate and Shane to take babies into their room to get them settled while Brenda and Linda did a tour of the new home.

'Well what do you think?' Brenda asked as she put the kettle on in the new kitchen, while Linda opened and closed cupboards, reacquainting herself with her new/old space.

'Think, I think this is wonderful, this transformation is just, well it's just an Iris House repeat. It is what I hoped for, when Shane told me he was doing this I worried a little, but knew with you, Kate and Rebecca around it would be fine.' She smiled then as both ladies could smell the gardenia and realised Iris was happy too. 'What's this?'

Linda had found the 'Bottle Bank' as David called it, was in its own space, it had a sink with constant hot water and microwave, and all that was needed to make multiple babies bottles stored above or below it. Linda was happily making the first batch of bottles, as she heard the first baby cry. Shane wheeling out with Louise in his lap yelling her disquiet at her empty tummy.

'Oh, that is a happy sound,' Brenda said, taking the baby and putting her over her shoulder, while Shane helped Linda. 'It is never just one with multiples,' as he heard both of the other babies starting. Kate and David came out with a baby each, smiling, 'Susan thinks they just need to settle in, this place came out all right. Are you happy with it Shane?' Kate said as she took a bottle from him to sit in the lounge room to feed the by now indignant squalling infant. 'All right, all right noisy boots, it's coming just let me sit down!'

Everyone laughed and settled to a quiet discussion of what the routine was going to be. Susan came out to join the family and wonder at the people she was working for, being treated as part of the group, being asked for her opinion, and counsel, was a novelty for her.

Brenda, Kate and David left after the babies were fed and put in their cots for the first time. Making sure they all knew they were only a phone call, or across the parking area away if needed. Leaving the adults to get to know each other a little better, and settle into their new quarters.

David invited Kate and Brenda back to his place as Dennis was making dinner for them all, and Dennis had said he needed to go over a few things with Brenda. A glass of wine and good company was the perfect end to the day, Dennis filled Brenda in on how the refurbishment of the Seahaven properties was going.

'I have to ask you to clarify something, as Leonard wanted me to check the plans he had from Peter and this young man,' pointing to David who was refilling glasses, 'in regards to the changes you have put down for our two houses were right?' Brenda looked at him and had a sudden insight into what he was about to ask.

'He wanted me to check that the basements were definitely to be knocked through? I wanted to check that as well, are you really sure, oh and he advised that he would have the apartments for Mary Beth and John ready in about two weeks, but there was a slight hold up from Brent in getting the right sized lift and the glass to put on the outside of the property, and encase it as they did at Iris House. He promised within the month they would have a place to call home.

Brenda turned to him, 'Dennis luv, of course I am sure, we need office space for the Iris House Retirement Properties Group, why not utilise the space under both our houses, it saves having to pay exorbitant rents here in the city, and it makes for a brilliant commute for you! If structural wise a complete knocking down of the wall is not feasible and I understand that it will be a load bearing wall, then just large cased openings, to give the semblance of one office would work. I will not be needing a basement, what would I do with one, a wine cellar? I prefer to have my drinks in company that is what the pub is for, and I am looking forward to being able to stroll there and stagger back when I visit.

I suggested a doorway direct to the street, with signage I am sure Patrick would love to design and execute on the big window and glass topped door that is being put in. Just make sure that Matt fits it out for yourself and at least three to four assistant's equipment wise, problem is then solved! Can I suggest once it is finished, and Matt has completed his electronic wonders, check with Gus and Janet if they know of anybody that has office experience in the area and needs a job, employ locally and we show the council we mean business.'

'Oh, I had not thought of that aspect, yes that would be a good use of the space, it will be a big office, the basements areas at street level, are huge in all the buildings along the sea front. I will tell Leonard to go ahead, he has a green light and the plans are good, thank you.' Brenda nodded and raised her glass in salute.

Dennis continued as they watched the light change on the water, 'I also found out that Mary-Beth has been bunking in one of her best friend's places. When her mother died, last year, she found herself homeless. She has been sleeping in various friend's places since. I hope you don't mind Brenda but I booked her a studio room at the closest apartment hotel I could find, booked it in for the next two months, to be safe. I offered to do the same for John, but he and his wife and baby son, are living with her parents at the moment, they have the room so will be happy to wait till either of the places is ready for them at Seahaven.'

'Mind, of course I don't mind, I didn't realise Mary- Beth was living like that. Thank you for organising that so quickly. How is she for transport, can we help with that as well, please check with Larry and Hugh; we need to give her a car fitting in with her capabilities, or van might be better and call it her work car, listed against the Care Homes. If it is based there once all the building is done then she and John can share it when on duty. What do you think?'

'Already done, so I have Mary-Beth meeting with Leonard on Monday, she wanted to get started as soon as she could. Thought that would be a good way for her to begin, looking after the situation and giving her a home to work from, am I doing, right?'

'Of course, you are, Dennis. Just what I would have done. Now what is the news from the council, any further problems, or can I leave that situation in your capable hands?'

Laughing Dennis was relived the measures he had taken were ok with Brenda, he had been a little unsure in the beginning, but then just stopped and said to himself, 'WWBD' – "What Would Brenda Do!"

Walking into Iris House, Brenda could not but say thank you for the blessings that had come her way, and hopes that it would continue. A flashing phone meant messages, so she and Kate logged onto the system to see what had arrived in the email in box and on the phones.

A message from Glen, inviting them all down for Sunday lunch if they were free, there had been developments at the estate, and needed to see her on Monday if possible. They had closed down the site early as they could not do any further work until she had seen what they had uncovered. She was instantly intrigued, Kate suggested they go with David to lunch at Glen's then drive down to Broadmeadows from there, there were no guests due for another week, so could spend a few days rusticating. Brenda agreed, saying what a good plan, asking Kate to ring David and see if he had a few free days to ferry them around, and quickly phone Glen to accept the invitation if David was free.

There was an email from Norman, he would also be down at the Estate on Monday, he was very happy Glen had called him in to check things out, hoping to see her there. Raising an eyebrow at Kate as she had not known that Glen had called on Norman for advice.

Michael Dranish Fawkes, was another email, he had booked a room for Max Jones at the pub in the village, until his permanent accommodation could be finished. He had found out here was another returned vet living on the kindness of friends. He had also suggested he visit the site on Monday to check in with Glen, and Norman, whom he knew was going to be there. He might even pop down himself as he was intrigued by the reports he had been receiving, he also wanted to be there if Brenda was, as he was sure the Commandant of the College would also put in an appearance.

Laughing at the connotations conjured by Michaels dry comment, after sending replies closed everything down, and went to bed content that life was very good indeed.

Chapter 23

Sunday Lunch at Glen and Julie's with the whole family was a lovely experience that Brenda always enjoyed. To be amongst friends, that were closer than any family she had, apart from her children, was a rush to the system she welcomed. Also, there were babies to cuddle, and make a fuss over. Iris and Edward were now toddlers, and came running to have cuddles from Brenda when she arrived, Kate and David making a fuss over them as well.

All going well until a nappy change was required for Edward, with Iris following, 'it's never just one at a time, toilet training is taking longer than I thought, ok come on you rascals!' Charlie said picking up the very pungent child with Iris being corralled by Gabby, yelling her unwillingness to be changed at the top of her lungs.

'Oh, my she has a good set of lungs on her, I can still hear her!' Kate said, 'were, we ever that loud mum?'

'Louder love, but I had the space for you to do it in.' Laughing she took a sip of the wine Glen had poured for her. 'Now Mr. Master Builder what is this mystery you have for us at Broadmeadows. We are heading there later on, so what should we look out for?'

'No lass, you are not going to get me to tell you, I have to show it to you. Norman is also very excited, so I don't want to spoil his fun either, please do not poke around in the dark either!' Glen put his finger on his nose, and laughed at her frustration. 'Now what is it I hear about you hiring a body guard?'

David and Kate stiffened, 'Body Guard, what do you mean Glen? Mum what does Glen mean by a body guard?' Two very concerned siblings moved closer to their mum, concern for her in their voices and mannerisms, bringing a lump to her throat.

Laughing at the way Glen had phrased it, making it seem more of a big thing than it was. 'Body Guard for Broadmeadows that is, not for me. Don't worry loves, Michael has found a couple of ex-military blokes who need a job, and both of them are outdoors men, so thought they would be brilliant recruits to help keep the estate safe they are Max Jones and Roger McAllister. Max is a single dad, so will be having visits from his son, another Charlie', as Charlie walked back into the room, a now very happy Edward wanting down from his arms so he could sit on the floor and play with the toy Brenda had brought him.

'And?', David said very interested in this new development for the estate.

'And, Roger is married to Mary, have a son George who is five I think. Roger, grew up on a country estate in Scotland, his father was Estate Manager, he will I think make an excellent Gate Keeper/Estate Manager for Broadmeadows. Roger has a job that he hates, Michael told me, in an insurance company, so can't wait till he can move out of the small flat they are living in at the moment. Max is an erstwhile Gardiner and Odd Job man, apparently has green thumbs right up to his shoulders, and can grow or turn his hand to almost anything. Michael has booked a room in the pub at the village for him, as he found out that he has been sleeping on friend's couches, unable to find a job to let him get a home. He will be coming over tomorrow Glen, so when he turns up, can you send him up to the Mini Manor, then I can introduce him to everyone. Definitely both men know how to take care of themselves, and will be a great addition to the estate, still that is a way away, but at least I know the estate will be safe, and I can stop worrying about all the oak trees, and sandstone just sitting there begging for people to take some!'

Glen nodded and hid a knowing smile behind taking a sip of his wine. Julie with a happy Iris on her hip came into the room to declare lunch was ready, and everyone moved into the dining room to enjoy the feast.

'OK what are you two thinking' she asked David and Kate as they drove away from Glen's towards Broadmeadows. Brenda was in the back of the car, nursing leftovers for their dinner Julie had insisted, even though Brenda could not fit another bite in, the basket she had given her had enough food to feed a whole village.

'What do you mean Mum,' Kate said all innocent, with a sidelong glance at her brother as he drove along.

'I know you two, come on get it out in the open, what is going on? You were very interested when Glen called Max my Body Guard? Why would you think I would need one, come on give?'

'It's nothing mum, really, just some silly nonsense thing. You know that Larry has invited us to this 'do' in a couple of weeks' time, well I have done some digging, it's at a rather exclusive estate, and there will be body guards the whole nine yards. Some pretty influential people really, so when Glen said 'Body Guard' it triggered my memory when he mentioned it!'

Brenda, let it slide, realising she was not going to get any more out of them, her children protecting her. So, turned the discussion round to the twins, and wondering how the McGill family were faring over the weekend.

Kate jumped out of the car with Brenda to open the gates, and let David drive through, in the twilight not seeing much of the area around the gate house, but very happy to be back at the Mini Manor.

Chapter 24

M ONDAY MORNING, AND IT was a glorious morning, Brenda woke just as the dawn did, it's beautiful peach glow giving a mellow quality to the air. Glad that David and Kate were happy to share the second bedroom with the twin beds, wondered if she could tweak the plans for the gate lodge and somehow turn it from two bedrooms to three? Quietly coffee cup in hand exited the manor, to take her morning walk through the grounds. Enjoying the space, and sense of serenity, turning to see the vista from the terrace as the sun rose, and bathed the morning in a glorious golden glow. Was very surprised to hear her name being called, she turned towards the sound and the road that went from the back of the house out towards the greenhouse. Yet as she made out who it was, realised he would not like being cooped up in a pub.

'Max, what a pleasant surprise, I was not expecting you till much later, but I should have known better. How did you get on the grounds, ah, another access to be checked, I think I have a lot more exploring to do!'

Glad that his presence wasn't taken as an intrusion, Max realised he was home, and he liked the feel of the place, what he had seen on his rambles over the weekend and his hike over from the village.

'I hope you don't mind Ms. Chalmers, oh sorry I should say your Ladyship?' he smiled and gave her a little bow.

Laughing at his confusion, she shook his hand, he was really surprised again at the strong shake it was. 'No Max please I am Brenda, yes there will be times when your Ladyship will be right, but as I said in Michaels rooms the other day, I am still getting used to all of this' and she spread her arms around to encompass the estate, 'I won an Inheritance Lottery, which is allowing me to do some fantastic things, but I am still Brenda underneath.' He nodded his understanding, wondering again at his good fortune, and hoping like all other good things in his life, that this one did not disappear on him.

'I am so glad that Michael managed to get you a room close to the estate, of course if you want to you can always bunk in at the Mini Manor,' at his confused expression, 'it's the mobile home my builder put on the estate so I could visit, he disapproved of my tent. I will show you it shortly, now, why are you up so early, and where did you come from?'

Putting all the questions that wanted to be asked first aside, he put down his backpack beside the stone wall on the terrace, and turned Brenda slightly in the direction he had come. 'It's a good nearly an hour walk that way, and you get to a break in the fence, that leads into the village, it's an old stile type arrangement, very broken down, but still gives access to the estate. It was probably how villagers got onto the place ages ago, I was thinking of asking your builder Mr. Haddon?' at her nod, 'if he could spare some bits and pieces and I could fix it up so would not be a hazard.'

'Thanks Max, yes that would be good, as people are beginning to know that the estate is being fixed up, I don't want someone to sue me because they could. Come on my coffee is cold, and I could use a fresh one, how about you come and meet my children before the hoards descend, and I will try not to confuse you completely.

Picking up the backpack and holding out his arm for her to walk with him, across the uneven ground he was fascinated by the woman, and her perfume – gardenias were his favourite flower. As they neared the Mini Manor, Max chuckled as he saw it, a car pulled up in front, out jumped Norman, and one of his workers.

'Brenda my dear, what a wonderful glorious day to be out in the country!' he moved over and enveloped her in one of his hugs, leaving Simon to introduce himself to Max, twin grins on both their faces.

'Norman great to see you, what brings you here this early. You have even beaten Glen and Dan this morning?'

'Simon here only knows one speed, so I think we may had done the trip in record time, but I am parched for one of your famous coffees?'

Laughing she opened the door into the Mini Manor ushering Simon and Max in before her. Grateful that she had set everything out before she left, but very happy when Kate greeted Norman as he moved inside. David coming out of the bedroom shocked at the people already up.

'Ok who's giving away the free beer?' he asked as he took the cup from Kate, looking at his mum, and the stranger in their midst, instantly recognizing Max, not just from Brenda's description, but the sense that this man knew how to take care of himself. Laughter rang out as introductions were done, Max was a little unsure of himself until he told David about the stile, and how he wanted the means to fix it, Norman became very interested, Max realising that this was the man from Kew Gardens that Michael had told him about, and to seek out when he got here. So, the two of them, with Simon adding a couple of comments were soon in deep discussion about the scope of the land on the other side of the manor house. You could see that Norman was positively twitching to get going, but realised he could not, as he was there to show the family what he had been doing.

There was a perfunctory knock on the door, Glen with Ben, Matt and Dan crowded into the room. Motioning the big men to sit, as it was too crowded for them to stand, served tea and coffees all around. Then introduced Max to everyone as the first staff member of Broadmeadows one of the estates resident Gardiners, stunned Max smiled, how did she know that was what he was hoping. He then told the gathering of what he had been doing in the short time he had been in the Village, he had done a lot of walking, and found not only the Stile that was broken, but two others as well. He already knew about the one to and from the College, but didn't think he should say anything about it at that time.

The welcome he received from the group in the room was warm and friendly, he was going to enjoy himself for as long as he could. Not really trusting that he had found where he belonged yet, it was just so difficult to trust, then he had a whiff of that gardenia fragrance again, and wondered. Both Glen and Dan knew what it meant, and they relaxed, yes Max was a personable man, not a young man but not old either, he had seen a few things that had hardened him, you could tell it was going to be difficult for him to realise he was home, but Iris had just confirmed it.

It was a happy group that walked down the driveway following Glen and Dan's cars to the gate lodge, chatting and explaining the history so far, to both Max and Simon. One thing that struck Brenda as they came over the rise and could see the entrance clearly, something was missing. It took a while but she could see that the container with the wood working machinery was still there but the oak trees, beams and trusses that had been steadily building beside it were all gone. She made a mental note to check with Glen, when they arrived at the office.

'It's ok lass, no one has stolen the trees or the timber. I got worried myself, so checked with the timber mill, they were happy to take them to start preparing the trees, for the beams and rafters and all the timber for the doors and windows we are going to need. They are also refurbishing the original oak beams and trusses we took out of the ruins, they are very happy with the quality of timber so they are safe, and where they should be.'

Relief flooded through her, but then as she moved further down the driveway noticed the clean and cleared site that was the Stable yard, with the cleared space in what would be a garden area from cottages to the now clearly seen dry stone wall that lined the road side of the property. The area showing Glen had as promised buried the utilities conduit and replaced the soil, there were also the steel skeleton frames of the Gate Lodge, and the two cottages rising out of what was the bomb site. She danced a jig at the sight of construction at last, oh she so loved to see progress, and this was a major step forward. Everyone getting caught up in her excitement; Dan and Glen grinning along with her 'I could not see this last night when we came through the gates, this is wonderful oh gentlemen all I can see is progress, where I was beginning to despair. Now David,' Her son looked at her, smiling knowing that a change was about to be made, 'I know Peter is not here, but you know the plans for this place, can I make this Lodge a three-bedroomed home, can you check please it would make more sense, as it looks like we are making more space, what do you think?'

'Judging by the footprint of the building mum, I think Peter has read your mind, I will just go in and check the plans, and see if what I think is happening is correct!'

As he moved into the office leaving everyone still taking in the space found behind the gate lodge, Brenda moved forward and stepped onto paving stones that yes, she could see some had been damaged, but oh what an area it covered. The stables also had a few pieces of steel uprights coming out from the bomb damage, the area was clean and neat, Brenda doing another jig, grabbing Kate in her dance of joy.

'Oh, this is marvellous, no more explosive surprises I take it,' at the shake of heads all around her. Brenda moved over to the first of the cottages with its skeleton frame, just waiting for floors, walls and a roof. Glen and Dan then explained they were waiting on the Oak timbers for the inside structure, with the fabricated panels, to put in place, insulation and wall all in one. They were expecting deliveries of those, and they had the sandstone ready for the face of the buildings, the special solar roof tiles were also expected to be delivered within the next couple of days, they were very sure that next time she visited, there would be houses where skeletons now stood.

'Ok, well the progress is what I expect of you all, but what is the urgent matter that is holding you all up.' Brenda did a 360-turn spreading her arms out to encompass the space.

Dan laughed moving over to her, gave her a hug. 'You remember that Fred put his foot through the floor of the Gate Lodge that first week?' at Brenda's nod of remembrance, 'well Glen had to wait to check all bomb damage had been checked.'

'Bomb damage, did someone say bomb damage?' Max who had been looking around the area, trying to comprehend the buildings quickly being completed before his eyes. He was impressed, and was instantly alert as bomb disposal was one of his special areas, but doubted anyone but Brenda would know that.

'Sorry Max, you would know from College History that the Manor was hit by bombs during the war, well this whole area was bombed. I wonder if they actually were after the college and hit the manor house by mistake!' Everyone looked at Brenda as she leapt to this conclusion, Dan and Glen looking at each other as if to say could be. 'Any way we will never know, but this area was also hit, demolishing the stables, gateway and cottages. We had General James Richardson, perhaps you know of him,' he nodded and grinned, 'with his bomb disposal squad down to give the place a once over. They found two "unexploded ordinances", put in General Richardson terms, which we detonated on site. So hopefully there are no more surprises, but once I get people actually living here, and that means you and Roger, I am going to get you to do a full and comprehensive check of all the grounds. I think we might see if we can rope in some of the cadets from the college to assist, in the mapping it out and making sure there are no hidden surprises in the area. Sorry Dan, please you were saying?'

Dan just chuckled, and motioned for everyone to follow him back out to the Gate Lodge. Brenda could see that the original footprint of the space had been expanded, but still stopped short of the paved roadway into the stable yard. They had extended it out to the side into the stable yard, and down to the actual gates as well turning it into an L shaped home. It would make a fine addition to the buildings on the estate.

Jack and Fred were standing by a couple of ladders that had been lowered into the cellar. Nodding and smiling at Brenda when she realised that Dan was descending, Glen following suit. Not saying a word, but with matching grins on their faces, they motioned for everyone to go down. Once in the cellar Brenda could see the quality of the building, and wondered at the light years this family had been ahead of the building game. Once Norman and David had arrived,

Dan and Glen handed out flashlights and moved over to a very solid oak door. Dan motioned to Ben, David and Max moving over as well, to help them open the protesting door.

'You knew that we had found this tunnel,' Dan continued after seeing Brenda nod 'well I didn't want anyone fumbling around down here.'

'Humph you just wanted to be first through the tunnel.' Glen muttered, Brenda chuckled as she heard the comment, with Max who was sticking quite close beside her and Kate. There was a click and the light bulbs that had been strung along the ceiling, came to life, Matt fiddling with a generator making sure it was humming away correctly, in an alcove just inside the tunnel.

'Well I can tell you when I got to the end, I was flabbergasted, that long forgotten Lucas relative, was born in the wrong era. Anyway, come and see for yourself, I still don't believe it!'

With that Dan moved easily down the corridor, Brenda looking at Kate and David, as gardenia floated around them all, she could hear ghostly laughter, and wondered what they were going to find.

Chapter 25

THE TUNNEL WAS A decent length, the debris that Glen had told her about had been removed, but Brenda counted three still debris blocked alcoves as she followed Dan. Could they be access from the cottages, and there were three of them, she thought. The tunnel ended abruptly, the remnants of what would have been a gas light sticking out from the wall. Turning ninety degrees to the right at this dead end and opposite the wall with the access from the cottages, was another wide oak barn door, this one also needed persuasion to open, although Dan had oiled and treated the hinges, the doors needed to be removed and the dust and grit of ages removed properly. Once open they flicked on flashlights, as Matt had only been able to light the tunnel, and a few feet into the area, the space they moved into was vast. In the beams of the flashlights and from shafts of sunlight through holes in the ceiling, they could see all different shapes and sizes of carriages, and even right in the front under oiled covers, were what could only be a couple of vintage cars. All lined up ready to drive out, but drive out how.

'What, oh my giddy Aunt, I don't believe this, what, who how?'

Glen came and put an arm around her shoulders, Norman was doing his usual happy dance, he knew the value of what was sitting in front of him. Kate and David just looked at each other.

'You could see them from the top, when you cleared the debris,' Max said moving into the main body of the space, Glen looked at him and beamed.

'Yep, while we were clearing the debris away, nearly lost Fred again,' and he pointed back to Fred standing in the doorway, who was grinning fit to bust. 'The load he had in front of the digger suddenly disappeared, so he stopped and got out realising it had fallen down a hole. Once we realised it was the garage, or whatever you want to call it surmised that there had to be a way to get them in and out. So, we called Dan to check and Matt to help give some light, and we found this.'

They followed Dan over to what looked like an alcove, but really was another room, Brenda could see there were another two doors along this wall. Following everyone into the room the lights in the corners powered by another generator that Matt had fired up, showed a very large room with a cog and spindle arrangement in the centre, with a bar jutting out, perfect for a horse to be attached to; a very big Clydesdale Brenda thought.

'No, they didn't, did they?' Brenda asked incredulous. Looking at the grinning faces in front of her.

'I am still working on fixing it up to an electric motor Brenda, nearly there but not quite yet', Matt said pulling a cover off the mechanism.

'I believe they did, now it was covered with this old tarp, we have oiled and cleaned this so with all this manpower how about we open the roof?' Glen motioned to the men in front of him, and at the bar, where the horse would have been.

Happily, the men all grabbed a space on the bar, with Kate and Brenda giving encouragement from the sidelines. It took some persuasion and there were creaking and groaning sounds not just from the mechanism, but from the men trying to move the ancient lever, then there was more groaning and grinding, slowly very slowly a door slid partially back into the wall opposite to where they were, you could see that a ramp in the side of the wall tried to lower into place, but could not for the area was overgrown and stopping the movement, for the first time in decades. From the gap that had been made, there was fresh air and dappled sunshine in a place that had been in semi-darkness.

Dan let out a YES at the top of his voice, 'See Glen I was right, you did not believe me but I said the ramp or whatever could not be in the stable yard, it was all the wrong angle. I was right, yes,

yes, yes.' He was skipping around very pleased with himself, Brenda going and giving him a hug, he pointed 'You see when we were checking for the extra steel for the rebuild of the stables, we could see that this was here,' and he pointed to where the very big lintel across the wide doorway could be seen, but that was all we could see.'

Brenda looked at Glen, 'not the roof, this is much better, there must be a road behind the stable block we have not uncovered yet. That makes sense with the flat space we found to the bridle path that was uncovered as you remade it for the bomb disposal. Ah, now I realise that is why you are here Norman, you are going to turn the jungle into manageable space again!'

'Yes, well I am happy to help in that regard Brenda.' Norman answered her, 'I just love being here when Iris or Lord Lucas decide to give us another gift; and I am sure that all of you would be eager to see the area cleared, but that is not why I and the team, who should be here by now, are here. Can we go and see then I can show you what I have discovered?'

David, Max and Ben had gone to explore where the light and air was coming from, coming back chattering to each other.

'Completely blocked by shrubbery, and trees, they have had a long time to grow in the space, the ramp has not lowered properly, so the door cannot roll back fully, needs to be cleared out to let it drop. Very clever, you would have thought they would have had a ramp like they have in the conservatory, Mum. Hmm, but then again that would be too steep, so they went out under the stables and round to either the bridle path, or I wonder if we will find another section of paved area further up the driveway. Very, very clever!' David came over to his mum, and grinned. Everyone was enjoying himself enormously.

Leaving Glen, Dan, Ben and Matt to see that the area was safe, she didn't want pieces of the ceiling falling on her head when she explored the area, Kate and David were happily exploring the carriages David itching to see what was under the covers, 'Don't have too much fun without me,' she yelled as she, along with Max followed Norman back along the tunnel.

Sure, enough when they had climbed the ladders back to the drive way, Normans team were waiting, hitching a ride with them back up to the main house, Brenda enjoyed saying hello to the familiar faces. Leaving the bus beside the Mini Manor and Simon's car, they pulled out backpacks, and tools pulling Brenda and Max with them following the new road to where the stream had been filling the depression. She stopped suddenly, Max nearly bowling her over, the area was dry, well relatively, she could see that a lot of work had been done. The culvert was blocked again, a lot of the bushes and shrubs, grass and foliage were gone, in its place and coming back to life was a wonderfully proportioned man made hollow, she could see the large deep blue tiles in the bottom, where the workers were trying to replace broken and cracked ones with similar in size and colour, then the coloured mosaic tiles under the balustrade, about two feet down meeting the larger ones. She could see the Kew people were restoring the balustrade running around the walkway, reminiscent of the walkways Brenda had seen in documentaries of the areas around Lake Como, flanking the water. In the centre of what could only be a lake once filled with water was a folly, that would be a focal point from the windows of the manor when built, you could see remnants of the building and an elegant bridge leading from the path that ran around the edge onto the island.

'Well what do you think?' Norman had come up beside her to pull her around to the best vantage point to see what they had done, everyone moving off with purpose to finish refurbishing the area to bring it back to life. 'Sorry we had to block up the stream again, but we could not get rid of the plants properly with water in here. It won't take long to fill to the right level once we have finished fixing the folly and replacing the bridge.'

'Oh, Norman it is just wonderful. I did not realise that this area was so vast, I can see it goes further on out into the estate, but this is just beautiful. I wondered if there was a water feature on the property, and you have given me a beautiful one, thank you.'

They spent an hour going around the area, Norman explaining that they did not want to do too much until the manor was rebuilt so were concentrating on the area closest to the Manor House, just fixing up the walkways around the lake so it was safe. He was planning on something special on the far side of the lake away from the house. He also wanted permission to explore the grounds, as they wanted to find where the stream began, old maps of the area seemed to show a waterfall, he was not sure exactly where that was as the maps were definitely not to scale, but he was not sure if that was the beginning of the stream. The terrace and grass areas would wait till building was complete; then just watch what they could do.

'I might have to buy myself a ride on lawn mower, always wanted one of those' Brenda said to the startled glances she got from Max, and the Kew team, Norman just smiled knowing that she liked to be hands on, even if Brenda professed to not knowing much at all. 'Well at least that is a skill I can do, going up and down on a ride on mower might be therapeutic. I will leave the masterpiece of design and plant management to you and the crew Norman, can I leave Max with you, I want him to know what you have in mind for this place, as he will be one of the main ones here maintaining it all, trying to keep everything under control! I think he might have some questions on repairing the stiles there are on the estate. Oh, catering for lunch is still happening and will be down by the Gate Lodge from about 1.30 onwards, please come down and enjoy.'

After receiving thanks from everyone, Brenda made her way down the bridle path, going back to the stable yard, she walked back with an eye to see where the road out of the garage could emerge. There were a couple of places that she thought was a little odd and the bushes and shrubs had not grown back correctly, and no large trees. The oaks she walked amongst were beautiful, and she hugged a couple in her exploration, thanking them for being there. She was standing in contemplation of a mass of rhododendrons when they moved. Moved with not very polite words emerging from the middle of the mass.

'If you can't say anything nice, don't say anything at all,' Brenda yelled, to which she received a belly laugh in return. Ben, Matt and David all appeared coming around the large bush, spades and pick axes in hand. 'Don't you think you should wait till Norman and the

Kew Team can remove that beautiful plant, it has been here longer than you?'

'Mum, well if you want to get those carriages out of there and use the garage as it should be, this' and he pointed at not only the rhododendron, but a few more shrubs and small trees, 'and these will have to go, they are blocking the entrance!'

'I realise that love, but there are ways, to remove plants without destroying them, even almost indestructible ones like these. Norman and the gang will be down for lunch, very shortly, and he can give you his expert advice, Max is the one who will be dealing with this. I am not going to be able to use any of the carriages in the 'Garage' as you called it, no horses, so until there are some to actually use them they are better left where they are, and you two,' pointing to Ben and Matt, 'have I am sure better things to do with your time?'

'Aw Brenda, spoil our fun you do. But you are right, just got caught up in David's excitement, and wanted to make sure the ramp could move up and down correctly, while we had the people here to turn the mechanism.'

Brenda nodded, walking back along the track they had cleaved towards her, dodging around some very mature plants, but awed by the size of the doorway into the garage when they got close to it, the road out of the garage was quite a drop from the curving bridle path that came out of the stable yard. Matt explaining that as the door moved back into the wall to open, ramps on either side of the pathway were dropped from side panels to give a firm base until you drove onto the bridle path and then round to the road, only one had partly dropped when they had worked the machinery that morning, now with the work to remove the foliage from the area, both of them were flat and level, the curve in the bridal path now made sense.

'Well I saw a couple of places that might be access to the main driveway, on my walk from the lake that looked odd, so will get Norman and Max to check them out after lunch,' Brenda said as she viewed the work they had done in clearing the access into the garage. They had pulled out the ground cover that had stopped the ramp from dropping correctly into place allowing the door to open fully, which had uncovered the entrance in all its glory. Moving into the garage to find Kate trying to clear out the debris that had fallen through the hole Fred had discovered, also noticing that all the holes had now been covered over, making the place a little dingy with only the light from the doorway.

'Have you thought how you are going to light this place for me Matt?' Brenda asked as she moved the boys over to help Kate. 'I know it's a while away before we can use anything down here, and your small generator will not be up to the task, but I will need to have everything inspected, and valued. So, will need lights to be able to see. I hope the solar panel roofs we are installing on all the cottages and the stables, will be able to cope with electric demands, I don't really want to rely on mains electric, very costly.'

'I am looking into it Brenda, don't worry I will come up with something. I don't want you to rely on mains anything, so leave it with me.'

It did not take long for them to clean out the debris, even the old stuff from when the holes in the ceiling were made. Glen saying the holes had been made by the blocks of stone, from the buildings shattered in the bomb strike. They had found a few rather large blocks in the clean-up. It gave them all great satisfaction to see it at least tidy, there were layers of dust on every surface and the carriages, Brenda told them to leave, as the holes were covered, what was there would be cleaned soon. They were attempting to close the door, when Max appeared from the tunnel to tell them the lunch van had appeared, giving just the right amount of extra help to have the ramps and door click into place sealing the area once again.

'I will work on the new motor for this as well as the lights. One of my techs is relishing the challenge, won't take long. Now Max did you say the lunch van was here?'

At his nod, they all moved to the doorway and closing it after them, moved down the tunnel, Matt switching off the generator before closing the door into the cellar behind them.

Chapter 26

MAX WAS ENJOYING HIMSELF, here with this very diverse group of people, that somehow were a cohesive unit. They all had purpose, and lives that had meaning, and they all adored Brenda. He could see that, as they sat in the sunshine eating lunch, Brenda made sure everyone had their fill, chatting to everyone, Max doubted she missed anyone. Chatting as easily with the new faces just being introduced as the old guard. Glen and Dan, he noticed treated her as a daughter, not an employer, and that is exactly what she was to both of them. Michael Dranish Fawkes had of course told him and Roger, some of the story behind Brenda's enterprise, and he thought the right person had in fact won that Inheritance Lottery, as Brenda had said. He had also asked Norman about the Gardenia fragrance he detected when Brenda was around wondering if she had her own perfume. The explanation he did not believe, but he could not denounce his sense of smell.

Norman, with Glen and Dan, slowly followed Brenda up the driveway, after they had finished eating, Max and Kate following along.

'How are you this afternoon Max, we haven't frightened you away yet I hope'

He smiled at Kate, that same 'home' feeling as he got around Brenda was there in her daughter, he wondered if she realised just how much she was like her mother, he decided that she would be proud to be told so, unlike some daughters he had known.

'It would take a lot more than this to send me packing Kate. This may sound crazy, I feel as though I have at last found a place that I can call home, I hope Brenda will let me stay. I can see where I and then Roger when he gets here will be able to help keep this a place of sanctuary for all of you, *and at last be useful again'* But that last thought was in his head.

'Of course, you are staying, I can see that this is going to be more of a home to you than either David or myself, we are quickly becoming townies. Please don't get me wrong,' as she saw a question on his face, 'I love this place as well, not as much as mum of course, but then she has a reason to love it. The Inheritance is allowing her at last to help people on a big scale, how big, well I don't think she even knows just how big. We have the right people in place to see that no matter what she does, she will never lose this place or Iris House in London, and will never have to think where the money is coming from to pay the bills. Oh yes, we have been there as well,' again interpreting the expression on his face, 'that is why mum might be Lady Brenda Lucas, on the peerage rolls, and friend to royalty, but will always be Brenda Chalmers, mum, friend and entrepreneur. I am probably saying this badly but if you have a problem, tell us, tell mum. Nothing believe me will shock her, she has been through so much, we' she pointed to David standing next to his mum as she was pulling very easily the foliage along the side of the road, oblivious to the remonstrations being made by Norman and Glen, Dan just standing back with a smile on his face. 'Know what she went through, although she tried to shield us. So please you are home, once it is built of course, and that will be soon if Glen et al work their magic and at their usual pace! 'he chuckled. 'If you have any requests for your home, please tell us, Glen will help get them incorporated. Have you seen what is being built by any chance?'

'I would be happy with a tent in this wonderful place Kate, and I can see first-hand, that this group work wonders, and fast. Thank you for the welcome, and chat. Michael told some of the story to Roger and myself when we took the jobs. I know Roger is just itching to get down here as well, he is the 'Organiser', that was his nickname in the squad, and he will love the challenge of getting this place back to its former glory. Do you have any idea what Brenda is wanting to do, apart from rebuilding the manor house and here?'

Shaking her head, saying she doubted Brenda had even thought that far ahead. Kate took him into the office, and showed him the plans for the three bedroomed Gate Lodge, this time Peter had beaten Brenda to the alteration, she told him. Also, the plans and drawings for the cottages and stables. 'Do you ride?' he asked Kate.

'Never been on a horse in my life, neither has mum. That will not stop her of course, she will give it a try, and probably enjoy it. Certainly, everywhere we go animals just roll over fawning, when she gives them a pat. We were visiting friends once, many years ago, they were in Country Victoria, so had all manner of animals. All the dogs, and these were working animals, just followed her around all day. They had a mobile farrier visiting at the same time for the horses, and he was having trouble with one of the two big Clydesdale's they had, he was being very skittish. Our friend, was turning us away as the look in this big fella's eye was not friendly at all. Mum just shook him off, marched over to the big boy, looked at him took hold of the bridle and he stopped, calmed right down, her hand on his nose, and her talking to him, will be something I will never forget.

Max nodded, he could see Brenda standing next to the big animal telling him to stop being silly, it would be over soon, he just knew that was what she said.

'Well Roger and I can help in that regard, I think of myself as a competent rider, Roger is the expert horseman. Lessons would be no problem, once we get the horses of course. I suppose the buildings will have to be completed before we can even think of that!'

'I think that might be a good idea,' Kate laughed, 'now let's go and see what mum is cooking up for us all this afternoon.'

Picking up his back pack, moved out of the office, seeing the buildings completed in his mind's eye, and nodding at how right and fitting they would be in the space.

Brenda had taken the men up the driveway where she had seen a gap, there buried in the bushes was a hitching post, it had a horse's head and a ring for reins, you could not really see it as it had fallen or been pushed partly over. As they moved out from where they had found the first post they came across another smashed to pieces, this one looked more substantial and they were wondering over it, when Max and Kate came up.

'Oh, that would have been part of a mounting box', Max said as he took in the pieces lying around. He bent down and started to pull out another post, David and Glen bending to give him a hand, as it was very heavy.

'Look at this Brenda, that is made of Steel.' Dan pointed to the very tall post now being supported by David and Max.

'Mounting Box Max, what do you mean?'

'Sorry Brenda, but I have just been talking to Kate about the stables, and here is something that you would find in a stable, must have been blasted out here on to the driveway. It's a Mounting box, Ladies would never just sling their leg over a horse to get on its back, that would be frowned upon. This box would have a couple of steps, this to allow a Lady to slide on the back of a horse, especially useful if riding side saddle, it's just an easy way to start your ride. He lowered the post they were holding, David helping him to put it on the ground, here let me draw it for you!'

He pulled out a sketch pad, very quickly and skilfully drew the high post at the corner of a set of steps, everyone nodding as what he had been saying made sense. Norman had been ferreting around in the undergrowth and shouted. Max moving quickly over to where Norman was, halting everyone's progress with a shout and holding up of his hand.

'Norman please very slowly move back towards the road, please everyone don't come any closer. Can someone please dial the college and ask to speak to General James Richardson, urgently!'

Brenda started to speak but then saw the fin sticking out of where Norman had been bending down. Immediately moved everyone back onto and down the road a few steps, urging Glen to ring the number. 'Please don't take any chances Max', she shouted, as she realised he had not come with them. It was great that they found the shattered step, but not what was right beside it, an unexploded bomb.

For the second time, they waited for visitors from the college, it was not long before the trucks, and jeep appeared in the driveway.

Max hearing them came down the driveway flagging them down before they went too far up towards the bomb.

'Lady Lucas,' General James said as he came towards her, smiling and taking her hand. 'A pleasant surprise, but what have you found? What do my eyes deceive me; is that Thumper, what the devil are you doing here man?'

Max came forward, a sheepish look on his face, going bright red at the nickname he had not been able to shake. 'Thumper hmm,' Kate said, giving him a wink. He moved over to the General giving a smart salute and then taking his hand.

'Sir, glad to see you and the troops.'

'Me too, but we did a sweep of the area and came up clean, what have you found?'

'Not sure sir, but I think a lot more fell on this place than the history books will have us believe. I am also going to be going over this place with a fine-tooth comb once we get rid of this little package.'

With that, they saluted Brenda, and moved up the driveway, she turned to everyone, and moved them further back towards the gates, she didn't want to be close to whatever was going to happen.

'It's an incendiary device, still would pack a punch, but really designed to burn, anything.' Max said as he and the General came back to the group standing by the office.

Glen, Dan and Norman had sent the teams home, Brenda was grateful that Normans team had finished what they had to do at the lake before lunch, and had moved the bus down to the main car park to help tidy up around the garage entrance in the afternoon, to depart after they had finished, not sure what was going to happen for the rest of the afternoon, so the site was quiet and they had closed the gates.

'Do we need to move it, I am afraid the depression is now not available to detonate it in. Norman has been very efficient in transforming the space!' Brenda said, and then smiled, as Max was smiling too. General James had given orders to the troops, and they were taking equipment out of the trucks and stealthily moving up to where the bomb was.

'Lady Lucas, can I please ask you and the group to stay in the office, for a while, we can dispose of this piece of nastiness in-situ. Max here said you wanted the ground cover cleared, so let us provide the assistance; just for safety though please stay inside. Max coming?'

With a grin, after seeing that Brenda, Kate and the rest were relatively safe in the office, handed Brenda his backpack asking for her to keep it safe, as she nodded in acceptance of the trust he was placing in her, he smiled and headed back to the site. It seemed to take forever, but was only thirty minutes, and then they heard a bang, then a rumble, as though someone had set off a large fire cracker.

A few minutes later Max appeared in the doorway, taking his backpack, motioning everyone that it was safe to come out.

'You will be pleased to know we have found another driveway to the garage!'

'It was there under the foliage, wasn't it?' Brenda with a strained laugh was relieved that the emergency was over for now.

'What's wrong Brenda, it's all ok, there was not much of a charge in the bomb, it was the incendiary material that was dangerous, but it has been neutralised.'

'No Max its ok, I realise this crisis is over, but how many more are out there. Without your eagle eye the outcome might have been completely different. Thank you by the way, you seemed to know exactly what to do. I think I have the right man for the job definitely.'

'Job what job, ma'am?' General James came up to them, after seeing the troops and the trucks out of the gates and back to the college.

'Mr. Jones is one of the first employees of the Broadmeadows Estate, General. He will be helping out here in a general capacity, but his talents will be appreciated in any way he can help. Or should I call you Thumper from now on?'

Laughing with them all, Brenda suggested an inspection of the site, on the way up to the Mini Manor, for afternoon tea or something stronger.

Chapter 27

JULIE'S LEFTOVERS CAME IN very handy, as Brenda had enough to feed everyone. It was an interesting evening in many ways, as she watched the dynamics in the groups. Norman, and Simon discussing with Max and Glen what to do first in reclaiming the newly discovered road to the garage. There was the interesting tete-a-tete between the General and Max, then the group discussion of where the building went from this point. Brenda making sure that Glen and Dan instructed their teams to keep an eye out where they put their feet, until a full and comprehensive check of all the grounds they were working on could be done.

'General James, sorry to intrude,' as he was having a chat to Max, 'I was wondering if I could request some assistance from the college?'

'No intrusion Lady Lucas, how can we help?'

'I am going to ask Max to start a search of the grounds, no not all of them yet,' as he took a breath, 'just the areas that will have hobnailed workmen doing their jobs, they have enough to worry about without wondering if they are going to set off an incendiary device or a full-blown bomb, the area say from the gates to the top of the first rise, for a start. Could I request some help from the Cadets in this, as it is too big a task on his own? I would also like to find out if the rubble that was once the manor house may have some unexpected surprises. As we are now finding out, there were more than a few bombs dropped on this area, a lot more as Max said than the history books tell us. I need to check with the Heritage Council if clearing the main site with a view to safeguarding the area, would be in contradiction to their plans, however I think they can have no objection to us checking, for those safety reasons, if you will back me up?'

Glen and Dan just looked at her, they had been itching to take apart the rubble from the main house for two years, and had been wondering how they were going to keep the workers safe, with this afternoons little lesson in point. Then Brenda with her intuition had come to a conclusion and an option that would allow them to do exactly what they wanted; start the clear out of the manor, and keep the men safe. Iris was around she approved of what Brenda had said, they both had no doubt that what Brenda said would happen, would in actuality happen, especially when she continued.

'I also think a word from the Commandant, in regards to explaining what was found here, may be beneficial, in helping us get the necessary clearance from the Heritage Council, and of course the Shire Council. Please', as she saw excitement and eagerness in everyone's faces, 'please, just let us make sure that we do this right, and we may even be able to start what I have waited two years for; can we do that?'

The gathering broke up not long after that, but not before Brenda was invited to the College the following day for a tour in the afternoon and dinner. Max saying, he was going back to the college with the General to organise some troops to start checking the areas that Glen and Dan's men were working on.

Brenda had taken a couple of minutes to ring Larry and asked him to check if what she had just proposed was feasible, he was most concerned that another explosive device had been found, and he assured her with Hugh's assistance they would make sure all the documents would be rubber stamped.

'Do you need moral support Brenda luv, I can come down tomorrow if you do?'

'I think I am ok at the moment Larry, what I would like you to do is get that paper work done, and then come down. I think Kate and David are driving back tonight, so have no transportation to get home with. Although I can use the train, I did enjoy my trip down a while back.'

Laughing with her, he said he would see what he could do, just be safe, and went off to ring Hugh and Michael to advise them of the latest developments in the Broadmeadows project.

Everyone seemed to leave at once. Kate worried about the guests due to arrive the following afternoon, and David wanting to check up on the plans not only for Seahaven but also now for Broadmeadows, they had some rethinking to do.

Peace, blissful peace, and quiet, descended on the area, Brenda was restless, and could not sit still, she picked up a flashlight and wandered down the drive way making sure that the gates were securely locked. She would also have to get Max to do a complete perimeter check, which she had no idea how long it would take, as she really had no idea how large the estate was. She had only seen this one small portion of it, and realised to see it properly would have to be either on foot or on horseback, as she realised that even a four-wheel drive might not be able to get to some places.

It was another early morning start the following day, Max true to his word arrived with a contingent of cadets, a mix of first years and a quite a few older. Eager and willing to use the equipment they had in real life not just in practice scenarios. They smiled at her as she opened the mini manor door, every one of them looking very young to Brenda's eyes. A fleeting thought of how did they get on the grounds stopped her for a second, then she realised they had come over the stile that linked the college and her estate. It was quite a hike, was the second thought.

'Morning Brenda, sorry for such an early start I just wanted to do a thorough sweep again of the stable and cottages site before Glen and Dan arrive with their teams. I want to check a wider area as well, but that area is a priority, just to make sure, and can do that better if no one is around.'

'Please don't apologise, I applaud your dedication Thumper, and no I am not going to ask how you got that nickname, and I promise not to use it again. I will be here doing paper work if you need me. Feel as though I should be here and not in town, so I will try and help where I can. Here is a key for the gate padlock, keep it please, don't forget lunch at 1.30 I have arranged for them to come for as long as the building works are ongoing.'

Max nodded and left whistling a happy tune as he marshalled the troops for the walk down the driveway to the gates.

He knew he had to cover the area from the gates to the first rise, around the driveway, bridle path and entrance to the garage, where all of the work was being done. As he moved through the undergrowth, marked the trees and plants to be left, and those to be taken carefully to replant them, or put on a compost pile, so the clearance of the stable driveway and making the bridle path even easier to navigate, would be accomplished relatively quickly. They did find another two intact incendiary devices they were removed carefully, and found to be duds. Moving out towards the road way, the trench that Glen had dug to get the extension of the large services pipe in place for the cottages, just inside the wall that ran from the gates along the road, he knew would be clear, or Glen would have asked them to check that area first. They did a wide perimeter sweep around the gates, and behind the office and containers, finding shrapnel but no intact bombs. It was a very tired but happy band of cadets that Brenda met at lunchtime. Glen and Dan also adding their thanks for the hard work that they had put in that morning.

'It was fun, the equipment we have is spot on, and although we found a lot of shrapnel only the two duds, intact. After lunch, we will tidy up what we demolished, so you can actually see where you put your feet, as Brenda said.'

Laughing with them all, Brenda relaxed feeling a lot better with the sweep being made. 'Thanks Max, oh that is good timing, come with me for a second!'

Wondering at what was happening, he followed, with Glen and Dan moved out to a car and van that had pulled up outside the gates.

'Ms. Chalmers,' the young man in a suit asked as he got out of the car, clipboard in hand.

'Yes, that is me, thank you for being so prompt in your delivery. Where do you want me to sign?'

The young man smiled, pointed out where her signature was needed, 'and the other driver?'

Motioning for Max to come over to where she stood beside a small blue van, asked him to sign next to her. The salesman and driver of the van, acknowledged the signatures, handed over the two sets of keys to the van and left in the car.

'What?' Max said, as Brenda deposited one set of van keys in his hand.

'Well I realised, even if you did not, that you would need some form of transport. I know you like the exercise, but there will be times when you will need to transport materials and goods. I asked Michael to organise for vehicles to be leased to the estate. This is the first one, I dare say that we will add more once the need is there. I asked for something sturdy that can go off road, as I think you will need this to get you to the stiles that need repairing, and yes I know there are more, in fact there are six of them altogether,' at his startled look, 'and the one from the College you used this morning, one of the Lucas lords was a bit anal in documenting everything on the estate, that gave access, when walking or horses was the norm, not the transport we have today!'

Glen and Dan congratulated him, walked over to inspect what had been delivered. Brenda just nodded, and walked back to the office, to say goodbye to the caterer, and asking for extra the next day, as she knew that deliveries were to be made to turn the steel shells into buildings once again.

Chapter 28

IT WAS AROUND THREE in the afternoon, Brenda had changed into one of her favourite outfits navy-blue pants, with matching lighter coloured shirt, adding a cashmere jumper, as it was still a little chilly in the evenings, with the longline jacket thrown over a chair, sensible laced up brogues, she was in the country after all. The Iris necklace and earrings a lighter touch to the outfit. When a car pulled up outside the Mini Manor, and to her surprise Michael Dranish Fawkes, and Max jumped out. Max looking very formal in his uniform, with a lot of ribbons and medals on his chest.

'Michael what a surprise,' and she turned to a grinning Max, 'and you, my you do scrub up well, to what do I owe the pleasure?'

'Well Max here mentioned last night when I rang him, that you had been invited up to the College, and as I have the titles to the blocks of land you are giving back to them, thought I would escort you. Max offered to drive us in my car, so dressed for the occasion, as that is surely what it is!'

Laughing at his comments, picked up her coat and clutch, and moved out to the car. Max motioned her into the back seat, with Michael beside her, moved into the driving seat, carefully turning the car and heading down the driveway. Stopping at the office, to make sure Glen and Dan were finishing to be back in the morning, ready to really build some houses. Deliveries had been happening all afternoon, piles of materials were filling the once neglected stable yard, the final deliveries due the following morning, with an even bigger crane.

Michael marvelled at the progress he could see there seemed to be workmen everywhere he looked. Already buildings had appeared where once there was just destruction, he mentioned to Max as they drove in, that he would not be in the pub for very long.

'I did not believe that anyone could build a house this fast. Brenda warned me that Glen and Dan made a formidable team, and by heck they do. Ben and Matt not very far behind either, Brenda is all that you told us she was and so much more. Thank you for the chance you have given me.' Michael just smiled and nodded as they parked in front of the mini manor.

Max very easily drove to the college, being stopped at the gate, and saluted. He was handed passes and motioned through, once Brenda and Michael had been checked. He gave a description of the grounds as they drove up to the main building, Brenda could see that the architect of this building had to be the same that had built her Manor, but the original building in this case had been expanded for the college, was on an even larger scale. She was gently held back by Michael, while Max got out of the car, putting his cap on, and smartly moved round to her door, to open it for her. Realising she had to assume the persona of Lady Lucas for the first time, smiled at Max as she got out of the car and he saluted her, giving him a wink in return.

On the steps of the main building stood the assembled hierarchy of the college, with Michael and Max flanking her she moved forward, General Richardson was the first to approach her, taking her hand and welcoming her to the College. She turned as he smartly saluted Michael in welcome, a little bemused but realising that Michael too had attended this college. Turning was introduced to the current Commandant, who welcomed her with such a flowery speech, she was hard pressed to not giggle. She was then asked if she would like to have a tour of the College, and was very glad she had worn sensible shoes two hours later when they finally made it back to the main building. Was very grateful when asked if she would like a pre-dinner drink, taking the sherry gratefully as she mingled amongst the two women, and six men in the group. Having requested a rest room break, was returning to the room when a familiar voice hailed her.

'Lady Lucas, hope the commandant and college are looking after you today?'

'They are indeed Raymond, just had a very interesting tour of the grounds, and was about to make the Commandants and the Colleges day, did Michael warn you by any chance?'

A chuckle escaped him, 'you can't fault the old boys network Brenda, thank you for your generosity, he told me about the extra parcel of land we were not expecting.'

'I am only righting a wrong Raymond, and I can't use that land, it rightly should have been the Colleges all along. Let see if we can't give a certain je ne sais quoi to the proceedings?'

With that he opened the door into the meeting room, and escorted her, with the military staff saluting smartly his progress with her across the room.

'Commandant, thank you for your hospitality this afternoon, and also can I express my thanks to the expert and efficient assistance I have had from this college in making my home a safer place to live in. I have been aware of a wrong that was done to the college a long time ago, I am happy to say I am in a position to right that wrong.' Turning to Michael who handed her a rolled, sealed and ribboned parchment, 'may I present the deeds to the block of land noted, as well as,' and another was put in her hand, 'this block that was the Lord Lucas stake in that infamous card game so many years ago. I hereby for now and future generations bequeath the two parcels of land back into the College grounds.'

There was a quiet hush, as though they could not understand what was happening, the Commandant was stunned, not expecting such a formal return of the lands, he knew that Brenda was thinking of returning the Card Game Land, but to have the second parcel added into the mix, well that just made his plans expand that bit more. Then cheers and congratulations resounded in the room. Brenda smiled, as she handed Baron Phipps the envelope that also had Trust Fund documents to build the three-new live in buildings, and training /teaching facilities on the land just returned, along with Glen and Dan's business information. She was not going to let this opportunity pass them by, if they did not actually get to build anything, they could be consulted on their new more efficient building methods. 'Open this later, please. I am happy with this as a thank you.' He nodded to her, and let the congratulations and thanks of the room take them into dinner.

Max drove them back to Broadmeadows, a grin that he could not wipe off his face leading them home, what Brenda had done for the college and himself he could never repay her, but he realised that she would not want any payment, she was just righting a wrong that she had seen was happening. Inviting both of them in for a nightcap, Michael asked for a small one, Brenda made the drinks for both of them, giving Max a water. Discussing the different aspects of the evening all of them had gone through, and their thoughts on how the college would now progress. Once she was seated, Michael reached into his brief case, saying he had a surprise for her. He handed her a folder, the smile on his face matched Max for different reasons, but the main one being that finally he could see Brenda beginning to live the dream.

'Oh, oh Michael is this what I think it is?'

He nodded and sipped his drink, remembering that Brenda's idea of a small drink was half a tumbler. Chuckling as she opened the folder to see the limited confirmation from the Heritage Council for the clear out of the manor house known as Broadmeadows. There was also an official looking letter advising that this was undertaken to ascertain if the area was safe, the exploration mainly to be done to check for further explosive devices.

Brenda could not contain herself, she jumped up and pulled Michael into a hug, laughing and crying at the same time. Gardenia floated around, both of the men realising that Iris was also approving the confirmation received. 'Oh, Michael thank you, thank you, you don't know how much this means to me. Max, it looks like your workload just got bigger.'

'That I don't doubt Brenda, I will help Glen and the teams in any way I can. As for the Manor, well I think we had better be a bit cautious there, as that ruin is a different kettle of fish. I may need a couple of workers, but will wait till we get the cottages and gate lodge fixed up first. It has waited this long, surely another month will not make any difference?'

'Of course, Max, you are right, just to have this permission is just wonderful, it has taken a very long time to get even this far. I can't wait to tell Glen and Dan about this, but I had better warn them I don't want anyone running up here to start clearing until you have had a chance to look at it all first. I also have to show you something in the morning, so can you be here early, well your usual time, as that is very early in anyone else's life?

'Of course, I can, now if you are ok Michael, I will take myself off to the pub, have to get a change of clothes and some sleep before Ms. Brenda here has me working like a navvy!'

Laughing at his words, Brenda saw him out as Michael assured him he could drive himself home.

'Thank you!' was what Michael said when she had come back into the room, and sat back at her drink.

'Thank you what for Michael, I think I had better take that drink away, especially as you are driving. Although you are most welcome to stay the night, the sheets have been changed in the spare bedroom?'

'Thank you, no I will head back the traffic is easy at this time. I said thank you for Max, you have given him hope and a purpose. The change in that young man is remarkable. Roger will be very pleased to see his best friend back on an even keel again, he was the one that proposed him for the job, when I offered him the Estate Manager job here, and wanted it to start immediately, if he could. I am so glad he is here, he is needed more than ever.

'Michael, you know that thanks are not required, I have a need for trustworthy people, that not only I trust, but Iris and Lords of this place et al., do as well. Iris has given her benediction to Max, whether he believes in Iris or not, Norman told me he was sceptical after he explained about that,' and she stopped as the gardenia was floating around again.

Michael nodded, and realised that he no longer thought of Iris's presence strange, she was as much a part of this enterprise as Glen,

Dan and the others in this strange mix of people. 'I also wanted to talk to you there is no easy way to start this, I have been contacted by the Australian Federal Police!'

'The Australian Police, what on earth for, am I being deported or done something wrong?'

'You, no of course you haven't done anything wrong. I believe they were contacted as a general check with all the legacy business. I also believe Kate and David have been contacted!'

'Michael what is going on, why have my children been contacted by Australian Police, they have not said anything, *a sudden flash of the conversation in the car driving from Glen's went through her mind*, or done anything wrong, I would know it. Come on tell me please?'

'Apparently, charges have been laid against a Mr. Greg Wilmott, serious grievous bodily harm being amongst the charges, and he has skipped the country!'

Michael was sorry he had been so casual with his words, as Brenda had gone very white, and Iris was there he could feel the change in the atmosphere, and the strongest gardenia scent he had ever encountered. He moved over and sat closer to Brenda handing her, her drink, and making sure she took a sip.

'I am so sorry Brenda, I did not mean to shock you and I apologise. Was this man that bad?'

'In the beginning Michael, no he wasn't, I just didn't realise till too late that a very handsome exterior didn't mean a caring person underneath. He did give me my two greatest treasures,' he smiled as she continued, 'I don't think I could have endured life if not for Kate and David, I continued for them. Eventually moving as far away as I could, living a nomadic life till the divorce came through, and moving ever since. I have now found my home, this,' and she spread her arms out to encompass the estate, 'is so far away and I changed my name, so he could not find us. Do you think he knows?'

'I honestly don't know Brenda, and I am checking with Hugh and Larry tomorrow to see what we can do. I really do think it may have been all the security checks, that were done on your background for the legacy and peerage. Although I thought that for security purposes no names were released in the course of the checking. The fact no public service has gone through does not mean that questions were not asked in your home town, they would know you were once Mrs. Brenda Wilmott, why the change to Chalmers, your parents were Digby?'

'It's my maternal grandmothers name, also in the hospital when the twins were born, I registered them as Chalmers, he never saw the official birth certificate, I had a duplicate made for him to see, which was just a useless piece of paper. I had also changed my name by deed poll, the year before I could get away from him. It took a long time for me to stop defending his actions, and a longer time for me to get away. Thank god I met Dennis, he has been my saviour in so many ways.'

Michael was shocked, he knew that Brenda had escaped a bad marriage but had never realised how bad for her to take such measures. Assuring her she was safe and determined to make his words a reality, he was going to have a word with all of the people she had around her, to make sure that this mongrel of a man would never be able to hurt her or the children again.

He did not like leaving her on her own but did not think she was in any danger at the estate, surely this man would be more likely to start in London. He took his leave of her, making sure she locked the door and that he would lock the gates on his way out, headed back to his home, wondering at the cowardice of a man who would ill-use such a generous woman.

He was very grateful as he drove out of the gates, that he had a word with Max that afternoon, realised the safety measures he had instantly put in place for the security of Iris House were not the only measures he could employ.

B RENDA DID NOT SLEEP well, her dreams were interrupted by flashbacks to a two-faced man, one soothing and loving, one beresk and violent, switching in her dream from one to the other pain was predominant. She woke in a sweat, forcing herself into the shower to speak her mantra and wash away the past, moving into the kitchen to make coffee, sitting at the table to read how her future would now move forward in the documents that Michael had given her, welcoming Iris's presence calming her down.

She was ready when Max knocked on the door, offering him a cup of coffee which he accepted, sitting at the table listening to him expand on his idea of how he was going to proceed with the clearing of the site.

'I hope you don't mind but I invited Roger and his family down this weekend. Thought he would like to get a feel of the land so to speak. I also want to run a couple of things by him, security wise!'

'Michael told you about my ex., didn't he?' at his nod, 'well not much I can add to it, except he and I parted not amicably a very long time ago. I actually wondered at the time if he knew I had left, oh he would have realised when his meals were not prepared, but as I said to Larry once, his sort always had a standby to warm his bed. He probably does not realise or possibly accept we are divorced, I have the documents and it is all legal, and I know copies were sent to him, whether he chose to read them I don't know or care. Still I know that Michael and the others would worry, so I am going to offer this to you Max,' she handed him a spare key for the Mini Manor, 'would you like to bunk in the spare room, just until your cottage is finished of course, and I am going to make sure Glen, Dan et al., finish it first. You need the permanent place to call home, you can also put the back pack in the wardrobe in here to make it official. I know that all you own is in that backpack, at least the precious things that you hold dear. It's ok, I have a bag like that as well!'

Shock ran through him, that she knew about the backpack and that she had one too, then another when he realised that she was offering him a space next to her. 'What about Kate and David, wont they be upset you are giving away their room?'

'I think they will be ok, and you have not seen the speed that Glen works at, when all the pieces fit together. He and Dan are a great team, and I love watching them work, that is why I am here most of the time. I think I am a frustrated architect really, as I see plans for buildings in my head, I can see how they could function, just don't know how to get them down on paper, that is why I was so glad David took Architecture as his profession, with Peter and Shane I get to have talented people draw what I see! Oh, you have to meet Peter and Shane, and you will, once we have a building that I can host a party in…oh what a party it will be. Now let's put a lid on the past, I am not going to let it worry me, in public anyway. Go and put that backpack into the wardrobe, you won't need it for today, and you can bring your stuff over from the pub later. I have something I want to show you.'

Putting action to Brenda's words, Max put his back pack in the spare bedroom, enjoying the fragrance that surrounded him. He took the flashlight that Brenda handed him and followed her out of the Mini Manor, surprised when she picked up a broom, and moved along the path that a fallen oak tree had made towards a structure behind the ruins.

'There are only a few people that know about this place, but once you start pulling the ruins apart you would have to know, so let me start at the beginning.' As they made their way through the undergrowth that had grown in the two years since the storage space was found, Brenda told Max the full story of the Inheritance, and the secret of the Glass House. Sweeping aside the debris, she opened with Max's help one of the doors, careful to not disturb too much of it, moved over to the side with the steps, and opened the trap door.

Dumfounded Max was, he had wondered just what Brenda was doing, but as always realised she had a purpose to whatever it was. When they descended into the storage place, he just stood there shining his torch in all directions in wonder at the structure he was standing in.

'The Lord Lucas and his sons that built this structure many decades ago, to prove a building technique mind you, never realised that it would be me, a commoner, that would rebuild their world. The interior of their home, is here down to the wood panelling and hand-made nails, and I intend to reuse every last bolt of it to see their dreams of a future Broadmeadows built with steel, become my reality. I will need your help Max, and Roger's too, once they do start to rebuild, to keep this place guarded, until it can be put back into the building I will be calling home. Can I ask you to do that?'

They had been wandering through the corridors made of the pieces of a grand house. He recognised panelling, beautifully carved and plain, stacks of furniture, boxes and crates. Awed he turned to Brenda and for the first time in a long time, he actually put his arms around someone and hugged. It was all he could do, as words were not enough to let her know the faith she had shown in him, would not be in vain.

They carefully retraced their steps, making sure debris covered the trap door in the Glass house and pushing it back against the door again. Walking quietly back along the track, Brenda explaining that all of the fallen trees around the estate had been taken by Glen to the timber mill to be turned into the beams for not only the cottages, but the main ones for the manor house. Making Max laugh when she described the sight of Glen and Dan measuring the lengths of the downed trees, and delighting in the spans they could cover.

'But isn't the structure going to be steel framed, that is what I saw on the plans Kate showed me?'

'Yes, the frames and main structure are going to be steel, but the original house would have had oak as the frame, and internally I want to be able to see and feel age under my palms. The outsides too, will be faced with stone, the actual walls will be of a type that Glen has patented, at my insistence. Once you can move into this home of yours Max, it will be cool in summer, and will be able to be heated in winter with just the ground source underfloor heating system that Glen put in place at the same time he dug in the big amenities pipe, what seems a life time ago; or the wood burning stove, or a candle, depending on how warm you want it!'

They got back to the Manor and with cups of coffee in hand, walked down to the Gates, welcoming Glen, Dan and the full teams of workmen eager and ready to bring the first part of the dream into reality. With what Brenda thought a very large crane, Glen had unloaded the internal oak beams for the cottages and Gate Lodge, Brenda could not help it, she wandered amongst the piles noting the different tags on each one denoting which house they belonged too, laying her hands on the timber, enjoying the feel and smell of the wood. Seeing the oak folding doors for the access to the small yards on both cottages, and the gate lodge, and the solid front barn-doors, touching the equally solid double glazed windows just waiting to be slotted into place. Deciding not to notice when Max took Glen and Dan aside, to have a little chat.

The rest of the day was all she could hope for, by lunch time all the internal oak had been installed, the floors were already in place with the underfloor heating, the wall panels, then the floor of the upstairs in place, with walls again, and then the roof panels with their integrated solar systems. Within the day, Mike's cottage had been built, and was teaming with workmen putting final plumbing and electrical systems in place, Ben and Matt whistling happy tunes with their work teams, as they worked in areas they could and waited for the installation of the oak stairs and the spiral stairs to the basements. The internal fittings for the cottages were in boxes or piles in the stable yard; just waiting to be used. Wood burner stoves, all the bathroom and laundry fittings, along-side the oak flooring which was stacked ready to lay, the kitchens in their boxes waiting to be put in once the tiler had finished laying the kitchen floors.

'You told me it would be quick Brenda, but I did not believe you. How on earth do these guys do this?'

'Teamwork and planning my friend. I promised you that the stay in the Mini Manor would not be long!'

'Nor yours either, the Gate Lodge is being built just as fast, I have never seen such efficiency.'

'Thank you, lad, I appreciate the vote of confidence.' Glen walked over to them cup of tea in hand, 'I think the changes you made to your cottage are going to work well, and we should be finished by the end of the week, do you have any furniture to go into the house yet?'

'Ah well no,' Max stammered, realising that he had not even thought that far ahead, not wanting to jinx himself with the possibility of needing furniture.

'Hmm, well then, I think this afternoon you and I are going shopping!' Brenda looked at him, and tilting her head smiled at him. Everyone around that heard her laughed and smiled when gardenia floated around.

They returned very late in the afternoon, the stable site was quiet, and in place of bare steel structures were two cottages and the almost finished shell of a Gate Lodge. Even Brenda was stunned, Max parked the van alongside the office, and they walked the site. Glen had put signs on the doors '_Do not enter, yes Brenda that means you!_' So, they contented themselves with enjoying the feel of the area, yes, the stone on the outside of the buildings needed to be done, and she could see that there were a couple of panels missing in the upstairs of the second cottage, but there were at last buildings in the neglected space. Getting back into the van, drove up to the Mini Manor, for dinner.

Safe she felt safe, knowing she had a champion sleeping in the next room, she had assured David and then Kate when they had phoned her, that she was ok, asking about both of them. Saying to them that it would be her that their father would be angry with, as he did not really know them at all, and would have dismissed them as inconsequential. Breaking the news that their room at the Mini Manor was being used by Max, was the best assurance both of them had heard, realising that he was the Body Guard that she needed, even if their mum did not realise it herself.

'I might come down at the weekend mum, I can bunk in with Max and Kate with you, we have done it before' David said, 'I need to check on a couple of things with Glen and Dan, are you staying there?'

'Yes love, come down Max has also invited the other new Broadmeadows employee Roger and his family down for the weekend, so I get to introduce you to them, please see if your sister wants to come as well, to check up on me? You might even have your room back in the Mini Manor by that time, as Glen is doing his usual magic trick and all the cottages are really looking good.'

Chuckling, David said he would check, and he would definitely see her on Friday night, wishing her good night, don't worry, rang off. Brenda sighed and making her usual preparation went to bed, and was asleep almost immediately.

Chapter 30

THURSDAY MORNING, DAWNED ANOTHER early start, and summer had arrived. Brenda realised that as a warm breeze with a smell of promise wafted around as she and Max enjoyed the long walk down the driveway towards the sounds of industry. He whistled as he saw the teams of workmen in each of the structures, you could tell who was who. Matt's electricians were in their familiar blue coveralls, Bens plumbers were in green, Ben had adopted Matt's coveralls as a means to keeping his team clean, and at one stage admitted to Brenda, it also eliminated the ubiquitous 'Plumbers Crack Syndrome', she had laughed in spite of herself, which is what Ben wanted, but once bought and worn all his colleagues admitted they were functional and comfortable to work in.

Glen and Dan's work teams, were everywhere else.

'Ho, there Lady Lucas!' Brenda turned to find John James the railing man striding toward her, hand outstretched.

Laughing she accepted the hand shake, introducing him to Max, walking back into the midst of organised chaos to find Glen and Dan.

They were talking to another two new faces and she was very pleased to be introduced to Brian Goddard the master stone mason charged with making sure the stone they had recovered, or sourced was ready to clad all the buildings. Then Stephen von Riddick who was the owner of the timber mill, that Glen used for the timber work in all of his projects. Chatting to them all, and thanking them for their expertise.

'We are just using these buildings as test cases, for the rebuilding of the Manor House Lady Lucas.' Stephen said, 'hopefully by the time you finally get the permission to rebuild, I will have the final timbers ready.'

'You will have time to be ready, Stephen, as I have received the permission we need, to at least clear out the rubble from the house!'

'What!', was the general comment from all of the gentlemen in the group, Max just stood back a little and watched the general mayhem that ensued.

'Hold on Gentlemen, please hold on!' when they had all calmed down, 'there is no rush, this is just permission to check the rubble, we cannot do anything, and I mean anything on the main manor house until it has been cleared by Max, and his team. Yes, I said his team, he will be recruiting a couple of people to help him shift through the rubble, then with your help Glen and Dan, to move the rubble he deems safe. I will not be rushing the clearing of the site, I value your lives even more than my own. So, Stephen, Brian you will have time to get everything ready, we may even find intact stones and timbers that can be reused, at least I am hoping we can. We will take the time to do this properly, we have waited for two years, the house has waited longer, gentlemen be calm, I can see the light at the end of the tunnel, walk with me till we get there.'

Morning tea was called to celebrate, and bring everyone up to speed on developments, Ben and Matt hugging Brenda to congratulate her on getting over this really major hurdle towards getting the house built.

During the rest of the morning, it was as though the news of the permission to clear the manor house filtered through to all the workmen, gave them an impetuous to finish the cottages and gate lodge at break neck speed. Brenda walked around the site, slowing down the pace of the work, making sure that no mistakes happened, assuring the workers that nothing could happen on the manor for a month or more, till all the permits had been received, and to do that, although the permission to clear had been given the final ok to rebuild would not be received till the buildings they were working on at the time, had been inspected, and deemed appropriate to the era.

A sigh seemed to echo through the site, and the frantic pace slowed to a more normal one, although even that was a lot faster than the average building site, but that was just how Glen had trained his workers.

Brenda was in the office when Glen, with Dan in his wake walked in, again ever present cups of tea in hand.

She turned to them both, a smile on her face, 'Max is inspecting his cottage he just keeps on saying 'Wow', and can't stop touching everything. I thought I should just leave him alone for a while so he could get used to it. I told him to fire up the wood burner in the living room, it would help dry everything out, I passed it by John first Glen, and he said it would be fine. Ah, there is the first wisp of smoke out of the chimney.'

They all looked out the window, and saw the tell-tale smoke rising from the chimney, the stone masons working on the cladding putting thumbs up to Max who came out to check they were ok, with him firing up the burner.

'It's fine lass, it is nice to see someone so excited about having a home, and one that deserves the best. Oh, did you get some furniture sorted for him yesterday?'

'Yes Glen, although he thought I was mad when I asked if we could have it delivered on Saturday, two beds, a table and six chairs, a sofa and two comfortable chairs are being delivered. Did I just see the carpet layers going into the cottage?'

'Yep, Ben and Matt are just in the pipe, making the final connections. There will be gas, water and electric in the cottage by the end of the day. We get the inspectors out tomorrow, and all will be well. Now we are going great guns on the Gate Lodge, we will probably have that finished by Wednesday next week. Are you staying down here for that long, we both think you should!'

Dan moved over to her, giving her one of his usual back breaking hugs, 'it will be safer here we think. Do you want us to leave a couple of workmen here over the weekend, they could do some finishing touches? We haven't even started on the stables yet!'

Brenda returned his hug, then moved over to the coffee pot, and refilled her mug.

'Thank you both of you, but I will be fine. I doubt that my ex., will find me here easily. He is more likely to start in London, I worry about Kate and David more, although it will be me he will be wanting to humiliate. He will be subtle more than likely go to the tabloids to discredit me, or something like that, at least that is what I told Michael. I refuse to let him affect me again, but I worry about the people around me, as it is them that he will strike at to hurt me.'

'You just have to whistle you know,' Glen said, disturbed for Brenda, that after all she had been through and achieved, this mongrel could be upsetting her again. 'We will be here till Saturday, might even get Patrick back down to paint over the weekend!'

'Patrick is here, you didn't tell me, oh he is in Max's cottage, I am so pleased that he was able to fit me in. Thank you both of you, I appreciate your concern but I am not even going to dwell on what my ex-husband is doing besides I have a secret weapon he does not know about!'

Both Glen and Dan nodded as they caught the whiff of gardenia that floated around, knowing that Iris would be there to warn Brenda if anything was amiss.

She immediately dragged them out of the office to say hello to Patrick and see if she could help in anyway, going over and checking on Brian who was inspecting the damage to the cobble in the stable yard with Greg, as they realised that they had been laid in a grid pattern on a steel bed that was the roof of the garage, trying to see how they could repair the damage and give the roof its security back again. As Brenda pointed out, the crane was giving the cobble pavement no bother at all, but would be happier when all was repaired.

Max was standing outside the cottage holding up a swatch of paint colours, 'Brenda your help please.' She moved over to him, both Glen and Dan being called to check on a couple of things. 'How can I help, and how are you doing?'

'I just did not believe you, these men are magicians. Do you realise that all that is needed is the certificate of occupancy, and I can move in. This is a miracle, I thought it would be weeks away, before I have to pick paint colours, but Patrick here wants me to pick now, as he will be painting over the next few days, and he has just told me that he is finishing the wooden floors today, so no walking over them tomorrow, but they will be ok on Saturday, barefoot no shoes, he is trying a new technique, thanked me for starting the wood burner.'

Brenda laughed, and moved over to Patrick, giving him a hug, thanking him for being there. He laughing with her, saying you don't miss Rebecca until it comes to choosing paint colours. Although she had given him only the colours that would fit in the period of the original house, the new tenant only had to decide which one he liked, and it would be put in every room, just to make the job easier.

Going back to Max, then helped him decide out of the six he had which he liked the best. Brenda suggesting that in the main room, they make one wall two or three shades darker to give an accent wall. Patrick accepting the choice and alteration to the shade for the accent wall, happily went to tell his team, that they had the colour once the preparation was complete.

Suddenly it was four o'clock and everyone was packing up. Brenda looked around at the changing landscape down by the gates, and knew it was right. Her camera was going to melt she took photos of everything, to record the changes, the only thing that stood out was the stables themselves, as Glen and Dan had made sure the cottages and Gate Lodge were the priority. The stables would be fixed in their usual efficient manner, she was sure of that. Glen had taken her inside the Gate Lodge, there was a hitch with the oak internal stairs, John James apologising saying he would have them finished in the next day or two, the spiral staircase down into the cellar was in place, Brenda smiling as she saw the familiar Iris panels in the railings. The space was wonderful, there were the two bedrooms upstairs, each with their own shower room, the master downstairs in the new section with its own shower room, spanning from the original footprint into the new space taken from the stable yard; with the open plan lounge room and kitchen downstairs, a separate powder room come laundry completed the space with a small study off the entrance. She had through the afternoon had a talk with Patrick about the paint colours she could use, agreeing with him on what she would like to use, but asking him to wait till Saturday to speak to Roger and his wife about colours for the second cottage.

She waived the happy workmen out of the gates, thanking them for their efforts, and asking them all to return the following day. She was planning a surprise for all of them after work on Friday, a traditional topping off ceremony for completion in full of one building, and just so close for the second.

Chapter 31

MAX WAS ON A mission, after his talk with Brenda over dinner the previous evening, information he had received about a couple of his comrades prompting this early morning departure, he had reluctantly driven out of the gates before dawn. Brenda assuring him she would be fine, that she would very soon be surrounded by people he trusted. Nobody could get into his cottage today, Patrick had shut the site down with his floor sealant.

Brenda wanted him to see if he could find the buddies before their situation got too bad, to see if they might be interested in coming to live in the English countryside, and help him with his clear up. He also relaxed when he received the text message from Roger, and his reply confirming the whereabouts of both their friends, that needed a little help.

Brenda had surprised him, he was going over the discussion they had as he drove through the morning mist, that she was making sure his own cottage was finished first, he had said it didn't feel right.

'Oh, my friend, it's not that it is right or wrong. Just the way things work out. Look I will be in the Gate Lodge by the end of next week. Glen and Dan have assured me all is nearly complete, and I could see with my own eyes that they are nearly there. Even Roger's cottage will be finished all bar the painting, which we are only waiting on Mary to choose. I think we will leave this Mini Manor in place and it can be a home for your two buddies, until the manor is built, may be a bit noisy for them, but they will be close to the action, so to speak. So, go on take a break, I will be fine, I expect Larry, David and Kate will be here early tomorrow afternoon, or late morning. So, go, see Charles, tell him what a great job his dad is doing, show him the pictures, and see if we can't help out a couple your buddies!'

Brenda was just walking out of the office, having checked on a couple of items on her to do list, when a hail from the closed gates stopped her.

'Lady Lucas, I am early can I gain access?'

'Roger, I wasn't expecting you this early, how are you?'

Brenda could see that Brian's men had spread pieces of stone across the driveway in their zeal to selecting the right pieces to slice and place on the outside of the gate lodge blocking the opening. 'Hold on a second, I will clear some of this,' on her words, as she bent to move the first block, Brian himself came out of the office, saw what was happening, and berated her for trying to move the heavy stone, grabbed a couple of his team who were having a coffee break, admonishing them about spreading everywhere.

'It is fine Brian, I understand they want to see what they have to finish, but we do need the driveway free, especially if the workmen want the lunch trucks to arrive!'

He nodded, and opened one side of the gate to allow Roger entrance, who Brenda introduced to the stone mason, with a smile.

'Well, I have to admit that Max's description of what was going on here, did not do it justice. I am gob smacked, and that is the truth!'

Brenda laughed, and taking his arm moved him around the industrious stone masons, and up the driveway to the entrance to the stable yard. 'Where are Mary and George, I thought they were coming with you?'

'We arrived last night, using the room at the Pub that Max had, George had a bad night, so Mary stayed with him and will come over later. I think she just wanted a chance to look around the neighbourhood, I have talked about this area so much. I enjoyed the walk over here, the village hasn't changed much, still the picturesque English postcard scene, although the modern but restrained shopping centre on the way out of town, is quite a different scene altogether. I think she was heading over to it once George woke up to do some shopping!'

'Then it will be well timed, come and meet the rest of my gang. The men and women who have helped me over the last two years to live a dream, and help me to keep on living it.'

Glen and Dan, were at that moment standing in front of the stables, Matt, Ben, Peter with Rebecca looking at plans on a trestle table. Introducing her Estate Manager to all of them, Roger looked at her when she said the title, until that moment, he had not known what role he was to play. Michael had said he was there for security, Brenda's mostly and the estate after, he realised that Brenda had other plans for him, that Michael had endorsed but not told him about. With a shock, when she said Estate Manager, realised that if felt as though it was meant to be. He saw the smile in her eyes, and understood instinctively he was home, smiling back understanding what he was there for, his family background was going to come in handy *"Thank you Dad"* he thought, looked at the details on the plans, looked at Brenda who nodded to him again, as she had seen what he had.

'Sorry, but can I put in my two pennyworths straight away, I don't know if you do, but I have a background in raising horses, and been riding them before I could walk. I have to say this is a wonderful building, but it will not work for today's lifestyle, for one thing it is too big!'

Peter looked ready to argue that the plans were as the specs of the original, then the whiff of gardenia came around him, so he turned to Roger. 'Oh, I just copied the original templates that were found, so what would you change?'

Brenda nodded, smiling at the expressions on the faces of her friends, as a new friend entered the mix. She could also smell the gardenia, so she took Rebecca off to the office, to check a couple of items she had found online, that she thought would go in the Gate Lodge, which was rapidly being finished. Walking past the two cottages, the bottom part of Max's barn door was closed and Patricks 'keep out' warning sign she noticed had *'This means you Ben'* in big black marker across the bottom, pointing it out to Rebecca who laughed with her.

It was lunch time, and the stone masons had cleared the driveway, the Gate Lodge was looking as it once had, a lot larger, but a building that could have been there since the beginning of the estate. The sandstone they had used had the original patina that only age can give it, and Brenda could not stop running her hand over the window sills, and walls. She was standing in the doorway, talking to Patrick, when a familiar four-wheel drive stopped beside her.

'I did not believe you last night Brenda,' Larry leaned out of the driver's seat, gesticulating to the building she was standing beside. 'But to see is to believe, want to hop in,' as a toot came from behind him, she looked at Kate and David's grinning faces, waving from David's car she ran around to say hello, then jumped into Larry's car, to take them up to the Mini Manor.

Walking back for lunch, all three of them wanting to see what had been going on, and to say hello to what was an old friend's reunion. Introducing Roger to the three of them, David interested in seeing how he had altered the plans for the stables for this modern age to accommodate horses and people with a couple of innovations he had from his father's stables. Both Peter and David saying the changes while not major, to the actual space the stables took, had changed the use for this modern day. First, he had cut down the number of horse stalls that the original plans had, saying that they would not likely need to have the twenty or so horses that the original estate had used, so cut them in half, basically into two separate zones. One part could be used as accommodation utilising the methods he had seen being used in the cottages, to make a townhouse arrangement at the end of the building within the original foot print, with a large tack room and storage, as that would make more sense with a space for large barn doors in the middle to the stable yard, leading to the horse stalls. The structure went from the entry on the driveway, to the ruins of the gate way it was a huge space. This would free up the gate house out to the bridal path for storage or even more accommodation.

Larry wanted to meet the man, Michael had said would be good for Brenda and the Estates security. He was not disappointed, the manner in which he talked and held himself showed an assured person, he had that quality of 'you can trust me' about him, that Larry knew he would do so.

They were standing in front of the second cottage when 'Daddy' rang out. George McAllister, ran into the stable yard, and Roger, pride shining in his face, ran and picked him up, giving him a hug and putting him down on his feet. Mary following in his wake, a general what is going on here look on her face. Introductions all around, with Brenda reinforcing that she was Brenda, and only at certain times was the Lady Lucas title to be used, making sure that Mary understood, seeing Kate and Rebecca take her under their wing, was happy when Iris also gave her benediction.

Lunch was a general halt to all the work, and Brenda enjoyed mingling with all the workmen, asking how they were, and thanking them for their hard work. There was an atmosphere of calm and belonging that was felt by all of the men and women sitting in the sunshine enjoying the feeling of accomplishment.

George was clearly feeling better, and Mary relaxed realising she did not have to shush him, here was where he needed to be, he was his father's son after all, Roger just loved being outdoors, and had even suggested they move down and pitch a tent in the grounds till the house was finished. She could not believe that the cottage that Lady Lucas, no she had to stop that, Brenda she was Brenda, was offering as their home was nearly complete. Rebecca and Kate had taken her inside, so she could pick paint colours, Rebecca explaining that they had a small colour selection as the cottages and Gate Lodge were test cases to prove to the Heritage council that they could rebuild in original style with up to date and modern features. She was stunned at the open feel and loved the timber frames with the old features, marvelling at modern touches put into the original looking property.

It was a happy time, George curious child that he was, made the rounds of all the workmen, Mary worried at first, but realising she was among a group of people who knew the vagaries of children. Relaxing even more when she saw Brenda intervene as he was about to walk into the path of a skip being used to tidy the remaining building materials. Putting the child on her hip as she talked to him, Mary stunned as he snuggled down relaxing in her hold.

'That's my mum for you!' Kate said coming up beside her, 'any child or pet is not safe around her. I take it George does not take to strangers very well, usually?'

'That's an understatement Kate, he runs and hides. I have never seen him like this, it's as though he has found a place he can have fun in. I have never seen Roger so happy either, I think I may have been holding both of them back, but it was helpful being close to my parents, especially while Roger was away.'

'Don't worry, you will come to realise that this place will welcome you if you let it. There is a job to do here, that is going to take more than builders to accomplish. These neglected grounds need to be tamed again. I have no idea what my mother has going on in her head, but I am sure she will have plans brewing to keep Roger, Max and whoever else she takes on working happily for the foreseeable future! What do you do, when not looking after an energetic toddler?'

'I am a teacher, and have been seeing if there were jobs around here that I might be able to get back into teaching. George is due to start, in fact has been going to Kinder School for the last six months, I think I should find out about a spot for him sooner than later!'

'I doubt you will have any problems getting him in around here, ask mum I have a feeling that when she realised that staff would be needed once buildings were finished. In her usual fashion, will have done some research already to help her staff when employed to fit in, I have no doubt she has already found out some information for you and have a couple of options for you to choose.' The stunned look on her face, gave Kate satisfaction, people did not understand that her mum looked at the whole picture, not just the main characters. 'Speaking of staff there is Max, I wondered where he was?'

The van pulled up outside of the office, Max got out and was followed by the second tallest man she had seen unfold himself from the passenger seat, a sprightly woman about her age joining them.

'Max, you were quick,' Brenda, George almost asleep on her hip came walking towards them. Mary moved over and took her son from Brenda, thanking her for looking after him the smile of contentment on Brenda's face stopping any further comment, she smiled and moved off to find Roger.

'Brenda, well when I found these two reprobates, they were very keen to see what we were up to. Keith Butcher, June Sawyer may I introduce Lady Brenda Lucas, her daughter Kate. I take it David is here as well?'

'You are right Max, welcome both of you welcome. Keith what did your mother feed you, how tall are you?'

Laughing at the direct approach, 'I top out at seven feet Lady Lucas,' the very deep bass voice replied, and her hand was shaken in a massive paw.

'I have to introduce you to Greg, he is one of the steel men helping with the rebuilding of this place, you two are twins!' Kate echoing her mother's comment.

June dropped a lovely curtsey as she was introduced, having not believed Max when he was telling who their prospective employer was, that this person, who clearly had been helping in the building going on around them, was Lady Lucas. Brenda accepted it and took the strong hand in hers.

'Now we have the formal introductions out of the way.' Brenda began, only to be interrupted by Roger and Mary joining the group, a grumpy George with them. Once the hellos had been said, 'as I was saying, now the formal introductions are out of the way, please people, my name is Brenda. Yes, I have the honour of being, and the title of Lady Lucas, but that is what it is a title and an honour I am proud to bear but I have inherited both; and yes, I am going to be your employer, but I hope also your friend. While there will be formal times that Lady Lucas will be appropriate and I am very sure you will recognise those, all other times I am Brenda, is that understood, please!'

The group in front of her, were not ordinary people, even Mary had been raised in a military home, utmost respect to anyone with a title was inbred. Brenda realised that it would take a while for them to get to know her, but hoped there were enough people around to encourage the Lady Lucas to be the title only, that she wanted.

'I was not expecting you to return with people Max!' Brenda had taken him aside as Kate took the new people, to introduce to the gang still working in the buildings.

'Sorry Brenda, I just could not leave them in the hostel they were in. Roger and I have worked alongside these two for many years, we came through the academy together, fought in various places I still can't even talk about, I trust these two, as much as I trust Roger with my life; we were, are a team. June is a better horticulturist than I am, she actually has a degree in botany, obtained through evening classes and some hard study, I just can't wait to introduce her to Norman. Don't let Keith's height fool you either, that man is the typical gentle giant, his trade is carpentry, learnt from his father. Can take offcuts of timber and make tables, chairs, cabinets, he has fine fingers'

'All well and good, but where are they staying, there is not enough space in the mini manor for all of us. I suppose I can ring the pub and book another couple of rooms, if they have them?'

'Please don't worry, you see that patch of land that Glen found when he was clearing the bridle path, where the Garage road comes out and meets the path?'

He pointed out the area on the far side of the stable yard through the trees, and sure enough now with the some of the undergrowth gone it was flat piece of land, that led to a large pasture area. Brenda realised that it was the access point Glen had bulldozed to get into the paddocks to bury the ground source heat pipes, he had dug up at the same time the main big pipe had been put in.

'Well we stopped by the college and I borrowed a couple of things, come and see!'

Moving Brenda over to the back of the van, opened the doors, inside were a couple of heavy duty tents. Brenda looked at him, 'you can't be serious!'

'As serious as it gets. Just leave us the office keys, for access to water and loo's, and we will be right as rain. As long as I get into my place tomorrow, which everyone has assured me will happen, for one night or even more we will be fine; it is summer after all who doesn't like camping.'

Laughing Brenda had to admit it solved a couple of problems. Glen and Dan came over to see what was going on, Max asking for their assistance to clear the undergrowth that had sprouted in the time since the initial clearing, Glen organising for the roller to be wheeled out and make sure the space was flat, and a secure place to set up the tents. Of course, as with everything this was done with very willing hands. The arrival of a van from the college with camping equipment, including beds and chairs, tables etc., was the icing on the cake. June had a smaller tent with a separate bedroom sectioned off from the main area, and was happy to move her couple of bags in. The larger tent had two sectioned off bedroom areas, which Keith and Max were happy to share for the night at least. The furniture just adding to the holiday feel of the place.

While this was being achieved with the newcomers being introduced to everyone, Matt arrived with the additional lighting Brenda had requested. He happily took over a couple of strings of lights and a portable generator to give the campers access to lights if needed. Then he was assisted by whoever was left to string up the lights Brenda had requested in the Stable yard. The caterer arriving with tables and chairs, setting up the spit roast in the corner away from all the industry going on.

It was a very happy group of people, that settled in for the second party held on the estate in a very long time. When Brenda announced to all and sundry that food was ready, they all moved back to the stable yard that had been transformed, the building supplies had been stacked over by the main building ready to begin the construction on Monday. The smell of roasting meat drew everyone in, it was not late only around four pm, everything that could be finished was, another sigh seemed to echo through the area as workmen and friends descended on the food.

Glen stood as everyone was sitting eating, turning to Brenda, 'Well lass, you can do what you want over the weekend. I have just received the certificate of occupancy for all three buildings, we have also had the Heritage Council people out visiting today, they were very impressed, I think that is only a rubber stamp formality. We only have to wait for the paint to dry to move in!' A cheer went up from everyone around, there was a holiday festival feel to the gathering, that this happy news was the icing on the cake.

It was with reluctance that people started to leave, the caterers packed up their gear, leaving the leftovers on a table in the shade. Around the only other table were the people that now called Broadmeadows home. George was asleep in his mother's arms, Max, Roger, Keith and June were discussing plans for the weekend, with thoughts and questions asked by them and answered by everyone. Brenda and Larry were enjoying the atmosphere, the lights when switched on as night fell, the food and general feeling of 'this is right' pervaded the area.

'As this is a topping off ceremony of sorts, and I am sorry most of the builders have gone, the beer we had with them was good, but we did not have enough champagne for everyone,' David stated as a pop of a champagne cork echoed round the yard. Startling everyone, but happy cheers rang out as he and Kate handed out champagne to everyone.

Brenda stood as she took her glass, looking at the faces smiling happily at her, 'I salute the valiant members of the Broadmeadows Staff, may your employment with myself and my persona of Lady Brenda Lucas, the memories of the Lucas Line, sustain and encourage you for many years to come, Welcome Home everyone.' Cheers rang out, from everyone, gardenia and ghostly laughter could be smelt and heard.

After a while, Kate and Mary, came over to Brenda, 'Mum we can't put all this food in the Mini Manor it won't fit,' Kate said she pointed out the leftovers on the tables

'Are the fridges in working order in the cottages?' Brenda asked.

'Yes mum, Rebecca was saying before she left that all of the kitchens are finished and appliances are switched on and ready to go, Glen gave us the green light in all of them, apart from a couple of things and finishing touches in the Gate Lodge. What are you thinking?'

'Well I know Patrick had said we could not walk on the finished timber floors, but if we go through the double doors from the gardens, we can walk on the tiles into the kitchens, in both of the cottages, if we take off our shoes, and only one person goes through the doors into the kitchens, we can pass this to them to put in the fridges. Breakfast for the troops in the morning, as you will be able to walk on the floors by then, Max, Roger are you ok with this?'

Max looked at Roger, but it was Keith with his longer arm span that went into both kitchens one after the other, to deposit the leftovers in the fridges. Keith proudly saying he had not touched the timber floor in both places, taking a stuffed roll as his midnight snack, bid adieu to everyone, looking forward to the following day to explore the area and see what could be done.

The goodbyes, did not even stir the slumbering George; Roger and Mary left very shortly after, but promised to be back in the morning. Mary wanted to make sure the measurements she had taken were correct, for her furniture to fit into the cottage.

It was a happy group that bid good night to the campers, the smile on Max's face seemed to be permanent, he was home, in the truest sense of the word. He also had a challenge, and that was the best part, as it was a challenge he was looking forward to with good friends, old and new by his side.

Chapter 32

THE KNOCK ON THE door the following morning was expected by Brenda, the rest of the family still sound asleep in their beds. Max, with Roger, Keith and June behind him eager to see what this small area of the estate had to offer.

At the look he got from Brenda, Roger advised he was an early riser, and had walked over after Max had told him to be here, as he had something to show him. Offering coffee or tea to them, which they grinning declined as they offered up the mugs in their hands as a salute, smiled as Brenda picked up her own, and joined them on a walk around the grounds. Telling them about Norman and the team from Kew, that were helping in the rebirth of the grounds. Showing June, the area now named The Lake, as that was what it would become, they were nearly finished with the clear out of vegetation, and patching of the tiles. The walled and kitchen gardens, June impressing them all with comments on what could be added and how she with Max, could help assist in the rebirth and keep the area blooming, healthy and productive. They skirted around the main manor, Keith, Roger and Max exchanging looks, with big grins on their faces at the task that lay ahead, heading as Brenda directed to the Glass house.

'This is an area I have been keeping people out of, for security, but as you four will be the main ones directing the removal of the stones and timbers near here in the house, I ask that you keep an eye out for any of them that might be salvaged to be reused. You will need to know what is here.'

Max had the broom with him this time, and happily showed the way to the storage area. Gasps came from all as they moved down the steps, wonder in Keith's face as he could see some of the fine furniture and panelling stored in the pristine conditions. Brenda took them over to the door way that would lead into the manor itself once the rubble was cleared, the oak door was buckled but still whole, a piece had been blown out of the door giving a view of a rubbish filled tunnel.

'This is why you had to know about this place. I told Max, I am planning on putting everything back in the manor as it was. On the outside this place once built will look exactly as it did when used as a family home, only the structure of it will employ modern day techniques and materials so it will be functional, without costing an arm and a leg to run.'

Nodding in acceptance of the fact she turned them back to the stairs, 'I will get David, to show you what we mean, the current plans are in the office. A lot of the modern energy saving techniques that we will be using in the rebuilding, have been incorporated into the Cottages and Gate Lodge, all unseen but worth every penny spent.'

June had gone up the steps and was walking the garden beds, 'No one has been in here for a very long time the Kew people have not catalogued anything?'

'No, June and I give this as your domain, once we can get to this place, it has taken a very long time to get the permission to actually rebuild, and that is a tale that a nice dinner and several glasses of wine will befit its telling. But, we have the go ahead now to a point, and I am hoping that between the four of you, you will be able to help me see the place safe, and give Glen and Dan a helping hand in the endeavour they have waited two years to begin.'

They had moved out and respread the detritus of ages back to cover up the area, and happily were walking back to the manor, chatting away, ignoring the ruin that they skirted, it had waited this long, it would wait a few days, they had to see what equipment they had to help lift the heavy blocks of stone, that had fallen inwards when the bombs had hit.

Kate was up and coffee brewing when they all returned to the Mini Manor, laughter roused both David and Larry, they emerging asking did everyone know it was a Saturday!

As they were leaving to head down the driveway, Max excused himself, reappearing with his bag and backpack, Brenda smiled at him, knowing that he was eager to get into the cottage, and make it a place his treasures would be safe in. Discussion was going on between everyone, June, Roger and Keith continuing to ask questions of Kate and David, Larry adding in his part of the story of the Lucas Line, they were not surprised when they got over the rise to see Glen's distinctive truck, parked next to the office or when Rebecca appeared in the doorway, cup in hand.

Rebecca laughed, giving hugs all around, 'I thought you might need me to place the furniture I know is arriving this morning. Just thought I had missed out so much that Ben and Matt had been talking about, my taste yesterday was not enough. You don't mind do you, also thought I should balance the scales so to speak!'

'Mind how could I mind, love that you are here, you will need to know the new team at Broadmeadows.'

Turning to Glen, 'I thought you were having a day off today?' Brenda said as she gave him a hug in welcome, 'that there was not much needing your expert touch?'

'Hm, yes well I got to thinking last night, that these four might be needing some help with accessing some of my trucks and skips here onsite, and I wanted to check that they were clear and licensed to use them. Not that I could stop them of course, being who they are,' all of them doffed imaginary hats, and smiled. 'Besides I have been thinking about the manor itself and I think we might need the assistance of a crane to move some of the big blocks you can clearly see in the rubble, so just wanted to check with them what size they would like so I can get the organisation of it to the site?'

Bowing to the fact that she was not needed went out with Rebecca to find Kate, David and Larry talking, wondering what else they could access to check what was needed. Keeping to herself what else she thought the men and woman in the office would be discussing, her!

While they waited, they made a tour of a nearly completed Gate Lodge, not sure what was missing, in bare feet they prowled the building, the main bedroom was quite spacious, the compact bathroom very elegant. David and Kate declared their bedrooms also perfectly adequate, and apart from the missing banister on the upstairs landing and stair rail, carpet in the bedrooms, everything looked ready to go. Brenda smiled at Kate 'You know what this means don't you luv?' A big broad smile from Kate and Rebecca 'Shopping Trip!' punching the air, Larry and David just looked at each other, groaning.

The groan was heard by the gang coming out of the office, with a beaming Glen behind them. 'Well did they pass?' Brenda asked.

'Of course, they did, never doubted it, but what was the groan about?'

'Shopping trip, coming up. The lodge is just about ready, so we will need furniture, and I haven't been shopping for ages.' Kate said and did a little dance, so like her mother.

'Roger, did Mary actually get to the shops yesterday?' at the negative shake of his head, 'well call her up, she can come with Kate, Rebecca (our resident expert) and myself, June you are welcome too, so you can discover what is in the area. Let's see if we can have fun, oh looks like it has just begun!'

A furniture van was stopping at the gates, the driver jumped down, Larry going and checking that he was in the right place, motioning Max over to sign for the furniture about to be delivered to his new home. They reversed the truck into the stable yard, many hands moving nearly all of it into the cottage, the setting up of the beds, and positioning of the sofa was accomplished in record time, there was a spare bed, a small four seat table with matching chairs, and sofa sitting in the yard once the van was waived away.

'Roger, Mary I hope you don't mind, but I could not see Keith and June living in the tent, when your cottage is sitting empty for the next couple of weeks. I thought that they could use it till you get here, but I will now have to go and order another very long bed for him!' pointing at Keith who bowed in return.

'Mind of course not Brenda,' Roger turned to her, 'I was just remonstrating with the fat lug, that he should move in, June too, you have made it impossible for them to decline.'

'Actually friends,' Keith had come up to them very quietly, 'we have enough beds, I don't fit in a regular bed, so June can have that one, I will just move the extra-long cot that I am sleeping on in the tent, that suits me just fine, and Roger thank you'.

Brenda went over to this gentle giant pulled him down into a hug, that surprised him at first, but he welcomed. He, as with the others, felt that this was right, this was where he was meant to be, he was home. Max came out of his door, saying late breakfast was to be served in his place once he found which box the frying pan was in. A grin on his face that no one was going to remove, he ushered everyone inside, no one had to be told to leave shoes at the front door. They helped to unpack the boxes of towels, sheets and kitchen goodies that Brenda had insisted he purchase. Brenda bringing out from the cupboard beside the front door, two shopping bags with stuff for the pantry, as well as the needed washing up bits and pieces. Kate arrived with a bag of milk, eggs and butter, from the mini manor, and they used some of the leftovers to serve a very substantial breakfast indeed.

Leaving the men having a pow wow as to what should be done the following week, and for them to show Roger and Keith the Garage. Brenda piled Kate, Rebecca and June into David's car stopping by the pub to collect Mary, June offering to ride with her so George could be safe in his car seat, the convoy set off to have fun shopping in the local centre.

They were strolling through the shopping centre, when Brenda stopped the group.

'Mary, I need to explain, that the Cottage is only temporary for you and Roger. I fully intend on you to be living in the Gate Lodge, once the Manor is completed. Then June and Keith can share the cottage, if that is ok with you June? Although the more I think of it, I may just make the new town house arrangement Roger suggested in the stable a lot bigger so Keith has his own place as well. Sorry just thinking out loud. I suddenly find myself with employees I have to house, this is so strange. So, I am only buying basic things, beds, a sofa, dining table and chairs. All that will make the place liveable for David and Kate and myself, when we visit but not so much that it cannot be transferred to the cottage, when we do the swop. I know it is an inconvenience and I apologise, but I hope you understand.'

Mary and June stood there, as George ran off with Kate following, leaving her mother with two very confused women. Both of whom could not understand why this wonderful person was apologising to them, brought home the comment from the day before, that Brenda was Brenda, and the feelings she had for others were not fake, Lady Lucas was just the title she said it was. Realising that she was worried about what they thought, was interested in their attitude to her. Both, of them engulfed Brenda in a three-way hug, tears running down their cheeks.

'You are worried about us,' June was incredulous, 'you who have given me, and the guys a purpose again. We will never stop thanking you, please we are here for you now and always. Thank you sincerely, I speak for all of us, right Mary?'

Mary just nodded, tightening her hug, as words alone would not convey what she was feeling, then wondered where George was, they all wandered over to where George was being entertained by Kate, sitting in one of the mechanical cars all shopping centres have laughing at the antics the movement made.

It was a happy group that returned to the estate, shopping completed. June and Mary drove into the stable yard, parking next to their cottage, happy to remove the groceries, and moving the bags of linen, and accessories they had been encouraged to buy, at Brenda's insistence, into the house. Brenda, Kate and Rebecca driving up to the mini manor to do likewise, once the shopping, groceries and goodies had been put away, Kate and Rebecca were keen to see what had been happening while they were away, Kate happy that she saw Matt's car as they passed the parking area, leaving Brenda checking emails on her laptop.

<h1 style="text-align:center">Chapter 33</h1>

IT WAS THE SOUND of breaking glass, that made Brenda sit up. In the silence that surrounded her, it was unmistakable. Wondering if the wind had picked up debris or there were young children making mischief, she moved out of the manor, the faint smell of gardenia made her cautious, but some compulsion made her move towards the sound, along the path towards the glass house, as that was the only place that had glass left to break.

Too late the warning from Iris made her look around, she was grabbed from behind, picked up and thrown to the ground beside the glass house, being cut on the shards from the destruction that was lying around, she turned to look into a face she knew very well, a surreal peace descended on her, now the uncertainty she had been living under was gone.

'Surprise, my dear wife, I have come to get my share of whatever you are into, Brenda my love!'

Brenda did her best to avoid the kick he sent in her direction, 'Greg, how nice to see you again,' as shocked as she was, Brenda was not surprised, and a trifle relieved, as now she could stop being frightened of shadows, here was the evil in front of her.

Delay, delay was the word going through her head, gardenia was surrounding her, looking into that cruel handsome face, the pent-up words she could not stop tumbling from her.

'You don't deserve a share of anything, apart from a spell in prison. How did you find me, I thought I had covered my tracks really well'?

Brenda tried to stand to keep out of reach of the fists she knew so well, and as she glanced down recognised he was wearing steel capped work boots not his usual sneakers, knew he had come to do serious damage to her. She had to play for time, keeping her ex-husband at bay by playing on his vanity, and self-belief in his god like existence?

A slap across the face, moved her back towards the structure, trying to keep out of his reach.

'Why did you leave, did you think I would not miss you? You took the children away, why not let me see them, raise them with you, I could have taught them respect, but then their mother never gave me any respect.' She tried to stand using the wall behind her, to get out of the way, but he pulled her back by the hair, punctuated this speech with more body punches, slaps to the head and kicks. Brenda had a deja vu moment was sure she could smell the red earth of the outback as she took a blow to the cheek, knocking her back down to the ground, as though he could not speak without a physical attack; what she realised as years of pent up anger at the universe was being released, at her.

'I hear you have stepped up in the world, what scheme are you running to be here. You were never any good at any job you were in, have you not learned your lesson, learned where you belong? Is this just another lie and you are just a hired hand working as a navvy', at every statement he kicked and punched no longer worried where bruises would appear, 'keeping to your station, cleaning house where you belong!' She realised he was not alone, another person was laughing coming into her view.

As she recognised him, she laughed inwardly, knowing that Greg would not have the brains to find her, but had found one of the two persons in the world that she knew with a grudge against her, willing to do bodily harm. Again, she tried to rise and make an escape, being knocked to the ground with punches from both men in front of her, realising she could not escape and hoping rescue would soon be coming as the looming figure of Bill Gardiner moved in beside Greg.

'I can see that you have acquired a likeminded friend.' This was danger, one psychopath she could try to keep at bay, but two was a whole different ball game, keep talking Brenda, keep talking was going through her pain filled brain.

'What hole did you crawl out of Bill, heard you had done a runner, rather than cleaned up your act and become more than you were, I would like to say nice to see you again Bill, I wish it were in better circumstances, but I can see you are not interested.' She saw the blow coming and raised her arm to shield her head from a large stick. Brenda screamed, as her fingers tingled, and she realised he had broken her arm. Then she was struck on the side of the head, sent bells ringing and darkness circled.

Using all her will power not to black out, focusing on the rage that was in both of the men in front of her, trying to avoid most of the blows, that were aimed at her, Gardenia surrounded her, knowing that help was on its way, she kept talking while she could.

'If you want something from me, better not beat me to death Greg, or you Bill, satisfaction of seeing me bleeding will not get you a penny of anything. Neither of you are entitled to even my pity.'

They stopped, stepping back looking at each other, greed overcoming there need of physical abuse for a moment, with a snide smile, Greg bent down closer to her face 'oh and what were you going to offer, Bill here tells me that you are a 'Lady', I can't see it, looks to me that you are living off the land, like a hermit, or worse. I have heard, that you have moved up in the world, to what this pile of rocks, don't make me laugh. What exactly where you going to bribe your way out with, my wife. Don't think a bit of paper saying otherwise will help you, till death us do part, you are mine to do what I want with!'

Brenda steeled herself, she could see her defiance was only fuelling his anger, but she could not help herself, years of keeping quiet were gone, 'as usual not doing your homework correctly, and taking information from sources that also only do half a job. No matter, the children are safe, and you and your cohort will not get anything out of me!'

Another kick to her head was somehow deflected slightly, the blow rattled her teeth, and she almost blacked out, hearing Bill grunting beside Greg, *well* she thought *at least I am making them work for the beating!*', then Brenda felt the wisp of breeze and smelt the fragrance she was expecting, knowing the troops were on their way.

As Brenda heard the glass break, and was walking along the path, the troops, were down in the garage. They were all helping Matt fix the motor to the ancient workings for the garage door. Max dropping the screwdriver he was holding seeing Roger do the same, both of them had lost sight that the most important person in their lives at that time was missing, a sense of foreboding, one they both knew so well, they could not dismiss overcame them.

Max felt a disquiet like he had a few times when on patrol, he looked around as Kate and Rebecca walked into the garage, he stiffened there was something. Roger too looked up, and their eyes met, gardenia floated around, '*Help Brenda*' loudly they heard the words in their heads.

The ramp had just dropped into the open position, Max with Roger close behind was out of it like a pistol shot, everyone surprised at their exit, suddenly Larry, then everyone was looking around, gardenia the strongest yet, was there.

'Where's Brenda?' Larry said, realising she was not with them. Kate and Rebecca turning to say she had stayed at the Mini Manor checking emails. Kate suddenly had the urge to run.

'I think we had better go and find her,' Larry said to no one as everyone had taken off after Max and Roger a feeling of foreboding filling them all with dread, gardenia was around all of them, a vision of the glass house everyone heard a voice saying "RUN". Urgency seeming to propel them all out the lowered garage door and along the bridal path, following the shadows that were Max and Roger. They heard the scream and then Brenda's voice, turning along the path to find the two men just pulling back to land viscous blows on Brenda lying at their feet.

Both of them had no chance, Max got there first with his head start, Roger next, took the two men out, making sure they would not get up in a hurry.

Moving over and cursing that they had left Brenda alone. Kate and David were beside their mum, Rebecca and June telling them not to move her, Kate tears running down her face, David stricken that he had not protected her better, Larry in shock, also saying don't move her. Through the haze of pain, Brenda could see Iris hovering around her, she reached up '*Thank you!*' it was a thought and a whisper towards the vision, knowing that she had helped save her, the hand moved then pulling her children close, making sure no harm had come to them or family she could feel running towards her, breathing through the agony of just raising her unbroken arm to them, trying to see them and Larry, making sure they and everyone was ok, a fleeting glimpse of Roger and Max manhandling her attackers to the ground, then the darkness overtook her.

Kate and Rebecca went in the ambulance with Brenda, she had not regained consciousness and they could clearly see that she had a broken arm at least, she was covered in blood from the cuts and bruises coming out all over her. Kate would not let go of her mum's good hand, Rebecca having to be the strong one keeping the fear at bay, that Brenda may not recover, she had lost a lot of blood.

Max and Keith had left the two downed men in June and Rogers not so tender care, taking Glen, Matt and David to see if anyone else was in the area, finding the car that Bill and Greg had arrived in parked beside the stile into the village.

Larry having called for an ambulance, was intrigued that they arrived with two police cars at the same time and very quickly! The paramedics praising the fact they had not tried to move Brenda, saying as no one knew what damage had been inflicted extreme care had to be taken. The Police he was expecting but not the two cars, one of them being a divvy van the two men had been moved into it not gently, no one mentioning the bruises they were sporting. One of the policemen, mentioning in an aside that Larry overheard, they had gotten off lightly, compared to the damage he could see they had inflicted on their victim.

He was also surprised when General Richardson arrived with some senior cadets, realising that Roger or Max must have called them asking for their help to check if anyone else was around.

It was late in the afternoon, and the happy mood had turned to one of disbelief, that the attack had happened so suddenly, when everyone thought they and Brenda were safe. Max offering to resign, as he was useless in protecting the very person who needed him the most, while he was having fun. Larry looked at the mortified faces around him, while they waited in the office, for the police to finish their reports.

'Resign, don't be bloody silly. That would be the last thing Brenda would want. How do you think I feel, I love the woman, and I could not keep her safe, knew the type of man that she had gotten away from, still didn't help! I don't think any protection would have saved her from both of those men, vengeance was in both of their hearts, we can be at least grateful that we don't have to keep looking over our shoulders.' Everyone looked at him, realising the truth in his statement.

'Max, don't be a fool, help me help you, all of us get through this, please don't give up on Brenda's dream. She would not want us to, so come on, we need to get to the hospital, David,' he moved over to David sitting in the corner of the office head in his hands, a stunned look on his face.

'That was my father, my father.' David could not stop the words tumbling from him. 'Oh, my god, I did not believe that he could be like that. Mum never spoke ill of him, when we were very young, but realised when we got older and started asking more questions she said he had died. It was only recently we realised he was still alive, mum had been protecting us by telling us the lie. We moved around a lot, I never realised at the time why we did, I now know it was to keep us away from him. How could he be so cold, and brutal, especially to someone he supposedly loved!' They could all see the tears running down his face, shock was running through all of them.

Glen came into the office, after seeing that Roger, June with Keith were helping the police, realised he was not needed. Taking in the sight of Larry and David, stunned faces, he had seen Mary take George into their cottage to distract him, realised they all had to be at the hospital, Kate would need the support.

'Ok, Matt turn my car around, we need to get to the hospital.' He turned to Max, still shocked standing by the door, 'Max come on man, can you and Roger take charge here. We need to make sure that no one else is around, I know those two would have gone for Brenda but we need to make sure no one else is around. Can you do that?'

Max coming out of his fog, realised he had a job to do, he needed to help with the college people, and the police more of whom had just arrived, nodding and taking Glen's hand taking strength from the firm grasp. 'Yes of course I can, I have my team to help. Larry, did you say you had called the college or Roger? No matter we will do a check of the grounds. You go, you all need to be at the hospital, Kate and Rebecca will need you, go!'

They arrived at the hospital to find Kate and Rebecca in the waiting room, David engulfing his sister, Larry comforting them both.

Rebecca going over to Glen and Matt, 'latest report Brenda is in surgery, they think only her arm is broken, although a lot of cuts some quite deep have led to substantial blood loss, and bruises some of them they think may be internal, and not sure if bleeding, with a massive head trauma, they have no idea how bad that is. They are going to place her in an induced coma, in intensive care, that's the best they can do, oh dad did you see the mess of her face, how can anyone do that to someone they supposedly loved?'

She broke down then, tears running down her face, Glen putting a comforting arm around her, not having an answer to that question. Matt going and putting his arms around Kate, she accepting the comfort his secure presence gave. They all sat waiting for someone to let them know what was going on time seemed to drag, then suddenly gardenia was floating around, the door opened.

The surgeon looked at the group that stood at his entrance, after introductions confirmed that Brenda would be ok eventually, physically there was blood loss, but they could not see any was internal, the broken arm was a clean break which was the only broken bone, and a miracle with all the blows she had sustained. There was some swelling to the brain, the cat scan they had done and x-rays were encouraging, they could not say how bad it was, she had a hairline fracture to the jaw that the x-ray had revealed, until she woke, they could not give any better news, to help Brenda heal, they were keeping her in an induced coma for at least 24/48 hours.

The doctor looked around the room, seeing hope blossom, advising they should just go home, the hospital had their contacts and if any developments would contact them immediately. Telling them come back the following day, he would arrange for the immediate family to see her, but for any other visitors, they could not get to see her till she was out of ICU.

Accepting the inevitable, and with Iris keeping them calm, they nodded and reluctantly went back to see what was going on at Broadmeadows.

Chapter 34

B RENDA WAS FLOATING, IT was a strange experience, not
sure exactly where she was, then she realised she was
floating through wood panelled corridors that were vaguely familiar.
Laughter was around her, she felt so good. A presence, floating
beside her, she stopped and floated down, her feet touching, but not
touching wide oak floorboards. Turning to see Iris standing beside
her, taking her hand and leading her up the corridor.

'Where am I,' the words formed in her mind, she didn't speak
them, but knew they had been heard.

'Silly you are at the Broadmeadows of my father and grandfather,'
the reply from Iris in her mind, she looked around and could see
out of the windows to the distance, the lake and folly, the oak trees
majestic and tall, the beautiful grounds spreading out before her.

'Am I dying?' the question was asked before she could censor it.
Laughter was around her again, it was comforting, and she relaxed.

'No silly, you still have a lot of work to do. I am sorry I could
not spare you the beating, I tried to help, but it was necessary so you
could be rid of that man for ever, you had been carrying him with
you for years, did you know. Do you forgive me?'

'Forgive you, sister of my heart, there is nothing to forgive. He
would have found me one way or another, yes, we had unfinished
business, I ran rather than facing it. The children are they ok?'

'Yes, don't worry, they are fine, it was malice against you that
drove both of the men. They were not thinking of anyone else. I
tried to divert as many blows as I could, please relax, let your body
heal, I will be with you always, the family too, you are doing so well,

thank you Brenda. Now is a time I and the family can answer your questions, if we can, and let us show you what you are rebuilding, this place of my father and grandfather's youth, you can only see so much from drawings and plans, we can explore this place together. I only have their verbal accounts to go by, and of course the pictures in the journals, I enjoyed just like you have. My family seat was always just a memory to me, this way we can both see what it was like before.'

Brenda sighed, a slight smile seemed to form on her lips, tears were running down her swollen cheeks, the nurse in ICU wiped them gently away, noting that her breathing had settled, and blood pressure and other vital signs were coming back down to normal, the induced coma was doing its part.

It was a subdued group that were surrounded when they got back to the estate. There were people everywhere, Max and Roger coming out of the office, with General Richardson the question they did not want to ask on everyone's face.

'She will live,' Larry said, 'not sure what damage has been done, she has a broken arm at least, may need some facial reconstruction, she was badly beaten. We won't know for the next 24 to 48 hours, she is in an induced coma. We will have more news when she comes around, the hospital will call us if any developments. Now what is going on here?'

General Richardson heaved a sigh and breathed with the rest of them. 'Good news, oh that is good news. Thanks for that, ok I am going back to the college, have a few things to check over, I will leave a few of the cadets here Max, Roger, if you don't think they are needed send them back tonight, the hike back to the college will be good for them'.

Max breathed again, at least she was alive. Saying goodbye to the General, he turning his shoulder as he left, saying quietly to him as they shook hands 'They need to know!'. Max motioned for everyone to follow him, ushered them all into his cottage, a quiet place in amongst the rapidly diminishing sea of people outside.

Roger went and gave Kate a hug, 'She will be fine, you can't keep a strong woman like that down for long, just keep the faith'

'Thanks Roger, thanks for being here, all of you, now where is everyone, all I see are new faces, what's up?'

Roger said, that Mary had taken George back to the pub, not wanting him around the negativity, he would head over there shortly, he was just waiting for news.

'The college offered to help, after I called them, I didn't realise how many would turn up.' Roger turned then handing over the conversation to Max

Max made sure they were all sitting down, offering tea or coffee or something stronger, nodding to Roger accepting he was given the lead in the conversation, because of his area of expertise, as the news he was about to tell them, he did not want them standing.

'We have done a complete sweep of the grounds, at least the areas that have been cleared and are being worked on. We found some interesting toys, and a few trip wires, apparently those two had decided to turn the Manor ruins and around the glass house, into very small rubble. We think they were planning, after taking their frustrations out on Brenda throwing her into the manor ruins and exploding the shell of the building around her. Making it look like she had been exploring and triggered a bomb, so it would be called an accident, and killing her. The amount of explosive that General Richardson has safely taken away would have left only small rubble, and decimated the storage area, with the over the top amount used. We will not be seeing those two for a very long time, attempted manslaughter will be the charge, we still have the Police, and the forensic people up at the glass house.'

'I am not sure I can take very much more,' David said, Kate looking at her brother, going and sitting on the arm of his chair to give him a hug. 'To find out that my, our father is a monster, how do I know I am not like him, they say like father like son.' Bitter doubt assailed him.

Everyone gasped at his comment, 'how could you think that,' Kate said shaking him,' you only become like someone, when you watch what they do, copy their attitudes, live with them. We never lived with that monster, and I refuse to call him father, as far as I am concerned, our father died, just after we were born just like mum has always told us, that man is no relation to us. We have a new life to live, let's just see that we live it, and help take care of mum, continue with this legacy she has started, make it prosper, that will be the best way to get back at that asshole, and she will need us now, more than ever.'

Leaning into his strong sister, he wept tears of relief, feeling the same drop onto his head, as Kate released the tension she had been feeling. Larry stood as he heard a car pull up outside, thinking it would be a Police car went out the open door, Sir James and Michael Dranish Fawkes, meeting him on the threshold. Taking the two men into the midst of the group, bringing them both up to date. Sir James visibly paling, and being ushered into a seat by Kate. June in the kitchen opening the bottle of Brandy she had bought and handing glasses around to everyone, they all needed it.

Glen took Rebecca away once they were sure everyone was ok, Matt staying to be close to Kate, and be a presence from the family if needed.

Sir James saying that he had come down with Michael to see what was going on. Michael nodding at Sir James, continued telling he had been given a cryptic message from the Police that they knew Greg was in the country but was not alone then had lost him, Michael had called Sir James and Hugh, with the worrying news. Hugh had then suggested that both of them had better alert Larry, he would stay in London to relay any news, agreeing with him both men decided to carry the warning in person. They had been on the road to them and had received a message from their contacts and Hugh, when Larry called for the ambulance and police assistance, wondering if they would be too late to make a difference, very sure they had made the journey in record time.

Michael also told the group, that he had the contracts for June and Keith to sign, making them officially part of the Broadmeadows team. It was a subdued celebration for them both, after the police and cadets had left, the stable yard so happy that morning, was a different feel in the evening, it was an empty feel, there was someone missing.

Kate was sitting in the small courtyard, that both the cottages had, trying to sort out her feelings, the anger she felt against the man who would do such terrible things to someone he loved! It was so foreign to her, she who had been surrounded by unconditional selfless love from her mother from the day she was born, was having a hard time working it out. Suddenly a breeze floated by her, gardenia surrounded her, she felt light and knew that her mum would be ok; Iris was there, and with Brenda she just knew it.

'Are you ok love,' Matt was on the doorstep, wanting to comfort but unsure of how to do so. 'There are sandwiches, so glad there was all that food left over from last night, Keith and June make a formidable team in the kitchen.'

Kate moved over to him, feeling the security as his arms came around her, understanding that here was a man, who although felt frustration at times, would not take it out on the person he loved, and that was her.

'I am getting there, how is it, who is left, I am not sure if I can face a lot of people!'

'Sir James was asking about you, he and Michael have organised rooms at the pub, they will be back tomorrow, Roger has gone with them. Larry just spoke to the hospital, Brenda's vital signs have stabilised, they will be moving her out of ICU to the recovery ward quicker than they thought if she keeps up the good work, then from there a private room. Michael and Sir James were talking about getting an air ambulance and moving her to London,' as she started to speak, 'no need love, Larry and David vetoed that idea. Saying Brenda would not like to be moved out of the area, this is home, and she was getting the best care. I think they may send for a specialist once they have found out exactly what injuries Brenda has, but they have at least calmed down. Now, it is getting late how about we attack that pile of sandwiches and then head up to the manor, we are going to need some sleep, to tackle the next few days?'

Knowing what he said would be true, and that Iris was already helping Brenda, Kate nodded and moved back into the cottage. June and Keith had moved into the second cottage at Rogers insistence, taking people to help them fold up the tents, putting them safely in the garage till they could be returned to the College, giving them something to do. The fact that rain clouds had appeared helping with the decision. David stood and gave his sister a hug, with Larry holding out a plate of sandwiches to them, making a smile appear on all three faces.

Larry looked at the faces surrounding him, 'Good, that's what we need to do, smile. We know that Brenda will recover, it sucks that she is not here to celebrate the fact people were actually living on the estate again! This is a milestone people, Brenda would want us to be happy with this fact, so here is a toast, to the Lucas Line, and Lady Brenda Lucas, may she be happy in this her home.'

A resounding 'Here, here' sounded in the room, gardenia floated in the air, all were aware of a presence, if not more than one, but it was fleeting, just enough to confirm what they were doing was right. Everyone felt a lightening of spirit, and a renewed sense of purpose, they had to succeed to make Brenda proud of them all.

Chapter 35

MATT WAS UP BEFORE dawn the following morning, leaving Kate sleeping, he had to check on something that was niggling at the back of his mind. Remembering the conversations, he had with Brenda, to somehow give cheap self-sufficient power, rather than link to the grid. Matt intended that the whole estate would be giving back to the national grid, not taking from it, he knew that the solar/battery system he was installing would be good, but there was something better that was niggling him, he wanted to check the journals, on Brenda's Broadmeadows laptop.

For her Christmas present the year before he had borrowed every last journal, scrap of paper, hand drawn map and with Kate's help, had transferred them to a new laptop, Brenda had been so happy with the "Broadmeadows Laptop" as a present the happy hug she had given him he could still feel. Wondering if she was going to be ok, he could not dwell on the previous day's activities, shaking his head, he turned his attention back to the journals.

Searching for a reference he remembered around 1775 and the late 1800's, he had been flicking through the journals as he loaded them, and remembered the names Richard Arkwright, Lord and Lady Armstrong, noted they had been frequent visitors to the estate, the son at the time had been very interested in a new process that they were developing. The more Matt researched this Lucas family, the more he was aware they were ahead of their time in everything. Wondering if there was more information he had missed in the journals, Matt was engrossed and didn't realise Kate was awake till she sat beside him.

'Sorry, didn't mean to make you jump, what are you so engrossed in, that you didn't hear me?'

'Oh luv, don't do that again, or I will end up in hospital next to Brenda. No I am not sharing at the moment, I am researching, just wanted to check on something. Now, how about breakfast, I will cook, want to go and wake up David and Larry, we have a lot to do today!'

They were not the only ones awake, as they drove through the drizzle down to the cottages. It may have been a Sunday morning, but the smoke rising from both cottages, told them everyone was awake, even Roger and Mary were there, as they saw the car parked out the front of the cottages.

Roger was the first to speak after good mornings had been passed around, and George had been given a hug. 'Any news?'

'Brenda is resting as comfortably as expected, she is being held in ICU for another day, but the doctor said the induced coma was doing its job. He is allowing us to visit briefly this morning, which is good. I am going to take Kate and David here off to the hospital, Matt are you coming too?'

'If you don't mind Larry I would rather be here, I really need to make sure that motor on the Garage door is working correctly which is what Brenda would want I believe. Do you mind luv?' this he asked of Kate.

'No, I realise you are working on something in that brain of yours. I will be fine, and I know that mum will be fine. Go on have fun'

Roger and Mary said goodbye as well, they were heading back to their little flat to organise the move down to the cottage, and Roger said 'for me to resign with a smile on my face from that soulless occupation I had been in.'

After waiving the family off, Matt gave Kate a hug, and with well wishes from everyone, they drove off to the hospital. Matt took Max, Keith and June down into the garage to tinker with the motor, Matt explaining to all three that he wanted if possible to do a little exploration of the estate in a particular area.

Brenda could not move, what was going on, she wondered if she had slept in, why could she not get the thoughts straight in her head. Had she slept on her arm, as it felt numb, and as though in a vice, and pain, oh that was not good. Someone was bending over her, what had happened, the children!

'Lady Lucas, Lady Lucas can you hear me, Brenda, open your eyes,' a voice female pleasant, she could hear words, but they did not make sense. She could not remember where she was, then she remembered Greg and Bill, made a sudden move, pain reverberated through her. 'Lady Lucas, please do not move, you are in the hospital, you are safe, open your eyes if you can, or squeeze my hand, please just lie still'.

Slowly and with great effort, Brenda opened one eye, a mere slit, the other she could not, as it was completely swollen shut, and she realised was covered by a bandage that covered nearly all of her head. The nurse was being so gentle but the warmish water she was sponging her face with smarted.

'Good thank you, I know this stings a little, but I am trying to clean off the blood from your face, this solution is my own concoction and usually helps in reducing the swelling. There now that is better, and good morning, you have a lot of people worried about you. No don't talk, or move too much, there are lots of cuts, some very deep, bruises and muscle tears, you also have a broken arm, and fractured jaw, you are in ICU, it is Sunday morning, you have visitors waiting to see you!'

Realising she could do very little to stop any of the ministrations from happening, Brenda relaxed, she was safe. Suddenly memory of what had happened returned, and she flinched as the nurse washed more of her swollen face. She tried to put the events to the back of her mind, she would not give those two monsters the satisfaction of thinking of them more than she had too, she had survived that was enough.

The doctor took the nurses place, standing where her barely open eye could see him, saying he was so pleased with her progress but they were holding her in ICU for another twenty-four hours, be better for her, telling her again about the broken right arm, which was in plaster and the reason she could not move it. With difficulty, she tried to concentrate on what he was saying, 'we found a hairline fracture to the jaw, may be difficult to talk for a while but we believe that will repair itself in time. Multiple cuts, bruises and torn ligaments, so you look a mess, sorry but true.' Moving away from the bed, he continued telling her she was going to be in hospital to make sure there were no complications for a few days, she was to tell the nurse if she could not cope with the pain.

The Nurse replaced the doctor as he left the room, moving into her line of sight, stood so she could see her, 'I am Ann, please I will be here, just raise your hand to alert me. Do you need anything,' Brenda quietly breathed no, 'your family are outside, they need the assurance of seeing you, please do not exert yourself, and I will remove them if you try, they can only be here for a very brief visit, can I bring them in?'

A small smile flicked across her face, taking that as a yes, Ann left the room, while the other nurses checked information on the monitoring equipment.

In the waiting room, Larry was pacing, wondering why they were being held for so long, it had been ages since they arrived, and they had not been allowed to see her.

'Am I speaking to Kate and David, you must be Larry?' Ann walked into the waiting room, she was not dressed in normal nurse's uniform, but was in pale blue scrubs, as the ICU nurses wore, she carried herself with the assurance of one who knew what she was doing, Kate and David immediately recognised the self-assurance this woman had.

'My name is Ann, I have been hired by Mr. Michael Dranish Fawkes, on behalf of the Lucas Estate to be Brenda's private nurse. I have to warn you that she is not a pretty sight, those mongrels, and yes, I know the names of the gentlemen, the Police have already been around, did a good job before being stopped. So, I say, she will heal, but it will take time, look beyond what you see, and just be happy she is still with us, it was touch and go last night believe me!'

Forewarned, still did not stop them gasping as they were ushered into the room, Brenda was a mess what they could see of her, bandages covering her shaved head and over half of her face, her face itself was swollen like a balloon, right eye covered, left eye nearly completely closed, purple bruising covering the side of her face they could see, cuts over the rest, her arm in a sling and propped up at the side of the bed, you could see the way was lying that the bruising and cuts were everywhere. Lifting her left arm to them, murmuring words of comfort, Ann left them as she heard footsteps outside, and voices questioning the policeman at the door.

In the corridor, Michael Dranish Fawkes and another distinguished gentleman turned to her as she walked up to them.

'Sir,' she smartly gave Michael the salute he was expecting, and then put her hand out to him. 'Please she is ok, come with me, the family are with her at the moment, come let me make you a tea or coffee, she is safe at the moment.' Nodding at the Policeman that was standing to one side of the door.

'Sir James, may I introduce Ann Darfmeir, I have been talking to her for some time in regards to another area, for now I have hired her to look after Brenda, I was just lucky she was between deployments and available.'

Sir James stirred himself, he had advised Shane and Linda of the developments, and stopped them from piling everyone into a car to head down. Being the voice of common sense, saying that was silly what were they going to do, Brenda was in the hospital, and they had the two villains in custody, he would see they would never see freedom again if he could. But his anger was useless, all the precautions they had taken, were nothing, Brenda had still been injured. He had worked through his anger while talking to Shane and Linda, he was calm, and relaxed even more in the presence of this very lovely and capable woman.

'Army?' he asked.

'Yes sir, and happy to help in any way I can.' As she brought him a cup of tea, handed one to Michael who sat to listen.

'To bring you up to speed, I checked with the contacts in Scotland Yard you gave me this morning. They were not sure when Brenda's ex left Australia only picking up a trace in Spain, they had again lost the contact with Greg Willmott after he had met up with Bill Gardiner in Portugal, they think they used one of the ferries to get to the UK. Checking passport control, they know when they arrived, both of them vanished, that was nearly three weeks ago.

They have been setting up what happened yesterday for a while. How the two men knew each other, well the Police were 'pursuing their enquiries' was what I was told. They also assigned the police officer to Brenda's door, outside ICU all night and I have been told there will be a police presence here for as long as Brenda is in the hospital. If you have anything further, I would like to keep Brenda up to date.' At their gasp, 'oh yes, she is not exactly awake, but she keeps talking, well it is really muttering, but I hear 'Iris' a lot, so I talk to her when I am in the room.' Both of the men looked at each other, understanding that comment, but realising that Ann would not, relaxed a little more. Ann continued 'from what you have told me sir, she will not be in that hospital bed any longer than necessary.'

Sir James relaxed, hearing Iris's name knew that she was around in some form, whether Brenda was aware, well he would keep that to himself, sceptical as he was of Brenda's unseen friend. He also knew she would hate to be termed an invalid, as he would.

Michael nodded, 'we have been told they don't know how many people were in on this little caper, so that is why the police are posting a guard. Only people to be admitted are family,' he smiled to himself, 'that might mean you will have to limit the visitors, as everyone is family to Brenda.' That brought a smile to Sir James face as well, he sipping his tea, trying to relax. 'There is possibly another player in this scheme, although with both of the main characters in custody, he might just slip away. I hope he does, but we will be vigilant.'

The door to the waiting room opened, Larry coming into the room, a concerned look on his face. 'I came to find you Ann, can you come and check on Brenda, she seems to be suffering, but won't admit it!'

'Just like her,' Sir James commented, as he moved over to Larry, gripping him on the arm, 'are you ok son, look at me, she is alive, just remember that.' Larry looked at this man he held in high regard, Michael coming to stand beside him, feeling the strength and maturity bolstering his flagging confidence, he just could not match the two pictures of Brenda in his head, one of her pliant and full of love in his arms, and the one he had just seen of her bruised, battered and in pain, but not willing to show it.

Kate and David, came into the room, grateful for the hugs they got from the two gentlemen, 'Ann wanted to check on mum, I think we may have outstayed her time line, and I don't think we will be allowed to stay longer. Mum is like a mummy, covered in bandages from head to toe there is still swelling at the moment, Ann thought they might be too tight. We just have to wait a few moments.'

David moved off into a corner, thinking that Glen and the family would want to know what was going on. Coming back when Ann returned, a smile on her face. 'That is one tough mother you have there. Now I suggest you go in say hello's and goodbyes and then let her rest. That is the best thing for her, I will be here, and looking after her, so relax, nothing will get by me!'

Knowing instinctively that Ann would be vigilant, they all, Michael and Sir James as well moved quietly into the room, Brenda trying to smile when she saw Sir James and the stricken expression on his face.

'Sir, please don't, I look worse than I am, please I am still here and will be up and about in no time.' Brenda her voice no more than a whisper tried to reassure the people in the room. Grimacing as she made an involuntary movement, that sent the pain through her arm. All of them realising that what Ann had said was right, after holding her left hand, as they said goodbye, and feeling the strength there, they started to move out of the room to let her rest. Kate beside her head hearing the sigh, 'it's ok mum, sleep we will be back tomorrow, we just have to go and check up on what Matt is up to.' Brenda tried to look at her daughter, and a small smile played on her face, she squeezed her hand, gardenia floating around them. Kate squeezed back, watching as the eye closed and Brenda slipped into sleep, slipping back into the dreams Iris was showing her how Broadmeadows used to be, and pieces of the puzzle were starting to fit into her plan of what the house and the area should look like.

Ann standing beside her, smiling 'thank you for being here, are you one of the recruits Michael is hiring for mum?'

'Yes, I am, so please be assured I will be here when she needs me. Go, and smile, all will be well, I promise.

Chapter 36

J UNE CAME OUT OF the cottage as she heard the cars arriving, hoping they had good news, and knowing it was when they all got out of the cars. Seeing the smiling faces, still with a bit of worry, but they were smiling. After being brought up to date, Larry looked around asking where were the men?

'All three of them, after they had fixed up the motor on the garage door have gone to check on something that Matt wanted to follow up on. Please don't ask me what it is, I volunteered to stay here for when you returned, but Keith and Max were really excited, that was a couple of hours ago, I am expecting them back for lunch, so please let me offer you the hospitality of the cottages, which I am very happy to share. This place is just amazing.'

David and Larry said they had to make some phone calls, one was to Dennis, as they had just left a message last night, so would just go back up to the mini manor for a while, to catch up. Leaving Kate and June to entertain Michael and Sir James with a tour of the cottages, Gate Lodge and using the spiral stairs in there moving down into the Garage.

'We know there are entrances to the Garage from all the cottages, showing the access points being cleared of the debris only Max's was completely clear, and also from the stables,' Kate was saying as she moved the two gentlemen into the cavernous space. Happy with the awed expression on both of their faces. 'but we won't be able to reach the stable one until all the debris has been removed, which is taking a little longer as mum wanted the cottages cleared first. Also, the stables were remodelled by Roger, new plans had to be submitted, there is time for us to check the area out. Both Peter and David know of the area it could be in, we can see it from the garage, but are waiting on the go ahead of the revised plans, and then Glen and Dan to find it for sure. What do you think?'

Sir James was stunned, and moved amongst the finest carriages he had seen, in the torchlight they were magnificent, yes, they were dreadfully filthy, but whole. Only one had sustained damage to its roof, from the block of stone which had created the hole Fred had found. He wandered over to the shrouded shapes under the canvas. Jumping when June started the motor to open the garage door. Marvelling with Michael at the workings, and pointing out to June and Kate the door they could see in the corner of the room.

'Yes, that is where they think the access from the stable is, still have to clear out a lot of debris, and rebuild. Roger has plans for the area he knows will be there, as the original ones showed storerooms under the horse stalls, which are all at stable yard level.' June was looking forward to the challenge, and it clearly showed to the people around her.

'Ah yet another convert to the 'Cult of Lucas.' Sir James chuckled, the first time in the last three days he felt happy, seeing the confused expression on her face continued, 'all of this,' he took in the estate as a whole, 'is just part of a cunning plan going back centuries. You get infected by it, the fact that everything we are discovering about this family only points to one thing, they were time travellers, for everything we have discovered, sorry Brenda has discovered, about this family says they were centuries ahead of their time. Anyone who even comes into contact with them, via Brenda and now you young Kate and David, just want to see the families vision renewed and their achievements and techniques reborn. You know what, I don't blame them either, this is wonderful, and I want to be here when you get better light to see what there is. I would suggest you don't move or take covers off anything till you can do so. Now how about another cup of tea, and I am starving!'

Laughing with him, they closed the door, now very easy to do with Matt's motor. Moved back to Max's cottage using the cleared-out tunnel that Brenda had seen, on her first trip to the garage. June telling Sir James and Michael to move out into the sunny yard, while she and Kate prepared lunch for everyone.

Setting up a couple of the caterer's tables in the shade of the stable yard, they were just putting out plates of sandwiches and fresh fruit when Larry and David walked in, with Max, Keith and Matt in the estate van following them into the yard. When they came towards the tables looking very muddy, and dishevelled, but with grins on their faces as they had found what Matt thought was there, but would not say anything, as Matt did not know if he could get it to work again and needed to do more research, with Max and Keith having to do some grunt work, to clear what they had found.

It was a happy, but subdued group that had lunch, Sir James and Michael putting forth the opinion that the Garage should be left for a while, until they could get proper access from the Stables and light to see what they were doing in there. Making sure that the Gate Lodge was finished in time for Brenda when she was released from the hospital.

Sir James passing on the message from Linda to Kate, to take all the time she needed, the Guest House was closed, they had cancelled the next two visitors, to allow her to be there for her mum. Both of the men going back to town, after a quick stop at the hospital, checking in with Ann, getting an update on Brenda's progress.

Kate, David and Larry going in the evening, to find Brenda looking much better. Ann making sure that their stay was not long, only long enough for them to be sure she was going to recover, Ann assuring them she was getting stronger and better by the minute.

The routine was set, a morning visit to the hospital, back to the estate, and the afternoon evening visit to make sure all was ok. The moving to a Private room from ICU was a red-letter day, and allowing Glen and Dan with other visitors in to see her, so they could report back to the troops, that she would slowly recover. Urging her to stay put, until they could move her into the Gate Lodge, which was not quite finished yet. Not voicing the opinion that they wanted her closer to her protectors, with one of the trio they thought masterminded the attack still on the loose.

For Brenda, her milestone came when Ann said she could have a shower. The bruising and muscle tears, she advised was something that Mother Nature would have to fix, but had brought some of her special solution for her to use. Her jaw was another problem, as it was still very difficult for her to speak and chew, a dental surgeon was called, he suggested a realignment would be needed, and repairing of some teeth, this they did without telling Larry or Kate and David. Going back into surgery, after their visit in the evening, she felt much better on the Thursday morning, and then Ann asked if she wanted a shower?

All tubes had been removed, her caste sealed in a plastic bag, she was gingerly moved into the bathroom in a wheelchair, Ann standing by just in case when she stood under the water, but it was heavenly, to remove all the grime, bits of debris and blood. Being careful as they removed the big bandages that were protecting the stiches on her shaved head, but she felt a million dollars, and a whole lot lighter when she put on a nightgown Ann had brought in for her that morning, had lighter bandages replacing the original ones on her head, crawled back into bed. Pain was now being monitored and managed by her, and with tablets not drips in her arm. She insisted from then on, she would use the bathroom, and walk a little more each day. Her face thanks to Ann's magic mixture, had reduced the swelling a little, and she could just see out of both eyes, she knew she was over the worst of it, when Ann gave her toast with her scrambled eggs for breakfast on the Saturday morning, and it did not hurt to chew.

Chapter 37

KATE ON THAT FIRST Monday after the attack, was sitting at the table in the Mini Manor, waiting for everyone to wake up, coffee in hand, reading through the notes that Brenda had been adding to the notepad at the side of her laptop, smiling a sad smile, at the conundrum that was her mother, old fashioned but embracing technology in equal measure.

As she read the notes, shaking her head at the old-fashioned sense of writing on paper and having a laptop at the same time, wondering if her mum would ever only use one, realising that it would never happen as Brenda liked the feel of physically writing her ideas down. Seeing under the heading of 'Reminder', her mum had noted to ask Peter and David, about altering the space in the stables, that area closest to the Gate Arch, that Roger had split from the original with the large barn door in the middle being the dividing point of the space. Turning the area from horse stalls and storage to a one or even a two-bedroomed apartment, or as it would have steps a townhouse for Keith.

Running underneath from that, to check if they could turn the Gate Arch into a dormitory with a number eight, for number of beds, Kate thought. Accommodation for extra staff that might be needed, with two bathrooms, and kitchenette; with a line of question marks after this with a cryptic check Brent for lift access, as though Brenda had been unsure if it could be done. Typical, Kate thought, her mum was not going to be caught again, with people turning up and having no where to stay.

David arose next, Kate pointing out Brenda's notes on the pad, with David smiling,

'The Stables Apartment, oh you bet it could be done and is being done, might have to make adjustments to the bedroom space, Peter has already put on the plan, he will need to fit a king super-sized bed for Keith in there. I can't believe how attuned Peter and mum are, he saw the space after Roger suggested the changes to the original plan, and realised with more staff arriving, they would need the extra accommodation. Also, realised that mum would want it to happen, so the plans for the new super duper stables are down in the office. Glen and Dan were with Max and Keith's assistance,' at Kate's confused look continued, 'checking for bombs in the debris,' at her nod of understanding, 'going to clear the basement of the stables this week, to see if we can uncover the doorway in to the Garage again. Still waiting on that boyfriend of yours to give us light down there, what is he up to?'

'I don't know he won't tell me anything, he went home last night, to get a change of clothes, he was filthy, and don't ask me where he had been, both Keith and Max were the same. I think he was going to pack a suitcase and bring it back with him this morning, you don't mind, do you?'

'Of course, I don't mind, I like the bloke as well you know, one of my first friends in the country. I am just getting used to Larry snoring,' this said as Larry came into the room, laughing at the comment.

'Me snore; never had any complaints from your mother, still my hay fever down here is bad, do you have any antihistamines Kate luv, or I will be sneezing my way around today!'

They all made their way to the office, Kate wanting to check on the plans for the Stable apartment, double checking they had not missed anything that Brenda would see, and pulling Peter to the plans, after giving him a hug, he was very upset about Brenda.

'She will be fine, I know she looks awful, but Ann said most of the worst blows were diverted somehow, and no real damage done to any major organs, only superficial damage, but that is enough, please don't worry. Keeping the thought that Iris may have helped in that regard to herself. She is in the best place, resting and getting better. Can I ask you about this Stable space?' pointing to it on the plan.

'Well I thought when Roger mentioned that there would be space to make one, there will be ample, and not just an apartment, a two storied one bedroomed town house, as it is just the type of thing Brenda would ask me to do and it will fit into the space. What don't you like it?'

'No Peter luv, it is just as mum would want, but I think we need to expand the bedroom if we can, and make sure the bathroom has enough height,' at his blank look, Kate turned and pointed to Keith, sitting next to the men in conversation across the office he was still taller than everyone, 'he will need a super king sized bed which I will be ordering for him today, and the bedroom and bathroom sized to fit his tall frame! Also, how do you access this place?'

'Well the door is here in the Stables - oh I get your point, we need a front door from the yard, if it is to be a townhouse, for additional access, thank you David would have pointed it out, but thank you. Let me at them I will show you a revised plan very soon.'

A message from Matt on her phone, saying he was fact finding, and would see her tomorrow or the next, made her curious, but she was so busy from then, helping Rebecca and June to source some more furniture for the Gate Lodge. Rebecca wanted to get some vintage pieces found only in Antique shops, which were abundant in the area, that would fit in with the time period of the building. June said she could not really assist in the grunt work, of removing the debris, would rather leave it to the men and machines that loved that type of thing, asked if she could go with the Ladies, and could they please stop by a few garden centres, as she just had to do some planting, or would bust.

Max and Keith, had reconnoitred the area of the stables, in their efforts to discover any unexploded bombs, and could not see anything. But when they started to remove the blocks of stone, and timbers that filled the area, were doubly cautious. Using the crane, and starting at what they knew was the garage wall, making sure the workmen removed the stone blocks and timber sections, piece by piece they dug down, carefully sorting through shrapnel and stone, halting work if unsure to take the time and be safe. Once down to the floor, which was covered in the same stone pavers as the rest of the space, clearing from there to the outer wall, amazed when they found the very wide, sturdy and thick oak beams and planks, Keith stunned at the age and size of the planks, that had been flattened in the explosion, they had clearly been used to divide the space into rooms, as lining and support wall in one. They had fallen inwards on top of everything inside the rooms, but remained intact. By the end of the day, the rooms and there were originally three of them, were turned into one, the new steel beams and posts from Dan able to hold anything above, replacing the ancient timbers.

Dan in his element once Keith and Max had given the all clear, needing to take measurements to fabricate all the beams they would need, and of course for a new set of stairs, the original was not a circular stair, this one came straight from yard wall in the stables above, down to a landing on the back wall, then turned at ninety degrees, to complete to the floor, underneath where the stair case originally was were wooden boxes and barrels most in pieces, but a few of them whole, and had been converted into a mouse or rats heavenly abode over time.

Dan wondered about the stair case, conversing with Keith and Max, 'you had better call Roger,' both of them said, 'he is the stable man,' Max continued, 'this is his number. Knowing him this will be the excuse that gets him down here by the end of the week. I feel sorry for Mary, although she does have her mum and dad, close by.' Everyone laughing the sound in the space sounding hollow, the clear out complete when the last of the shrapnel was removed, the door into the garage now seen again from the other side.

It took a while for Dan and his team to remove the buckled steel door from the frame in the garage wall. Fitting a temporary set of steps into and out of the cellar at David's suggestion, until they could talk to Roger in regards to what should be permanent. They had continued putting in place the beams they had available, when Max approached them on the Wednesday, as they stopped for lunch.

'David, Peter can I have a word?'

'Sure Max, did you visit mum yesterday?'

'Yes, I had too, to say sorry, that I had not looked after her properly. Do you know what she did?' David just smiled thinking he knew what was coming, 'She told me not to be stupid, nobody could have stopped those two, not even Iris could. She thanked me for stopping them, even though I could see she was in pain just talking to me, she thanked me. I have never been thanked by someone who took as savage a beating as that. What could I do!'

'You went to see her, my friend, she would have appreciated that. Now what can we do for you?'

He motioned them into the office, and pointed to the plans for the Gate Arch and the roadway out to the bridal path. Noting the second set of plans for the dormitory room across the top, 'Brenda?' he asked.

'Yep she was mortified that you, Keith and June had to sleep in a tent! I know it was only for one night, but she realises that there will be times when there will be the need for extra staff, so thought about altering the plans, there is room for eight beds, and two bathrooms, with a kitchenette. Drawn up, but not confirmed yet,' at Max's raised eyebrow, 'Mum hasn't seen them!'

'Oh, right, well can I ask for a change to the building and possibly the stables, before they get too far along, as well?'

'What,' both of the architects said together.

'I am expecting a couple of four wheeled drive buggy's, to use as farm vehicles. Michael authorised and ordered them for me on Monday. They will be delivered by the end of the week. They will be fine in the yard while the weather is good, and we can cover them in tarps., but I was thinking, and Keith agreed, if we extend the gate way, to the end of the stables, joining the two buildings we can use the ground floor of the arch as a buggy garage, with access from the ground floor of the townhouse, do roller doors into the garage from the yard and again on the other side, making a bridge across to the bridal path to give access but not interfere with the original road to the garage underneath, and from there on to the estate. Then with the extended space above it, this will allow us to extend Keith's abode to a larger bedroom for him above the buggy garage, and the extra height it will need possibly adding skylights, and even adding a second bedroom perhaps?'

Max stopped at the silence from both of the men beside him. David smiled, clapping him on the back, going out to the door way, shouting for Glen and Dan to step into the office for a minute. Rebecca and Kate following in their wake, interested in what had gotten David so excited. Glen and Dan were all for the scheme, Rebecca moved to the drawing board where Peter had already roughed in the new addition.

'Ok folks let's just take a breath a moment. Please remember this is a Heritage site, as well as a building site. You cannot just go adding bits and pieces to plans, they have to be passed, especially if not original. I would love to see this happening, but we have to be careful and build it in such a manner that it fits. If you extend this side to the stables, you will need to extend the other side to match.' She had picked up a pencil and was roughing in her idea, that as she spoke just felt right.

Kate then put in, 'if you do that, it also gives a second storey to the stables, to make the area complete, do we have any information in regards to that? It would be great though, as Max said it gives the stable Townhouse, space for two bedrooms on the upstairs; as well as a hay loft for extra supplies above the stables.'

Rebecca nodded, looking at the drawing, pencilling in the upper level to the stable block, turning to Max.

'When you checked this side of the area, did you find any blocks of stone on the cottage side of the gate way by any chance?'

'Yes, yes, we did, a lot of them come to think about it, actually there was enough for another cottage, to be attached to the gate way, what is going on in that head of yours?'

'How do we know that the original gateway was just that, a gateway. Did it once extend to the buildings either side, to make it an enclosed space, with gates on both sides, there is no one living to tell us? So, I say, let me research this some more, I like the idea Max, it is very practical and a good one. We could actually make good use of the space, better than the original builders, and I know Brenda is worried about having places for the workers she may need.

You lot being point in fact, pitching tents indeed. Let me see what I can find, talk to Peter and David here, to see what we can draw up. Why don't you go and order a gazebo to put over your toys when they arrive until we can build them a proper home?'

She took everyone out of the office then, over to where the gateway was, asking for Dan and her dad to check on the footings, to see if the flash of vision she had in the office was there. Glen immediately called a halt to the work, until Rebecca had the revised plans for the architects, and until Roger arrived.

Kate following on behind them all, wondering just what Iris and the Grandfathers were up to now.

Chapter 38

I T WAS OVER THREE weeks later, Larry went to the hospital on the Friday to collect Brenda and bring her home. Not really surprised when Ann had bags to put in the back of the Range Rover.

'I am Brenda's nurse Larry, where she goes I go. Until she gets a clean bill of health, and checking out of hospital on just a bare three week stay, after the injuries she sustained is not a clean bill of health.' Understanding between the words, he nodded and helped Brenda into the car.

Brenda was quiet as they drove back to the estate, Larry respecting her silence, the smile on Ann's face when he glanced in the rear-view mirror reassuring.

Brenda gasped as they drove through the gates, her dreams had become reality, almost.

'Are you alright Brenda,' Ann asked gently touching her arm.

'I am fine Ann, don't be such a worry wort, it's just I got a shock seeing the buildings again, nearly all finished. This is wonderful!'

Larry turned the car into the parking place at the end of the Gate Lodge, carefully helped her out of the car, getting the wheelchair the hospital had given them out, but immediately folded back up again, at the look of disdain Brenda gave him. Kate put her arm around her mum giving her a gentle hug to welcome her home turning her towards the door way into the Gate Lodge. Brenda still felt self-conscious, the swelling had gone down a lot, but the bruising and cuts were still there, glad of the scarf covering her shaved head, that

244

had been done in the hospital to allow them to see the extent of the injuries. Glen and Dan were next to welcome her home being a select welcoming committee, they had both sent their workers home giving them an early mark.

'Where is everyone, oh I want to see what you lot have been up too without me!'

'You can't see anything until you have seen this place, so come in coffees on, you have to see what Rebecca, June and Kate have done,' David came to give his mum a steady arm to hold onto, with Kate on the other side, to be there if she needed them, as walking, he knew was still painful for her with the torn ligaments, cuts and bruises on her legs, Ann had told him about the extent of her injuries, on his last visit to the hospital. They urged Brenda slowly towards the new and improved Gate House.

Knowing she was not going to get far, yielded to her children's wishes, and walked into a warm welcoming hug of a home. Gardenia was there, but also Nona's mixture, the biggest bunch of Iris's on a table in the small hallway, and then Rebecca and June coming towards her to give gentle hugs of their own, holding back the tears that they wanted to shed. Vowing that Brenda would be her old irrepressible self in no time, this house and they would make sure all was ok.

The tour of the Gate Lodge was everything she expected, well at least the ground floor, Ann voicing her relief that the master bedroom was downstairs, and standing in front of the stairs to stop Brenda from climbing them, as she knew she would try. Brenda turning to Rebecca, giving her a hug, there was a wonderful mix of antique pieces with modern convenience, she particularly loved the way the kitchen area opened out to the courtyard garden through wonderful oak French doors, loving the fact they were timber this time not steel. The garden itself was completely finished, June had out done herself, there was a tinkering water garden feature, a whole row of Gardenia's along the fence line, hanging baskets filled with flowers and herbs, the whole area was designed to be relaxed in, the table and chairs even two loungers invited you to do so. Brenda was encouraged by Ann to try out one of the loungers, and have her coffee in the warm sunshine, not surprised when she drifted off to sleep.

'Is she alright,' Rebecca asked as they quietly moved back into the house, Ann smiling at their worried faces.

'She will be, the trip from the hospital, although she will never admit it was a struggle. Her muscles are still healing, that is why I stopped her trying to go upstairs, and sleep when she can will be the best medicine. She has refused any of my medications I can offer her since last weekend, so Brenda is doing this the hard way. Although I think I may offer her a couple of pain killers before bed tonight, she may even accept them!'

When Brenda woke, she was in a calm state of mind, no more did she have the doubts or worries that she was doing right. She knew she was, Iris and the Grandfather Norman's had shown her what this wonderful place should be. She now only had to get fit enough to enjoy it, and she would, with Ann and everyone's help she vowed she would.

Trying to loosen up her stiff muscles with some gentle exercises, she went to find where everyone was.

'Hey there sleepy head, how are you feeling?' Larry had been working on his laptop on the table, and rose to envelope her in a hug.

Brenda welcomed the solid, dependable feel of her anchor, back again in her arms. She could feel the strength in him, his mute apology he had not done more.

'I am home, and will get stronger every day. Now where is everyone, and I am hungry is it lunch time yet?'

Lunch, it turned out was set up in the stable yard, with a buffet feast and tables for all. Brenda gasped as she moved into the area, her good arm through Larry's as they moved into the yard, noted the look that Ann gave her, 'It was hurting my neck,' she said interpreting the look at the absence of the sling. Ann shrugged, 'let me know when you want it back on', she said. The arm was healing, it could still get mighty sore, but she found that the sling irritated her more, she would have a weather-wise ache in that arm for the rest of her life, she knew.

She also gasped for the structures that now surrounded the stable yard. She had been expecting the Gate Lodge, and two finished cottages, but was un-prepared for the works in progress of a third cottage and the Stables and Gateway, which seemed to have doubled in size. Max, Keith and June came to help her to a seat next to Kate and David, with Roger, a very cheeky smile on his face pulling out the chair.

'Ok you lot, just what is going on, and how on earth did you see my dreams?'

Puzzled, they all looked at each other, Rebecca and Kate first ones to realise what Brenda meant. 'Mum,' Kate said quietly, 'what do you mean what have Iris and the Grandfathers shown you?'

Giving her daughter a kiss on the cheek as she hugged her, sat in the chair next to her, smiled at everyone. 'I am not sure if I was shown what I have wanted to see for the last few years, or it was my own imagination working while I recovered, but, the shock I got when I saw the gate lodge, not the same size mind you, realised that I had seen it before, was startling. Now I come into this area and see the next part of the dream. Well, I have to ask who else has been hallucinating, hmmm.?'

'Not exactly hallucinating, just a feeling that we were missing something, and it just felt right,' Rebecca came up with a plate of sandwiches and some fruit for Brenda, hearing the last part of the conversation.

Pulling her down into a hug, Brenda whispered in her ear, 'you were right'.

She continued including everyone, 'Now if my visions are to be believed, and I need to check on a couple of things, the wings of the gate way did extend to the cottages and there were three of them not just two, as it seems you have worked out, with fences and gates between them, the last one being attached to the gateway. The extension on the other side from the base of the gateway to the stables originally was just a wall; I am so pleased to see my visions have been upgraded. I like the structure to the stables, a much more efficient use to make this an enclosed space, so the horses could not bolt!' Roger nodded, it now made sense, where it had not before.

'I am so pleased that you have started the alterations, and want to see if I can't tweak the plans a bit, I know Peter is just waiting for me to do that,' everyone laughed, 'but I know what was originally designed for this space, and we can make it better. Now come on everyone eat up, then I can check on what you have been doing, and make you start again!'

Chapter 39

AFTER THE RELAXING LUNCH, Brenda immediately wanted to be shown everything that had been achieved. She enjoyed having her extended family show her what was going on even though it was going to take forever with everyone trying to slow her down. She looked at Ann, the look on her face and shake of her head made her realise that if she did not take notice of what her body was telling her she would go back not forwards in her healing process, but it was just so frustrating.

Brenda slowly walked out of the gateway through the arch which was almost completed with its stone veneer there were a couple of large pieces missing at the base. Around towards the bridal path passing the posts in place for a bridge coming out from the buggy garage that was the new addition to the arch base on the stable side. Commenting on how good it was going to look, and asking Dan about the time frame to the finished product. He just chuckled at the comment realising Brenda had instinctively known it was being made in steel.

Ann watched her, making sure her veto on the use of any steps at the moment was being adhered to, had not been surprised when Brenda had tut tutted her suggestion of the wheelchair for the look around the stable yard. She realised she was going to have to watch Brenda like a hawk, and repeat again her request to wait at least another week, for the exercises that she was doing to help free the muscles to let her go up and down the stairs.

The entrance to the garage had been completely cleared out by Max and June, trimming and making the area neat and weed free.

It was totally different and Brenda could see the magnificent door working from the other side, as Matt had fitted it with automatic controls.

'I knew someone is missing, where are those talented sons of yours Glen?' Brenda asked as they all moved into the garage, Dan and Glen coming from the tunnel side, she could see that lights had been fitted in the ceiling one in three working, giving a gloomy aspect, cabling running from them into the old machinery room.

'Not sure what they are doing to be quite honest Brenda, both of them with Max and Keith here, have been pretty quiet on that front. I would love to know what is going on?'

'We are sworn to secrecy, and not quite there yet. We thought you might have been in the hospital for another week, but we should have known.' Keith said coming over to her side, 'this place is the best place for you. Please we will amaze you I promise but we need at least a week or two to finesse the system!'

'Hm, a new system, well Matt did tell me he was working on something, ok, now can I please see the rest of the place?'

Ann started to remonstrate with her, saying it was enough for the first day, it was starting to drizzle after the sunshine of the morning, and continued walking could be too strenuous for her.

They were walking out of the garage, Brenda ready to argue with her, when a four-wheeled buggy, pulled up in their path. Max's grin clear for all to see, 'your chariot awaits mi 'lady!' he doffed an imaginary cap. Ann threw up her hands, all hope of getting her patient to rest disappearing as Brenda moved quite quickly to take Max's hand to help her into the passenger seat of the buggy.

'Don't worry,' David said quietly in her ear, with Larry nodding beside him, 'she is just excited and she will be the last one to admit she is tired. Just let her see what has been going on, Max won't let her do too much. He can take Brenda around to see everything, without her sneaking off on her own, and undoing all your hard work!'

They waived her off, Ann making sure when she returned that rest would be the top of Brenda's list, not the bottom.

'When did you get this?' Brenda asked Max as he slowly drove her up the bridal path towards the manor and lake, pointing out the meadows that were now looking good after June had repaired the damage from the ground source heating system Glen had put in for the manor, and cottages, way ahead of time, but with his usual efficiency. He was waiting for Brenda to glimpse what Norman and the team had finished only the day before.

'I realised that we would need something a bit more rugged than the van, once Matt showed me what he is up too, and no I am not telling, he would kill me! I asked Michael for a four-wheeled farm buggy to help with getting materials and people with ease around the estate, of course he ordered two, this one with four seats for people, and a second with a tray top!'

Brenda laughed, and nodded taking in the changes that were appearing around her, she could not believe she had only been away for three weeks. There was now a structure to the wildness that was there before, the bridal path once overgrown and unusable, now was easy to negotiate, Brenda could see how it would again become the main access into the estate. Then they rounded the bend onto the new part, originally cut by Glen to dispose of the bombs found, but now the major access around the lake, realising that he had used parts of the old pathways, and expanded on them, she gasped.

Larry stopped the buggy at her gasp, realising this area of the lake was new to her, and opposite the area so manicured on the Manor House side. She had seen the lake and folly in all its glory. 'Norman said he hoped you liked what you saw, there are still a few finishing touches to do, but in the main, till the main house was completed and they could gauge the vistas, this was the best he and the team could do. He also wanted to be here, but realised you needed the peace and serenity this area would give you to heal!'

'He was right,' Brenda breathed. Her dream had come to light, yes there were slight difference in interpretation of the folly, the new modern day version was quite severe in its simplicity, not the ornate edifice she had seen in her visions. But, it was beautiful in its classic setting, once the trees and flowering shrubs re-established themselves, it would be wonderful again.

'Now what do you think of this?' Max asked as he reversed the buggy to go back down the road, driving towards the ruins, and

Brenda gasped again, the site was being cleared. There was a massive crane parked beside the Manor, and in neat piles she could see recovered stone and timbers stacked opposite the mini manor. 'No I am not letting you out, you don't have your hard hat, and you are in no condition to be scrambling around. We have not completed the salvage yet, Keith, myself, and now Roger is here, plan on continuing next week, slowly. As we have found a couple of incendiaries, in the rubble, but we have begun."

'Begun you have, oh thank you Max, this is wonderful. I meant to ask Roger how come he is here, and where is Mary?'

'Well when we realised the stables were not going to be exactly as first thought, both Dan and Glen with Peter, kept ringing him with questions. Mary in her wisdom, sent him on ahead. Actually, Keith and June have moved into the mini manor, as the time frame for their apartments has extended, they are very happy, at least it is not a tent. Then when Mary arrives next week can have the second cottage as planned, I would have been happy for him to bunk in with me. But June would not hear of it, moved Keith and herself out so Roger could get acquainted with his new home and to find out what furniture he wanted to keep.'

Brenda was taking it all in, the way the Broadmeadows family was beginning to look after itself, and work together. The work being done and how it was being done, a credit to this group of people, 'So what are the plans for next week, have you any in place?' Brenda asked as Max turned the buggy down the drive way, Brenda may not have said anything, but she had gone a little grey, he realised she needed to rest, the brave face she was putting on, was still hiding someone in pain, even if she would not admit it.

'Well, we have Peter arriving on Monday, now don't look like that,' as she drew breath to remonstrate the delay. 'We are not rushing this, we needed to get the Gate Lodge finished for you to recuperate in, close to where we can keep an eye on you!' he turned his head briefly to look at her, and she smiled, 'so no work over the weekend, we can plan, and I would like to get your comments on our ideas. Peter did leave the plans he had drawn up, and three pencils, so you could alter them?'

Brenda laughed then, knowing she would, and the fact Peter knew she would.

'Then we can check on the stables, we are waiting on the steel and Rebecca I believe has been combing Libraries and archives still researching details to not annoy the Heritage Council. We have got this far, so now is when we slow down slightly so we can get the planning permission to rebuild the Grandfather Norman's and now your dream.'

Ann had taken one look at her when she had returned from the buggy ride, and marched her into the bedroom, saying a lie down would allow her to be awake this evening. Putting a couple of tablets in her hand and closing the door on Brenda's remonstrations, singing La, la, la, as she walked down the short hallway to say she did not hear her.

Watching as Max and Brenda disappeared for her quick tour that afternoon, Ann turned to everyone, to make sure that they realised the extent of the damage that had been done, the bruises and healing cuts, they could all see only a small part of the whole. The two men had put in a lot of damaging kicks, and Brenda was just lucky nothing else was broken, or any vital organ had been severely damaged. She would have to slowly build back the muscles that had been damaged, and ease back into her 'normal' life, although she would argue all the way, rest and gentle exercise would win the day, but it would take time.

'She will recover, just as she was?' David voiced the worry they all had, that somehow Brenda would be altered by the attack. He still could not believe it was his father that had led it!

'Of course, she will, please people she will recover, and this episode will just be a dark memory very soon. I just do not want Brenda exerting herself too fast, her leg muscles were nearly torn in two with the blows they received, just think when you pull a muscle what physical pain that is, well Brenda has that over most of her body. So, are you with me, in trying to slow that whirlwind down, so her body can heal?'

There was a waft of Gardenia as the chorus of yes, filled the room, everyone but Ann knew that Iris would be helping too.

Chapter 40

I T WAS A RELATIVELY quiet weekend, for Brenda's standards that is. She insisted on going over all the new plans and designs that the team had come up with, as it kept her in her study or at the dining room table with plans spread out all over it, with the visitors coming to her, Ann's request for people to visit Brenda, kept her at her desk or table and seated, Ann did not make a fuss. Brenda agreed with a little but changed a lot, her ramble through Broadmeadows in her dreams/hallucinations while in hospital, giving her a clearer insight into what should be, but very difficult to tell people how she knew.

They also quickly ran out of room for the flowers that were delivered, having spread them around the Gate Lodge, and the Cottages, even into the Mini Manor, Brenda being touched by the thoughtful cards from everyone, especially the arrangement and note from 'E', knowing Baron Phipps would have advised the lady of what had happened. She rang the florist and asked that she keep the cards and deliver them, if she also took a picture of the bouquets and arrangement, she could then in all honesty thank the sender for their beautiful flowers, but could she take any more flowers that were ordered for her to brighten up the church, the hospital and aged care facility that was attached to it. Laughing the Florist said what a lovely idea, and would do so.

Matt and Ben put in an appearance on Sunday afternoon, Brenda had been dozing in the courtyard, the sound of the water tinkling, and the warmth of the sun, lulling her into a snooze. The sound of a sibling squabble woke her, 'Oh, the prodigals have returned,' she said moving to give them a hug, but being held at arm's length, they were covered in mud.

'Oh, my goodness, where have you been, covered in muck like that?'

'Doing things his way,' Ben said and pointed to Matt, as both of them were trying to remove their mud cacked boots in the door way.

'What do you mean,' Matt continued his squabble to Ben, 'there was no other way to do it, and you know that, if the dam you had built, had held better we would not be in this state, and no,' he turned to Brenda, 'I am not telling you at the moment, because it is not working and I am frustrated because I think I know, but don't really know why?'

Frustration was clear in his entire being, it oozed out of him just like the mud that was oozing off the boots now outside the door. Kate went over and offered them both a cup of tea or a beer, knowing that he had to work through it himself.

'OK I will not ask, but I am insanely curious, what has gotten you two so het up? Now thank you both for the work you have been doing, and is there anything I can do to help you?'

Matt carefully moved himself up the stairs, saying he would go and change, before he said anything.

David coming out of his room, took in the scene, came half way down the stairs, laughing at Bens state.

Shrugging his shoulders, Ben looked up the stairs laughing with David as he turned to Brenda, 'May have to borrow a plastic bag from you Brenda, for my car seat, I don't have the luxury of having a change of clothes here!'

'Don't worry Mate, hang on a minute', and David disappeared back up to his room, coming back with some tracksuit pants, 'here, go into the laundry and change into these I think they will fit. At least they will be clean to get you home, you can hose off the boots but I am not sure if they can be rescued!'

Brenda moved everyone out to the garden, while the brothers changed, when Ben joined them in his stocking feet, she started to ask again, if she could help, realising the boys would not ask, they were also in on the conspiracy of keeping her inactive. Laughing as he told her the edited version of how they had both gotten so muddy, but not the reason why they were playing in the mud.

'There are some beautiful spots on this estate of yours, and I hope to be able to explore more of them, if I get invited down for weekends, when you are in residence?'

'Of course, you will be luv, and I will insist you bring at least a change of clothes to be here for you, for just such emergencies.'

They both laughed, Kate coming out with some afternoon tea, Ann, Larry and a clean Matt joining everyone in the garden.

'Now I am going to say something and I don't want you to argue!' Brenda started, everyone looking at her, wondering what was coming next. 'I thank you for being here for me, but we have work to do, and for some of us that cannot be done from here. So, I am getting fit and healthy, thanks to Ann,' a round of applause broke out, making Ann blush just a little, 'I do not need mollycoddling, or the extra attention. So, David, Larry my love, you can both toddle off home. David, you have to get on top of the Seahaven proposal with Dennis, so thank you for being here love, you can ring me every day, but you have to go.'

She had been reading with satisfaction the reports from the Seahaven group getting geared up to start the final massive clean-up and excavation of the site. Leonard, had jumped through so many hoops with the council, he was thinking of becoming a contortionist, he told Dennis one day. Mary-Beth, John along with Gus and Janet from the Pub, had all put in good ideas for the working arrangement of the site. Dennis had been down to see her in hospital, he not shy in telling Larry what he would like to do to both Greg and Bill, it was not nice, but he had assured Brenda she was to rest, and he with Mary Beth, John and Leonard, would make sure all would be well. Larry, David and Dennis saying they would be her eyes and ears at the council meeting to be held the following week, Brenda arguing that she was well enough to attend she wanted to be there; the look Ann gave her, quelling her enthusiasm a bit.

Reinforced when she could hardly move on the following morning her scrambles around the stable yard and garage being a bit too much, also although the swelling had gone down she was still very puffy in the face and body, the bruises had not diminished either. The headgear she had taken to wearing only empathised that she had been beaten, she did not want pity to sway any decisions, decided to listen to Ann and her body telling her to slow down. Frustrated that she could not just step back into the life she wanted, silently cursing the foibles of men, who did not acknowledge their own shortcomings, but took them out on others, resigned herself to the second-hand news.

'Kate, I suggest you go to check up on Iris House, I know Linda said they had cancelled the next couple of guests, but she will want an update on me, and I need an update on the babies. Larry, you have to continue to check up on our two felons, and the missing one to the trio; yes, I know they are looking for him, and you can do that with Hughes help over the next week. Come on people don't be down in the mouth, I will have Dan, Glen with Max, Roger, Keith and June, around me, as well as all the workmen. Think what we can achieve, even if I am sidelined a bit, over the next weeks. Life has to move on, I will not let those two mongrels dictate what I do next!'

Kate looked at her mum, the strength in her, just made her so proud. She was going to argue, but what was the point, and she was right. She needed to be back in London, they may have cancelled a couple of guests but they had a full house coming up in a week. Going and giving Brenda a hug, she asked the question they all wanted to ask, 'Are you sure Mum?'

'Yes of course I am, look at me, well look past the bruises and cuts on my face, please, but I can only get better, and I can do that here as I have a purpose to being here, you really don't need me in London do you luv?'

Kate laughed, knowing again Brenda was right, she really ran the Guest House, and that was what Brenda was doing, saying for all to hear that it was Kate's baby.

David started to argue, but Brenda just gave him a hug, whispering, 'Don't you dare feel guilty for what has happened, luv. More importantly don't let the knowledge of him change you. Now we need to get on with this life we are making!'

He nodded, unable to speak, resolved to put the man named father, out of his mind, as Kate had said, she was going to keep on with the idea he had died just after they were born, and had never been in their lives which was the truth.

'Are you sure love, I...' Larry started to say, but Brenda went to him and carefully put both her arms around him.

'Yes, I am sure, and I need you, as I said, with Hugh to keep on with the case of the missing conspirator! I will be fine, Ann can move into one of your rooms, if you don't mind,' to Kate and David, 'then I can get back my study.'

'I don't mind the murphy bed, Brenda it is quite comfortable.' Ann said as she came out from the kitchen with some more nibbles.

'I mind, I still have to check things, and as it is a sedentary task, my study is where I prefer to do it. So, thank you one and all, but Ann alone is enough to drive me bonkers with her restrictions, you all get out of here, then you won't feel guilty when I do something she does not approve of!'

Everyone laughed, soon with bags packed, with a little bit of encouragement, toots of car horns and waves they had all departed, suddenly peace descended on the Gate Lodge. Brenda moved back in to find Ann moving her belongings out and up the stairs, the murphy bed folded back up out of the way, her study awaited. Quickly before Ann could come back down, she carefully, moved her papers from the bedroom, giving a sigh as she sat in the chair, enjoying the feeling of the room.

'Didn't think it would take long, I have a suggestion, and am only making it because I am sure you will do it yourself. How about we take the buggy, it is such a beautiful warm evening, and have a dip in that lake of yours. I have been told, that Norman turned part of it into a swimming pool, with a shallow spot to be able to walk in and out. What do you say?

'Ann, that would be wonderful, what about my caste?' she stopped as Ann produced a hospital plastic cover as they used in the shower, and a roll of tape. Moved Brenda down to the bedroom to put on bathers, and then tape up the arm.

They purloined the two-seater buggy, wondering where the second buggy was Brenda enjoyed the excursion through the grounds. Slowly till Ann got used to it, they moved the buggy out onto the bridal path, and up to the lake. Finding the second buggy and a lot of shouting; Max, June, Keith and Roger were already happily splashing around in the shallows. Moving to assist her out of the buggy and into the cool refreshing water.

Chapter 41

MONDAY MORNING, BRENDA STRETCHED saying thanks for her life, as she did every morning, then realised she had muscles that were still healing, but she did feel better after the swim, and vowed it would be a regular occurrence at least through summer. She also had to ask Ann about the caste, wondering if she could get it changed to something lighter, it weighed a ton!

She was in the kitchen enjoying the feel of the space, finding out where everything was, trying to make coffee when Ann appeared.

'We have a doctor's appointment this morning Brenda, I think we can take off that caste replace it with a lighter removable one. Do you think Max would mind us using the van?'

She moved round and gave Brenda a quick hug, taking the coffee pot out of her hand and shooing her out of the kitchen and onto one of the stools.

'What, is the matter. Oh, have I been reading your mind again?' at Brenda's nod, she laughed. 'No not reading your mind, just seeing you in action. Thank goodness that arm was a clean break, as it is healing remarkably well. You don't need the heavy caste it is putting, as you said, a strain on your neck and back. So, we head back to the hospital, and see what the surgeon thinks? It will also be easier to remove it for your swimming, which I would like you to continue, ok'

'Very ok, thank you Ann, so how long do I have the pleasure of your company? Don't get me wrong, I would not have survived this time without you, but your time is valuable Doctor Darfmeir, you have better things to take care of than me?'

'Oh, done some research have you. Knew I should not have moved out of the study, or given you that laptop so soon. What gave me away?'

'Your manner, the way many of the junior doctors in the hospital gave way to your requests, immediately, no nurse would get that kind of treatment, although they should. The fact you have more blacked-out pages in the resume I asked Michael to send to me, and he only sent it grudgingly, also the fact that Baron Phipps appears in the pages. Special ops, and more, you are not only my Nurse/Doctor, but also a body guard as well, am I right?'

'Partly right, my contacts are correct, but I had been approached by Michael and Dennis,' at Brenda's start, 'I have had a couple of meetings with Mr. Brookes. To be the head doctor at your new Seahaven Care Home. As I am due to retire from the military, fairly soon, I was mulling it over as it were, when I got the urgent call to get down here pronto, as what everyone thought might happen had!'

'What do you mean, everyone thought, who thought what?'

Ann patted her hand, 'please don't get upset, but Michael, Hugh and Larry have known for a few weeks, David and Kate too, that your ex-husband was on the loose. David and Kate had known he was looking for you even before you came to the UK,' at Brenda's start at hearing this she looked at her, 'Oh have the children been keeping secrets from you? Anyway, he had not been subtle in vowing to find you, which became more intense when all the security checks had been done in Australia for the legacy, he really went to town for a while and then disappeared. It was just bad management that no one had thought to check the background of why you moved and divorced him, before they started their cross checks. Believe me there will be a shakeup in that system, following on from this.' Ann shook her head, and sipped at her tea, gathering her thoughts, wondering if Brenda was ready for the full disclosure.

'And?'

'And, they really became concerned when Greg's current bed warmer, I think was the term you used for his partner's, oh and he has had many in the intervening years, some of them realising what he really was, and got out before serious damage was done I should think. Well the newest 'bed warmer' was found barely alive in the house, the neighbours called the police as well as an ambulance. She is alive but with a broken arm and leg, the doctors believe she was picked up by the arm and leg and thrown against the wall, her parents and family are the main ones pressing charges against him, she is just twenty years old!'

Shock ran through her, dear god she was even younger than Kate, was the thought that popped into her head. Tears were streaming down Brenda's face, she could not help them, wondering if she could have done anything different all those years ago to stop this man.

'Now, don't you dare go and blame yourself for what that man has done since you ditched him, please, as I said there have been quite a few others in between that could have come forward. You also had the children to look after, and you will be pleased to know he only fathered Kate and David, just think of him as a sperm donor and not their father, it will help. I have to tell you that I took photos of you when they brought you into the hospital, for the court case, we don't want either of these men to get away with what they did. The police are also going to be here during the week, they will want a frank and full statement from you, now you are able to speak coherently.'

'What do you mean speak coherently, when did I not?'

'Well you kept talking to someone called Iris and Grandfather Norman, during those first days, so not sure what that was all about. I have now with the help of the team worked out who Iris is, I am sceptical on that point, but there was something that kept you from organ damage, the steel capped boots both men wore, should have inflicted a severe even deadly outcome. I kept the police out of the room at the time, you were in no state to make any kind of statement, helped by a phone call to the Police Commissioner from Baron Phipps, I do like having contacts,' and she looked at Brenda and winked, making her laugh and come out of her retrospection.

'Now, I can hear the troops massing, it seems it is going to be another busy day, please once we get the caste off, do not think you are superwoman. You still need to take it relatively easy ok?'

'OK and thanks for telling me, I promise to listen to what my body, is telling me, and take a nap when I can.'

Ann looked at her, and smiled, not believing her for a second, but was going to be around and watch her like a hawk.

Brenda could hear the workmen parking cars, and the heavy sound of another large crane being moved into the stable yard. Peter was first through the door, with Glen and Dan following, Brenda going to give him a hug thanking him for his work, and advising him it had changed, slightly.

He was shocked of course, the shaved head, without the headscarf she had taken to wearing, showing how many blows and cuts had been inflicted, from her face down the side of her body, looking past the caste on her arm, he could see she was still covered by an ugly purple and red bruise, fading slowly across her face to the yellows of healing. There were a couple of deep cuts on her face as well, she had tape holding them together, and a few other taped cuts on the rest of her face and down her arms. But she was alive, and that was the main thing, Brenda held him from her, 'I am here and determined we get this right, are you ok?'

'Now I am,' he said forcing a smile, and hugging her gently again, 'Rebecca said you had made some changes, like what?'

With that Rebecca walked in demanding a coffee before they start, and where was the stack of papers she had left on Friday.

Brenda waved Max and Roger off to the main manor house, asking them to say good morning to June and Keith, also remembering to ask if they could use the van later in the morning.

They parked the van in the only spot they could on the return from the hospital, on the spot beside the gate lodge. Ann, saying she would take the added medications she had picked up at the hospital and make lunch. Brenda advising her that she had a lunch van coming on site at one thirty, so no need to fix anything. Nodding her head in acknowledgement headed into the gate lodge as Brenda walked towards the stables, Ann realising she would not be able to get Brenda to rest, until she had checked everything out.

Rebecca, with Glen and Dan were standing next to the crane watching as a steel beam was lowered into place to extend the back stable wall to the Gateway. As she approached to see what was going on, Matt, still with a look of frustration etched in his face came out of a door of the stables that Brenda had not seen before.

'Hey Brenda, where is your hard hat?' He said as he made a beeline for her. 'You just wait there I will go and get it for you!' With the words he was off, and returned very quickly with Brenda's hard hat from Iris House, giving a very graceful bow and flourish when he handed it to her.

'Thanks luv, I didn't realise I would need it, your father never ceases to amaze me. I knew he and Dan were a formidable team, but this is just another level. Now, what is frustrating you so, and don't fob me off, I know something is getting your goat, tell me please let me help. If it means using my head and not mucking in with my hands, well one at least, let me, as I will suffocate with all the cotton wool everyone is wrapping me in!'

He laughed with her, the laughter alerting the others to their presence, they were welcomed into the group Glen and Dan wanting to show off what they had achieved and Rebecca and Peter wanting to check with her what they had designed fitted in with her dreams.

Max, Roger, June and Keith found Ann standing in the entrance to the stable yard, watching as Brenda interacted with the workmen, watching the byplay between Glen, Dan, Matt, Ben, Rebecca and Peter with Brenda, a bemused smile on her face.

'Don't worry, they will not let her do too much, family is the best in that regard, and contrary to popular belief, family don't have to be blood relations,' Max said, 'we are living proof of that,' coming up and standing beside her.

Ann turned as the lunch van pulled through the gates, not surprised when a second one followed the first, moving out of the way, as the workers put down tools and out to have lunch. 'I was at first worried, but seeing the way Glen and Dan hover over Brenda, she is their elder daughter really, and I can see that. I also see that both of those gentlemen have not really forgiven themselves for what happened the other week, and will be doubly impressive in the feats they are planning in the rebuilding of this place; just to make it up to her. Now how about you folks, how are you doing?'

Max nodded at Keith, June and Roger, 'we regret it happened, realise that we could not have stopped the two determined gentlemen, but we did before very serious damage was done, that is what we are telling ourselves. Brenda is giving us a chance to make a life here, doing what we love, a chance no one else has even offered us. This is home, and we will make sure no more fruitcakes try and destroy it, or our benefactor, who is family.'

The others nodded in confirmation of what Max said, Ann hearing the sincerity in his voice, he had come home, the others as well. Wondering at the feeling of family that had surrounded her since she had stepped onto this estate, liking the feel, but still unsure if this was the place she needed to be.

Brenda arriving to give Keith and June a hug, they pointing out the new caste, and reminding her it needed to be on her arm when she was outside, broke the mood around them.

'Ann, have you seen what these miracle workers have done. Honestly, I cannot thank Dennis enough for putting me in touch with this family; now my family. Ok enough talk I am starving what's for lunch today?'

Chapter 42

MATT CAME UP TO her after lunch, Brenda knew he would, in his own sweet time, wondering at what he was puzzling over.

'Brenda, can I ask you something?'

'What is on your mind luv, come on I need to check something walk with me back to the Gate Lodge, and tell me what you are searching for?'

'Well remember I said I was working on the electricity for you, and promised you something better than going on the grid?' Brenda nodded as she steered him into the study, knowing that they needed privacy, to work out what Matt's problem was, the smell of gardenia as they walked in telling Brenda she had made the right call.

'When I loaded all the journals and papers, into your laptop for your Christmas present, I was reading them haphazardly as you do, and I remembered one of the Grandfather Norman's commenting on a series of people his son had invited down for visits that lasted a month and more at a time. I remembered the comment because he stated he had hardly seen them while they were there. Well when I found the entry, it stated they also had repeat visits from a Michael Faraday with Lord and Lady William Armstrong; Lady Armstrong helping with the redesign of the gardens around the lake. Once I got to explore here, realised who the first person was, and what he and the son were doing for the month, and then the next few years. It is also what I and my team, Dad and Dan, Max, Keith and now Roger are trying to work out why it is not working.' He got up and paced the room, which was not very far it was not a big room.

'Ok so you are following up on a lead from one of the journals, I might be able to help you better if you tell me the name of the first person that got you so excited?'

'Oh, yes sorry, Richard Arkwright – he was a Mill owner in the Derwent Valley around the 1770's, I can hear the question, what has that to do with the family Lucas? Well you might be interested to know he ran his mill machinery with hydro power!"

Brenda looked at him, wondering at what the connection was, Iris was also a little confused, as she sent another wave of gardenia around the room.

Finally, the penny dropped Brenda turned excitedly to him, seeing the smile on his face. 'Oh, I see, you think the son and this Richard Arkwright started a Hydro plant here on the estate, and then Lord and Lady Armstrong also had information on the scheme, but you would need either a fast-flowing river or a dam on a lake to be able to get the pressure to run something like that. What, you don't think I know about hydro plants, I do read you know?'

Matt looked at her, and then realised she was trying to tease him out of his doldrums, he had to laugh at the tilt of her head, and cross eyes she was staring at him with.

'Ok I am the first to realise that I have not had a chance to see all of this estate, but I intend to from now on. As I also made the decision that here was going to be my permanent home, but don't tell Kate or David. They need to be in London on their own, without having Mum watching over them. Oh, I will still be a frequent visitor, have to have my cuddles with the triplets, but I am stepping down from my role with Pickworths.' At his frank look, 'Well at least I say I am, never know what will happen, do we. So, how do we fix your problem, and I will take a guess that it's a distribution one am I right?'

Stunned that Brenda had put her finger on his dilemma so quickly Matt nodded, 'do you have the map of the estate around, I need to show you something?' Brenda pulled out from the flat drawer fitted under her desk, the original map of the estate, 'Do you have the most recent one as well?' he asked. Folding them so they could lie next to each other on the drop-down desk that was attached to the Murphy bed, Brenda could see the difference between the two immediately, following Matts finger as he outlined the river on the original, then hovered over the latest map.

'Here, see on the original that river, well if you compare with today's map, that is The Lake, and yes that is still part of Broadmeadows. I have to take you on one of the buggies to see this place, it has formed one of the boundaries of the village and the estate. The villagers will tell you that it is public ground, as they have been using it for decades, but, it is not. The lake is man-made, by the Lucas family, the lake and the village are all part of the Lucas estate. I found the original very substantial dam, which had been built up from a small natural barrier to make the high dam wall, and the shell of a power house, flattened by a couple of the bombs we are finding bits and pieces of all over the place. It had been blended into the landscape so well, if you were not looking for it you would miss it, probably the work of Lady Margaret Armstrong, and it is very good. The bombs also cracked the dam wall not badly, but enough to allow a natural feel to the falls that developed from the breach. Over time people forgot it was there, having become overgrown and disused. The point is I, and everyone else I could rope into it, have been trying for the last few weeks or so to fix it, as it is a great solution to your power needs. Hell, if I can get it up and running with the new equipment I am trying to add, it will probably be able to supply the Village and the College as well, I just can't seem to find out what the problem is!'

Brenda was stunned that the family she had inherited, were so forward thinking, she could not help but think they were wasted in the era they lived in. Just for a moment, thoughts of what they could have achieved in this day and age, stunned her.

'Right, you have a problem then, as now you have told me about this I want it, not just for me but for everyone!'

Matt looked at Brenda and smiled, happy that he now had the ally he needed to help him figure out the problem.

'Who do you need, and what do you need. Let's go back to the basics, and from my perspective go over everything. I am sorry but I am going to state the obvious, but I have to go to the source as it were!'

For the next hour, Matt told Brenda about the way Glen and Dan had repaired the original Power house, built a second structure and repaired the dam wall. The Experts he had brought in were amazed that the ancient machinery with a few extra bits and pieces would still be generating power. The new generation batteries and transformer that he had added in the new building, next to the original plant to store power. The electricity board had agreed to buy back the extra they didn't use, and at the moment that was a lot, as he could not get the power from the plant to anywhere?

'Well if there is not a problem at the plant, then it has to be in the cable, I take it there was originally cable laid to divert the power?' at Matt's nod, he smiled as Brenda had gotten up to pace the study as he had done before, absently rubbing her arm, she had taken off the caste the moment they had walked through the door. 'So, forget trying to find the ancient stuff, which I take it is where your frustration lies; it probably got chopped to bits by stray bombs or farmers digging the fields not knowing what they were doing, heck even critters chewing on it over the decades. I doubt when they laid it they were thinking of where it could be laid to avoid those erstwhile ancient or even modern farmers with their powerful machines, in the future, so let's just lay modern cable, upgrade the service then we can lay down pipe work in the right places to be the conduit we need, or had you already thought of that?'

'We had just recently it was the only solution to the problem, and have been working on it, I am hoping that the new transformer, and burying the new cable when it gets here will solve the problem. Oh yes, I will be burying the cable, and have started the process; I just knew you would not like power poles to mar the landscape. The only hiccup in this, the cable I want, to be able to handle the load is only manufactured in China, of all places, for the amount I need it is taking an age to get here, I think that is the root cause of my frustration!'

'Well then we will be patient, I know you want everything to be perfect in an instant love, but I am learning with this place slow and steady wins the race. You are in front as far as I am concerned, you have found and repurposed something that was lost and forgotten, we are putting in solar systems as a backup, and hey, let's give the electricity commission some funds before we tell them bye, bye; I can afford it I think. Let us, just make sure that everything you can do before it arrives to give us the power it is generating is up to your high standards, so when we can flick the switch, gratification is instant.'

She hugged him, liking the strong, capable feel she got from him, 'now how do we purloin a buggy I want to see this place like right now!'

Laughing he told her to put her caste back on helping her tie and fix it properly, picked up her hard hat, holding out his arm to take her out to the buggy. When they emerged from the Gate Lodge, Glen, Roger and Max stopped them insisting they accompany them, when they found out the destination.

Brenda enjoyed the traverse across the estate this was the first time she had ventured out of the area of the Manor house, and the space was as mind blowing as it was beautiful, taking her across the areas she had envisioned while looking at the map of the area, it was large and diverse. Through a forest, past a farm only a small part of which was working, Roger pointing out the very modern facilities and saying he had already chatted to the Farmer, and others in the area. Then past another that was very forlorn and derelict both farms she had no idea were part of the estate. She was stunned when they topped a rise approaching the estate side of the lake, was expecting a small pond and building, seeing the lake spread out before her from a hilltop, with the edges of the village in the distance. Understanding how it had come into being with the damming of the narrow end that housed the machinery, and wondering at the patience the family had, as it would have taken a long time to fill the area with water. Not really prepared for the sight of the magnificent falls, and power house rebuilt, attached to what looked like a rock face, wonderment and awe filled her, gardenia surrounded them as they walked the path to the newly built and restored original buildings.

Matt explaining that the falls were perfect, the two sluice gates that had been built into the original dam wall still functioned as designed, were again working to generate electricity that was being stored in the new age batteries in the transformer house built next to and mimicked the design of the original power house.

It was a very tired but very grateful Brenda that crawled into her bed that night, enjoying remembering her afternoon trip over areas of the estate, she had not realised were part of her inheritance, vowing now that she was here would try and add her part to the legacy.

Chapter 43

T HE HIGHLIGHT OF THE next week was the arrival of Mary and George, with a small removal truck, heralding another step forward in the reawakening of the estate. Many hands helped to move the furniture and bits and pieces into the cottage, Brenda being told to entertain George while the others did the heavy lifting and moving. Mary endorsing the request, after she got over her initial shock at Brenda's appearance, which was getting better day by day.

Later in the day she found Mary in the midst of unpacking boxes in the kitchen, giving her a hug asking if she could help.

Mary took one look at the tired face in front of her, and realised that Brenda was doing just a bit too much, Ann's request for help to slow her patient down so she could heal ringing in her ears.

'Thanks Brenda but I have this, I think I am about due a coffee break want to have one with me?'

Pointing to the lounge room after making the coffee, moved them both over to the sofa.

'Where is the irascible George? This place is so quiet without him?'

'He and Roger are inseparable at the moment, and he is following him everywhere. Did you know that Glen has given him his own little hard hat, he looks so cute in it, he follows everyone around insisting he can help!'

'Well I am glad he is not here, as I wanted to talk to you, and please tell me to butt out if I am intruding, but I did a little bit of research, and networking for you, in regards to Kindergartens and teaching jobs, I apologise I was going to give you this before you went back to pack up, but' Brenda held up her arm in the caste, then handed over a folder, with the information she had gathered in it. 'Not sure if you want to get back into the saddle so to speak, but you and George would be welcome at any of the three places around here. That is if you don't mind teaching at the same school as your son is attending?'

'Brenda, thank you, I was just looking around for places, as I now have time too. I was waiting for the Teachers Association to contact me, as I really did not know where to start, thank you. Now is there anything I can do for you, I know that Ann is keen that you don't overdo anything, and you need to heal slowly. I have also heard that Norman and the gang from Kew have altered the lake slightly and it is a good place to escape this heat, in a freshwater pool? Once the workmen have gone for the day, I am insisting we all go for a swim, want to go and see if Ann is free, George just loves the water!'

The Vicar and his wife were another couple to visit, curious to say the least and to say thank you for all the flowers that had been donated to the church. Asking quite bluntly exactly what she was doing, a direct approach she liked and approved of. Stunning them both, when she advised she was rebuilding the Manor house, and would hopefully be able to help the community with more than flowers for the church or the luncheon business she was employing.

Roger also initiated morning meetings which as her Estate Manager had insisted be a daily occurrence and what would by tradition have been happening with the Lord/Lady of the Manor, adding she could bring Max, Keith and June into them as well to bring them up to date on events, but usually it was just the two of them. It was also a sedentary task that gave Brenda an overview of what was happening without her exerting herself too much, Ann had approved.

After her sojourn out to the falls, Brenda had done some research herself, in regards to the estate, and what was still operating to maintain it. She asked Roger to check with the farmer who was working the farm they had passed, asking him to organise a visit. Roger, Max and Keith all had sung his praises, having had several visits to the farm and also some businesses in the area, as they got to know the locals.

Brenda talking to Michael invited him down after he checked his records to join in this meeting of minds. She asked him mainly to check if what she wanted could be done; not to evict Bruce the Farmer, but to formerly employ him for the Lucas Estate, which the records showed he was not at that time.

Bruce Hudson, was mid-forties he arrived dressed neatly, as his wife pressed him to be polite, not sure of his welcome even though he knew Roger, and liked the man. Knew he had been installed as the Estate Manager, which had surprised him and most of the village, after the time the place had been in ruins.

When Roger ushered Bruce, into the study at the Gate Lodge, Michael was seated chatting to Brenda, Bruce was nervous looking at Michael wondering what was coming, as he could tell he was a lawyer so he was ready to fight for his place. To argue that his father, and his fathers, father and even further back had worked the farm, and she would have to fight him if she wanted to evict him; as he loved his place, the farm was in his blood, and he had so many ideas with so little time.

Roger smiled at his vehement attitude, knowing what Brenda was intending to do, as she had asked his opinion, and told him of her thinking, that they had to start giving back to the area, not as charity, but to see that any ideas these people had could be developed.

Michael nodded and smiled, 'Can I interject, I am not sure if you are aware but you are paying rent or should I say tithes, to the Lucas Estate, and have been since your fathers, fathers and a few fathers back farmed this land. Oh, not much by today's standards but it was a substantial sum for your relatives in the day.'

Bruce looked at the faces around him, dreading what was coming next, yes of course he knew about the tithes that were paid, and never begrudged them, being a very small amount per year. He looked at Brenda, she was smiling at him, asking him to sit while she explained her thoughts. Seeing the scars still very visible, that the recent events had left on her and rumour had spread, the lunch ladies loved to gossip. Brenda then outlined what she envisaged, requested that the reasonable tithes be kept at the same level no increase at all, she did not want or need anymore. In fact, if he had problems with the amount, she would be as happy with payment even being made in fresh produce if that's all he could give, as his greats before him would have done. Also, if he had any ideas of how to improve or expand the farm with inviting family or friends to help him in the expansion and improvements; perhaps even revive the derelict buildings she had seen, with family or those friends. If he had any ideas to diversify; for him to come and see her in a week with those ideas written out so she could do her own research on them.

'Bruce, I will be a hands-on Landlord, this is my home, I want to see everybody's lives improve as I improve the estate, we will be rebuilding the Manor House it will be available for everyone to use and enjoy, not only the house but the grounds as well. So please pass it around that the Broadmeadow versus Military College Inaugural Cricket Match will occur the first year the house is finished, and then I plan on seeing that and a few other celebrations happen every year!'

Wondering at his good fortune, when he left with the formal tenancy agreement to the farm in perpetuity for his family, now making it legally his and not just the word of mouth that it had been down the ages, but still owned by the Broadmeadows Estate. Realised that the rumour mongers in the village had got it all wrong, this was a good deal for them, not some trumped up townie ready to ruin their way of life, someone who meant to live on the estate, and rebuild it to what it was or even better.

The week went by very quickly, they had visits from General Richardson and the Commandant, also the local member for Parliament, the Vicar and his wife again calling to see if Brenda would be free to join them on Sunday after services for lunch, something she left hanging, not sure about diving in to that aspect of village life.

The staircase down to the store-room under the stables had been decided, and Brenda was surprised when she saw it being built with a fairly substantial space in the middle that she immediately realised was for a lift. Applauding Peter and David for the inclusion, telling her son he was a genius when she rang him that evening.

'We are coming down at the weekend mum, have to bring you up to date on Seahaven, so don't give my room away please.'

Chapter 44

LARRY, WITH KATE AND David following behind, arrived just as the workmen knocked off for the weekend on the Friday. Brenda enjoying the fact she had her anchor's back in her life. They marvelling at the progress not only in the building, but in their mum! Yes, there were still bruises and the deep cuts, but they were fading and healing slowly. Larry approving of the close cap of new grown hair, with dashes of distinguishing grey. She was also moving very easily, and they wanted to know how she had achieved this.

'A tour of the estate is required for you to find that out,' Ann came into the conversation, with drinks as they sat in the garden. So once refreshed, they purloined both of the buggies, and reacquainted themselves with a place being changed daily. They were amazed at the lake/swimming pond, vowing to return after getting changed to have a dip in the cool water. The change in the main house was the most startling, Max, Keith, June and Roger had done a sterling job in clearing out the debris. Piles of stone and timber now stood opposite the mini manor, David whistling as he walked around them.

'I can see that quite a lot can be reused mum, have Brian and Stephen seen this lot?'

'I believe that is on the cards for next week, they only finished the clearing this morning, you should have seen the size of the crane they used. I believe Dan and Glen are happy with the temporary support structure to hold up the basement walls so they don't cave in with the rubble being removed. They are organising some scaffolding for some temporary stairs to be put into the basement level, I am not allowed to go down the ladders yet!'

'Oh mum, give yourself a break,' Kate went over and gave her mum a hug, 'I would not be scrambling up and down the ladders either! Did they find any nasties, your crew when they were clearing the rubble out?'

'They found a few bits and pieces, nothing bad, thank goodness. These three pieces they rescued, I am particularly pleased with.' Brenda moved over to what looked like a pile of stones, when they got closer could see they were four very ornately carved pieces of granite, two side pillars and an extravagantly carved mantle-piece that had split in two.

'I think this is the mantle for the main fireplace that was in the hallway, I am so surprised they found it in only four pieces it is massive, I am hoping that Brian will be able to repurpose it, and find others?' Moving through the pieces of not only stone but timber that were in neat piles, agreed that the massive piece would have to be reused. They moved back down the driveway, following the smell of a BBQ to the stable yard.

'Hey welcome back to the fold,' Max said as they parked the buggy under the awning, and returned to the tables set up outside the cottages. 'We thought we would eat al fresco this evening, here try this beer,' handing a cold bottle to David, 'from one of the local breweries! What do you think, looking good isn't it?'

'Looking brilliant, wow, so different from the first time I saw this place, we have a community happening here, you have to show me around in the morning, so I can get my bearings, things have changed in a week!'

Larry just looked around, the non-existent stables and gateway of a month ago, now looking like buildings again, with all the steel beams in place showing where the finished buildings would be very soon, the area they were in now felt right.

'Great work on the manor rubble, did you find any problems?' he asked, accepting the brown chilled bottle handed to him.

Keith moved from the cramped position he was in while playing with George, to get another beer. George voicing his displeasure of him moving, Roger picking up his son, and telling him dinner was ready, he needed to wash his hands.

'We did find a couple of incendiary devices, that had not gone off, but we disposed of them. I was more fascinated by the fact that many of the oak timbers, especially the massive front doors had survived, did you see those. Oh, probably not, I think Glen took the doors to Stephen yesterday, he was going see if they could be restored to be reused as the main entrance doors, we found them flattened to the floor. Must have been blown inwards by one of the first bombs, and then everything else landed on top of them.' Keith said as he walked around making sure everyone had drinks. 'I can't wait to start the rebuilding, there is still a lot of clearing out in the basement area to be done, it is bigger than you think from ground level, although Dan has warned that he needs accurate measurements to be able to fabricate the steel required, and there will be a lot, this place was massive as a stone building, will be even more so with steel. So, we have to wait for the scaffolding to make the set of stairs down into the basement, and there is still a bit of debris down there to move.'

There was no swim that night as the company enjoyed the evening together, the first of many Brenda vowed. Ann had given Larry a couple of tablets for her knowing she needed them but would not ask. The ache in her arm would keep her awake, she had done a lot that day, Ann had seen her swinging George to her hip a couple of times to get him out of trouble, which was really not smart with her healing arm.

Larry pulled Brenda into his arms as they laid in bed, the night mellow around them, a feeling of all is right in the world filled the air. This was a good place and getting better, Iris had enjoyed the evening as well, gardenia floated in the air along with the tasty smells of the BBQ.

'Luv, are you awake?' he asked, a non-committal hmmm, came from Brenda, 'they have found John Hemsworth, he won't be bothering anyone for a very long time.'

'That's nice,' in a murmur, came from Brenda.

Larry smiled and snuggled down switching off the light, a very contented man.

It was an early start to the morning, with Brenda walking everyone to the pool for a swim. The swim and walk starting the day off right, with a breakfast around the BBQ, bacon, eggs and toast had never tasted so good.

They had just finished the inspection of the new steel work, when a seven-seater van pulled up into the stable yard, Linda being the first one out running over to give Brenda a huge hug. Brenda in shock having to calm her down, telling her she was fine, and looking a great deal better than she had. Everyone moving over to help Shane and Susan out of the van, with the triplets. Morning tea was called Brenda happy that everyone relaxed once the initial shock of her appearance was gone. She had to reassure both Linda and Shane that really, she was getting better, her hair was growing back, although she did like the convenience of the close crop style, the purple bruises across her head and face then down the side of her body, now moving into multi hues. The worst one on her face, was still a deep purple but was morphing into a rainbow, and her arm well, she wore the fiberglass caste just as a precaution outside, but did not use it indoors. Still Linda was shocked at her appearance, and Brenda was glad she had not been able to visit before.

It was no surprise to her that Sir James, Michael and Norman arrived in the afternoon, all concerned that she was doing ok. Sir James and Michael very much pleased with her appearance, from the last time they had seen her in the hospital, Norman in shock, as this was the first time he had seen her. The second tour of the estate followed, along with another swim, as the summer had really found its way to the area. Mary and June, left for a short while, having to go and replenish supplies for the gathering that was happening at the Stable Yard. Keith and Max, taking Shane, Sir James, Michael and Norman out to the Dam, to see the reawakened Hydro Plant, saying the "experts" were amazed at the workings, and the fact they still functioned. Max, pointing out the deep trenches along the fences seemed to be going everywhere, with lots of pipes piled here and there, explaining they were waiting to lay new cable to utilise the system, hoping to be able to power not only the estate, but the village and college as well. Roger taking David and Larry in the van to get more beer and some cider that this very lucrative cottage industry produced, situated just outside the village, still on Broadmeadows land.

Brenda grateful with the fact that she could go to the Gate Lodge and close the door to take a nap, once she had seen that Kate, Mary and June were helping Linda and Susan with the triplets, Ann endorsing her move, smiling and closing the gate behind her. So many people in her quiet space, a bit much, on top of the exercise of the morning. Later she was glad, she had her nap, as the evening was wonderful, she had family around her, and life returning to the neglected space. Iris also enjoying the evening ghostly laughter and the presence of family past around them as well.

Michael came and sat beside her, with Norman and Sir James on the other side, Larry hovering, watching as George had roped in as many people as he could to play ball with him.

'Now there is one young man, who is enjoying the open space and life,' Michael said, laughing at the antics of both young and old children. Ann came up to ask if anyone needed anything, Michael motioned her to stay.

'Now I am not sure if you are aware Brenda, but the police have arrested John Hemsworth, trying to get out of the country.'

Brenda turned to him, not sure how to take this news remembering vaguely Larry saying something the night before, looking at the smiling faces around her. 'And?' she finally asked.

'Well he was found with correspondence linking him to Greg and Bill's plot to do you damage, he is swearing that he had no knowledge of the physical attack, and thought they were going to discredit you, and try to extort money only. We finally know from him it was a twist of fate, or information given by his police cronies, that Greg had seen your new address and Bill's details on documents in regards to Iris House and his subsequent sacking, which had been left lying around when the checks were done on your background, and they struck up communications, I won't call it friendship, as that would be wrong, all three of them, wanted revenge of sorts. The workers from Bills defunct building company, they used to obtain and spread the explosives, that Max, Keith and Roger found after the attack, are also in custody. They giving up all three of the ringleaders, saying they did not know that you were to be in the middle of all this, one even asked if his apologies could be passed on, saving their own necks. As far as the Police and Scotland Yard are concerned the crooks have all been rounded up, and the case is closed. The investigation of how Greg had been able to read classified information on you, well that is another matter. Are you alright?'

Brenda had not realised but tears were streaming down her face, gardenia floated around, she smiled, 'Sorry people, just tears of joy, that we can now come out of this cloud that has been over us. Thank you for the news, Michael, I think a toast should be made, David!'

David looked up and saw who was around his mum, realising something had happened, extricated himself from George and the ball game, going over with a question on his face.

'We have just got some very good news, can you and whoever George will let go from the game, go down to the cellar in the Gate Lodge and bring up some champers, we need to celebrate!'

Curtailing his curiosity, grabbed Kate and Ann, to organise the drinks.

'I take it I will not need my bodyguard then, I will miss her company?' Brenda said as she watched the trio move through the garden gate to the gate lodge.

Larry looked at Brenda, smiling, she had figured it out that Ann was more than the nurse employed. Wondering if she was going to try and persuade her to take the Doctor in charge job at Seahaven? Realising almost immediately that was not how Brenda was, she offered, gave a chance, and if the person wanted to continue, wonderful, if not their choice; no repercussions at all, so Brenda would let Ann make up her own mind.

The toasts made, and everyone relaxing in the twilight, the news having spread around everyone, making the evening even more special. After a last cuddle and feed, Linda Shane and Susan left, vowing to return and enjoy the space once there was accommodation available to stay. Shortly followed by Norman, Sir James and Michael, they also vowing to return once rooms were available. Happy with the alterations Brenda had made to the Stables and Gateway, so that there would be rooms. Of course, once the Manor was rebuilt there would be no shortage of rooms available. Brenda making a mental note to check on how she could update the nursery wing, knowing it would be needed in the future.

It was a laggard group that woke on the Sunday morning Brenda was the first with Ann following shortly after.

'It was great news that Michael gave last night, don't you think?' Ann said as she walked into the kitchen to help Brenda make coffee and start breakfast. A summer shower just refreshing the air and cleaning the ground, keeping them inside.

'Great news, especially for you, my friend. Of course, if you have no-where else to go, you are quite welcome to stay a while, as long as you don't mind changing rooms when the kids come to stay?'

'I think I might stay a little longer, you keep using that arm of yours, and it has still not healed completely, so I will stay just to make sure you don't overdo it, although I am really not required in my other capacity, which I am very glad of. So, what are the plans for today?'

'I have to go over a few things with mum, today.' David said as he came over and gave Brenda a hug good morning, moving into the kitchen for a cup and some coffee.

'Oh yes, Seahaven, what happened at the meeting last week luv?'

'I would rather wait till Dennis gets here mum, oh yes he is coming down, he feels pretty bad that he only managed the one visit to the hospital, and he swears you won't remember him being there. So, Shane and Linda worked out yesterday was the best day for them to visit, Dennis is coming down today. In fact, I think that is him now!'

Sure, enough the door opened and in walked Dennis, the biggest bunch of roses and Iris's Brenda had ever seen. The hug she got from him one of the most welcome she had received. 'I am so sorry,' he murmured in her ear, 'I am so sorry, I could not stop that mongrel. Are you ok?'

Brenda moved him away so she could look into his face, Ann taking the flowers, and asking David to help her find a vase. 'I am fine,' at his snort of doubt, 'really I am, just ask Ann, she has been hovering over me like a mother hen, making sure I don't do too much, but really Dennis, I am fine, healing really well, soon will only have the scars and memory to remind me of what happened. Did you hear they caught John Hemsworth, so all the gang is now in custody! One of Bills lackeys who did the distribution of the explosives even apologised. They did not know I was the main target of two vengeful men, and were sorry!'

Dennis had known about the arrest, but not the rest of the story, grateful for the coffee that David handed him, and then motioning them to the dining table, so they could chat.

'How has she been, truthfully?' Dennis asked Ann as she sat beside David, smiling at the doubt she heard in Dennis's voice.

'She has been the model patient, not as diligent in wearing the arm brace as I would have liked, but at least she does wear it, when she is outdoors. Resting is another thing that is not in her vocabulary, but then, I don't think her brain switches off even in her sleep. We have got along better than I thought, and she is about as tough as old boots, heals very fast!'

Brenda raised her coffee cup in salute, smiling at Dennis who grudgingly realised he was not going to be told any different. Welcoming the intrusion of Kate and Larry arriving demanding tea, coffee and breakfast.

After the dishes had been cleared away, Dennis brought out his briefcase and laptop, ready to bring Brenda up to date on what was happening in the just recently opened care homes, all of which was good news. He wanted to check over some details with not only Brenda, but Ann, in her capacity as Medic to the Lucas line and hopefully Chief Medic of the Seahaven Care Home. Leonard and Wayne, had been working diligently with the plans they had put before council to demolish the buildings and infrastructure that was on the site, to allow the new up to date modern facilities the site was due. They had a bit of a struggle trying to sell the utilities in a pipe idea that had worked so well at Broadmeadows, but the pictures that Larry had shown them of the before, during and after of the installation done by Glen and his team, had sold them on the idea. They had the go ahead to completely clear the site, remove everything, down to the broken and rotten sewerage pipes that were, Leonard had found to his disgust, depositing the waste directly into the sea. That information also made the council agree to the upgrade to the utilities; the fact they did not have to pay for it helped. The trucks and cranes required would be on site tomorrow, beginning at last the moving forward phase of the build. Dennis added he was very happy with his new house and office space, now that he had moved some furniture in, wondering when Brenda was going to be visiting to also check and move at least a bed into her place.

Brenda laughed, advising that she had asked Rebecca and Mia to visit next week to see what they could do, knowing they were assisting Dennis as well. When there was a gentle knock on the door. It opening with a giggle announcing George had arrived, 'Brenda, Brenda come see, come see. Oh' he stopped as he saw a new face in the mix. The smile returning when Brenda moved over to him, everyone following her out to see what George was so excited about. Mary and Roger being introduced to Dennis, Brenda being dragged over to a new bike and George standing proudly beside it. Before anyone could say be careful, he was on it, and off up the driveway. Brenda gasped, smiling and laughing with everyone.

'That child is definitely your boy Roger, absolutely no fear in him at all. Not even training wheels, he does know it has brakes, doesn't he?'

'I have shown him Brenda, and when I said I would put the training wheels on you should have seen the look I got. I put his helmet on him, and we came out here as its flat and even, the cobbles in the stable yard not good for beginner learning to ride a bike. No sooner had he realised what he had to do, and he was off. I have no idea how we kept him quiet in that flat for so long, this is where he belongs!'

'As you both do, and Mary too, this is home, and I thank you for being here for me. '

George came flying back down the driveway, stopping quite sedately beside Roger, the grin on his face wonderful to see. They watched him a little while longer, then asked if he would like to show Dennis what had been achieved, before they could move, a familiar four wheeled drive pulled into the driveway. Kate smiling, as it was Matt, parking next to the office, getting out and saying hello to everyone.

'I wasn't expecting you till next week, Matt, what's happened?'

'Well I got some good news, the cable has arrived in the country. It could be here by the end of this next week. I just wanted to check that what I have done is all in order, want to come and see what I have been tinkering with?'

With a happy George running before them, they all went through the new stable door and down the stairs to the basement, Brenda a lot slower than she would have liked, but at least she was going down the stairs, Ann looked but did not say anything. *Another step forward,*' Brenda thought.

They crossed the garage and into the control room, that Brenda did not recognise. A new slate tiled floor had been put down with the removal of the old horse wheel that was no longer needed, the dust and dirt of ages past gone, in this clean and airy room. There were new panels of dials and switches, cables going in and out, that this room at this time was to be a control centre of the new electricity system there could be no doubt. Matt moved over to a switch on the wall, and flicked it on, all the lights came on, the once dim and dark interior now flooded with light.

'Don't get excited Brenda, that is mains electricity I am using, you said you wanted to see if it worked, well it does. Once we get the new cable laid, and linked to this system, we just flick this the other way, and we are on Hydro Power, neat eh?'

Chapter 45

WITH THE LIGHTS NOW up and running in the Garage, Matt also opened the door, they could explore all corners and everyone scattered to see what treasures they could find.

Brenda, Larry, Dennis and David gravitated to the first of the covered shapes, she just had to see what was underneath, the undisturbed dirt of ages lay very thick on the top. Brenda stopped by the first one, and pulled up a corner, the wire spokes of a very flat tyre, and red paint were the first thing she saw. Everyone at this stage had come over to where Brenda was, Keith and Max had joined the troops in the garage, eager to see what was there. Larry, David, Roger and Keith grabbed a corner each and very carefully lifted the cover off the beautiful car. Taking the tarp straight out the garage door and depositing the debris out where it belonged in the garden.

'Wow mum, that is one very sweet car!' Kate said as they all admired the pristine pillar box red paintwork. 'It's as though they just parked it yesterday. What's under the other one?'

As she spoke, the boys had repeated the lifting and taking out of the cover to the garden, uncovering a twin to the first but this one in English racing green. 'A pair, oh my, they are beautiful.'

'Beautiful and very rare,' Max said, as he ran his hand along the car, looking at Brenda who nodded, he flipped the catches on the hood, flipping it up to show the engine a bit grimy but still looking good.

'Well that looks really good, Max, or am I hoping it is. They are Singer's made around 1930 if my memory serves me well.' At their astonished looks, Brenda laughed, everyone had been holding their breaths it seemed as everyone gave a sigh, with the smell of gardenia floating around. 'Actually, Singer Le Mans, with the very latest aluminium accessories, and they should have a tool kit just under the hood!'

'Ok Brenda how on earth did you know that, I didn't know that, who here knew that?' Larry asked, still thunder struck at the pristine condition of the cars.

'Well I do, and Keith,' Max looked at Keith who was very carefully opening up the hood of the green car, an awed expression on his face, and looking as though he was handling glass, not a motor car. Keith realised he was being spoken too, and turned as he realised he was also being watched.

'One of my father's hobbies is restoring old cars. The one and only Singer he worked on, so badly neglected, it should have been scrapped, it took him a long time to repair. So yes, I know just how rare these two are, and I am itching to see if we can get them running again, if we can. Would that be ok with you Brenda? I would love the task of restoring them, not that I think much restoration will be needed, but I won't be able to drive it,' at everyone's gasp and why not, he then moved and stood beside the car,' can't get the seat back far enough, my knees will be up around my ears!'

Everyone laughed again, and the spell was broken. The inspection turning to the practical, and even more excited when the store room on the other side of the refurbished power room, was accessed. There still in the boxes from the manufacturer, were replacement parts for at least 3 engines, down to the last bolt and screw required.

'*Thrifty and forward thinking those Lords of Broadmeadows,*' Brenda thought as Max and Keith went into ecstatics over the find. Calling a halt to them starting immediately, stopping Larry, David and Dennis, from even opening the driver's door.

'Ok I knew they were here, as I have had time to finally read the journals, and one of the last entries was how they had bought two of the new-fangled cars and had put them in the garage till the son came home from his military training, we all know what happened then. I will give my permission for work to be done, and I want to drive this red one so badly, but fellas, please let's be practical. Where is the hoist to lift these babies up so you can work on them? The equipment you need to lift the engine out and check it? This garage has to be moved into this century first, before you can start pulling apart these splendid machines. Am I right?'

Grudgingly all the men, agreed that she was right. They slowly covered the cars again, hiding them from view, a last pat from Keith and they moved over to the carriages that George had been climbing over. Roger explaining what function each of the four would have been used for, and how many horses would have been required to do so.

'These also are in remarkable condition,' Roger said, 'once we can get them outside and washed, they will sparkle. I know a company that can repair the roof of the Town Carriage Brenda, although it might be better to wait till we have a horse to put in them so we can move them, or more men!'

Mary and June suggested that Brenda show Dennis around while they organized a late lunch, early dinner on the go from the leftovers of last night's celebrations. Shooing Larry, Ann, Kate, Matt and David out the garage door onto the bridal path, along with Dennis and Brenda.

Brenda had to agree, walking the bridal path gave one a sense of belonging, she now had a very good idea of how big this estate was, and wanted it to shine again.

Dennis being very impressed with the work Norman had done, and vowed to bring his bathers next time he visited, the water looked so inviting. The ruin of the manor house now that the removal of the debris showed just how big the house was, impressed him most.

'This is going to be one very large house Brenda dear, are you sure you want one this big.' He spread his arms around to signify size.

'Well love, I think ten bedrooms might not be enough, when you think about it, I need four for just us, then a nursery suite with bedrooms for visitors with babies, and then at least another five for family, when you work it out, I will have to farm people out to the gateway if everyone turns up at once!' Laughing they all slowly began the long walk down the driveway, mulling over her words, and coming to the conclusion that she was right. David wondering, if there could be a way to increase the bedroom numbers when, as Brenda said everyone turned up at once, but still have spacious rooms the building deserved.

Around the meal table discussions went on in regard to how equipment could be purchased to bring the garage up to date, Larry, David and Dennis all weighing in with Max, Keith and Roger. Brenda just let them go, knowing that what-ever was organised would be for the benefit of the estate, and another step forward for them all.

Chapter 46

THE START OF A new week, Brenda welcomed the arrival of more steel beams, and she was pleased to see oak framing had been delivered to get the stables and gateway moving forward. Leaving Glen and Dan to supervise, telling them they knew where she would be, she was feeling just a little tired after her exertions of the weekend, gratefully went back to the peace of the Gate Lodge.

She was in her study catching up on emails, and rechecking the information on Seahaven that Dennis had left her with the night before, when Ann knocked on the door.

'Good I am glad to see you are not out helping Dan, move those pieces of steel that were just delivered. You have visitors, the Police want to interview you, are you ok to do so, I can send them away if you don't want to face them?'

Brenda hesitated for a moment, but realised putting off the inevitable was very silly, of course they wanted to speak to her, they needed her testimony to make sure the charges laid would stick. 'It's fine Ann, just ask them to wait for a moment, I will be out shortly!'

Composing herself, removing the scarf so they could see scars on her scalp, through the stubble of hair that had regrown, ready for whatever was to come, Brenda was surprised to see Larry and Michael, along with a plain clothed policeman and a police woman, sitting around the dining table.

'I was not expecting to see you both today, what a lovely surprise!'

Brenda gave both men a hug, and Larry kept a hold of her hand, as he pulled out the seat next to him.

'Had to come and give moral support, also we are your lawyers, so came to be of assistance, Michael had information that he needed to give as well, so it was a good excuse to get out of the city, you don't mind, do you?'

'Of course not, don't be silly. Now who am I speaking with?'

Once the introductions had been made, the detective started with a very blunt, 'At what time in your relationship, did the alleged violence from your husband begin?'

On her mettle immediately, and with gardenia floating around, Brenda had a thought that Greg's charisma had been working again, that man could charm the birds out of the trees.

'Not in the first instance, I point out to you he is my ex-husband. Here are the papers to prove it, even if he does not believe it, legally we divorced over twenty years ago!'

The atmosphere in the room, had changed, both men sitting either side of Brenda had stiffened at his opening remark. The detective had been introduced while they waited for Brenda to arrive, he knew of course who the gentlemen were, having read the statement Larry had made at the time of the attack. The warning from his supervisor before he left to do this interview, which had been considerably delayed, and to walk carefully around Lady Lucas the title having thrown him a little, as no previous mention had been made of this piece of information. His reports had identified the victim as Brenda Chalmers the supposed ex-wife of her attacker, he had to go back and research the gap between the various names. Also, having one QC never mind two, present as her 'lawyers', just set his hackles up. He could see that the beating she had been through had been very severe, if the injuries were still this bad. Now wondering at the version of Greg's story that Brenda, his wife, was prone to 'accidents', he rethought his plan of attack, realising this woman wasn't the prima donna that he thought she would be, or had been led to believe again from the report he had from Greg, with all the warnings and information he had gathered. That she had produced papers to prove her point, and there were more in the folder she had brought with her, made him sit up, Brenda got in first.

'Detective, you may think you know my ex-husband but believe me whatever he has told you will be a fabrication of his life, what he believes the world owes him, his due, his right. Oh, he was sweetness himself, when we were courting, he swept me off my feet and we were married really when I was just out of high school, my parents did not want me to marry so young, but I was in 'Love' and didn't listen. Things were fine for a couple of years, mainly because I was working full time, and could pay the bills, he did odd jobs around the town, and had a few 'private jobs' he did that I found out about. Women in a small-town love to gossip. Then things got a little tight, and he started taking his frustrations out on me. That's when my nightmare started, I tried to leave him, went back to my parents. They had an accident, not sure how that happened, as dad was a very good driver, it came out of nowhere. After protestations that he had changed and been to counselling, which I was made to believe, I went back to him, he was good for about six months, then the beatings became more savage.'

Brenda took out hospital records she had kept, pushing them across the table, 'and before you ask, yes I thought it was my fault for a long time, you have met him?' he nodded, 'and I am sure you believe everything he has told you, in his twisted mind he is always, always right and you the object of his ire are very wrong and deserve to be punished. You forget he is a very persuasive person, his arguments that it was all my fault sounded so reasonable. When after a particularly nasty evening I arrived at the hospital with a hairline fracture of my arm, the nurse on call phoned the police! That was a big joke, as Greg was mates with the two police officers at the station, at that time. They dismissed my case out of hand, as they had talked to Greg, and he had said I had fallen down the stairs, which was ridiculous, as there were no steps at the house. At that hospital visit I found out I was pregnant, it sealed my fate for the next few years. Oh, the beatings did not stop, but of course he was so proud of the fact I had fallen pregnant, it proved that he was a man, he was careful to not do too much damage, just enough to keep me in line, and respectful – his words.'

'After one particular bad evening, before I found out about my pregnancy, it was about a year after my parents died, I realised I had to get away, in a small town it is not easy to hide things. I started planning and saving what I could, while keeping Greg at least calm. It was going fine, until I found out I was pregnant. I was working at the local hotel, as the events co-ordinator and assistant manager, the manager on one occasion after he saw the bruises on my arms, and this time a black eye, which was a rare bruise, tried to help and offered me accommodation at the hotel, needless to say, six months pregnant I was going to take it, but Greg intervened. That was about the time I met Dennis Brookes, whom arrived out of the blue, you see I had my champions, but Greg always won in the end.'

'I used to be thankful when he did not come home on a night, especially towards the end of my pregnancy, when I got very big, I ended up in hospital for the last month, as they realised I was having twins. That was just bliss, I had a surprise visit from Dennis, who helped me through the births, not Greg.'

Ann sitting at the end of the table was horrified, getting up and putting a glass of water in Brenda's hand, telling her to drink, before going on, also putting a box of tissues in front of her, as she could see the tears running down her face, as she remembered the nightmare she had escaped from.

'Why did you not seek help, if the beatings were that severe?' the detective asked in the lull.

'You forget this is a small country town in outback Australia, Detective. Everyone knew what was going on, but you don't interfere, help if you can, but oh no, don't actually state anything in the open. Besides, who was I going to call on, Greg, persuasive as he was always had a plausible excuse for my black and blue state, I was clumsy, never watched where I was going was always walking into doors or tables. He always made sure that he made friends with any police that did their tour in the country town. All this time my preparations were quietly ongoing, I had to go back to work quickly as I was the only one earning, so I used to take the twins with me to work, when they were small it was easy. I would not leave them at home, especially after I saw how Greg picked up David one time, and acted when they cried, his rage never far from the surface, as he had been replaced in his mind as the Alpha person. I managed to shield the children for a couple of years, and my plans were finally coming to a head, I had changed my name, to the official name on the children's birth certificate, 'she handed both documents across the table, 'had even managed to buy a second-hand station wagon, which I had parked at the hotel. The manager had offered the space, he also had lined up a new job for me with a friend of his over in Western Australia, as far away from Greg as I could get. It all came to a head the night my neighbour had offered to take my toddlers for a night, so I could get some sleep, by this stage I was existing on about three hours a night. That was a night I will always remember, as for some reason, whether he had an inclining of what I was doing, small town remember, but realising the children were not home, he went to town.'

Stopping for a moment, as the painful memories were dragged up again, Larry requested they stop, horrified by what he was hearing.

Taking his hand, 'it's ok luv, they are memories but see how far I have come. I need to do this, I am not the only one with a story like this. Hopefully I can help in some way!' squeezing his hand and taking a sip of water, she looked the detective in the eye, noting he could not look at her, but was looking at his notepad, reading his notes.

'Well after he left the house, the neighbour came over to get something for the twins, and found me she immediately rang for an ambulance. I pleaded with her to keep the twins, to take them to a girlfriend of mine, in the next town, Greg did not know her, which I am grateful to say she did.

Greg of course tried to explain it away as my fault, but the surgeon who had done the emergency hysterectomy on me, and fixed up the other injuries, no broken bones thank goodness called the police. This time the intervention order was put in place, and I spent a few days in hospital, the doctors and nurses horrified when I checked myself out. But I could not stay there, Greg knew where I was, but not the children, they were his bargaining tools, and he was not a happy man, the gossip I heard from the nurses was that he was turning the place inside out trying to find them, he had to be forcibly removed from my hospital bed, trying to get me to tell him where they were, even threatening my neighbour, his police mates had turned against him.

I had been packing the station wagon for months a bit at a time, so I was dropped off at the hotel, early in the morning, and drove myself to my girlfriends in the next town. I managed to stay with her for a couple of weeks, in fact I had to, as she took one look at me as I got unsteadily out of the car, and took the car keys away. That was the beginning of my nomadic life, I had left no trail for Greg to follow, and meant to keep it that way. I began the divorce proceedings as soon as I could, made sure they were legal, and I made sure he received a copy. Moving from town to town, state to state to make sure we never crossed paths again. It worked till he arrived here with Bill Gardiner as his compatriot.'

The detective was impressed by the courage of this woman in front of him, she had documents to prove her story, and photo's as well. Once she had realised that Greg was full of bullshit, and blamed her for his mistakes, she had eventually got out of the merry go round that had been her life. It had not been easy, and taken longer than it should, he now realised that the story that Greg had given was as Brenda had put it a complete fabrication. He was really to be pitied, especially after he heard what had occurred only the month before. Brenda telling how she had met Mr. William Gardner two years previously, as the original builder of the Iris House refurbishment, and how she had dismissed him as incompetent, which had led to the owner of the building Sir James Pickworth, spreading the news. But it had been Brenda he had blamed not Sir James. Then, over a month ago, heard the breaking glass, and went to investigate, being surprised to see her ex-husband, and Bill Gardiner on the property, factually telling what had happened next.

Ann then added the photo's she had taken of Brenda as she laid in the hospital, adding her statement to Brenda's. Larry telling how they had missed Brenda at the new stables and went to look for her, to find Bill with a large tree branch in hand and Greg ready to plant kicks on Brenda as she lay at their feet, stopping them but not before she had been badly beaten,' Larry pointed to the scars and bruising still to be seen, 'but before very serious damage could be done.' Larry left out Iris's part in all of this, he did not think the detective would be a believer!

The detective and the police woman left after asking Michael and Larry a few more questions, they asked if they could take the documents Brenda had given them, she advising they were copies, she had the originals and yes, they could take them all, handing over copies on paper of her abusive married life. Releasing more than the documents, she released the guilt she had been carrying around, realising that there had been nothing she could do to stop Greg, or the thousands of men, and she knew a few women, like him. They would use whatever means they could, for their easy life, and hang the people they trod on, or abused.

She let Michael and Larry show them out, going into the bedroom to wash her face, and her hands, making it a ceremonial cleansing of her soul. Iris seemed to shimmer in her reflection, a benediction for her, gardenia floated around, and a breeze wafted her cheek. Ann knocked on the door, not opening it, speaking through it 'are you alright Brenda, do you need some more time? Larry and Michael and I, are concerned that was too much for you!'

Brenda shivered a little the benediction seeming real, and pulled back her shoulders, 'I am coming, Ann, I feel like celebrating, even though it is early, do we have any Champagne left in the cellar, can you go and check please?' hearing her walk down the hallway to check for her. Counting to ten, leaving her scarf on the bed, revelling in her new-found freedom, she would show her scars with pride from then on, followed her into the room, Larry immediately enfolded her in his arms, saying quietly in her ear 'I love you!' which brought a lump to both of their throats, just holding her anchor was enough to bring her back onto an even footing.

Michael coughed, breaking the tableau Brenda and Larry looking into each other's eyes, trust and promise in both of them. Ann returning with a couple of bottles asking for assistance, shortly they all had glasses in hand, 'To the Future, and may it be glorious!' Brenda announced, here, here was the rousing reply.

Chapter 47

'It's a bit early for Champagne, isn't it?' Glen walked in on the end of the cheers, 'what have I missed?'

'My liberation Glen, and it was a long time coming. I just had my interview with the Police, that is another page in that book done, so we were celebrating an ending of sorts. Now what can I do for you?'

Glen took in the atmosphere, and Larry mouthed *Fill you in later!* Knowing that he did not want him to push Brenda just then. Took the offer of a cup of tea, keeping his curiosity in check, telling them all what they had been doing, inviting them all out to see the progress they had made.

They followed Glen out to the stable yard, there were buildings in the once empty spaces. The stables Brenda expected, but now there was the start of another cottage attached to the gateway. The steel shell of the Gateway, was proud and tall arching across from one side of the yard to the other, already in place the second-floor uprights waiting for the cross beams, floors and then roof, but the biggest surprise was on the stable side, with the buggy garage, the side of the quadrant was complete. The "stables" ran from driveway to gateway, she sighed, it was as her vision, updated to fit into this modern world, but her vision non-the less. The men just finishing putting in the roller doors, Brenda could see the bridge in place to link this new garage to the bridle path, it was just wide enough for the buggies or people, and as Brenda could see was not solid steel, Dan had used the some of the punched steel plates from the

298

landings at Iris house, as the base, workmen were busy putting in the finishing touches.

The outside access to the stair case up the side of the archway still waiting for a door. Glen moving her into The Stable Apartment, 'I think we should call this a Town House, as it is multiple floors,' she said making Glen chuckle. Through the front barn door, from the yard, drinking in the space this building had, the tall ceilings matching the new tenant who was watching with interest from his doorway into the garage, the new roller doors being fitted. Keith moving over to them, a smile on his face 'what do you think Brenda, does this fit in with your vision, it is so much more than I even hoped for!' he was pointing out the space on the ground floor, just waiting for appliances to finish them off was an open plan kitchen/living room, with small office and laundry come powder room, a barn door led into the stables proper, through the tack room, an open space with the large barn door out to the yard, was the break before the stables themselves.

Brenda was speechless, as again her dreams were becoming reality. Larry handed her his handkerchief, as the tears of joy flowed. She walked back out into the stable yard, taking in the sights around her, and enjoying the feeling of belonging that was there. Walking among the mounds of supplies that had been delivered from new paving stones, for the stables, to the oak frames and stable doors. Double glazed window units, sky lights and everything glass. She stopped at what looked like a big stack of corrugated iron, with a pile of flat sheets beside it, it looked so out of place in amongst the oak and glass, asked the question 'What is this for?'

Roger had been talking to Dan they both moved over to her at her question, 'Well it's for a new compost area Brenda, we discussed the spot behind the stables remember, we are already making waste that should be composted. Max and June are really keen to use our own compost. When we get the horses, and I realise that is a way off yet, a good system will be worth its weight in gold. So, I have expanded the system my father had at his stables, and hope to utilise the space behind here flanking the garage door. Come I will show you!'

Taking advantage of a break in the installation of the roller doors, he led them through the new garage to look over the bridge railings, at the site he was talking about, behind the actual building, it was a sheltered place with the foliage of some big trees, a perfect spot for some large compost bins. They all followed him into the stable, and up to where Brent and his team were trying to install the lift, which was a little larger than their usual, saying hello to Brent, telling him to come and see her before he left was urged onwards by Larry.

'You can chin wag with Brent later, I want to find out what Roger is doing!'

Laughing, they moved to the back wall of the stables, Roger explaining they had used the space of a couple of stalls to redo the stairs and add the lift which would be big enough for a bale of hay to be moved. Leaving nine horse stalls, that should be,' he turned to Brenda seeing her smile, 'more than enough in this day and age.'

In the horse stall next to the stairs, on the back wall, she could see a steel frame, with a door that slid up and down, had been added; at ground level, the bottom of the door was flush with the floor.

'What I am hoping to do, with June and Max's help, is convert that space at the back of the stables into our own recycling and compost area with another small greenhouse, which there is room for. We make a ramp with the flat steel, from the edge of the floor here, into the garden, into a collection bin I am making with the corrugated sheets. When we finally do have a couple of horses, we just shovel the manure through the door to the ramp and into the compost bin. Then it can be moved into one of the several bins I am planning on building, for various stages of compost, that will benefit the grounds. I am following some guidelines from June already, and Brenda please from now on, please use the scrap bin I will bring round later for all your food waste, I am also working on a paper recycling idea as well!'

Congratulations was heaped upon him from all, Michael staying to have a word with him, as Larry, Brenda and Ann went back to the gate lodge.

For the next couple of weeks Brenda was happy with the pace of work, and very pleased to be where she was. Enjoying that she was healing every day, the bruises fading, muscles coming back with the swimming and exercise's, Ann gave her. The adjusted plans for the stables with the extra large bedroom for Keith going over the new buggy garage, second bedroom over the tack room. The third cottage being built next to and attached to the Gateway. With the addition of the lift she had discussed with Brent in the Gateway, met not only her approval but both the councils.

The debris was finally removed from the manor house, Max, Roger, Keith and June breathing a sigh of relief that only a couple of dud incendiary devices were found. It was a highlight of the week, when they used the temporary steps and could finally explore to the basement of the main house, finding the door to the storage area, cheering when Glen, Dan and all the crew moved the last blocks out of the tunnel, Dan checking that all was safe and secure to be able to use it again. Exploring the large area that the basement covered, not only the main part but the side wings that were not visible from above, seeing where the kitchen used to be, finding the well confirming Brenda's thoughts that the pure water that was giving her the lake, was originally also used in the house.

Finally, she could see what this house could become, and she was going to change the layout, as she had seen in her dreams, using the original kitchen for a different purpose. As she realised a new kitchen at ground level was going to be what this new modern manor house required. The servants that the Grandfather Norman's had were no longer a viable option in this modern age, but still having to have a kitchen that caterers could use and easy access to the terrace, where most of the summer extravaganzas were going to be held most important. Discussions with Peter, David, Dan and Glen, occupied many hours in the days to come, while she explained how she wanted to live in this new home. Cheering along with Ann, when David sent her the video of the machinery breaking ground at the Seahaven project. The removal of the shacks and buildings that were there and had taken so long to take away, another massive step forward in her dreams.

Her health all clear was another highlight. The surgeon happy with the healing of her arm, declared her fully fit, but to still take it easy for the next three or so months to just make sure they were no set-backs. Ann endorsing the surgeon's words, on the drive back from the hospital.

'Now please, don't start slinging any sledge hammers, although the break has healed the arm is still weak. We still have to be a little cautious, ok Brenda? Are you listening to me?'

'Yes Ann, I understand, and I promise I won't be doing anything foolish. I also understand that it will take a little while longer for the arm to fully heal, the ache it gives when I do too much is warning enough. Now what are you planning to do? 'at Ann's puzzled glance, 'well you hardly need to be watching me hand and foot now, and I am sure you have a life you want to get back to. Please I am not pushing you out, and you are most welcome to stay, but you stay because you want too, as my guest and friend, not because you have to!'

Ann suddenly realised that she did not want to go, had found a family of sorts, but still had that urge to move. 'To be quite honest Brenda, I am not sure what my next move is. I have found a place that for once I don't want to run away from, but still have that feeling I need to move. Thank you, I will stay until things become clearer if you don't mind, although I don't want to cramp your style too much!'

'Well the Gate Way Cottage will be finished soon, I am sure June will be happy to share, if you want, I am happy for you to stick around. It is especially nice to have my own doctor on hand without having to wait in a surgery to see you?'

Laughing at the ingenious expression on Brenda's face, both ladies relaxed and enjoyed the drive home.

Chapter 48

IT WAS RAINING AS Brenda sat at her computer, opening up the emails, that were not a chore to her anymore. Thinking back to times when having more than one email in her inbox meant a problem in various jobs she had worked at. The one from Gus jumped out at her, and as she read it, realised she had secluded herself for too long. She immediately made plans, she had word from Rebecca that the fit out for the house at Seahaven Village, was complete, just a couple of last minute touches that Mia was following up on that week, but it was ready for a visit, and Brenda was going to do just that.

She rang the car yard to arrange transport, asking them to deliver if possible later that morning. Then went to find Ann, who was working on her laptop on the dining room table.

'Are you free this week?' Ann looked up and wondered what was coming next.

'Yes, nothing I can't put off, and I want to put it off!' she continued at Brenda's raised eyebrow, 'a reunion, of sorts, and I can't stand half the people that will be there, but please don't breathe a word to Michael, he is among the people I like to meet at these shindigs!'

Brenda laughed and sat opposite her, noting that Broadmeadows had also worked its magic on Ann, who was relaxed and smiled a lot more. 'Well, I have to go to Southend; apparently, there is a growing movement in the Seahaven Village area trying to shut down the development, they believe it is going to be operated by a foreigner and will not be of benefit to the area!' Ann snorted, and made a rude noise.

'They are right in a way, it is going to be run by a foreigner, but one much closer to home. Gus and Janet would like to hold a meeting, in the Pub of course, to see if they can stop the rumours dead in their tracks. I need to be there, but I still don't like to drive that much, oh I am ok, here on the Estate, but that is a very long drive and I don't trust my arm for that sustained a trip. I was going to ask Max, if he would drive for me, but I would like you to come as well. To give another perspective to the meeting, please?'

'It will also give me an insight into what is going on there, and for me to meet Mary-Beth and John, hmm, ok yes why not. When is the meeting?'

Brenda stood to go and find Max, turning at the door to say, 'Tomorrow night!'

It was lunch time the rain had stopped and the lunch trucks were busy with making sure the hungry workmen did not stay hungry long. Brenda found Max, just taking his cup of tea, and sandwiches from the counter, looking around to find a spot to eat, seeing Brenda walking towards him a smile on her face, he approved of the short curly style her hair was growing back in, it suited her, apart from a few bruises, the main one that was around the jaw, she was almost back to normal.

'Hi there, good timing, were you coming to find me or did you want some lunch as well?'

'Both, can you wait till I get my salad, and can we talk a minute?'

Nodding he motioned her to the counter, and waited while Brenda was served, then moved them back down towards the stable yard, saying there was no-where else to sit.

'I need to ask your assistance please,' Brenda began as they sat on a couple of chairs Max retrieved from the stack in the corner, 'I hope it won't be too much of an imposition?'

'Whatever I can do to help you I will, what's up?'

'I have just had an email from Gus Lambert, he is the owner Seashore Retreat the pub at the new Care Home site in Seahaven Village.' Max nodded as he ate his sandwiches.

'They are having a Village meeting as someone is spreading rumours that the works being done are to benefit 'foreigners' and will not be good for the area, taking jobs and money away.'

'What, that is poppycock, who would do something like that. Talking out of their hats, or worse. So, what do you need me for, oh driver, you want me to drive you to Southend for the meeting right?'

'Yes please, my arm is still not as strong as I would like, and that long and sustained effort to Seahaven will not be good. I am taking Ann with me, as I don't think she really understands what I am trying to do, and need to show her, she will be vitally needed to explain her area of expertise and where she will be fitting in I hope if she takes the job. So, do you mind, being my chauffeur, for a few days, I would appreciate you being there?'

'Of course not, I could do with a trip to the seaside. Might even get Charlie to come and visit while I am there, would that be ok with you?'

'Fine Max, perfectly fine, Rebecca said they had outfitted the three bedrooms in the house with two queen beds and a twin, so we will have enough room for everyone. Now here is the twist, the meeting is tomorrow night, so we need to go this afternoon, I have a car being delivered shortly, can we leave here around two?'

'Don't give a guy much notice do you,' and he laughed, 'lucky I am always ready, and as I have finished my lunch will go and pack a bag. I suggest you do the same!'

The car was delivered on time, a call to Rebecca gave the information that keys had been left with Dennis, it seemed the most logical thing to do, she hoped that the décor was to her liking, and with that cryptic comment rang off. Then a call to Dennis to advise him she would be arriving some time that evening, and to have a light on in the house, that not to worry the cavalry was coming. The laugh he gave was one of thank goodness for that, and he rang off assuring her that she was welcome at any time.

It was a pleasant drive, the traffic Max said was light, but Brenda was very glad she was not in the driving seat. Discussions about who might be spreading the rumours were lively, and if she had not known that her two major antagonists were in jail, might have thought it was a movement on her recent attacker's behalf to discredit her. Common sense prevailed at one stage, and Brenda had a fleeting thought she might be the object of a rival Care Home company, she had been making some very big waves in those quarters.

It was just becoming dusk and the sun was a hazy ball when they pulled up in a parking spot opposite the houses. Vastly different houses from her first visit, a fresh coat of paint, and a lived-in appearance did wonders for an area. Lights were on in Dennis's place and also next door in Brenda's new home. They were just waiting to cross the road when Dennis came out and waved. Running across to give Brenda and Ann a hug, a strong handshake for Max.

'Oh, I am so pleased you are all here, how was the drive, how are you feeling?' Tumbled out as though the words would not wait to be spoken in order. Laughing Brenda caught his arm, and as she went to pick up her bag, had her hand knocked away by Max, who picked up her bag, and Ann's, after slinging his back pack on his shoulder, then motioned them all across the road.

Dennis made a ceremony of giving Brenda her keys for the house at Seahaven Village, laughing as he held her back to look at the stained glass that was above the front door a beautiful window with Iris's surrounding the words 'Iris Sea House'. She walked into another house that hugged her as she walked through the door.

This was a different feeling, not many antiques but comfortable and practical furnishings gave it a welcoming feel. She realised that some of the same techniques at Iris House had been employed in this new place, the double glazing, and insulation throughout. As Brenda was ushered through her blue front door, she saw the ground floor was one space, there was a living room at the front, moving into a family room and then modern kitchen at the back, tucked into the corner beside the sliding glass doors that led out to the small garden, was a compact single person lift, Leonard had pulled out all the stops, prompted she had no doubt by Mary-Beth. There was a walk-in pantry, compact laundry, and powder room, completed the downstairs. Moving up a flight of stairs to the first floor, the lift she could see went up to the top, a great addition which would allow her and her visitors, she was thinking of Shane mostly, to be able to use the house easily. The three bedrooms all had their own compact bathrooms, two rooms were fitted with Queen beds, Brenda took the front one, at Ann's insistence, with Max taking the compact twin room at the back. There was also another floor up in the attics, and Brenda was surprised to see two more bedrooms with a shared bathroom in between. Marvelling at Leonard's skill as a builder, equal to that of Glen's, Brenda made a mental note to never tell them she had even had that thought at all. The whole house was furnished in a contemporary modern, but comfortable style, that made you want to stay a while, and enjoy the view out of the front bay windows, to sit in the window seats and watch the world just flow by.

They toured the large basements that all the houses had on the shore front, and had been given over to various uses. Dennis was very proud of the fit out both his and Brenda's basements had undergone, they had been made into one space, and were now officially the registered main office of Iris House Retirement Properties Group Co.

Dennis turned to Brenda as they viewed the very modern offices in the basement, there were four desks, with space for a couple more, an area along the back wall where all the equipment that a modern-day office required, even a small tea room attached to the wall in Brenda's side. Turning to see the access, not only by the large glass fronted door to the street, but the two spiral staircases in the opposite corners at the back of the rooms.

'I thought we could go and have a meal at the pub, Gus and Janet were hoping you would arrive before the meeting tomorrow, would that be ok?'

'Fine Dennis, let me freshen up, that sounds good, I am starving!'

Brenda's words were seconded by both Ann and Max, so after freshening up, they all trooped up the street. Twilight had descended so Brenda could not see much of what was going on in the building site, but noted the area was very clean and neat, the high fence, screening the view to all.

Gus was the first to see them, and waved them over to the same window seat Brenda had been in on the first visit. She was happy to see there were not many people around, as she wanted to talk to Gus, before the meeting the following evening.

After introductions had been made, and drinks served, Gus stood by Brenda's side, a smile of hope on his face.

'Thank you, thank you for coming, I am so sorry I hope I didn't alarm you, but what you and your family are proposing for the area will only bring the good times back. I can't understand why there are so many problems!'

'I have an idea Gus, and I am sorry, it is because the care homes that I have opened have become very popular, that I think a couple of my competitors are playing dirty!'

Dennis looked at her, wondering why he had not thought of that. Realising as Brenda had said it, it was right. They had been treading on some very powerful toes, that did not like their bottom line being thinned. How were they going to get across their point, and stop those oddball rumours from gaining any more traction?

'Ok, I have a plan, stop me if you think it won't work?' Brenda asked to the thinking silence that surrounded her. 'I have invited the Mayor to visit in the morning, and I am going to have a quiet word with him in regards to the Council. I will make sure he is aware, that the home and any workforce for it, will be taken from people who need and want a job in the area; Dennis has already started with his staff, I am pleased to say. I want him to make the local Job Centre aware of this fact, that I will be needing not only trained office staff, but also cleaners, gardeners, cooks, handymen and electricians. I have already spoken to Leonard and he is on board with hiring local men or women during the building, and then we can keep them on staff as handypersons, once everything is up and running, Leonard also said he is coming to the meeting. Ann, I am hoping you can advise on the benefit of the centre to the community, as I will be opening the medical area for the whole village not just the home. They will finally get local competent medical treatment again, and not just doctors, I want them to know as we need for the centre everyone we employ will be available to the community. Such as dieticians, physiotherapist, hell I will even throw a couple of naturopaths into the mix. I want them to understand I will be diversifying and making what I build open to everyone. What do you think?'

'I am a believer' Max said, making everyone laugh, 'but then I have been your convert since you gave me this wonderful job. We have to convince a room full of sceptics it sounds like. I think I am not here only as a driver, if you get my drift?'

'Yes,' Dennis added, 'I am so glad you came as well Max, I don't like to think of people resorting to underhanded tactics, but with what Brenda has just gone through, I am glad you are going to be by her side!'

Shaking her head, Brenda gave Janet a hug as she brought out the meals they had ordered, Janet turning to her husband, telling Gus he had a bar to attend taking him away, to refill the drinks, and they enjoyed their meal.

Discussion went on through the evening, and Ann finally called a halt saying she was tired, not sure how Brenda was keeping her eyes open. Saying goodnight to both Gus and Janet, inviting them down for morning tea the following day to continue the planning strategies.

Chapter 49

BRENDA WOKE TO GLORIOUS sunshine, moved to sit on the cushioned seat in the bay window watching the world wake up around her. As was usual she was up before the dawn, was showered and in the kitchen with coffee brewing and making toast when Max appeared.

'I have put Charlie off, Brenda, when I rang his mum last night he spoke to me and sounded terrible little chap. He has a rotten cold, so told him to keep warm, although with this summer sun, that won't be a problem, and he could visit me at Broadmeadows when the long summer holidays begin in a few weeks. I have it all worked out with his mum, so hope that is ok with you?'

'Me, of course it is. I love having children around, they not only make me feel young, but also learn by watching what you do. He enjoyed his brief stay over Easter, didn't he?'

'Yes, he loved it, in fact hasn't stopped pestering his mum to let him visit again, we agreed on four weeks, out of the six. He is booked to go to Spain with his extended family last couple of weeks, so it works out fine. I also did not want him here if there is going to be problems, I hope you understand.'

'I hear you loud and clear Max, and I will be cautious. I just can't believe I escaped one beating, to be given another. All I want to do is help people!'

'That is the crux of the matter Brenda,' Ann stated coming into the kitchen. 'You want to help the general public, but the people who have made fortunes out of that general public don't want their fortunes diluted. They don't want the great unwashed, as it were, to understand they can get help, without an exorbitant cost. Therefore, as you stated last night, you have made enemies, and not just the two, sorry three scumbags that are in jail. It is going to be very interesting this evening, I don't think the antagonists are expecting you to be here at the meeting.

'I agree with Ann,' Mary-Beth said when she came through the open garden doors, 'I have been doing some checking, and whenever your name, or the Iris Care Homes come up, there is always a pause, as though people don't know what to make of you or what you are trying to do, it seems it comes down to them checking the bottom line every time. I have put feelers out through the Care Home communities as well, anonymously I assure you,' she added as Brenda gasped. 'The feed-back I get is all they can see in you is a very aggressive competitor, and one they don't want to understand or match, especially if you are going to cut their bottom line and take away potential profits from them. I just don't understand why they do not see that even with the prices charged we are still making money, oh not the enormous profits the others make, and are used too, but we also maintain every property correctly, which provides a higher quality service than some of them with their exorbitant charges. Still I am trying to stop the rumours, but it is difficult, what time did you say the Mayor was due?'

The mayor arrived at eleven as expected, with two others in the group, the woman who had smiled at Brenda, at the first meeting, and a gentleman who's bearing screamed 'Politician' at her. Tea's and coffees were supplied, Brenda enjoining the group to sit around the large table in the family room, to give the feeling of familiarity she needed, as that was where she sat back at the Gate Lodge when things were being discussed. If the Mayor or the council woman thought it strange they didn't show it, they also viewed Brenda's still slightly bruised and scared face with curiosity, the politician was ill at ease.

'Thank you for accepting my invitation Mayor George, I hope this did not intrude on your day?'

'Please Ms. Chalmers, call me Graham, may I call you Brenda? This is an informal occasion after all. Esther here, was most insistent that we should find out once and for all exactly what is going on with the site?'

Esther continued, 'We have heard rumours of dodgy building practices, and money being taken under false pretences,' she took a deep breath to give her final scathing retort, 'and jobs would not be given to locals, you are bringing in a work force from Korea!'

'I have also heard these rumours, and in the best interests of my constituents want to know exactly what you are proposing for this area, I don't think what you have submitted is exactly true!' Ian sallied forth, a pompous tone to his voice, clearly not to be outdone.

Brenda could not look at Ann, or Mary-Beth if she had she would have burst out laughing, but it was no laughing matter. Max just looked at her, and then turned away into the kitchen to put the kettle back on, he just hid his chortle under the running tap.

Before she could say anything, Dennis arrived a little out of breath with Leonard and Peter following close behind.

'Sorry we are late, just had to get some up to date figures for you Brenda, and Peter wanted to show you this!'

Peter and Leonard then carried in a 3D model of the revamped Seahaven Village area, complete with the Care Home and surrounds.

'Well timed Dennis and Peter, may I make the introductions; Mayor Graham George, Council Woman Esther Marshall, and Member for Seahaven Ian Daniel Ellis, my team; Dennis Brookes CEO of Iris Care Homes, Mary-Beth Walters who is one of the Managers of the home when it opens, Leonard Masters –Master Builder, Peter Mason who is one of the architects, my son David is the other. This is the prime team on the Iris Care Home Seahaven, and this is what is proposed for the area. That is one neat presentation Peter, when did you get that done?'

After handshakes, they all gathered around the model, Brenda was very happy with the detail it gave and scale of the buildings. 'As you can see what we have proposed is exactly what we are building, and no Mr. Ellis, it is has not been designed as some rich persons retreat, or to sell off the units for a time share. Yes, the units will be sold, or leased would be the better way to describe what I am trying to achieve. To the individuals as their properties, for over 55's, early retirees if you like, but still held by the trust. The funds paid are then put into the Seahaven Iris House Retirement Properties Trust Account, Dennis can show you the figures we have on the other properties that I have opened, it is all above board, checked on by Revenue and Treasury. The funds accrue, the interest allow the homes to then continue, paying for the upkeep of the buildings, and grounds; individual units pay their own utilities bill, just like anyone would have to in a normal home.'

'The main areas,' Brenda pointed to the two buildings at either side of the site, 'are the actual Care Homes, for our elderly, and not so elderly, people who need just that little bit of care as they move into old age, nearing the end, or even a respite period for the families. One of the units also has a dining room, Library, indoor swimming pool, all the amenities you would expect in a four to five-star hotel. The other is to be fitted out as a fully equipped medical centre and hospice arrangement on the floors underneath, the medical centre will not only be operating for the care homes, but I hope will be for the entire area.'

Dennis jumped in before the politician could, there was something about this man, that set his teeth on edge, 'this is the first time I have seen you in the area Mr. Ellis, where exactly do you live?' Not really the best opening gambit, but Dennis could not help it, the man antagonised him, his manner, his sneer as he just sat oozing hostility, he knew he had seen him before but could not remember where, but it had not been a pleasant experience he was sure.

'I don't think that is really to the point Dennis, where exactly do you live may I ask?'

'Next door, so I can be on hand to settle any disputes, and be on site to oversee the construction when it can move forward.'

'I have had to close down the site,' Leonard spoke into the glaring silence between the two men, 'my men were getting heckled by a group, that has been hanging around. Funny they are not here today, but we have had to call the police a couple of times. Mayor you know me, I have built houses for the council, would I get mixed up in anything dodgy, please how can you believe these insidious rumours?'

'Well I must admit that I have found it difficult to believe them, as I was very sure of the sincerity of Ms. Chalmers here. Where are you getting the funds to do this, as I know what you are proposing is not going to be cheap to build. Is the money coming from foreign interests if you can assure me that it is not I will be a happy man?'

'I can unequivocally confirm that funds are legal. Yes, some of it does come from overseas but only from companies that I control. You could class me as a foreigner, lived most of my life in Australia, but I was born just up the road from here in the next county over, and lived there for the first part of my life.' Brenda did not miss the stunned look on the politician's face, he had not done a very good background check, she would have loved to have been a fly on the wall when he got back to his office. 'So, the rumours have some basis, but not the full picture, the majority of any profit at all is put back into the Care Homes Trust, I do have to pay Dennis and the local staff he has hired, their salaries. I will not if I can help it, see our elderly, who deserve our respect die alone and uncomforted, which is happening because they can't afford anything else. If you require further clarification please call this number, advise you are calling in regards to Iris Care Homes, and the character of the owner,' and she bowed her head slightly to confirm ownership, 'I am sure you will be reassured not only as to my intentions, but also the financial stability of the scheme.'

Brenda handed over an envelope to the Mayor, knowing the information and contact details from Hugh would help ease the Mayor's mind, 'Now I think I have taken up a lot of your time. There is to be a meeting at the Seahaven Retreat this evening, if you are free, let me buy you a drink? You are also welcome Esther and Ian.'

The envelope was put into an inside pocket, you could see that Ian was very interested in what it contained, but the Mayor thanked Brenda and pointedly ignored him, a blind man could see the two men were not on good terms. Esther was also confused as she could see that everything was as initially given in the first submission in the chambers, how had doubt crept in, she also wondered why and who had started the rumours. She was going to get to the bottom of it have no doubt. They left not long after, passing Gus and Janet on the stairs.

They were very interested in the model that Peter had produced, asking how they could help. The upturn in business from the workmen in the area was good, but they needed to have a long-term plan to be able to update and grow the pub. Assuring them that long term was going to be good, it was the short term and all the rumours that were the problem.

Brenda moved everyone around the table, 'During my recent enforced down time, I have been doing some research of the area.'

'Of course, you have,' Dennis interjected to laughter from everyone.

A look at him and smile, Brenda continued 'this was once a very prosperous area, being where it is, and the, I quote "Healing Waters" the Georgian and Regency periods highlighted, the houses and coaching inn were built up with the affluence that flowed in. I also found that the property around the corner, beside the Retreat, which you have to admit is an eyesore, used to be part of the pub! In fact, the whole end of the block used to be part of the title, circumstances split the block in two!'

The gasp from Janet had everyone looking at her.

'Sorry, but I wondered, great grandad used to tell us tales of his childhood and his fathers with carriages rolling into the yard, but we could never figure out where this could occur, that building has always been there?'

'Not always, I think once we remove the detritus of the modern era, we will find the remnants of a stone gateway attached to the pub, at the front wide enough for carriages to go through, with a walled courtyard filling the rest of the space, to give room, where the buildings were, for a couple of stables and a yard. The original Seahaven Retreat was a carriage stop, that would have catered to the gentry that came from London for weekends away. Now I can't demolish the buildings that have been built stopping the traffic going through the old stable yard out the lane behind us, but I can help you both with this!'

Brenda handed them the deed for the full property, the pub and the land next to it watching as they read the documents, steeling herself for the jubilation she knew would be their reaction, as they both realised what it was.

'Brenda, what, what is this?' Gus asked, Janet jumped up and ran to hug Brenda.

'Thank you, thank you, thank you, this will be a boon to us. We can turn the area into a Garden Room, and possibly extend the pub to give me a proper commercial kitchen, oh the possibilities!'

'Hold on love, we have to think this through, it will take some money to do this. Taking away the mess that is there for one thing, checking that there are no nasties hiding in the area, not going to be a quick fix'. Gus, could not believe his luck, his dreams of expanding the pub were right in front of him, but his practical side was telling him to slow down.

Janet looked at her husband, realising he was right, the shinning future she also had been dreaming about, was again a dream. Where were they going to get the money from, to do the job properly.

Brenda watched them, with Max, Ann, Dennis, Leonard and Peter looking on, smiling as Brenda moved to be in-between them, they just knew she was up to something, especially with the gardenia floating around, putting an arm around Janet and Gus's shoulders, smiled at them both.

'You don't think I would offer this to you, if I didn't have a plan for you to build your dreams, did you?'

'Brenda, what do you mean, just giving us the title to this place is wonderful,' Gus turned to look at her, 'I will find a way to fix it up, don't you worry!'

'Me, I am not worried at all, I am going to make sure what you want to do, is put past an Architect,' she pointed to Peter, who smiled. 'Then checked with a builder,' Leonard nodded as they looked at him, 'and paid for by me!'

Janet started to remonstrate, Brenda held up her hand, 'I will pay for all the new works, and the refurbishment of the Retreat itself, but please keep the old-world charm, don't turn it into a glass and chrome edifice, or you will never see me in it again! We can organise a repayment of the loan, once you are on your feet, and this place is earning its keep once again. I will let the lawyers do all the paper work, but what do you say, partners are you in?'

The couple looked at each other, wondering again at their good fortune, the wonderful fragrance that surrounded Brenda was very strong, Iris giving her benediction, what else could they do but say, Thank you.

Brenda stood and dangled a bunch of keys, 'Let's go and see what is in store for Leonard then, as he will be the one tearing out that awful place next to the pub, I wonder if that is where the rodent problem is coming from. Oh, I know about it,' at Gus's intake of breath, 'talk to Leonard, he was most concerned whilst refurbishing these houses. Besides its lunch time, haven't you two got a pub to run?'

Chapter 50

AT SIX THIRTY PM, a half hour before the meeting began Brenda, Ann, Dennis, Peter, Leonard, Mary-Beth with Max following, made their way to the pub. A very crowded and noisy pub, Dennis spotted Gus, having a tough time trying to fill everyone's orders, slipping around to the kitchen entrance, deposited his bag, gave a kiss on the cheek to Janet, and slipped behind the bar, serving the next in line. Gus looked and realised who it was, smiling and checking to see where Brenda and the rest were, as he realised if Dennis was there so was Brenda. When he spotted her, motioned her also through the kitchen entrance.

'It is a skill once learned never forgotten, I would offer to help as well, but think I should stay in the background, so let me see if I can help Janet, you really do need to hire more staff Gus, we will address that tomorrow. Let's just get through tonight, shall we?'

Gus gave her a quick hug, and went back out to the bar, Ann started stacking the dishwasher with the dirty plates and cups, rolling up her sleeves to start on the stack in the sink, Peter picking up a tea towel to help, Leonard checking to see if there was anything he could help with, Janet asking him to gets some supplies from the cellar, Max checking with Gus, joined him. Mary-Beth smiled at Brenda saying she would go and do some networking, as there were some people she wanted to talk too. Brenda nodded moving into the kitchen asked how she could help, Janet was still aghast at the bruising she could clearly see, and talk she had with Ann, gave her the task of chopping and slicing ingredients for the few counter meals she was offering, allowing Janet to concentrate on the cooking of the meals.

In very short order calm had been restored to the chaos, and Gus left the bar to check on the area he had set aside for the meeting with a long table, and chairs, switching on the PA system he had rigged up. Asking the people that had made the space their own, if they could move so the meeting could begin.

'Ladies and gentlemen, friends and neighbours, if you will all quiet down, we can get this meeting started.' It took a couple of goes, but eventually hush came upon the gathering. 'Now I decided to call this meeting, as I have been hearing some very nasty rumours in regards to the rejuvenation of this area.'

'Selling out you mean!' was shouted from the back of the room by a male voice, 'No good will come of it, no jobs for us at least!' a female voice yelled. 'Foreigners will ruin us, taking everything and giving nothing!' another male voice was raised. Gus was a bit perplexed not sure of how to go on.

Then from the kitchen door, Brenda's strong voice reaching even the back corners of the packed room, bringing almost immediate silence.

'Tell me people, how long has that parcel of land been derelict, how long since you as a community decided enough is enough, let's do something about that eyesore? How long has it been that any of you that live here, have actually looked around and thought I could change this, make it better!'

Brenda came to stand beside Gus, taking the microphone from his hand, Janet joining her at the table.

'NEVER, is the answer, because you have been told all your lives, that there is nothing you can do, by the council, the politicians, your friends. Well, let me tell you this now, and I hope the hecklers at the back of the room, not showing their faces will take note. I DON'T BELIEVE IN THAT TWADDLE! My name is Brenda Chalmers, and I am the person who has bought the old Holiday Village. You can see I am not a foreigner, I was born about a hundred miles up the road, my parents emigrated to Australia when I was a child, and I have now come home. I have bought the land not to turn it into some rich person's personal money pit, or to build a car park, or an inappropriate shopping centre.' This being a dig at Ian Ellis, who Brenda had spotted at the doorway, she had found out that one of the bids the council had received, had his name on the documents. 'I intend to give back to this community if you will let me!'

'Ha tell us another one, going to leach us blind and then run back to Australia I bet' the first heckler interjected. 'Yeah no jobs for us that's for sure' the female voice piped up.

'Well if the legitimate residents of this area, are not interested in what I have to say, and will allow what I take are a few noisy interlopers to interrupt the very good news I want to tell you. Fine, I will take my leave!'

Brenda put down the microphone, and started to leave the table space.

Gus quickly picked it up, 'my friends, neighbours I want to hear what Ms Chalmers has to say, I promise you I have seen what she is proposing for this area, and it is good. You Beth and Will,' pointing to a couple of locals in the crowd, 'are already working for Mr. Brookes, see the locals are benefiting already, how long were you both out of work for? Are we going to be led like sheep, and not think for ourselves, I think it is time we stood up to be counted, and say enough, we want more!'

There was a general murmur among the very large crowd, Beth and Will being looked at and questioned, a few locals realised that the people making all the noise were strangers. Suddenly, the new faces were being made to feel very uncomfortable, and six people left the room very quickly.

'Thank you all, Brenda, please continue.' Gus handed the microphone back a smile on his lips, his faith in his fellow villagers being renewed.

'Ok, thank you. Dennis, Leonard can you please bring out the model.'

Peter followed the two men as they deposited the model on the table, putting plans on the stand that was next to it, they all moved to be next to Brenda. Leonard saying hello to a few of the faces in the room.

'This is what I am proposing to do to the site. This will be the newest of the Iris House Retirement Properties, if it can ever get off the ground. Peter Mason here,' and she turned to introduce him, 'is the main architect on the project. I think a few of you know Leonard Masters builder, Mary-Beth Walters will be one of the Managers of the home, and Mr. Dennis Brookes is the CEO of the Iris House Retirement Properties Group, and both are now residents of the area, you have probably seen them around? We are here to answer any questions, and I will ask Gus and Janet if I can leave this model here so people who could not make this meeting will have something to check.'

'But what about the jobs, are you bringing people in from Korea?' was asked by one of the locals Brenda had seen in the pub a couple of times.

'Jock, what do you think,' Gus interjected, 'does Ms. Chalmers look like she will be bringing in Koreans to work here?'

'You can never tell, Gus, I am just asking the question!'

'It is a good question, Jock, what is your line of work?'

'I was an electrician, a good one, till I got laid off, haven't been able to find a job since, that was two years ago. Not much around here to find a job!'

A chorus of here, here went around the room.

'Well Jock, if you want a job, then let us build this,' and she pointed to the model, 'if you or any of you skilled men or women, want a job, give your resumes to Mr. Brookes here. Mr. Masters will have the last word on if you are hired while the construction is ongoing.' Raising her hand to stop the questions beginning, 'and then I will have need of competent electricians, plumbers, gardeners, cleaners, office and kitchen staff, all the kit and caboodle to run this place once it is completed. I would rather use local talent, in fact I insist on using local talent, if you are willing to do the work, and do it well.'

There was a murmur of disbelief, Brenda took a sip of her drink, realising she almost had them, also that Ian Ellis had left with the hecklers.

'People please, if you want to check my credentials, go on the internet, and search Iris House Retirement Properties Group Co, I have four open and operating at the moment with another just being finished. This one will be the sixth and biggest, you ask why I am doing this, let me tell you a story.

My parents worked hard in Australia, they were not rich, but the three of us had a comfortable life, they died in a car accident just after I had left school. I worked and saved, investing not making a lot but enough to cover the bills. I worked reception in many retirement villages in Australia, the one complaint that would be constantly made was the cost. Whether the residents were full time, or booked in to give their families a break; it is very intense when you have a loved one, who cannot remember who you are!' There were nods of agreement around the room, 'I eventually made my way back here, I was working with my Uncle, tending bar in his pub, and found myself in London with a great job. Whilst clearing out some papers from the owner of the premises, I won the Inheritance Lottery, and became an influential person. I found out that owner of the building had died alone in the house at the age of 104. No one had taken the slightest interest in the lady for years, dismissing her as a recluse and cranky old woman. I vowed that the legacy I had been handed would not be used to make me rich, that is not a life I like or want, but that I would use the bequest to the betterment of everyone if I could. I started the Iris House Retirement Properties Group, to atone for Iris being alone when she died, to give families an affordable place their demanding elderly relatives could have respite care, or an affordable place if they needed care they could no-longer give. Each and every home, is set up like a hotel, but with specialist care as well. I urge you to check up on me if you are still sceptical, I am what I say.'

Brenda sat then, not sure if she could say anything more to persuade the crowd she was sincere.

'So, what benefit is this place to us then?' A woman sitting at the side of the room asked.

Dennis turned, 'Apart from giving you jobs, this area is going to be made safe for everyone, the beach cleaned and repairs made to the sea wall, and foreshore, so access to the water will be available not just for the residents of the Care Home, but everyone. The raw sewage that has been flowing into the sea for the last few years due to the breakdown of the Holiday Village infrastructure and vandalism, has already been contained.' A muttering of thank goodness, ran around the room. 'I have a leaflet which will outline the benefits of allowing us to continue, to the whole community. A medical centre is being built into one of the buildings, a chemist shop is already in the works for when we open. The closed-up restaurants, sorry Gus and Janet, will be reopened. These are not only for the Care Home tenants but will be open for everyone to use. There will be general repairs done to the roadways, and even the Station has been planned a face lift. People we are not trying to destroy this community, we are trying to help you grow and prosper. We need your help. Mr. Masters here has been heckled by groups of men, and a few women, over the last few weeks, forcing him to close down the site. The police cannot help as by the time they get here, they have disappeared. If you really care about where you live, and want the opportunities this centre will give you, can you please help us to stop these hooligans from returning?'

It was the right tone to finish the meeting, Leonard, Peter and Dennis were surrounded, and curious people stepped up to the table to see the model. Brenda saw Ann and Mary-Beth in the corner of the room surrounded by people, not sure if she should stick around ended up behind the bar, helping Gus serve drinks to the community.

As it turned out behind the bar was the right place to be, as Brenda could chat to people as she helped Gus; it proved she was what she said, an ordinary person, like them all, just trying to help. Esther was one of the people she served, Brenda being a little surprised as she had not known she was there.

'You are what you say you are Ms. Chalmers, and I thank you for what you are doing. I will do all I can to help you, and make sure that Mayor George knows as well what I have found out tonight, and through my checks today. Call on me anytime I will see what I can do!'

With that and a hand shake she took her drink and weaved away from the bar, Brenda losing her in the press of people. Eventually the throng died down, and when Gus called 'Last Orders Please' the pub, while still full did not have the packed to capacity it had during the meeting. It was a happy group that sighed when the door finally closed, everyone helping Gus and Janet to tidy up and put dishwashers on before they left.

'That went better than I expected,' Brenda said as she walked back to the house with Ann and Dennis. Peter and Mary-Beth had departed shortly after the meeting finished, and Leonard wishing them a good night walked back to his car. As they approached the house, she could see someone sitting on the steps, it was Max 'I wondered where you had got too?'

He smiled, 'Glad I was missed, how did it go?'

'Better than I thought, will wait and see. Leonard is starting up again in the morning, that will be the test.' They moved into the house, Brenda realising that she was being hustled inside, fairly quickly. She moved into the kitchen, watching as Max surreptitiously moved around checking doors and windows.

'OK, what's up?' she asked, Ann and Dennis looking at her as she confronted him.

'Up, what do you mean, up?' he could not avoid the look she gave, knowing that Brenda would not let it go, sighed. 'Alright, sit down please', they all moved to the table.

'After you got the residents to toss out the hecklers, I decided to follow them, especially when I realised Ian Ellis had left as well.' Brenda nodded, sipping her tea, waiting for what was to come. 'They exchanged a few words on the pavement, and then split up. I followed Ian to his car, he rang someone spoke for a few minutes and then drove off. The ringleader went the opposite way towards the back of the houses, after Ian left I followed him. I had asked a couple of police buddies of mine to ask around to see if the local coppers had heard anything, not sure if there was going to be a problem; glad I did,'

Out of his back pack he pulled a very nasty looking pipe bomb, with at least three more in the bag. Brenda and everyone gasped, 'they do like to try and blow things up around you, don't they!'

'Oh, my giddy Aunt, what do I do? I can't stop now, and I don't want to put anyone in danger. That nasty piece of work would have taken out the whole block, am I right Max?'

'It's ok Brenda, I was not the only one concerned, my query via my colleagues to the local branch, had the outcome that a couple of plain clothed detectives were in the pub during the meeting, they found me after it broke up and we had a conflab after I found and defused these. Let us just say the ringleader that planted, or tried to plant, these nasty pieces of work is, a person of interest. Leonard's complaints may have seemed to be ignored but they have not been. There will be a close watch made on this whole area now that they have shown their hand, and an underhanded one at that!'

'Here,' Ann said putting a whiskey in front of Brenda, cradling one for herself and handing one to Dennis, Max shook his head. 'You need that, you have gone white!' she watched as Brenda took a sip of the liquid, nodded as some colour came back to her cheeks.

'What can we do Max, any suggestions? I don't like the idea of Brenda being here if that is the sort of thing being found. What did the police say, and why have you got that nasty thing anyway?'

'I have it as I want to show Leonard in the morning, we are going to have to go over the entire site, as I don't think this is the only one around. I also know how to disarm them, so while I wouldn't want to find any more, I can handle them, also I am the only one qualified to deal with them. I want to contact Michael to check if I can persuade two of my old bomb squad buddies, I know jobs for the boys,' he added as Brenda looked quickly at him, 'but I think they would be handy to have around if we do keep on attracting people who want to blow you up!'

Brenda shuddered, she wasn't worried for herself, what ever happened to her while not being nice was just to her. It was the cowards who would do something so devastating remotely and hurt a lot of innocent people that made her so sad. She sipped the fiery liquid and listened to Max, Dennis and Ann making plans for her to return to Broadmeadows.

'I am not going!' she stated flatly, in the silence that followed, everyone looked at her. 'I am not running away, I came to support Gus, Janet and Leonard, you too Dennis, so I am not going. I want to enjoy my seaside break, in my beautifully refurbished home. So, we are staying, understand?'

Realising there was little they could do to persuade her, relented. 'Max; I like the idea of getting a couple of your colleagues here, so if you know where they are, call them up, I know its late but see if they can get here in the morning they can then help you in your search. Dennis, can they bunk in at your place until we get things sorted?' at his nod and of course, she continued 'Leonard has nearly finished a couple of houses in the street behind us, so I will get him to finish them quickly, and get Rebecca and Mia to furnish them. Then I will feel a lot safer for all the inhabitants of the area, they can keep an eye out on the shifty characters we are dealing with. I will check with Matt in the morning we should have clear shots of all the people at the meeting tonight, what?' she stopped as everyone looked at her, 'I took precautions as well after Leonard told me about the problems he was having, so I asked Matt to help with some security. He sent some of his team down a while back, and put camera's around the site, in the Pub, and has a couple from this and Dennis's house to cover the street, also out the back of here any area that skulduggery could occur I asked him to cover, we may even have pictures of that nasty piece of work being planted! I will check in the morning. Now I am exhausted, and will take a couple of pain pills please Ann, my arms certainly got a work out tonight, and then I am going to bed. See you all in the morning'

It was a restless night's sleep for all of them, Brenda heard Dennis leaving a little while after she had gone upstairs. She paced the floor for a while wondering how she could combat this maliciousness, if it was just against her, she would cope as she always had, but this mindless viscousness was directed against innocent people, just living their lives. Wondering at the thought process of the mindless, vindictiveness of greedy people, she smiled when gardenia floated around her, realising Iris was trying to calm her down. *'Ok, I hear you, leave it till the morning!'* took the tablets Ann had given her, and went to bed.

Chapter 51

L EONARD WAS ON THE doorstep as the first rays of sunshine appeared, Brenda who had been up for a while, directed him to the kitchen offering tea or coffee, sitting next to him at the table where she had been working on her laptop.

'Are these familiar faces?' she asked him moving the laptop so he could see the people on the screen as she flicked through them.

He looked at Brenda, then at the faces again, 'yes, those two are the main ones that have been making mischief. Oh, and her as well, what is going on Brenda?'

She was interrupted by Max, coming through the open French doors into the garden, followed by two new faces.

'Morning Brenda, how long have you been awake, no don't tell me, I know early!' She laughed and gave him a hug, looking at the two young men who were looking around and smiling. 'Let me make introductions, Andy Streeter, Anthony Doubette, everyone calls him Tony, Ms Brenda Chalmers, and Mr Leonard Masters, your employers!'

Brenda turned to Leonard after saying hello, 'there was a development after you left last night, and I have asked for extra help for you, but also to keep the whole area safe. I bet that Andy and Tony here, apart from being very fit and charming, also have a raft of skills, that they are not allowed to tell us about!' Both men in question looked and smiled,' but also some that would be useful on the construction site, so I would like you to add them to the crew, as they have to keep you safe.'

Leonard was just as confused after this speech, so Max told him what he had found on his check of the house and street, after the meeting; then introduced Andy and Tony properly and handing him their civilian resumes, which included dumpster and fork lift driving.

'Don't you people sleep at all, well I know Brenda doesn't, but still it is very early!' Dennis came into the kitchen, 'compliments of Janet, breakfast croissants.' He slid a tray of croissants onto the table, shaking hands with Andy and Tony, welcoming them to the Iris Clan.

'Dennis will explain that cryptic remark later,' Max said to their confused looks.

'OK I realise I need some extra workmen, and welcome your talents,' Leonard said to the two young men, 'but we will not move forward if I don't get out of here and open the site, so we can do a check for any more pieces of nastiness like that,' pointing to the bomb on the table. 'Let's just see what happens today, hopefully I get more of the work done, and I need to start on the place next to the Retreat. Come for a visit later, I have a hard hat in the office for you Brenda, as I know you will not be able to stay away!'

Laughing at the truth in his words, Dennis took Andy and Tony, via the gate in the back fence to his place to drop their bags, saying to Leonard he would bring the men over once they had settled in. Leonard finishing his tea, bid Max and Brenda good morning, saying hello to Ann as he went out the front door.

Ann joined Max and Brenda at the table, she had kept out of the way as the two new faces were introduced into the Iris Clan. 'Iris Clan, I like that, it encompasses everyone that you and Iris have touched! No don't you colour up, it is a good thing, and will be good for this place. Mary-Beth and I were talking to a group of mothers last night.'

'I saw you both in the corner, didn't know if I should rescue you or not?' Brenda asked her.

'Thank goodness you didn't, as we had quite a chat. They are very worried in regards to the rumours going around, your being at the meeting allayed most of them. Realising it is not a big business, mindless corporation that is proposing the refurbishment of the area. They were telling me that they had to travel for over an hour to get to medical attention, and don't even think about an ambulance coming to this area!'

'I assured them, that the Medical Centre would be for everyone, and it is a goer, confirmation of it going in had been received from the Council, all we needed to do was actually get the place built. One of them put forward that they had seen a couple going around the teenagers, and one that had been approached was her son, stirring them up. Offering all sorts of things, Gameboys, phones, expensive toys, for them to do some vandalism. She had put a stop to it, but wanted to know if what you were doing would be of benefit to them!'

Ann took a sip of her tea, looking at Brenda, who cocked her eyebrow at her, encouraging her to go on. 'Well I sort of said you would be starting an apprentice scheme, to give hope to the youth in the area, was I right?'

Max roared, laughter floating around the room, with gardenia in abundance.

'Seems like I will have to…. Max stop it, go and get Dennis for me will you, this I have to run by him. Looks like the Iris Diploma courses have just expanded!'

Max nodded at her, still chortling, before he went out the doors turned to her, 'oh and by the way Brenda, Andy was working part time in a couple of cocktail bars in London, thought he might be good to introduce to Gus and Janet, if you get my drift, although if you want him on the site, he was ok with that as well.' Continuing on through the gate, coming back with a slightly confused Dennis.

Brenda answered Max as he came back into the room, 'he would also be a bit of added security for them, yes that would probably be a better idea, and they do need the assistance. I am glad to see Dennis had not lost his touch, although I have, my arm is really sore this morning. I am sure they have room for him to bunk there, I will speak to him when I go over to the site later on. Thanks Max, ah Dennis, my love, I have need of your teaching skills!'

'Teaching skills, what are you going on about Brenda, after talking to Andy, just now he would really be suited to Gus and

Janet's place not the work site, although he was quite happy with that as well, he loves working with machines he said!'

'Already been decided, so will go and rescue him from Leonard in a moment, and take him up to Gus and Janet to introduce. Now Ann here has been promising things to the locals, and I like the idea. Let's see if we can do, what she promised!'

Brenda with Max went over to see Leonard later that morning, he handing her a deep blue hard hat, with Lady B on the side. 'I couldn't give you a silver one, that is for Broadmeadows, and I have been hearing good things from Glen on that endeavour. So here Iris Blue and all yours, come and see what we have accomplished so far.' Brenda looked at the hat, giving Leonard a hug, putting it on, moving out of the office to check on a different site than the last visit.

Mostly gone were the derelict huts, and the two main structures were slowly being demolished. Leonard saying, they had to go slowly as the ground was not stable, and he could not understand how they were actually still standing. They passed Andy who was helping a couple of Leonard's men filling a skip dumpster with rubbish, asking him to follow them. Brenda telling Leonard that she wanted him to help Gus and Janet, he would have a lot of help before long. Leonard nodding, as he realised Brenda was trying to give some sort of protection to the people she cared about. Max explaining to Andy where he was required that most suited his talents, a knowing look passed between them, as Max had explained to both men the attack on Brenda, which they could still see the remnants of, and the bombs found at the back of the houses the previous night. There was not much else to see, the wonderful view that was not marred by ugly useless buildings a balm to the soul, and Tony's smiling face and wave as he passed them driving the dumpster to the lorry to dispose of some more rubbish.

Brenda, with Max and Andy, walked up to the Retreat, meeting Janet as she put out the coffee sign. She welcoming, giving Brenda a hug, and inviting them into the pub. Brenda introduced Andy to Janet, then was surprised when Gus walked into the room!'

'ANDREW, is that you, my god man where did you come from?'

Andy turned, and gave the friend he had worked many hours with, well into many long nights, a shocked look and then engulfed him in a hug.

Brenda, Max and Janet looking on, 'I take it that you two know each other?'

'Sorry Brenda, yes you could say that, Andy here was one of the best cocktail makers I have ever come across, and I enjoyed working with him, but you disappeared, and I moved we lost touch, so how are you here now?'

'You know I said we would discuss you getting help in the bar; well here it is,' and she pointed to Andy, who was grinning fit to bust. He had no idea what Max was bringing him into, he just knew he owed him, and the challenge that he had given was too much to pass up. That he would have somewhere permanent to stay had also been a very good carrot, Max had dangled before him. The fact that he would be helping his old mentor in Gus, was the icing on the cake, oh he was going to enjoy this.

'I think we had better go and let you get reacquainted, come down to the house later, and we can formalise everything. Oh, and Gus, Andy's salary is being paid by me!'

On that note, Brenda left with Max going back to the house, a happy smile on her face, even bigger when she saw the line-up of people, at the site office. She could see Jock at the front of the queue; Dennis waved as he came out to take him in for his interview.

Chapter 52

T HE REST OF THE week passed, with more and more applicants appearing for interviews, as the word was passed around, not only for the site work, but just work in general, a few good applicants for the Seashore Retreat as well. There were a couple of incidents in the line-up of people patiently waiting for their interviews, a couple of scuffles, with the men and women involved being ejected and seen away from the site. Asked about it, a shrug of the shoulders, and the people in the line stating that they didn't fit, and were mouthing off, being given as an explanation. Leonard advising Brenda that the locals were policing themselves as Brenda had asked.

The eyesore beside the Retreat, had been removed, everyone cheering as they uncovered the original cobbled yard, walls and part of the stone gateway, that had been covered by years of additions and neglect when it was all removed nearly tripled the size of the property. Peter showing Gus and Janet what he proposed, after talking to them to find out what their hopes were for the pub. When the shoddy building, and all the detritus was finally removed, they found the outline of a bricked in double doorway from the pub into the yard, the footings for another part of the wall around the yard was also uncovered, both Gus and Janet stunned, as it proved the large yard had been part of the pub in the distant past.

Max and Brenda were sitting at the table, discussing the timetable of when they would be going back to Broadmeadows, Ann and Dennis coming in from the street, discussing very intently.

'But you don't know that,' Ann stated as they walked into the kitchen.

'I have a feeling and that is what I am going off, that man is linked, I know he is, with those three reprobates in prison at the moment!'

'You have to have proof, Dennis, not just feelings, god knows my skin crawls when he is around, but that will not stand up in court. I have contacts, let me check, although if he is involved in all this, he is a puppet too, he hasn't the brains to work this out!'

'Do I have to ask, or can I guess, would you be discussing our local member for Seahaven, perhaps?' Brenda asked trying to cool down the situation.

'He is as dodgy as, Brenda, I just know him from somewhere, and it is driving me crazy. Of course, I know he is being played, but I don't want to see all the hard work being put into this place, being shot down by dodgy people!'

Brenda knew it would do no good to remonstrate with him, making him a coffee sat beside him at the table, Ann sipping her tea, Max continuing to scroll through Brenda's Laptop.

'Ah here it is!' Max beckoned everyone over to him. 'You know the other day at the site, when the Mayor and council were being shown around; Mr. Ellis came too, and he admitted although he owned property in the area, making him eligible to run for the Seahaven seat, he had never lived in it apart from the six months required to make him a local. I asked Larry and Hugh to check with the titles office.' At Dennis and Ann's intake of breath, 'what you don't think that he makes my skin crawl as well! Well Larry advised me of the address, I was talking to Jock and some of the locals at the pub the other night. They thought all the trouble makers were in a house on the edge of the village area, just inside the boundary. Guess what, it just happens to be the house owned by one Mr Ian Douglas Ellis! But what I can't figure out is why he is being so stupid, surely, he would realise we would be checking. Or does he think it was buried deep enough we would not find out?'

'If he is the landlord, then he might not realise who they are. I know the many, many places I have rented I only once met the owner. We have to prove that he does know the hecklers, and it would be good to find out who he rang after that meeting?' Brenda went back to her seat, picking up some papers Hugh had forwarded her brain racing, trying to see the pattern in the world around her.

Dennis had been scrolling through some internet sites while listening to the discussion going, he suddenly jumped up yelling 'I knew it, knew it!'

Brenda turned to him, 'knew what, come on give, what have you found?'

'You know that Ian Ellis has been bugging me for a long time,' they all nodded, 'well I had the feeling I had seen him before, well I was wrong I have never met him, but the family resemblance to the person I have met, and also disliked is uncanny!'

'And' Brenda prompted him, knowing that the disclosure was going to be very good.

'You remember all those years ago, the Council Site Inspector that was on Bill Gardeners payroll?'

Brenda nodded and shivered, how could she forget him, he nearly derailed all their hard work on Iris House.

'Take a look,' and Dennis turned his tablet round so they could see, that Ian Ellis was the Inspectors nephew!

'Oh, that makes so much sense now, the hostility the tactics, he must be wanting payback for what happened to his uncle!'

'I also have something else, see here Brenda,' Max again pointing to the screen, 'in the photos taken on that night, here is clear proof that the ringleader and Mr. Ellis do know each other, I think there is a link with one or more of the other retirement groups here, we just have to find it, as that is where all this trouble is coming from I am convinced, whether the ownership of the house is known that is another question.'

'I know Max, I saw that photo a couple of days ago, but it is still not enough proof. We will have to go very carefully from now on, I know that Michael, Larry and Hugh are going through their sources, no matter how good they are the bad guys always leave a trail. We have thwarted them to a point, we are moving forward with the build. Thank goodness, we were able to allay the Mayor's and Council fears and squashed the rumours. Being vigilant, putting some competent people in place that can be watchful for surprises, will help.'

'But we now come to the question, can I ask you to stay here Ann, with your retirement from the military last month, and the decision of whether you take the Medical position when the centre is finished, I will not ask for an answer to that offer now. You have this house to use, but I need to have someone here, apart from Dennis, John and Mary-Beth I can trust to make sure the people are safe, what do you say?'

Ann looked at Brenda, realising that here were people she could trust with again, what they had been through and the future she could see before her. She had bonded with the locals she had met in the last week. Could sense the upsurge in hope they had started, she still had the doubt of taking the long term medical job, but could see where Brenda was coming from. Her medical skill may be required if more attempts were made to injure the locals to get them to stop backing the new works, so she could be useful, and leave the main job on the back burner for a little while longer. She could see the hope in Dennis's face, that he would have someone else, he could rely on, he had been doing it tough since he moved into his place. Yes, Brenda was on the phone to him, and emails were replied to quickly, but they were no substitute to a face to face discussion with trusted friends, and four heads were better than three. She could smell gardenia, and smiled, everyone did. 'I think my decision has been made for me!' she said, ready for the hug she was engulfed in from Brenda.

The following week, Max and Brenda pulled away from the Seahaven house with mixed feelings. Brenda happy that she knew Dennis had allies around him, so he and Leonard could move forward, and if Leonard's building pace was anything like Glen's, that would be very quickly.

Max was just happy to be going home, he had enjoyed his stay at the beach, but he had made the decision that Broadmeadows was his home, a place he could expand in, excel in, and was ready to prove to Brenda just what he could do.

Brenda going over the events of the evening before, as Max moved them through the traffic. It had been agreed that they would stop in at Iris House for Brenda to pick up a few more things, and check in on Kate, who wanted to know everything, being intrigued by her mum's phone calls.

Everyone had enjoyed their farewell dinner and the cocktails that Andy had developed for her to prove his talents in that area when they had been in the pub, some being whiskey based with amazing citrus flavours coming through, and one he had named 'Iris Twist' in her honour, she thoroughly enjoyed it, but realised very quickly it would be in moderation. The chat she had with Gus and Janet in the kitchen, explaining to them her theories about the situation, advising that both Andy and Tony were not just there as workers, but they had other talents that would assist if there were more problems. They were also to keep in close contact with Dennis, Ann, Mary-Beth and John when he was there, Gus laughing saying both Dennis and Mary-Beth were part of the furniture and they were looking forward to Ann and John joining the happy group. Also, advising the locals were policing the situation, as it were, they wanted the promise that Brenda had shown to be there, not the empty promises that vanished as soon as the people left. They both would keep in touch, and she had better come back in a couple of months to see exactly what they had achieved.

Iris House wrapped itself around her, as she walked in the door. Showing Max around, he looking everywhere at once, trying to take in the place he had heard so much about. Realising that this was where Iris had lived for the last part of her life, looked at the portrait in the alcove, it seemed to shiver in the sunlight.

'Max, what, oh Iris, meet Max, Max, Iris.' Taking his hand, she moved him to the French Windows into the conservatory, 'She has that effect on everyone, this is my pride and joy!' Brenda spread her arms wide to encompass the beauty of the area. 'Let me leave you here to explore, I will go and find Kate, and get coffee. Come down to the basement,' and she pointed to the door and steps on the landing, 'when you have had your fill.'

Kate was fascinated with the information her mum gave her over the coffee and lunch they had. Kate adding more news from the case against Brenda's muggers, saying the court case was due in a couple of months, and she would have to be back in town to testify.

When Brenda asked Max to take the two suitcases to the car for her, also realised that Brenda had meant that she would be relocating to Broadmeadows, as her permanent base. Not sure if it was something she liked or not, she had always had mum around. She had enjoyed being on her own, over the last few months but there was always her mum's presence around her. Gardenia floated and Kate smiled, *'I am being silly, I know, you and mum will always be her, in spirit. Mum at times in body, annoying the hell out of me!'* she heard the ghostly laughter and realised this was meant to be.

Waving Max and Brenda off from the doorstep, went to phone David, he just had to hear what their mum had been up to.

Brenda enjoyed the drive back to Broadmeadows, excitement built in her as they got closer, she could tell Max was eager to see home, as much as she was.

They arrived back just at knock off time, and had to wait for the cars to clear the drive way before Max could get in and park next to the gate lodge. He turned and said if he was not needed he would see her in the morning, Brenda thanked him for his help, knowing he was eager to reacquaint himself with his home again.

'Thanks Max, I will see you in the morning, we can do a full site inspection then.' She saw Glen and Matt coming out of the office, nodding to them,

'I am sure Glen and Matt will give me a hand, and I need to update them on what has happened.'

Both gentlemen agreeing with her comment said hello and go home to Max, they then helped Brenda unload the car and move into the house.

'Ann didn't come back with you lass, what exotic place has she gone off to now?'

Glen asked as he moved a suitcase down to the bedroom, he was very glad it was on wheels, as it felt extremely heavy, Matt and Brenda laughed and followed him depositing another suitcase and smaller bag on the bed, and motioning them out into the lounge, moving into the kitchen to put the kettle on.

'The beautiful and lovely area of Seahaven Village, is where she is going to be for a while Glen. She has not quite made up her mind if she is going to be a full time local there yet, but I asked her to stay and help Dennis. Can I make you a cuppa, and I can tell you what is going on, or do you have some place to get too, you too Matt, or would you prefer a beer?'

Both men asked for a tea, so while it was being made Brenda told the tale of her time away, 'so as we have settled the first lot of rumours, I was sure there would be more, I asked Ann if she could stay and give Dennis a hand. Max was a great help, and we have two new recruits for the 'Iris Clan', at their puzzled looks, 'we are the Iris Clan, anybody that has been touched by Iris or the Lucas's, Dennis is naming the Iris Clan, so you had better get used to it, as you two are part of it as well!'

Both men laughed, 'promise me you will not go wandering around tonight Brenda, and let us give you a grand tour in the morning. We have made very good progress, and Rebecca wanted to speak with you about the Gate House rooms, I shall bring her with me tomorrow, if that is ok.?'

Glen rose as she nodded 'I promise, I will just enjoy my space here for tonight.'

'Well I have something for you, can I have your Mobile, not the Iris phone, as that is programmed for Iris House.' Brenda handed over her own mobile, watching as Matt did some tinkering with it, smiling and handing it back to her, 'follow me!' he said.

Glen said good night, see you in the morning, getting in his car, tooted as he went through the gates, that had been altered Brenda realised. 'Ok now see the gate icon on your phone tap it!' She did and slowly the refurbished original gates closed meeting in the middle with a slight clanging sound and a click. 'Oh, Matt they are wonderful.'

'Tap it again Brenda, and they open. Very secure, I have it on my phone, Dad also, with Dan, all the Broadmeadows staff have it as well, I will update Max in a bit. Access should be limited to only people who belong here. Oh, and before you ask, if the power goes off it goes off at the gates as well, so they can be manually opened; tap the TV beside the gate app!'

She did and she could see the gates and the drive way, looking at Matt she just had no words. 'If you are ok with who is there, you tap the gate app and let them in.' He gave her a peck on the cheek, a see you in the morning, running in to see Max, before he left. Brenda checking later that the gate was closed giving her a sense of security in her home.

True to her word, she did not leave the Gate Lodge that night, although she did have welcome home visits from everyone. Promising her she would be surprised when the dawn broke, as there had been quite a few changes in the last few weeks.

She was awake and ready when she heard the gates opening, checking the app to see who was coming through them. Had tea and coffee ready and waiting for Glen and Rebecca, when they walked through the door.

'You look rested, how was the trip?' Rebecca asked depositing, bags and laptop on the table, giving Brenda a hug while accepting her coffee.

'It was interesting, and thank you for the décor at Iris Sea House, it is wonderful and really suits the house and me. Before I forget, I need you to work your magic on another two houses that Leonard has almost finished. We have more recruits for the 'Iris Clan', that need places to stay. Although I think one of them will be happy at the Retreat, until we start tearing it apart that it is, and then we will have to house Gus, Janet and Andy!'

At Rebecca's please explain look, Brenda gave her the abridged version of the past events, she looking at Glen to see if he was as gobsmacked as she was.

'Don't look at me, I just don't understand how such a wonderful person as our Brenda can make so many enemies, and they all want to blow her up to boot!'

'Who wants to blow who up?' Ben and Matt came through the door, going and giving Brenda a hug to say hello, and she giving tea's and coffee's in return. It was Jack poking his head in the door who moved them, 'Hey you lot, there is work to be done you know, stop blathering and get out here, don't we have to show Brenda what she missed?'

Chapter 53

WHO COULD DISMISS SUCH a well phrased invitation, going and giving Jack a hug and kiss on the cheek, he saying welcome home, in her ear. Brenda picked up her hard hat, and with everyone moved out into the sunshine.

George was the first one to run up and demand a hug from Brenda when she walked into a very changed stable yard, Roger and Mary with smiles on their faces following him, and being hugged in return. Max joining them as they followed Glen over to a table under the awning in the corner of the yard.

Brenda did a slow 360 degree turn to take in the first nearly completed structure on the Broadmeadows estate, the buildings were almost as she had seen them in her dreams while in hospital. The three cottages on the road side, all with fences and gates linking them together, the last one linked into the magnificent stone archway over the entrance to the bridle path looked as though they had been there for centuries. Yes, there were sections still to be faced, but the actual structure was complete, and workmen were everywhere, trying to get as much done as possible on this Friday morning.

'I was hoping to have the clock installed before you got home Brenda.' Rebecca was saying as she showed her pictures of other archways with a clock in the top part. 'But there was a delay in getting the parts, so it will be installed next week. The clockmaker is as frustrated as I am, it's the largest one he has made in this digital age. What do you think?' she asked as she spread her arms wide.

'Think I think this is wonderful, Keith where did you come from?'

Keith moved over and gave Brenda a hug, a smile as wide as he was tall on his face.

'My town house Brenda, want to come and see? June and I moved into our places on Wednesday, Rebecca has done a wonderful job.'

'As she always does, of course I want to see, and June's as well, ah here she is,' another hug, and Brenda moved out to inspect the two new homes. One that was original and one that she had made out of the buildings, adding her stamp to the past. They both had that new build smell, Keith's ground floor had a front door from the yard, leading into a spacious open plan lounge room, kitchen and dining area, with a laundry come powder room, and a study, with a barn door leading into the stables themselves, and on the opposite wall another barn door out to the buggy shed. Brenda commenting that he was living in a house of doors, had them all laughing. Then upstairs two bedrooms, the master being as large as the tenant, built over the new buggy garage, skylights in the roof line giving it a light and airy feel, with a huge super king sized bed dominating the space, a sufficiently sized bathroom, Keith advised Ben had done him proud, as he actually had a shower he could use, without becoming a contortionist. The smaller second bedroom had been arranged with two king single beds, and more conventional again modern bathroom.

June's new home, surprised Brenda as it was three bedroomed, the ground floor the same as the cottages, open plan lounge, kitchen and dining, French doors leading out to the small courtyard/garden, also a small study, laundry and powder room. She had a barn door into the ground floor of the archway, beside her front door, linking the cottage to the Archway. Peter had put two bedrooms on the second floor, and made the top floor into one master suite. Brenda approved, as it fit with the overall feel of the space, June commenting she was still trying to get used to the space she had. 'You have not even seen the best of it yet Brenda, come on!'

Mary picked up George, turning to Brenda, 'I will take this rascal and see you later, I will have morning tea ready when you have explored a little,' she said. George began to complain, saying he wanted to see Brenda. Mary just gave him a look, and walked out the door, saying see you later over her shoulder. Ben, Matt and Keith also said they had things to do, so it was Max, June, Roger, Glen and Rebecca who accompanied Brenda on the next phase of her tour.

June opened the barn door and Brenda walked through the small space connecting the two buildings and stepped into the base of the archway. Seeing they were still waiting to put in the door from the actual stable yard into the area, another one on the list of small items yet to be completed. The sandstone floor tiles were of the era, as well as the sandstone that had been put on the walls, echoing the outward skin, although Brenda knew it was only a skin and not solid sandstone blocks, it still felt as though they had built with the solid block. Then she saw the magnificent steel stairs, the Lucas crest interwoven with Iris flowers prominent, these wrapped themselves around a glass enclosed lift, a la Parisian style. Glen moving to open the ornate screen door, then the inside glass door, and opening the glass door, everyone with space to spare moved inside.

'This is magnificent, oh Rebecca you have out done yourself!'

'Not just me, I have just furnished these places, Peter and David designed them, Dad and the boys have executed them, but I am pleased they give me a chance to practice for the big one, and oh, just watch out when I get my hands on that!'

Laughing at her comment, the lift stopped, Brenda could see it went up one more floor, she moved into a small hallway, with windows that gave a view over the roadway, and the yard, it was light and airy, opening the door in front of her moved into the gallery that went across the bridle path. Oak floors made the place light, just in the entrance a small kitchen space, with a sink, microwave and fridge, just enough to make a tea or coffee, and some toast. Next to a compact shower room, Rebecca telling her they had duplicated the Bathroom space on the other side. In between, placed in two orderly rows, underneath the wonderful windows that gave incredible views over the estate on one side, and the yard and drive way on the other, were eight beds four each side, with half walls to the bottom of the windowsills giving a little privacy and dividing the space, but it was what Brenda had dreamed of, come to life.

Standing on the bridle path side looking out at the vista that was Broadmeadows, Brenda could not miss the new structure that was still being faced with stone, on the spot Max had pitched his tent so many months before.

'What?' was what Brenda said, to the group around her.

Glen smiled, 'I think we had better go and see, but there is more to see here, come on let's finish this inspection before we start another, shall we?'

Brenda smiled, knowing that she was doing this tour on her friend's timetable, not her own, gardenia floated around, and everyone heard the ghostly laughter, 'I think the grandfathers have just spoken, come on Brenda, the best is yet to come, I assure you!' Glen gave her a hug, and pointed out the amenities, which matched the far side, and then moved them through the door into the other tower. No lift in this one, but a set of stairs going further up and down to the ground level, to which Roger moved them and led them up.

The top floor, was just an open gallery, with the clock tower being constructed in the centre of the space above it being the focal point again of the stable yard, she realised it was going to be a four-sided clock, with the workings in the middle, it also fit her dreams. The fresh summer breeze ruffled her hair, and a caress of her cheek Brenda knew the Grandfathers were approving the construction. The view from all sides was magnificent, she could glimpse through the trees in front of her, the giant oak trees that denoted the place where the original manor house was and way away even see a portion of the lake. Glen moved them back across the top, using the lift to get to the ground floor. He being hailed as he came out into the yard, Brenda realising that they were about to put in the huge gates to finally enclose the space once again.

'Come on Brenda,' Roger pulled her over towards the stables 'Glen will give us a whistle when they are actually putting them in, but come and see what I have been overseeing!'

Roger, with Max and June, moved over to the big stable door, in the centre of the building, easily swinging it open. Brenda's senses were assailed by two prominent sensations, smell and sound, stunned she walked into a functioning stable complete with two horses!

Moving inside Brenda briefly took notice of a fully fitted out tack room, bridles, blankets and saddles arrayed in orderly fashion, before moving into the main part of the stables and standing for a moment to catch her breath and let her eyes adjust.

Before anyone could say a word, Brenda was quickly past Max, who was standing in the entrance to the stalls, she put a hand out to touch the head of a beautiful roan stallion, who had stuck his head out to see who was there. He was magnificent, but in a very serious state of neglect, very skinny, his coat patchy, she put her hand on his nose as he bent to smell this new stranger, snickering as she talked to him, softly soothing. The calming voice he understood, and he sniffed her knowing her, he settled, moving back into his stall happy with this new person in his life.

Brenda moved on to the next stall, a magnificent Clydesdale stood there towering over her, but he was as skinny as the stallion and in the same neglected condition, after giving the same benediction to this wonderful animal, Brenda turned everyone could see the tears rolling down her face.

'Oh Roger, thank you where did these two come from?'

Roger breathed again, he had wondered if he had done the right thing, but was sure Brenda would understand. He knew that she would be ok with the two Labradors he had rescued at the same time as the horses, who were probably, at that time making Mary's life a misery, being locked up in the house. Max was just watching in wonder, realising the story that Kate had said about her mum, was very true. He had been ready to pull her away when he saw the animals, and the shocking state they were in.

As she walked between the two animals, murmuring kind words to them, giving them the apple pieces Roger gave her to feed them. He told her how Bruce the farmer on the estate, had contacted him, in fact they had become good friends, after Bruce had got over the shock she had given him with the deeds to the farm. They had been discussing in general terms how they could move the estate forward, just ideas he assured Brenda, to be worked on and discussed with her now she was back and getting her health back, but they were looking forward and he did not just mean Bruce. Brenda hugged him, giving her approval, getting a nose on her arm, as she was still holding slices of apple for the stallion.

'Well about a week ago, Bruce came up to me asking for help, as part of his volunteer RSPCA work, he had been advised of a neglect case in the next county over. They had discovered a very neglected small farm, owner no-where to be seen, and the animals in a shocking state, a few of the horses could not be saved, but this fella who I have named Roan, and Oscar over there,' he pointed to the Clydesdale whose ears pricked in their direction making everyone laugh, 'were the last two and destined for the knacker's yard. I am sorry but I could not see them go, so told Bruce to bring them here, along with any tack gear that was salvageable; he added the goats and sheep to his heard, but I kept the dogs!'

'Dogs,' Brenda said, turning from Oscar, 'what dogs Roger?'

'The two black Labradors, that are probably making Mary's life a misery as they are in the house, they have come on a treat, we managed to farm out the puppies, but have the runt still with us, he is not very well. You really don't mind do you, I just could not bear to see the animals being slaughtered due to a human's neglect.'

She hugged him and after giving the horses another pat, and soothing words left the stable almost running across the yard to the house. Roger following with a smile on his face, June and Max shrugging their shoulders, said they had things to check on, left Roger to make the introductions, Max had already said hello to them the night before.

Roger moving into the house was assailed by two black bullets, he giving pats and scratches in return. Brenda moved to sit at the table waiting patiently till Roger had calmed the dogs down, waiting till they realised he was not alone. Hackles rose as they could smell a stranger. Brenda just sat making no movement slowly they moved over to her, and in the same soothing voice as she had used on the horses, calmed them, the hackles slowly lowered and they moved over to sniff, soon she was giving her own soothing pats, and crooning to them, gaining their trust.

'They were in a sorry state Brenda, Maverick he pointed to the male sitting at her feet, and Sable here, he pointed to the bitch that was trying to get as close to her as she possibly could without getting in her lap, 'were covered in fleas, and half the weight they should be for mature working dogs. Sable had a litter of pups, we think six of them about six weeks ago, she was in a worse state, trying to nourish puppies with nothing for herself. Three we think had not made it, two we managed to find good homes for, but this one, was not well so we decided to keep him.'

Into Brenda's lap, wrapped in a towel for warmth he deposited a small bundle of black fur, with a white question mark on the top of his nose. 'We named him Lucky!'

Brenda's heart melted, Sable gave him a lick, and sat her head in Brenda's lap looking at the pup, that she was automatically giving gentle pats and stroking the fur.

Accepting the cup of tea, and chatting to George who was giving his own brand of pats to the dogs, being extremely gentle, and getting licks in return from both of them, she spent some time checking that Roger had contacted the local vet, to come and see the animals, to advise on how to get them back to their peak physical conditions. Roger telling Brenda that the vet had been part of the RSPCA volunteers, and was helping as well. Mary giving Brenda a small bottle to feed Lucky, making sure Sable was ok and watching as the puppy eagerly took the nourishment. George sitting quietly beside her, saying he had also fed the puppy, and he had grown since he had come home. It was a lovely interlude, and Brenda made sure that both Mary and Roger realised they had done the right thing, neglect of either our elderly or animals not to be tolerated.

Glen poked his head through the door, Mav and Sable both giving him a bark hello, 'We are ready, want to come and watch, Stephen is really happy, he hopes you are too?'

Leaving the dogs inside the house, they all moved out to the yard, watching as the first gate was lifted into place, Brenda had a deja vu moment seeing the huge gate that she had seen in her dreams, and remembering the ruin of a gate she had seen many months before. Cheering with everyone as it fitted perfectly, then turning to watch the second one being moved into position. It was perfect, and Brenda bestowed hugs to everyone, but was surprised when Glen turned her around to face the driveway entrance. She had not realised that the stone pillars had been rebuilt on the ends of the Gate House and the Stables. Matt coming up to her, smiling asking for her phone again. 'What are you up to?' she asked handing it over.

It took a few more minutes, but he handed her the phone, along the bottom of the screen that had a screen saver of the Gateway, were boxes. 'If you tap, this one, 'which had a picture of the main gate. Brenda did so, and the screen filled with six boxes, three of which had pictures in them. The first one she realised had the gate and camera that Matt had shown her the previous evening. The second one was the Gate Archway, 'tap that' he said, Brenda did so, and two screens appeared, 'tap that one, and the second screen had a picture similar to the front gates.

From the stable side, a smaller single gate slid across from the opening, at Brenda's gasp, 'Well we had to make it safe to let the horses and dogs out, until they got used to the place, didn't we? Give me an hour or so, and I will have these,' and he pointed to the massive oak gates to the bridle path, 'linked to the first icon. Oh, you can open them manually if you want, same as the main gates, no problems, but why would I not wire everything for you, more efficient that way!'

He had the same smug expression on his face as he had when he had rewired Iris House everyone was laughing, Brenda giving a him a hug, telling him why not, and it was magic.

Brenda then led them through the gates and onto the bridle path, wanting to know just what was going on with the new building she had seen from the archway. Realising when she got closer it was a huge garage. Keith hearing them coming down the path, came out of the doorway.

'Hi Brenda, ok let me explain, you gave us permission to fix up the Singers,' at her nod he continued, 'well we realised that we could not really do that correctly in the original garage, we would be destroying the history, so Peter and David suggested we just make our own modern one, with' and he motioned her to walk through the doorway he had come out of, 'a fully equipped garage, that will allow us to keep the estate vehicles in tip top condition, and also house a few cars to boot!'

Brenda turned then and saw the Estate van parked at the far end of the garage, but beside her gleaming in all its pristine condition was the red Singer Le Mans she had uncovered in the basement garage. Max standing beside it with a key in his hand, 'want to see if it starts, Keith here wanted you to be the first to really fire it up, and take it for a drive?'

Eagerly Brenda took the key, Max opened the driver's door, she was assailed by a myriad of senses, sadness for the loss and age it had taken to finally have progress on the estate, of pride and achievement emanating from Keith, he bent down, as Max slid into the passenger seat, to make sure she knew where everything was, thankful she knew how to drive a manual car in this day and age, held up the key, grateful that Rebecca was there with her camera. Ceremoniously inserting and starting the engine, the roar was gratifying, she noted where everything was. Turning to Matt, 'please make sure the gates are open as I will go up to the manor and then come back down the driveway.'

At Max's quizzical look, 'no rego yet, not going to take it too far on this her maiden trip!' He nodded, Brenda slowly put the car in gear and manoeuvred it out to cheers from all the workmen who had come to see a legend in motion.

She was very pleased with the handling, but realised her arm was going to be a little sore, as no power steering to help her, but it was immense fun and she enjoyed the feel of the machine around her, she managed a respectable speed on the long straight down the driveway, turning to cheers from the workmen to cross the stable yard, driving into the garage, she wasn't quite up to reversing it in.

'Oh, that was absolutely wonderful,' she hugged Keith, 'you have done a great job, especially with this!' She motioned the garage with its modern equipment, 'didn't take you long to put it up, I like the fact you are facing it with stone to make it blend in.'

'Had to, Brenda, Rebecca wouldn't let us do anything else, but it is great to work in.'

They were interrupted by the arrival of Larry, David and Kate with the lunch vans, not realising the morning had disappeared so quickly Brenda curbed her children's impatience stating lunch first, then another more in depth inspection, she wanted to check what was going on with the main site. Tables were set out, Rebecca catching up to her asking questions, comments came from all enjoying the sunshine and the good food, while decisions were made for how to proceed, until Brenda changed it all of course was Glen's comment, with everyone laughing.

Chapter 54

Lunch over, Glen said he was going to check, but he was sure there was not much his workmen needed to finish, when they had tidied up he was sending them home, an early mark for a change. Besides he said, Brenda needed to reacquaint herself with the place, without others around.

Another inspection of the site, the three of them being introduced to Roan and Oscar, the gates both sides closed Maverick and Sable could be encouraged to roam a little in the safe stable yard, Brenda carrying Lucky and being shadowed by Sable at her side.

True to his word, Glen gave the workmen an early finish soon he and Ben had departed, leaving Matt with the Broadmeadows team to enjoy the space around them.

They were just finishing the tour of the stables, when another face appeared at the outside gates, Brenda checking on her phone, with Roger looking over her shoulder, 'Oh that is Merry, the Vet! Sorry Meredith Drew is the local vet that was with us when we found this lot,' and he gesticulated to the animals, 'and brought them back. Let her in please Brenda, I don't have my phone on me.'

Brenda duly opened the gates for the new comer, Meredith was a stocky, but lean middle sized mature looking woman, who could have been 20 or 40 she had one of those faces that you could not tell. Roger went to meet her, holding onto Maverick, seeing Brenda had a hand on Sable's collar, just in case the open gate gave them any ideas.

'Well met Roger, just thought I would pop around and check on the charges, especially the little one. I have brought that new formula we were discussing last week, but these two are looking much, much better.'

Roger made the introductions to the new faces, Brenda liking the strong handshake she received, and the quiet way she dealt with both Maverick and Sable once she bent to accept their welcome. Lucky even stirred to open one eye, when she prodded and poked him, commenting on he had put on some meat which was good, as well as Mav and Sable, their coats looking a lot better.

Brenda handed Lucky back to Mary, as she accompanied her into the stables, as she wanted to check that both horses would recover.

'It is my pleasure to see someone living on the estate again Lady Lucas,' at Brenda's raised eyebrow, 'oh yes I know who you are, please don't worry, I need to thank you for bringing back some joy to our lives. You have given all of us, in the village and even in the county new hope, that we can move forward, rebuild as it were as you are doing!'

Merry moved over to Oscar, after giving Roan a check, Oscar was a bit skittish so armed with pieces of apple that Roger always seemed to have Brenda moved over to him, holding his bridle, talking to him, calming him down. She asked questions of how she could help maximise both horse's recovery, as she could not bear to see them in distress.

Enjoying the discussion, Roger joining in with some information his father had sent him, getting approval from Merry, happy with how both horses had improved, advising a daily gentle brushing would help the coats come back, and remove the detritus of the past.

They moved out after making sure there was feed and water for both of them, Brenda advising that she was going to take separately, both horses out to walk the bridle path, she knew she could not ride either of them for a while, they both had to get their strength back, but she suggested, and Merry approved a walk or two a day, gentle exercise would get both of the horses aware of their surroundings for when they could be ridden. Brenda also asked that at her next visit she bring her scanning equipment as Brenda wanted to know if any of the animal's dogs or horses had been microchipped, and if not they were to be, she would make sure they were safe on the estate and anywhere.

Merry was encouraged by all to stay and enjoy the evening with the group, as Brenda wanted to expand on her comments in the stables, finding out that her father and grandfather had all been veterinarians in their days, but only the last two generations had actually acquired the certificates to prove it. Making the group laugh at the antics she had with animals of all sizes, dealing with the bulls and cows on the neighbouring farms, down to Mrs. Creighton's – the general store owner's Pomeranian.

It was fairly late when the group bid everyone goodnight, seeing Merry out of the gates and on her way, Larry and Brenda making their way back to the Gate Lodge, leaving Kate and David enjoying Matt, June, Max and Keith's company. George having exhausted himself with the people and animals, had been taken to bed some time earlier, Roger and Mary saying goodnight as they carried their sound asleep son into the house.

'Are you, happy luv?' Larry asked as they moved into the lodge.

'Happy, yes I am I have to admit my life at the moment is wonderful. Even with everything that is going on at Seahaven, and the trial coming up, at this moment I am very, very happy.'

'I hear a 'but'? he said as he took her into his arms, where she fit so well.

'But', she said moving back a little so she could look into his eyes, 'there is so much more to do, and I can't wait to begin the next stage of this adventure.'

'The Manor House?'

'The Manor House, and whatever the Family throw at me, the next stage is sure to be something to be savoured, and enjoyed!'

Table of Characters of The Iris Clan

Iris Fitzgibbon Boerchermier – (Deceased) Iris House Owner.
Lord Norman Lucas – (Deceased) Father / Grandfather et al. –
Lucas Line.

Brenda Chalmers – Lady Brenda Lucas
David and Kate Chalmers

Dennis Brookes – friend and confidant- CEO Iris House Retirement
Properties (IHRP Co.)
Iris Force /College ///Iris Clan / new recruits.

Linda McGill – CEO Pickworths – Brenda's Employer
Shane McGill – husband/ architect / paraplegic car accident.
Triplets – Norman Lucas, David James and Louise Brenda McGill.
Nurse/Nanny – Susan Swift.

Sir James Pickworth – owner of Pickworths – Linda's Grandfather.
Giles – Sir James - Major Domo

Stan, Nona and Poppa – Ace Cleaning Team

John Marshall – The Jewellery Shop
Luke – assistant.

Stewart Saunders - Locksmith

Glen Haddon – Master Builder.
Julie Haddon – wife
Benjamin and Matthew – (twins) plumber and electrician
Rebecca – Interior Designer.

Charles and Gabrielle Waines – Gabby Glen/Julie's eldest daughter
Twins- Iris Brenda and Edward Lawrence
Rob 2IC at Waines Glassworks

John Sark – Glen's Forman, Fred and Jack
Patrick Greenhill – Painter
Nigel Hawthorn – Master Carpenter

Dan and Helen Jones – Jones Steelworks
Greg Baines
Peter Mason – Architect / Structural Engineer
Beverly Mason – Dan / Helen's daughter.

Marcus Cannington – Glass
Brent Winegood – Winegood and Tate Lift Specialists.
John James – RailPlus – Speciality Railings and Stairs.
Brad Goddard – Stone Mason
Stephen Von Riddick – Timber Mill owner.

Norman Greenwell –Marquis of Trent- Kew Gardens
Tristan, Mary and Simon

Original Building Team:
Mia Farrington-Smythe – Interior Designer.
William (Bill) Gardiner – builder
John Hemsworth – Architect.

Guests of Iris House-
Nasser and Adelle – Loren (8) and Louis (10)
Doreen (Chef) and Pierre (Major Domo)

Legal Teams:
Lawrence Morecombe QC
Son – Andrew /wife Beth – Grandson Lucas
Son – Ewon
Secretary – Jo Seymour
Norman Lawrence Morecombe (QC retired) Larry's father
Hugh Pemberton QC
Wife – Phyllis
Michael Dranish Fawkes QC - Fawkes Inc.
Lucas Estate

Duncan Rogers – National Portrait Gallery - Doris
Lady Maybelle and Lord Vincent Dorsett.
Baron Raymond Phipps – Queens Equerry.
John Johnston III – Protocol Expert

Military College -
Colonel Richard Johnstone – Cadet Trainer/Leader
General James Richardson – Bomb Squad Commandant.

June Smith Lyon – Mama's Kitchen

Greg Wilmott – David and Kate's Father.

Broadmeadows Staff -

Maxwell (Max) Jones – Gardens/Stables

Charles – (12) son

Roger McAllister – Estate Manager / Stables
Mary – wife / George (5) son.

Roan, the Stallion // Oscar the Clydesdale
Black Labradors – Maverick (dog) and Sable (bitch)
Lucky – pup, black with white mark on nose

Keith Butcher – handyman/carpenter/explosive disposal.
Father – Joseph Butcher – carpenter, handyman.
June Sawyer – gardener / explosives disposal.

Bruce Hudson – Farmer Broadmeadow Farm.
Wife Karen – Teacher
Children – William, Claire and Henry.
Meredith Drew – Vet
Mr. & Mrs Creighton – General Store
Samantha(Sam) Sargent – Broadmeadows Catering

Seahaven Village Staff-
Iris Sea House – Seahaven Village home

IRIS House Retirement Properties Group Co. – (IHRPG CO.)
Dennis Brooks – CEO
Mary-Beth Walters – Joint Manager Seahaven Care Home
John Hunter – Joint Manager Seahaven Care Home.

Leonard Masters – Master Builder.
Wayne Swan – Foreman
Anthony (Tony) Doubette – skip driver

Seahaven Council -
Mayor Graham George
Esther Marshall – Council woman
Ian Daniel Ellis – Member for Seahaven

Seashore Retreat – Pub - The Retreat
Gus and Janet Lambert
Andy Streeter – barman

General Store
Mr. and Mrs Singh. – Leonora and John